BLACKHEART

PIXIE RELLA

Cover Art + Design by Jordyne Lucy

Scene Artwork Created by Ashley Griggs

———

This is a work of fiction. Names, characters, business, events and incidents are the products of the author's imagination. Any resemblance to actual persons, living or dead, or actual events is purely coincidental.

TRIGGER WARNINGS (Light Spoilers Included)

This tale contains mature themes such as violence, sexual content, emotional manipulation, strong language, coercion, and depiction of forced sterilization. Reader discretion is advised.

ISBN 979-8-9936278-1-6 (Paperback)

ISBN 979-8-9936278-0-9 (eBook)

First Edition, December 2025

Dedicated solemnly and tenderly to all of the Eloras out there, black as their hearts may be.

CONTENTS

Glossary

As written by the Golden Scholar of Lyonscliff, under decree of King Clarke Lyonaire

"His Majesty welcomes knowledge where fear once ruled. I record what others shun."

— Jon Harvington, Golden Scholar of Lyonscliff

Blackheart: Dark Natured being whose Nature manifests as a corrosive poison. Their blood itself is harmless, thank Fate, but when their Nature is released—by rage, defense, or despair, it becomes deathly. Even their tears are lethal. Common identifying traits include dark veins and eyes, as well as a black marking located on their hip.

Lyonheart: Light Natured beings able to wield healing and light magic. Typically identified by a brown, sun-shaped marking on their chest or back.

Dreamsoul: Light Natured dreamwalkers. If powerful enough, they can wield storm magic and even travel through their Nature itself. Identified by a unique constellation marking on their back.

Sapphires: A cult of those who have succumbed to blood magic. While their abilities are not yet fully known, it is believed they possess enhanced speed, strength, and illusionary magic. It is difficult to say how easily they can blend in with the rest of society—but if you see red-rimmed eyes, you've likely found one.

Flamecastor: Dark Natured wielders of fire. Can be identified by a red, shimmering mark on their face.

Nightcastor: Dark Natured shadow wielders. Typically identified by a crescent moon marking behind their left ear.

Stonesender: Dark Natured beings with the ability to wield earth magic and minor air abilities. They bear unique, stone-like markings across their palms.

Blackheart Pronunciation Guide

Amzee - AM-zee

Ansel - AN-suhl

Arielle - AR-ee-elle

Avan Shadewind - AH-ven SHAYD-wind

Castivian - Kas-tIv-ee-an

Clarke Lyonaire - kl-AR-k LIE-on-air

Clayvarie - KLAY-var-ee

Dayire - DAY-eye-er

Delaina - Del-LAY-nuh

Draker - DRAY-k-er

Drakington - DRAY-k-ing-tun

Draven - DRAY-vin

Dronis - DRO-niss

Elora Amona - E-lore-uh Uh-MON-uh

Fiera Poss - FEE-air-uh p-AH-s

Jocelynn Wrenavia - JOS-lin REN-A-vee-uh

Kostini - Kos-TEE-nee

Lestivia - Leh-STIV-ee-ah

Payn Vikesh - p-AYE-n v-EYE-kish

Riven Blacksword - RIV-uhn BLK-sord

Saffron - SAF-ron

Sitara - si-TAR-uh

Trista - TRISS-tuh

Xavian Steele - Ex-ZAY-vee-uhn st-EE-l

Valeska - Vah-LEH-skuh

Zephyros - zef-fear-os

PROLOGUE

"IT'S YOUR FAULT!" QUEEN DELAINA SCREECHED. "ALL of you!"

Hooded healers rushed away with the limp body of little Princess Clayvarie, who would likely never wake again.

There was a price to be paid for what happened to the sole heir, and thousands would pay it. Those of privilege called for the mass execution of the Dark Natured. They would have gotten their way if not for King Clarke.

Yearning to surpass those before him as a peaceful ruler, he forged a plan to "save" us. Instead of slaughter, he forced us into an isolated city within towering obsidian walls. For this, some would say he was the worst to have ever sat on the throne.

It was no home, but a cage. Once inside, we never came out. Three winters confined had tamed many—

but not all.

PART 1

"It is hereby declared, that the Dark Natured are undoubtedly wicked, and such sinister abominations have no reason to lurk upon the common lands. It is not only merciful, but necessary that the vermin be confined within the Waywards. There is no place more fitting for the misbegotten."

— *Marker Dane, Lord of Lawship*

CHAPTER 1

THE ACCUSATION

I MOVED THROUGH THE NORTHERN WAYWARDS earlier than most, skirting along the shadows with my hands shoved in my pockets. Inebriated bodies littered the doorsteps of curtainless brothels while rodents skittered nearby.

I cut to the left, down a narrow and uneven path.

Dangerously tall, haphazardly stacked buildings lined the streets. The towering structures were daunting, but no match for the stature of the obsidian walls. No matter where I stood, the barrier remained in sight. A reminder that this place was no home. It was a prison.

Dawn neared, and others trickled into the mud and snow-smeared streets. They shuffled about in black and brown sweaters, shawls made of crude wool, and roughly knitted hats. I tied the top half of my hair into a bun as I hurried along, the rest of my dark hair a shield to the back of my neck.

Tucked away in the tight corner of an alley, a half-rotted sign hung diagonally from rusted nails.

'Blackhearts Welcome'.

There were few places like that left in the world.

I pushed the creaky wooden door open.

"Mornin', Elora!" Trista called out from behind the bar.

My shoulders relaxed, stiff joints thawing. I claimed my seat at the weathered counter, yawning as she slid me a pour of blackfire tea. The steam curled into delicate ribbons, tickling my nose.

A few other patrons were scattered about the shop, chatting among themselves at small wooden tables. Lodge Dugspur, a regular who frequently tipped well, sat on a barrel once used to crate fish. His companion straddled a rotting chair with three true legs, while a broken broomstick filled in for the fourth.

Trista flicked a piece of fiery hair behind her shoulder and stirred her brew.

I held my cup close to my chest, my voice barely a whisper.

"Any news of Arielle?"

Trista glanced around cautiously before her hooded eyes landed on me.

"I paid a Draker with mouth and tongue, all for him to tell me she was delivered to the castle for a trial. She could've pleaded her case, but they couldn't settle her. She went entirely mad—even attacked a noble. No doubt, my niece is dead." Trista let out a soft sigh and returned to her stirring.

I took a healthy draw of my own tea. A strong mug of ale would have been better suited for this conversation.

Arielle had always been one to push boundaries, yet I hadn't expected her to be so foolish. There were rules within these walls, and she had broken the most dangerous one.

Using her Nature.

The seven Witchlords were rarely forgiving. It was even rarer to be sent before the *king* for a trial, and Arielle hadn't even made good use of the opportunity. She could have survived. All she had to do was give herself a chance.

"What a waste."

The front door of the shop swung open, a gust of cold air bursting in with morning light. Trista's posture stiffened, her eyes wide in warning.

Thin floorboards groaned beneath heavy, measured footsteps. I tilted my head imperceptibly, chest tight as a cloaked figure towered behind me. A Witchlord. I had never seen one in Trista's before. Casually, I took another sip.

"Blackheart," he snapped.

My cup jerked, tea spilling over the rim. I rested it on the counter and turned to face him.

Witchlord Ansel stared down at me with cold blue eyes.

He'd just arrived in the Waywards as a replacement for Lord Zerys. I'd never interacted with him—or any Witchlord—beyond standing in the crowd during his introduction ceremony. They hardly ever spoke to *us*, and certainly not during my morning tea. I always minded my own, controlled my Nature, and never once tried escaping the obsidian walls. The Witchlords had no need to speak to me.

Until now.

Lord Ansel's cropped raven hair was neatly groomed and framed his face in a way that complemented his angular eyes. A light blue pendant pinned his black cloak in the center of his broad chest.

He had no need for armor or fighting leathers. The Witchlords *were* the weapon.

Witchlord Ansel should have been out patrolling—reminding the Dark Natured of his presence. Instead, he stood before me, eyes roaming from my weathered boots to my ill-fitting pants, then up my chest before settling his glare upon my face. "You've been accused of using Dark Nature," he cited, devoid of empathy.

I mirrored him, crossing my arms. "Which liar said that?"

Lord Ansel scrutinized me carefully. "Charles the Imp."

Oh, for Fate's sake. The accusation was nothing short of an attempt on my life. I nearly flew off the chair as words came spewing from my mouth. "Charles is a drunk! And that little shit is just upset that I continuously reject his advances." I finally made eye contact. Perhaps he would detect the truth in my gaze.

The Witchlord's eyebrows rose as he slid his hands into his pockets. "And you think you're so desirable?"

I blinked, struggling to combine words that didn't include 'fuck' and 'you.' The Witchlord smirked. My Nature stirred, the veins along my skin darkening. Itching for release.

"No," I gritted through clenched teeth.

"Show me your hands," he ordered.

Trista sucked in a breath. We both knew what would happen if he didn't believe me—we'd not even enjoy one last tea together before my execution. A true shame.

I held my hands together protectively, fumbling for the right thing to say. "You're not scared of my poison hurting you? My hands are... sensitive. I could accidentally—"

The other patrons turned their attention to us, faces pale. One by one, they discreetly escaped the shop.

Lord Ansel cocked his head to the side. "Put your hands out, Blackheart."

Not once in the three winters of living in this hellscape had I ever been accused of breaking the rules.

As much as I wanted to argue further, I had no choice but to comply.

With shaking arms, I stood and presented my palms, pulling my poison in towards my core. Even so, my dark veins bulged, filling and rising on my skin.

The Witchlord reached for my hands, his fingertips gently bracing under my knuckles. An electric sensation raced down my spine.

He inspected my palms for all but a moment before dropping them.

"No trace of a leak."

My shoulders sagged.

Lord Ansel offered no goodbyes as he took his leave, slamming the shop door behind him.

Trista's freckled face was unnaturally pale. She held her dainty, blotched hand to her chest. "Mother of Moons, help us," she breathed. "I thought you were as good as dead."

I settled back in my spot, returning to my tea. With every sip, my Nature settled, and breathing came easier. I'd survived, unlike Trista's niece.

"I don't like him," I announced. I didn't care for any of the Witchlords, but he was somehow the worst.

"I don't think anyone does."

I rubbed my temples. "I know one person."

"Don't tell me she has her eyes set on him..." Trista shot me an incredulous look. "You need to tell that girl what just happened!"

"I'll try."

CHAPTER 2

THE TALLEST WITCHLORD IN ALL OF DRAKINGTON

"It is necessary for the Dark Natured to remain bound to the Church of Fate. Without such divine guidance, we are certain to damn ourselves. Heresy, the blackest poison, cannot be forgiven, nor overlooked. To guard against such corruption, I deem it vital that the Dark Natured be led in prayer before each day's labor."

— *KOLSON STRANGE, MINISTER OF SPIRIT*

MY EYES BLINKED OPEN TO THE DARKNESS OF MY stale apartment. There was no comfort in staying in bed. The makeshift mattress was hardly holding together these days. Once sewn with scrap fabrics and stuffed with dry leaves, now sinking in and popping along the seams.

I wrapped myself in a threadbare blanket and padded across the room to my pile of laundry. I hadn't dared to wash my clothes these past few days, for fear they would freeze. An abhorrent mistake I would not make a third time.

Footsteps shuffled from upstairs. A baby cried in a nearby apartment. A couple argued somewhere below.

The sound of families used to be a bitter reminder of an old wound. My mother, troubled and undeniably lacking in maternal instincts, was the only one of my family I could remember. She'd told me once that I had two brothers, but my father ran off with them before I was born. My mother ran off eventually, too.

I'd become numb to the morning commotion, despite how crowded our building became.

There was so little space within the 'Wards that most of us lived in compact cottages stacked on top of each other. Many people climbed the outer walls and slid into their apartments through tiny, carved-out windows because no builders would bother wasting materials on stairs above the third floor. Luckily for Luna and me, our place sat only three stories high, and I never went a day without being grateful for the luxury of stairs.

Luna shuffled in, rubbing her shoulders, and cursing at the door for getting stuck on the frame. I sank onto our only piece of proper furniture—a brown couch that one of Luna's *customers* had given her a while back.

A sympathetic smile slid across her face as she dropped her satchel onto the wooden countertop. "You're up early again."

With a blanket wrapped tightly around my shoulders and knees curled up to my chest, I shrugged. "I can't sleep. Too cold. And my head is killing me."

I had worked well past midnight at Widow's Way Tavern,

drinking my way through the shift. I should have been used to the headaches by now, but the alcohol always took its toll.

"Well, I was quite warm last night," Luna bragged, practically falling onto the opposite side of the couch.

"I'd imagine so." I leaned forward, weighing my words. "If I had your job, it would be solely for body heat. Nothing more."

Brothel work was understandably appealing. It paid well enough, and sometimes Luna seemed to enjoy being at work more than at home.

For me, it wasn't the act that was intolerable. It was the expectation of *entertaining*. I could count on one hand the number of people whose conversations didn't feel like torture. Pretending to enjoy them would wear me down long before the true service.

She bounced her shoulders and grinned. "It's the coin for me. While I suppose the warmth is nice, the brothel keeps me from looking like you. Hungover and freezing to death and stinking like ale all evening."

I winced. While I wasn't hungover *every* morning, she had a point. The winters were the worst. Maybe I would be better off serving my flesh instead of ale, but I wasn't like Luna—alluring and hospitable. People weren't drawn to me; they were deterred.

"I assume it was a good night then?" I rubbed my hands together between my thighs, eager to return to Trista's. She always prioritized firewood in her budget. It wasn't long before she'd open up shop, and I'd have plenty of time to warm up before my morning work.

Luna shrugged and sighed dramatically. "It would have been better if the new Witchlord had stopped by. Two weeks he's been posted here, and he's yet to come to Miss Soryl's. Are you aware of how tall he is? It's ridiculous."

I hadn't had the chance to tell her about my encounter with him. Luna had stayed at work for the last two days, and I certainly would not be stopping by Miss Soryl's to talk about a Witchlord. Especially when Luna had a dedicated paramour who might overhear.

"Pining after Lord Ansel when you have dear Riven warming your bed?" I asked, brow quirked.

Riven went against the rules by caring for Luna, and she loved it. As a Draker, he kept guard and ensured that we, the Dark Natured, behaved. She never admitted to actually caring for him, but too many times I had found the Draker sneaking into our apartment, his usual armor absent. Never leaving until the early hours of the morning.

I wasn't a fresh summerborn nor as dull as a soup spoon. She liked him.

Luna rolled her eyes. "Riven probably has plenty of others. Besides, if Lord Ansel came to the brothel, that would be work, and work doesn't count." She proudly tucked her mahogany shoulder-length hair behind her ear.

"Well. I guess you're right." I rested my elbows on my knees, innocently looking away. "I suppose you wouldn't care to know where Lord Ansel was last night?"

"Elora!" she squealed, kicking my leg underneath the quilt. "Tell me immediately!"

"I saw him yesterday morning, as he was *looking for me*."

"Looking for *you?*" Luna looked ready to strangle me if I didn't spill faster. "Tell me you fucked him. If anybody gets him before me, it's you."

Grimacing, I straightened my posture and cleared my throat. "No, I did not fuck Lord Ansel. The furthest thing from it. Charles the Imp accused me of using my Nature."

Her voice softened. "A Witchlord believed you?"

The question jolted me.

"I guess. He checked my hands and left. *But then…*"

"There's more?"

I nodded. It had been bothering me nonstop, which was probably why I was awake odiously earlier than usual. "He was at the tavern last night, sitting in the same corner he sat in a few days ago. Didn't speak to anyone, just watched and ordered one ale."

An ale he never bothered to drink.

"He didn't speak to anyone?"

I shook my head. "Just watched."

Paying attention to him felt weird, but it was hard not to. He was a brooding eyesore, Witchlord cloak and all. Everyone else had been drunk and reeking of barley and grime. His presence was off-putting.

Luna hopped off the couch and paced the small kitchen. "Perhaps I'll swing by the tavern this evening. It is my night off, anyway."

It had been some time since my best friend had visited me at work. I wouldn't mind some sane company. Plus, maybe she'd finally see for herself how intolerable Lord Ansel was. "You should," I said, forcing myself up.

Dawn was near, and soon the streets would be crowded with Blackhearts, Stonesenders, Imps, Flamecastors, and Nightcastors. The economy was rough in the Waywards, and *everyone* had a job to do.

I pulled my boots on and braced myself for the morning chill. "Enjoy your sleep," I called as Luna snuggled into the couch.

Once out of the grim apartment, I ventured onto the winding dirt and snow-speckled streets. Drakers were posted all about, their dark grey armor embellished with the Drakington falcon across their chests. Daunting black hoods and golden masks disguised their identities. I typically tried not to think too much about who might be under the masks. It was one of the many reasons I couldn't work in the brothel.

Luna often discovered too much.

There were countless Drakers, but only seven Witchlords within the walls. They didn't stroll the streets often, but they were undoubtedly lurking, checking for forbidden uses of magic and whatever other useless shit they did.

During daytime hours, I had been assigned tailoring duty. Tasked with sewing clothes for the Drakington forces without pay. Everyone worked in the Waywards as payment for living here and the supplies that were sent in. If we refused to do our assigned job, we might as well climb into the burn pile ourselves.

Besides our assignments, we still needed to make money, which was why I slung ale at night.

Thankfully, my day full of sewing went by fast enough, and I hoped for the same with my shift at the tavern.

Being a bar maiden was preferable to being a tailor, at least at night I was paid for my work. There were also no Drakers over my shoulder telling me I wasn't working fast enough, especially when I was already pricking my fingers from sewing too quickly.

I hurried through the back door of Widow's Way toward boisterous voices and clinking glasses. It would only get busier throughout the night.

I relieved the day shift barmaid and strolled behind the bar. The tavern was packed with not only various Dark Natured, but also a few unmasked Drakers and two Witchlords. We were one of the rare spots that welcomed anyone, no matter their Nature or status. It was an unspoken rule that what happened in the Waywards at night did not linger into sunrise.

Hours passed like minutes as I bustled up and down the bar, serving ale and collecting coin. Charles the Imp had been kicked out earlier and lay pitifully on the ground outside. He carried on wailing and singing sorrowful songs, each one more miserable than the last.

I had considered killing him, but every time I had a perfectly breakable bottle in hand, Drakers hovered nearby.

Luna sat at the bar, circling her finger around the rim of her drink, and swinging her feet. Her long-sleeved beige shirt had only a few thin spots and hardly any stains. It showcased the little bit of cleavage she had and complemented her dark brown eyes. She was on a mission.

I topped off a regular's glass and made my way to her.

"Where's Riven?"

She gave me a warning look, overly worried about people finding out she was sleeping with the Draker. Some rumoured that Riven was the king's favorite. Oftentimes, if there was a message needing to be sent to the capital, he was the one who rode to Lyonscliff.

I scoffed. "No one is listening to us."

"You never know."

There was a reason Drakers were disliked. They were Natureless people who did not care when we were sent into the Waywards. Beneath the masks were our old neighbors, business partners, and even lovers. It was a money-making opportunity for them.

When Luna was twelve, a lord's family bought her out of the capital orphanage to keep the house clean. She had three adopted brothers and was impossible to console the day she found out one of them was under a Draker mask himself. She wouldn't have ever known if he hadn't bought her time at Miss Soryl's.

She never hated Riven for being a Draker, though. She had him over to the apartment so often that he was the only one I recognized easily when maskless.

While Riven was quiet and likeable enough, he was not to be trusted. He was here to keep the Dark Natured in line and to maintain the peace. Any hint of an uprising and they burned everyone involved. The punishment was always swift. They'd slice the perpetrators' guts open and push them into the flaming pile of flesh.

My throat tightened.

"Did you hear about Arielle?" I whispered to Luna.

My discreet efforts were for nothing as the most prying Nightcastor I knew turned his attention to us.

"Where *is* Arielle?" Beck purred, slyly scooting his stool closer to Luna.

She smacked his arm and huffed. "Beck, you nosy bastard."

While the tall, bronze Nightcastor didn't frequent the brothels, he was a regular at most taverns. The low light caught glints of caramel in his soft curls. He tugged his full lips into a mischievous smile, the softness in his hazel eyes contrasting the sharp angles of his jaw and nose.

A regular or not, it was none of his business. "I'll tell you later, *Luna*."

"You two are the worst gossips I've been around in ages." He laughed and flicked me a coin for another round. Most Nightcastors loved gossip. They also all shared the same birthmark, a crescent behind their left ear. Some rumored the mark was actually a thief's hook for stealing secrets.

Every Natured person was born with some kind of indicator, making it impossible to conceal oneself. Mine was a dark design on my left hip. Some described the Blackheart mark as a flower entangled in sharp vines. Others described it as death overcoming its victims. Every Blackheart's marking was unique, but the hip placement was a telltale sign.

I refilled Beck's glass. "How about we trade? You tell me something, and I'll tell you something," I offered.

His inquisitive features relaxed into a saccharine smile.

"Deal."

I set his glass down as the three of us leaned in, our voices hushed within the blaring tavern.

"Go on," I nudged.

Beck's mouth twitched.

"The king is ill. He will not make it to summer."

Luna's eyes narrowed. "A lying little loser is what you are. Go away," she ordered, shooing him with sweeping hands.

I crossed my arms. The king was healthy enough, and only ten winters older than I.

"Tell me about Arielle," he pleaded, any trace of playfulness disappearing.

I'd never seen Beck in any sort of desperation.

I sighed. "She's dead."

Luna spat her ale out. Beck did not react beyond the slightest flare of his nostrils.

"I thought you'd say that," he said, turning back and scooting his stool away from Luna.

I was aware of the loudness of the room in a way I had not been before. Luna rubbed her temples.

"You look distressed," I noted.

She eyed me, dumbfounded. "Of course I am. Miss Soryl is going to make me take Arielle's customers. I'm going to need another drink."

"Oh, hell." I refilled her glass, offering loose promises of prayers and sympathies.

The front door flew open, and an unwelcome Witchlord sauntered in.

Third night in a row.

My frown settled promptly as he faced me at the bar, two coins in hand.

His tunic was noticeably wrinkled, bearing the marks from the day. His sharp eyes were framed by soft black hair, while his cheeks were cold and blotched. He was possibly the tallest man that had ever entered Widow's Way Tavern, his head nearly scraping the ceiling.

He shifted, staring down at me impatiently.

I eyed the coins, the wet spots he'd trailed in from the snow, and lastly, his cold, blue eyes. "What can I get for you, Lord Ansel?"

Luna gawked from the other end of the bar.

"Water."

"Water?"

He dropped two coins into my palm. "It's a clear liquid."

I clenched my jaw. "I know what water is."

He smiled, eyes twinkling. "Great. Water it is, then."

I dropped the coins into my apron and fetched a glass. If he wanted murky water from a barrel, then fine. Luna caught my gaze, wildly motioning at the Witchlord. I shook my head.

Lord Ansel waited patiently. As soon as the glass was filled, I plopped it down in front of him.

"There's a seat at the other end of the bar," I added, nodding towards Luna.

He leaned in to pick up the glass before standing to his full height. "I have a good view of what seats are available." He settled in the back corner of the tavern, just as he had the past few nights.

I exhaled and marched back over to Luna.

She excitedly bounced in her chair, sloshing her drink. "Tell me everything."

"He is *not* very fun."

"Those are the most fun!" she playfully whined. Swiveling in her chair, she peered back at him.

I wiped the inside of a dirty tankard, gritting my teeth.

"He ordered water, then practically taunted me when I said he could sit next to you."

She looked back *again*. "Perhaps I should go sit with him."

My eyebrows nearly hit my hairline. Perhaps she should not. "You're worried about being caught with a Draker? Imagine what the others might think, or *do to you* if you associate with a Witchlord."

She rolled her eyes. "Fine. I'm going home then."

I nodded, catching a coin as she tossed it. "I'll see you in a few hours."

With Luna gone, there was no one to distract me from Lord Ansel's peculiar behavior. For the rest of the evening, he sat alone in silence. He never asked for another glass of water; he'd barely touched the first.

Was he trying to catch me using my Nature? Did he so eagerly want a reason to add me to the burn pile?

He finally left towards the end of the night, like most patrons. While many went easily, there were always a few stragglers I had to practically drag out the door before I could clean up.

When I left Widow's Way, Charles the Imp was sound asleep on the icy street, and Lord Ansel stood with his arms crossed, leaning against a neighboring building.

"You're still here?" I whispered, the Waywards chillingly quiet.

He gestured to the little green shit sleeping on the ground. "Waiting for the Imp to wake."

The cold pricked my skin, snow dampening my hair. "He may not get the chance, exposed to these temperatures."

Lord Ansel shook his head. "Imps have thicker skin than you and I. He'll be fine."

We both stared at Charles, whose mouth bubbled with spit on every exhale. As pleasant as it was to think about him freezing to death, I needed to get the precious little sleep I could before dawn.

"Well, enjoy watching the Imp."

I had already turned on my heel when he spoke up.

"Do you want to know what he's dreaming of?"

I cocked my head to the side. "You're a Dreamsoul?"

All of the Witchlords had been Lyonhearts before, with magic of healing, light, and strength. Rare, especially in Drakington—Dreamsouls were the only Light Natured kind to exist aside from Lyonhearts.

He flicked out a wrinkle in his tunic. "With the gossip around here, I would've thought you'd know by now."

"Can I speak freely, Witchlord?"

"Sure."

"I don't give a shit what your Nature is."

Silence filled the space. Instinctively, I straightened my posture under his electric gaze. He was a Witchlord; I was a Blackheart.

"Respectfully," I added.

"Do you want to know what the Imp is dreaming of or not?" he asked again.

I shrugged. "I'd rather be warm, but if you must share, go on."

He rolled his eyes, flicking his middle finger and thumb together. A fuzzy grey cloud erupted from his hand and wrapped itself completely around me. Brief flashes of lightning buzzed gently, heating the Dreamsoul blanket.

I didn't move or thank him. I stared only at the charmed cloud, breathing in the scent of crackling air before a storm breaks.

Lord Ansel nudged Charles' head with his boot. "He's dreaming of Lyonsreach. Within the castle, he's greeting guests for a ball. He's wearing finery. A young maiden has called him handsome. He's discussing politics with noblemen."

The invasion of privacy was disturbing and fascinating, and all the more reason never to fall asleep near a Dreamsoul.

"Interesting."

I also dreamt of castles and nobles, except I was never in the dreams. I just watched and woke up every morning sick from it.

"Go home, Blackheart."

The word 'home' was laced with lies. I longed to escape, to even get a glimpse of freedom. But there was nowhere else to go.

I pushed against his cloud. "Are you going to take this back?"

"You don't want to keep it? A gift after our... misunderstanding the other morning."

Warmth flooded my body as the blanket held me tighter. I looked down at it, eyes narrowing.

"Take it back."

The corner of Lord Ansel's mouth twitched into an arrogant smile. "Very well." He snapped, and the blanket was gone. Crossing his arms, he watched as the cold practically punched me in the chest, goosebumps spreading across my body like wildfire.

I never knew the authorities to play games or ensure Imps woke up. Furthermore, I had never met a single Dreamsoul in my twenty-three winters. To my knowledge, they preferred living in the bastard kingdom of Castivian. It was bizarre that *he* was our new Witchlord.

I gave him one last skeptical glare before turning away, hurrying home while cursing the cold.

When I returned, Luna was asleep on the couch, entangled with Riven. I quietly closed the apartment door and tiptoed across the room.

The Draker sat up, her head falling off his chest. He checked out the window, where the moon hung high in the sky, before turning back to me. His face twisted in confusion as he ran a hand through his tousled chestnut hair.

I should have looked away first, but I didn't. I couldn't.

Luna groaned, breaking the spell. "Elora?" she mumbled, voice muffled with sleep.

"Yes?"

"Goodnight," she murmured, turning back into Riven.

"Goodnight, Luna," I whispered, ducking into my room and shutting the door a little too fast. As I drifted off, I almost thought I could feel the cloud once again wrapping itself around me, soothing me to sleep.

CHAPTER 3

A NEEDLE

"The Sapphires are remorseless and deadly, and must be held in dread. If that accursed cult sets foot upon our soil, let their passage be redeemed with blood."

— ANONYMOUS CORRESPONDENCE FROM LYONSREACH TO SIR RIVEN BLACKSWORD

WEEKS WENT BY, AND TO MY RELIEF, THE WITCHLORD stayed away. He no longer bothered to frequent Widow's Way, nor did he come into Trista's shop. He'd likely found other troublemakers to investigate.

With one annoyance gone, another emerged. Every night for a week, I'd dreamt of a sword in my hand. There was a man in front of me wielding one as well. Over and over, he'd perform the same attack, and I'd have to repeat the defense. The repetition was maddening. Again and again, just the singular move. I never attacked, only blocked continuously.

"You are the only man who would try this," the stranger laughed.

I am not a man, I wanted to say, but I could not speak. I was silenced, caged, and stuck in the same motion.

Over and over and over and over and—

Panting, I sat up in bed, clenching my quilt.

"I'm not a man!" I yelled out into the freezing bedroom. Sweat beaded down my forehead. Blinking a few times, my eyes adjusted to the darkness.

The floorboards creaked outside my bedroom. Footsteps far heavier than Luna's.

The soft brushing of knuckles weighed against the door. Riven had never come all the way to my room before. I was hardly dressed, only wearing my undershirt and underwear— the rest of my clothes strewn across the floor, desperately needing a wash.

Surely he wouldn't barge in, would he? I grasped the sheets, waiting anxiously for the knock. What would he say? Did he know I had a nightmare?

The knock never came.

His steps trailed back to the couch, silence filling the lonely space.

Riven seemed to spend every waking moment either working or tending to Luna. That couldn't leave much time for sleep.

Maybe he deserved to be exhausted. After all, he was a Draker.

———

A month passed with similar dreams. Always a sword, always repetition. I never should have complained about the years I'd dreamt of castles and nobles. At least in those I simply watched events unfold around me, always feeling like I didn't belong.

The dreams I had now left me exhausted during the day, as if I'd never slept at all.

I sat at a weathered table in the tailor house, tediously sewing a shirt that would be used as an undergarment for the Drakington forces. There were fifty of us Dark Natured working away, while only two Drakers paced around supervising, accompanied by a Witchlord lounging in the corner.

There was still no sign of Arielle's return to the Waywards, further confirming she was in the burn pile. Its ash carried the deceptive scent of hot coals and cooking meat through the city. I shook my head as my stomach growled, repulsed that I could still have an appetite with the scent of burning flesh plaguing the room.

We were the hungriest during the winter—the time of year with the most fatalities, resulting in frequent bonfires. The sickness season had marked its arrival eight nights ago, taking a wave of Dark Natured with it.

Witchlord Dronis watched us from his corner, wobbling an orb of light between his hands like a game. It must've been nice, being allowed to use his Nature so casually.

A Draker faced me as I rethreaded my needle. There was no telling whether he was looking at me or someone else. Behind his mask and hood, he could have been closing his eyes for all I knew, but it certainly *felt* like someone was watching. I stared back, just in case, imagining the little needle in my hand finding its way through that mask and straight into his eye socket.

I often wondered how those assholes felt being the middle class of the Waywards. The Drakers would never admit it, but the only thing they were good for was sitting and guarding. All the true power lay in the Witchlord's wield, who answered only to the king.

Clearly, Dark Natured were at the bottom of the barrel. Maybe that made the Drakers feel good. They would never be nobility, but at least they were better than us.

With the rest of the kingdom already harboring enough hate for the Dark Natured, I'd thought we might have some camaraderie with one another. I learned quickly that it was quite the opposite.

Blackhearts were regarded as alley-piss. It was a Blackheart who had led to us all being caged in the Waywards. The man who'd committed the crime was long dead, but those of us left would pay the price for the rest of our lives.

Even the Imps, despite being classified as creatures instead of people, were regarded higher than Blackhearts. They had been forced into the 'Wards, since they weren't Light Natured and possessed bits of magic. The kingdom took no chances.

Flamecastors and Stonesenders ranked above the Imps. Nightcastors, like Beck, lingered somewhere in between. No one ever trusted a Nightcastor.

Drakington guards were all either highly skilled in sword-craft, previous squires, or the kin of Drakers before them. All Natureless, and all reportedly well-trained.

Those ranking the highest within the walls were the Witchlords. Only they could use their Nature and were profi-cient at it, too.

King Clarke had never set foot within the walls, and surely

never would. When I was a child, he was merely a prince. Now he was a young king with a beautiful queen, Delaina of Jadehill.

Queen Delaina despised all of the Dark Natured for what had happened to Princess Clayvarie. The girl was still alive, but her condition, as they called it, was rumoured to be worse than death. Perhaps a new heir would be born, or someone else would be appointed. I'd likely be long dead before that day ever came.

I picked up my stone, pulling the thread taut before continuing to weave. Women seated nearby gossiped about the upcoming weekend festivities. It was our third year surviving here. The entire Waywards celebrated halfway through winter, hoping it would keep us going until spring. There would be another celebration for those who lived to see the flowers bloom.

It was difficult to imagine anything blooming in this place.

The Witchlords enjoyed the midwinter holiday, as they hosted a game themselves. Bets would be made, and we would be 'reminded' of why we belong here. That was their justification for allowing a few Dark Natured to use their Nature—to prove the danger of it. A handful of people usually died during the game, not that anyone cared.

The fatalities had no effect on the festivities. It was the most exciting night of the season without question.

I cursed as my thread snapped. Even though it set me back three steps, I had to be grateful. Life could be far worse.

Louie from upstairs had been assigned street duty. He spent his days cleaning bodily waste and carrying it off in buckets. He usually looked and smelled as if one or two had spilled on him throughout the day. We could always tell when he was climbing to his apartment by the stench wafting by.

Luna's chore wasn't ideal either. She had to scrub Drakington armor with nearly frozen water in the afternoons. Often, her fingers were littered with bruises and cuts scattered along her arms from slipping on the sharp metal.

It was annoying Riven wasn't able to get her a safer assignment. What was the point in her sleeping with the king's favorite Draker if she still had to endure daily torment?

The most sought-after job belonged to the hunters. They were allowed to leave the Waywards with Witchlord supervision for days on end, hiking through the woods in search of game. While still not allowed to use their Nature, they weren't sitting in a cold tailor house with rumbling stomachs all day, pricking their fingers while weaving men's clothing.

Trista sat next to me, sewing away and babbling on. "What business do the Sapphires have with Drakington anyway? They have their own lands to keep. Lots of 'em too, I'm told."

I was sick of hearing about the Sapphires' threat, especially because our workload had increased since our kingdoms were on the brink of war. The Sapphires had taken over Lestivia easily enough, but those were peaceful lands. Drakington was far larger, with far more resources.

Trista chuckled. "You know the madman calls himself a king now, too?"

Considering Saffron had taken over Lestivia, he *was* a king, though the Sapphires were more cult than kingdom.

"Focus on your work, *inkweeds*," a Draker barked through his mask.

The word *inkweed* stung no matter how many times we

heard it, because that is not what, or rather *who*, we were. They loved to call Blackhearts that, as it was easier than learning our names.

Witchlord Dronis dragged his attention to Trista's sour face before turning to the Draker who'd ordered her silence. His dark skin glowed against the orb of light as he paused his tossing, cradling in one hand. I almost thought he would challenge the Draker and order his silence as well, just because he could.

Then he resumed tossing the orb from one hand to another, like nothing had happened.

A scream pierced the air. I whipped around, dropping the garment. Everyone in the room stilled as more followed from outside the tailor house.

"Sapphires!" a voice cried, as if Trista had summoned them herself.

I clutched tightly to my needle as a knot twisted in my stomach.

"Hide yourselves," Lord Dronis ordered before storming out, the Drakers following close behind.

As everyone began rising and running to back rooms and closets, I walked to the window, tiny needle still in hand.

Dark-blue cloaks and red eyes flooded through the gate. Drakers charged towards them on entry, swords held high. My heart skipped as blood smeared the walls like paint. Hundreds of Sapphires pushed forward, blurs of navy and crimson coating the street.

"What in Fate's name," I breathed.

Lord Dronis drew out a grand sword, his veins rippling with gold. Transferring his Lyonheart Nature into the blade. It flowed through him with a blazing intensity until the sword was bathed in golden flames. Without mercy, he sliced into the first Sapphire to cross him, severing the man's head from his body through aureate, fire, and steel. He leaped to his next target.

Even with Witchlord Dronis striking them down one at a time, there were so many Sapphires—too many. Hooded and quick, they descended upon the Drakers.

Evidently not everyone had been warned to hide, because as Dark Natured ventured out of their jobs and homes to examine the commotion, the Sapphire's targets changed.

They weren't going for the Drakers anymore.

They were coming for us. Like insects drawn to an oil lamp, they hauled toward the Dark Natured.

I backed away from the window, hands trembling. Did they hate us as well? Had they come all this way to kill us?

It was early. Luna would still be at home sleeping. Vulnerable, with no idea what was coming.

I ran out the door into the bloody streets. Moving away from the gates, I sprinted past dilapidated buildings, ignoring the sounds of slaughter behind me.

The farther I made it, the more unaware people were. We were under attack, and they didn't even know.

"Get inside!" I shouted, never stopping. "Sapphires are within the gates!"

Some gave confused looks, while others appeared excited, as if they too might try to go through the open gates.

They'd never survive to see the other side of the wall, but that was not my problem.

I ran into my building and up the stairs, barging into the apartment only to find Riven leaning back against the kitchen counter with Luna's mouth around his —

I gasped as he shifted away from her, his warm face going pale.

"For fuck's sake, *I eat in here!*" I scowled, blinking hard as I tried to erase the memory.

Luna shot up, holding in a laugh and wiping her mouth while Riven pulled his pants up. I never knew his arms and chest were covered in tattoos, nor had I wanted to. He quickly reached for his shirt off the counter before running a hand through his hair, taming it back.

"You're supposed to be at work," Luna said playfully, offering a smile.

I did not return it. I had been concerned for her life. I *still* was.

Stone faced and anxious, I pulled the door closed behind me, pressing my back against it as if the lock wasn't enough to keep it shut. "Sapphires tore through the gate. We're being attacked. People are dead!"

Riven's eyes shot up, dark brows pulling together as he noticed my weapon—well, the needle tightly fisted in my hand.

Luna's face fell.

"Are you certain they're Sapphires?" Riven asked quietly. "Not the Dark Natured attempting another revolt?" It was rare to hear him speak. His eyes bore into mine, waiting for an answer.

Shoulders tense, my face heated. Never had I experienced such intense attention from a Draker, and certainly not from the one bedding Luna.

"I'm sure of what I saw. They're Sapphires. Lord Dronis is fighting them off," I insisted, tripping over my words.

Riven grabbed his Draker gear and sword, quickly putting himself together. I shuffled to the side as he rushed to the door.

"Stay here," he commanded, bumping my shoulder before locking the door behind him.

His steps faded as screams neared our apartment. The attack had made it far past the gate.

Sapphires were truly in the Waywards, and my already small world was closing in.

CHAPTER 4

AN UNNATURAL STORM

"The Dark Natured are curious things, ever teetering on ruin.
Deny them their Nature, and they begin to unravel."

— *HENVRI JOYE, HIGH HEALER*

PEERING THROUGH THE WINDOW, LUNA AND I STOOD
shoulder to shoulder. Our eyes nearly touched the pane as blue
cloaks filled the streets. Horns sounded, and Drakers charged
from the top of the hill.

Metal rang out against metal, the black cloaks fighting
against the blue. Their years of training displayed in battle. Even
so, the Sapphires wormed through the Waywards, stabbing
chests and slitting throats.

It was strange that they were using steel, as they had a reputation for practicing blood magic. They had taken over the
kingdom of Lestivia, never wielding a blade.

"Perhaps they're not Sapphires. They aren't using blood magic," Luna whispered, making the same observation.

"Who else would wear their cloaks?"

Why would they attack here? If they wanted the Dark Natured for their army, it made little sense. Most of us were practically useless. We became ill when using our Nature, and in the time it would take to train us, they may as well have trained their own Sapphires. The Lestivian territory was also weeks of travel away. They would never make it that far with prisoners.

Coming from downhill, Lord Dronis still held his flaming sword, now covered in blood. The brutality in his snarl told me it wasn't his, and he had every intention of spilling more. Yet, his steps were sluggish, and he visibly struggled against a trio of Sapphires, grunting through each swing.

He'd never be able to take down the army by himself. Drakers were assisting, but they too were being swarmed. He needed the other Witchlords' help.

Luna's voice was shaky, her fingers trembling. "I don't understand."

Throughout the streets, Dark Natured infested the area, as if they could protect the cage they called home. A Stonesender with greying hair walked into the chaos, raising his cracked hands in a gesture of surrender as he approached the enemy. His clothes were ragged and dirty, and his face was pleading. He *begged* the Sapphire to take him back to Lestivia.

I shook my head. "Is he fucking stupid?"

Still, the Stonesender supplicated, grey palms faced out. "I don't want to be here anyway!" he shouted over the chaos. "Take me! I'll fight for you!"

The blue-cloaked figure held his hand out—an invitation. Giddy, the Stonesender ran over, uncaring of consequences. He approached the Sapphire, so close he was within arm's reach.

"Give me a sword, I'll help you! I owe no loyalty to the falcon!"

I strained to hear what the Sapphire was saying to him, but had no success. He reached for a sword, and as the Stonesender smiled, the Sapphire slashed right through his face.

"Mother of Moons!" Luna and I both recoiled. She looked away. I could not.

The Sapphire rabidly sucked blood from the Stonesender's fatal wound. Luna stumbled away from the window, hand covering her mouth.

It made sense now why they weren't using blood magic. There would be no prisoners—they were here for fuel.

"We have to do something," I said.

I had no idea *what* to do, but sitting there waiting to be drained was not ideal.

Luna's lips tugged back as she stared in disbelief. "We need to get out of here, out of the Waywards entirely. We need to *leave*."

"And go where?"

They would swiftly catch and execute us beyond the walls, no questions asked. We needed to help secure the Waywards, at the very least, to protect our building. It was all I had.

Luna pointed at the window. "We need to go somewhere these people are *not*. I refuse to be a meal for those monsters."

What she was suggesting was not possible or rational. We'd meet death sooner if we escaped.

"King Clarke created the Waywards for us," I snapped. "Outside these walls, we are hunted. *We are nothing*."

Luna's arms were at her side, hands balled into fists. "He created a prison! Not something special for us!"

"I'm not denying that, but maybe we deserve it. Maybe this is better."

I'd laid my guilt out on display. Pain etched across Luna's soft face as if I'd slapped her. As if she'd thought the same thing, but never said it aloud.

I didn't want to hurt her, but I'd already said it. Blackheart poison rumbled through me, lurking in my veins. Never far from the surface.

"Last I checked, neither of us had anything to do with Princess Clayvarie, a man did!" she screamed. "Yet every male in the kingdom is not locked behind these walls. Whatever trench your self-esteem has made a home in *reeks* of weakness. We did nothing wrong, so get your things together. If the gates are open, we are leaving. *Now!*" Black streams of poisonous tears rolled down her face.

She acted as if I had given my life for the man who'd attacked Princess Clayvarie. Like *I* was the one fucking the men who treated us like *shit* in here. I tilted my head, silent long enough to make her shrink a little, then even longer as the tears ran down her neck. "Who died and made you queen?"

"Elora!"

"Luna!" I shouted back.

She wiped her tears away and stifled a pained smile. "Being queen would be nice," she joked.

"Oh, for Fate's sake," I sighed. Only Luna would joke at a

moment like this. She took a deep breath, pulling herself together.

"I'm not leaving, Luna. We have nowhere to go."

She nodded, finally understanding. The only place we could live free was an ocean away in the Bastard Kingdom of Castivian. If it were easy to get there, everyone in the Waywards would have gone years ago.

I glanced back at the window. Three more Dark Natured were being drained on the ground while Sapphires polluted the grim streets.

Witchlord Dronis ferociously roared as he cut through a Sapphire's abdomen with his sword of light. His brown skin gleamed in the sun, and his white teeth shimmered with a snarl as he headed for his next target.

A frail, redheaded beauty walked up the hill, barefoot and trembling. My heart sank.

"I thought she was dead," Luna whispered.

There Arielle stood, alive and in the middle of madness. She was so slender that her once full cheeks had sunken in. Trista would be overjoyed her niece was alive, if she stayed that way.

Selfishly, I wanted to know what had happened to her in the castle of Lyonsreach.

Arielle glared at the men around her. Drakers, Sapphires, and the Witchlord. She let out a blood-curdling scream, sending violet Blackheart flames barreling out of her hands.

I stood in panicked silence. What the hell was she doing? Using her Nature again, in front of everyone?

She had no control, not even attempting to aim. Some of her blows hit Sapphires, others hit Drakers. Scream after scream, Blackheart venom barreled out of her, the flames fanning larger and larger.

A Draker charged her, his sword held high. She didn't flinch. With a shaking arm, she bared her teeth at him and sprayed black mist across his mask and armor. He screamed as it burned through metal, skin, and bone. She stepped over his body as he collapsed on the ground.

Arielle thundered with rage, igniting a violet flame the size of a boulder from her mouth.

It hurtled straight toward our apartment.

Luna and I pushed away from the window. We were halfway down the first flight of stairs when it hit. The impact sent us tumbling, landing on the platform of the next level.

Above us, others rushed down, while some yelled for help from their windows.

Luna cursed, wiping blood from her lip, but we had far worse problems. Smoke filled the already dark hallways along with the echo of screams. Overhead, a violet glow of flames ignited, melting the apartments. There were twenty stories in this building. At least fifteen levels' worth of people would die at Arielle's hand.

"Come on!" Luna choked through a cough. We hurried down the steps, our palms skimming along the rough walls. The moan of the crumbling building surrounded us, my vision obscured by dust and debris.

I followed her through the exit, into the smoky and blood-soaked street. We had no weapons, no training, and nowhere to go. Only a sewing needle and a will to live.

"Please! Please catch her!" a woman yelled from above.

My blood ran ice cold as I looked up.

The apartments wouldn't last much longer. The highest floors were already sinking into the flames. Leaning her torso through the window a few stories up, a mother held out her child, heavily wrapped in blankets. "Please!" she shrieked.

I nodded, my throat too constricted with terror to produce words. I held my arms out, and Luna did the same. Was I strong enough to catch the infant from this height? Was the mother going to jump, too?

She dropped the baby.

I was so afraid. I wanted to close my eyes, but forced them open. Luna and I crashed into each other as we both aimed for the child, collectively catching her between our arms and falling to the ground. She wailed, but was safe.

A wicked scream rang out, and I didn't need to turn around to know it was Arielle. She had to burn out soon. We couldn't use our Nature forever.

As the flames engulfed the mother's floor, she jumped without warning. Luna covered her face, and I tucked the girl to my chest, turning us both away before the *splat*.

"Oh, Mother of Moons," Luna sobbed, slapping a hand over her mouth.

The Sapphires and Drakers didn't pay any mind to the burning building or the cries coming from it. The Drakers were outnumbered.

"I don't know what to do," I admitted as the neighboring building set ablaze.

Cloaks and steel continued to strike each other down, the bloodshed unending. Dark Natured cried for their fallen families, some even picking up weapons to use themselves. Against the Drakers. Against the Sapphires. Against their own throats, even. They had nothing left to live for.

We couldn't stay put. There was no telling which direction our building was going to fall, or how many others it would take with it.

"We need to run." Luna's words were shaky, her eyes full of fear.

"My baby!"

An olive-skinned man with an unruly beard and tears streaking down his face approached, holding out his arms. He must've been working when the attack began.

"I'm so sorry," I mumbled as I handed off the baby.

He hadn't made it in time to save his wife.

Taking one last glance at my apartment, I followed Luna. We ran along the outskirts of the havoc, blocking out the cries and carnage. All of the Drakers looked the same with their masks and hoods, making it impossible to know which one was Riven.

Maybe Luna knew.

Blue lightning cracked through the sky, and a ground-shattering thunder sent everyone falling to their knees.

It was no natural storm.

"*Enough*!" a menacing voice roared. A voice I was ashamed to admit I immediately recognized. Witchlord Ansel stood dauntlessly atop the hill.

Sapphires jumped to their feet in defense. Witchlord Ansel just smirked. Lightning erupted from the sky like a web, electrocuting six of them in one precise beat. Lord Dronis chuckled, raising his sword with pride. Lord Ansel eyed Arielle, then the burning building. My building.

Something like panic etched across his face, followed by a deadly darkness. He strode forward, sword in hand. Black cloak billowing in the unnatural wind. He pointed his weapon to the sky, swirling it towards the fire. The skies opened up with a torrential downpour.

I flinched at the bite of cold water.

Arielle stiffened, her jaw tight and face twisted. She wasn't done. She wanted to burn out. In her gaunt, emaciated state, she must have yearned for death, willing to take anyone she could with her.

"Enough," Lord Ansel repeated—a warning to Arielle. He offered her mercy, if only she would accept it.

A Sapphire attacked from behind, but he was quick on his heels, whipping around and slicing their head clean off. He turned to Arielle, whose mouth opened, a poisonous flame within growing rapidly. Lord Ansel's smile curled upwards.

"Sweet dreams."

His Nature was effortless. All it took was a blink, and she fell to the ground, unconscious. Her poison sizzled away like a bad dream.

"I want him," Luna breathed.

"I want this to end," I said, shaking my head, throat dry.

"That too."

A sword laid forgotten on the ground next to a Draker's corpse, glittering against the flashes of lightning. I dragged my hand along the cold alley wall, rain running down my face and heart pounding.

Those aggravating dreams had practically forced me to train myself to wield a sword in my sleep. I remembered the way my arms would arc through the air, and the force needed to drive the blade down.

Before Luna could convince me otherwise, I rushed out from the safety of the alley and grabbed the hilt.

I could barely lift it above my waist. My shoulder wailed in pain from the fall down the stairs. There was simply no way I'd be able to swing it.

Only a moment passed, but when I turned back to the alley, a Sapphire was cornering Luna. With her back against the wall, she stared at me with pleading brown eyes.

"I like when my dinner begs," the Sapphire said greasily. Only the back of his dark blue cloak faced me, but his voice was *ugly.*

The sword was too heavy. Entirely useless.

I threw my needle at the back of his head, but he didn't even flinch.

He closed in on Luna, blade nearing her chest. My instincts screamed at me, begging me to fight. I prayed the Drakers would forgive me.

I held up my hand and aimed for his head once more, only this time, I shot a pathetic, violet ball of mist. It flew right past him and hit the wall instead. He hissed, turning towards me, black eyes glowing under his cloak. There were no red flecks from blood magic. He was powerless, but worse, he was thirsty.

Shit.

He stalked towards me with a sinister smile, displaying an array of missing teeth.

"Elora!" Luna called out.

As if my name made the game more fun for him, more valuable, his eyes flashed in excitement. I scrambled to pick the sword back up, the weight of it sagging to the ground.

"*You* are for keeping," he said, the blade aimed at my chest.

The heavy sword had me tripping over my feet. Nausea overcame me, erupting from my mouth. I felt every bit of worthlessness as I spewed up the consequence of using my Nature.

The Sapphire chuckled darkly as he approached me.

Luna froze. This was how I was going to die, soaked in rain and bile.

She stood with wobbly legs, hands trembling and eyes watering. "I'm sorry," she mouthed.

Then she ran.

Time may as well have stopped. Her short brown hair flopped against her shoulders as she bolted, not bothering to glance back as she disappeared into the chaotic streets.

The air escaped my lungs. She'd left me.

Looming above, the Sapphire beamed. "I should use your blood. You clearly don't have the stomach for it," he seethed, towering over me.

I wouldn't die of hunger, or from the cold, or even from the sickness season. Thoughts of my family surfaced. I'd never find my two brothers or ask around about my father. I'd never get to tell them about our mom and how she too had eventually left me. I'd never gossip with Trista again, or live to see if Princess Clayvarie would rule one day. I'd never marry or have a family of my own.

The Sapphire gripped my arm, yanking me to my feet. My Nature boiled within me, the taste of it on my tongue.

"I'm not afraid of you," he said, rotting gums too close. His putrid breath would be the last thing I smelled in this life. I closed my eyes.

"But you should be afraid of *me*," a Draker growled before grasping the Sapphire's head and twisting it until his neck snapped. I knew that voice. It didn't matter that he wore the mask.

The Sapphire's body fell, nearly pulling me down with it. I regained my balance and protectively pulled my hands to my chest as if someone might reach for me again.

"Thank you," I said, chin tilted up at the man who'd saved me.

"I won't let anything happen to you," Riven promised. He gripped his sword, leaving me in the safety of the shadows.

It only took a moment to lose sight of him as violence littered the piss and rain-soaked streets. Thunder shook the ground relentlessly.

I tucked myself against a stack of meat crates. The poorly made building above slanted just enough to grant me the slightest coverage from the rain, my legs facing the worst of it.

Lightning cracked once more, followed by a resounding smack of bodies falling to the ground.

Another crack. Then another.

Nauseous and alone, I pulled my knees to my chest, pillowing my face into my forearm. I had no concept of time as the storm drowned out the sounds of screams and clashing metal.

It wasn't until the downpour slowed that I peeked out of the alley, catching a glimpse of Lord Ansel and Lord Dronis putting their weapons away.

The streets were finally calm. It was over.

Scooting further into the alleyway, I rested my head back against the wall. The nausea was subsiding, but the anxiety was not. My home was gone. Luna, the only person I thought I could count on, had left me to die.

I flinched as steps approached, black boots splashing through red-soaked puddles.

"You have a leak, Blackheart," Lord Ansel said.

I frowned, glancing at my hand.

Sure enough, poison was seeping out, begging for further release.

Well, fuck.

CHAPTER 5

BEYOND UNFORGIVABLE

"Though I concede that Blackhearts may feel affection, lust, or even the madness of obsession, I find it unlikely that such creatures are capable of love. Their hearts are black indeed."

— *ANONYMOUS CORRESPONDENCE TO*
LYONSCLIFF

SOAKED TO THE BONE BY RAIN AND THE SENSE OF complete failure, I sat silently against the alley wall.

"Quite messy of you, really," Lord Ansel lectured, eying my clenched fist. It was a pathetic attempt to stop the flow.

I pressed harder. My home had been burned, the Sapphires attacked us, and Luna left me. She *left* me. Attempting to use my Nature was the stupidest thing I could have done, and most infuriating of all, the obsidian wall was still there, taunting me.

Lord Ansel loomed above me, not a single drop of blood or

water on him. The only dry person in all of the Waywards, letting the storm pour on everyone but himself.

If only the rain could have washed my Nature away with it.

"You need to go home until you get that under control, Blackheart."

"I don't have a home." I clenched my hands tighter, desperate to contain the poison I would never be free from.

He glanced back at the building. Bodies were being dragged out of the destruction, but I couldn't bring myself to look at their faces. Maybe Fate favored Arielle, because she was no longer lying in the streets. How she had lived while so many others died, I didn't know.

"Hm."

"What?" I snapped.

"Get up."

I did, letting the poison drip from my palm as I stood before him, body aching and refusing to meet his eye. I could run, but where? Fighting would be comical. He'd just brought the sky's wrath upon a small army of Sapphires.

"We have enough bodies to add to the burn pile."

I looked up, brow scrunched. "What?"

He extended a hand. "Do you trust me, Blackheart?"

"Do you want an honest answer?" I would trust Charles the Imp before I trusted a Witchlord.

"No." He gripped my hand, and the world around me became blue with mist and fog. It was as if we were floating in a cloud, yet moving too fast.

I tried to scream, but he was behind me, placing our joined hands over my mouth.

Swatting him away, I lost my balance. Somehow, I was tripping, my hands smacking onto a hardwood floor.

Large windows poured soft light into the well-kept living room. Bookshelves and blue velvet couches filled the open space. Artwork adorned the walls, and a mug was left discarded on the table.

The floor sizzled as poison pressed into it from my palm. I recoiled, grabbing my own wrist.

"You know, it's rude to burn a hole in someone's floor," Lord Ansel said.

His floor? I scrambled to my feet, backing away. Outside the window, the house across the street was black with a golden-tipped domed roof.

This was Keeper's Street, an exclusive area for the Witchlords' homes.

He tossed his cloak onto the couch and stood in his tunic, black hair shining under a chandelier.

"I'm not supposed to be here."

"Says who?"

"The Witchlor—" I stopped as he raised a brow, challenging me. *He* was a Witchlord. Within these walls, what he said was law, and he answered only to the king.

Lord Ansel left for a moment down a hallway, returning with a thick cloth. I'd probably made it myself in the tailor house.

"Wrap your hand. There's a room upstairs to the left you can use until you find suitable arrangements. I'll be back later." He tossed the cloth to me and headed for the front door, his cloak still on the couch.

I gawked. I would rather sleep in the streets than a

Witchlord's home. Discomfort was no stranger to me, and I would not be inconvenienced by it now.

"I can find my own sleeping arrangements, and you're forgetting your cloak!" I called out.

"I don't need it where I'm going," was all he said before letting the door shut behind him.

This was not how things were done in the Waywards. If I were caught in his house, the Dark Natured would eat me alive. Drakers were one thing, but to be acquainted with a Witchlord was beyond unforgivable.

CHAPTER 6

AN EXCEPTIONALLY SHITTY DAY
IN THE WAYWARDS

"The punishment for wielding Dark Nature must be nothing short of grand. For if mercy takes its place, rebellion is but a breath away."

— *MARKER DANE, LORD OF LAWSHIP*

WITH MY HAND WRAPPED AND THREE HOLES ACTIVELY burning through Lord Ansel's floor, I ventured outside, fleeing Keeper's Street as quick as a thief.

The Waywards had never been in such disarray. Blood, bodies, and smoked flesh coated the air, the stench stinging my nostrils and irritating my eyes. I rubbed my face with my sleeve, blinking harshly a few times before pushing on, keeping an eye out for Luna.

The Drakers worked their way through the destruction, evaluating and loudly reordering the defenses still left in place after the attack. With the possibility of remaining Sapphires within the walls, many threw paranoid glances over their shoulders while families boarded-up windows.

Bodies lay all along the wet ground, most unrecognizable beyond their attire. Among the dead were Drakers, Sapphires, and far too many Dark Natured. Not a single Witchlord had fallen, their Light Nature serving them well. Lord Ansel's had served him *too* well. That mattered little, though. I had the living to worry about, not the dead.

I checked on Trista first.

She was inside her shop, physically fine, and tending to her unconscious niece. A few of her nephews had helped carry Arielle back home, unseen. Believed by others to be deceased.

Trista promised to handle her, and while I'd turn a blind eye for her sake, I wouldn't shed a tear if someone slit Arielle's throat in the night. Families had lost their homes and their lives. The Waywards weren't large enough to hide in forever. Her punishment would come.

Satisfied at seeing Trista alive, I moved on to looking for Luna.

My poison had yet to settle. I was on edge, the possibility of exploding seeming more likely by the minute. Lord Ansel hadn't killed me, but I would not be free from punishment. Not when there was a horrible aching in my limbs—the cusp of release I couldn't reach.

Stepping around bodies and moving through the somber Waywards, I headed back to the debris of my apartment.

I wasn't sure where to go for the night. If it weren't so cold, I would sleep outside. Luna could at least stay at the brothel. Maybe I'd talk Mister Archwindle into letting me stay at

Widow's Way after my shifts. Or maybe I just wouldn't sleep at all.

While I'd hoped Luna and Riven would be waiting for me nearby, they were nowhere to be found. An uncomfortable knot dug into my stomach as Drakers stacked unidentifiable bodies into a pile of rubble. Scavengers sorted through the ruin, stealing anything salvageable. If Luna were here, she'd surely be one of them. She was always fond of the principle of *"finders keepers."*

Perhaps she was just ashamed to show her face so soon. It shouldn't be too difficult to find her. After all, she had to be somewhere within the walls.

My pace quickened as I searched the soot-covered streets, gaze shifting from ruin to the surrounding solemn faces. As smoky air burned my throat, I coughed into my elbow. This was an exceptionally shitty day in the Waywards. After so many fatalities, they wouldn't have to worry about us outgrowing the cage anytime soon. I winced as I passed the body of an old acquaintance, but pushed on.

I'd walk every street in the city to find Luna if I must.

And I did.

Every. Single. Street.

The sun had set by the time I circled back to where I'd started. My legs and injured shoulder ached, though my heart rivaled both. Once again, I hoped to find Luna sitting outside of what was left of our apartment, maybe waiting to apologize, but all I found was Riven, appearing as defeated as me.

He stood with his mask and hood off, his grey and gold armor coated in blood. Wet tendrils of chestnut hair clung to both sides of his tan face.

He wiped sweat from his forehead with the back of his hand, grimacing at the dark clouds overhead. The worst-case scenario floated to the front of my mind, my stomach twisting with each silent second that passed.

"She's gone," he said at last.

My heart dropped, poison swirling inside of me. "What?"

"She left the 'Wards."

"What?" I repeated, snapping my head to the gate. It was once again shut and guarded.

"I confronted her in the woods myself. She wouldn't come back. She's gone."

It was as though an arrow had struck me through the chest.

She was the closest thing to family I'd ever had. I didn't think she'd truly leave.

She was a coward.

"She'll be hunted out there," I whispered, more to myself than him. The walls were too high to climb. Too difficult to break through. Many had tried.

Riven shook his head, jaw tensing. "I asked if she wanted to know whether or not you'd survived. She told me to fuck off. Let her face the fate she chose. It's not for you to worry about now."

My poison was on the edge of *boiling*. If Luna didn't care about me, then no one did.

My heart cracked.

———

Two miserable days passed.

I lay curled up on the wood floor of Widow's Way, tucked

behind the bar where there were no windows. Thieves were everywhere. If someone broke in, I wanted to see them first.

Mister Archwindle had agreed to let me stay in the tavern for a few nights, but it was no permanent solution. I didn't need long anyway, just enough time to find a way outside of the walls.

Two dish towels were folded and pillowed under my head while I hugged myself for warmth. Thank Fate that the floors behind the bar weren't soaked in ale, especially after an exceptionally busy shift. Everyone had needed a beverage to numb their mind after the Sapphire attack.

I forced my eyes shut, but my thoughts were unyielding.

Where was Luna sleeping? Was she alive? What about my mother or brothers? Were they all dead? Did they wonder if I was alive? Did anyone in the entire world care about me? Did I even care about myself?

"Stop," I whispered, flinching.

The world wasn't ending, not yet anyway. The midwinter celebration would be in two days, which meant I could at least look forward to watching the annual game of Orb Hazy.

Luna always loved watching, even when it got gory. I hadn't wanted to go last year, feeling insecure about my appearance. I recalled getting ready in my room, just an hour before the game would begin.

"You're so pretty," Luna said.

She gave compliments like gifts, wrapped in soothing tones and always right when you needed them. I sat in front of our cracked and rusted mirror. I never looked at my reflection, but that day, something had willed me to look, and I did, as if answering an order.

"Help me with my hair before Riven leaves and goes to the celebration by himself," Luna joked.

I sat behind her on the floor, brushing through her pin-straight hair, bravely glancing up at the mirror every so often. Luna's warm caramel skin practically glowed. Her hair fell just below her shoulders, making it quick work to braid.

While I appreciated her compliment, she was the pretty one. My skin was fair and lacked her radiance.

She had soft brown tresses, while mine was a devouring black. My face was longer and narrower. We both had brown eyes, but mine seemed like a void, while hers were inviting like chocolate. My cheekbones were more prominent, but her lips were fuller.

She always looked happy, while my face sat in a natural state of misery.

"Stop comparing yourself to me," she snapped.

I met her gaze in the circular mirror. "I'm not," I lied.

She sucked her teeth and rolled her eyes. "Blackheart women are beautiful. We are beautiful. Don't trick yourself into believing anything less." While her tone was sharp, there was something else behind it, too. She wasn't only trying to convince me, but herself as well.

The squeak of the door startled me out of the memory.

Sitting up, I listened closely, perfectly hidden behind the bar. Only one set of footsteps entered, quiet but heavy. Reaching for a low shelf, I carefully grabbed the paring knife. The floorboards creaked near the bar as my heart pounded. I was vulnerable, but I wasn't entirely helpless. I jumped to my feet with my weapon ready, knowing I'd aim with the pointy end and hope for the best.

Lord Ansel lifted a brow. My back hit the wall, knocking over a glass. It shattered across the floor.

I scowled. "What are you doing here?"

It was late into the night, yet he was polished. He hadn't bothered to wear his cloak. Instead, he stood in a black tunic and matching pants, no weapons in sight. Not that he needed them. He silently assessed me and the mess *he* had caused. Unamused by the knife in my hand, he snatched the blade and tossed it down the bar.

"Blackheart, explain why you're here."

I grabbed a broom. "I'm trying to sleep." It was bizarre speaking so familiarly with a Witchlord, but he did not *act* like the others.

"You prefer the floor over a perfectly fine bed?"

"It's not perfectly fine," I argued, shards clinking together on the ground.

He raised his chin. "Oh? It's not? You never went into the room to know."

"I don't need to see it to know it's unacceptable. It's in a Witchlord's home!"

I'd shouted, *and loudly.*

If he was angry, he didn't show it. "Find somewhere *hospitable* to sleep by tomorrow night, or you'll find yourself where I put you," he warned.

"You can't tell me where to sle—!"

A grey cloud surrounded him, then he was gone—like he'd evaporated.

I clenched my teeth, yanking the broom once more to finish sweeping up the glass.

After locking the door and placing a chair in front of it, I returned to the frigid floor.

His definition of hospitable and mine were entirely different. Anywhere I could lie down was hospitable enough—anywhere he was, was not.

I hummed, a trick that sometimes soothed me to sleep. I'd been doing it since I was a little girl. Other times, I gently scratched my arms, imagining it was someone else.

Since failing to lift the sword, I hadn't dreamt of wielding or training anymore. In fact, I hadn't dreamt at all. It was as if my own mind was disappointed and didn't know what to say to me.

I was truly alone.

CHAPTER 7

A POSSE OF IMBECILES

"They must be punished. All of them!"

— *ATTRIBUTED TO QUEEN DELAINA*
LYONAIRE, AS OVERHEARD IN THE COUNCIL
CHAMBERS

I BANGED ON TRISTA'S DOOR WELL BEFORE OPENING, asking for forgiveness as I hurried in.

She gathered a pitcher of water. "If Arielle killed someone close to you, add yourself to the list. I can't be bothered to hear about it anymore."

I shook my head. Arielle wouldn't be receiving a solstice gift from me, but killing her was the least of my worries. "I've witnessed enough death this winter. I need your help with something."

Trista wrapped herself in a brown blanket, her hair a frizzy mess and bags drooping under her eyes. Dawn was hours away, and usually I'd wait for the shop to open. But uncertainty haunted me. Even being allowed in provided a semblance of relief.

Sometimes, I wondered if I bothered people just to see if I was worth the burden.

She plopped two mugs onto the counter with a *thud*.

"Help with what?" Her veins were a little darker than usual, protruding from her temples as she lifted the pitcher. I might not have been the only one forced to use my Nature. It would have been rude to inquire about such a thing, and unless I had a way to fix it, there was no use in pointing it out. She was probably well aware.

"I need to find a new place. A temporary one."

I had only one night left to sleep in the tavern, and no intention of ending up in a brothel.

Trista filled our mugs, an audible sigh vibrating against her pursed lips. "Well, do you have any coin saved up?"

"Does anyone?"

She scratched her head and yawned again. "Nope."

I didn't think so.

She tapped her finger on the counter for a moment before letting out an excited gasp. "Just find one of those wealthy gentlemen who live in the Pearl and marry him! You're not half bad, you know? You're young enough, too. There would be a lovely bed to sleep in, and probably a fireplace, and—well, Moons of Glory, I hardly know what they have, but I'd bet it's nice."

I frowned. While the idea of an actual bed *was* nice, the thought of living on that end of the Waywards attached to a wealthy man was nauseating. I just wanted my apartment back... and my best friend.

"There are poor men with beds, too," she offered.

I gulped my tea down. I would have to brainstorm more on my own.

I thanked Trista before venturing back out into the city. It had been some time since I'd visited the Pearl. There would likely be apartments available for rent there, but I rarely concerned myself with the unattainable. Perhaps being surrounded by the wealthy would attract some coin into my life. It wouldn't hurt to look.

The moon guided me through the alleyways. The walk felt short enough at night when there weren't a million screaming beggars and petty arguments taking up half the muddy street.

The Pearl wasn't much different from everywhere else in the Waywards, but it had slightly nicer homes and exclusive establishments.

The wealthy had tried buying their freedom three winters ago, but no amount was high enough. Despite it all, they still found ways to feel superior, elevating their status even within the walls. Several had fronted the cost of labor and materials to build better homes, then rented them out at a higher price to their fellow socialites.

Their buildings were still grim, but also polished with rare luxuries such as stairs, fireplaces, and even the occasional balcony.

The stars twinkled, but they could not steal my attention from the queen of the sky. The crescent moon shimmered. What must it be like for her to wait all day for her chance to shine, just for the world to be sleeping?

A hand grabbed me, shoving me down. I shrieked as my palms and knees slammed into the wet ground of the alleyway. Turning over, I shuffled backwards frantically until I sat pressed against the cool wall, with four men looming over me.

My eyes widened at the strangers. The looks I received in return were of nothing but hatred.

"She's a Blackheart," one said, gravelly and sure. My markings were under my clothes, but my traitorous eyes and veins were a dead giveaway.

Most Blackhearts could camouflage their veins with a mixture of practice and not using their Nature. I'd tried that for years, but it didn't matter. My Nature demanded to be known. A heart as black as mine would know many things like animosity, shame, and fear, but I would never know what it meant to be looked at and not judged by my Nature before anything else.

I glared up at the four men. It was easy to hate them back as they stood together like a puddle of dicks awaiting their turns for a buttered sock.

My nostrils flared. A chuckle escaped from one of the men's lips as he cracked his knuckles. While his hands were noticeably dainty, he was the largest of the group. Most certainly due to pie and a lack of training. The blond rodent's nest on top of his head was almost as unruly as the wispy display of a beard on his face.

"Of course she's a Blackheart. Look how filthy she is."

Three of them laughed darkly, while the fourth observed with wild eyes and a continuous brow, sizing me up like prey.

I shot back a deadly glare and scrambled to my feet. "Save your giggling for when you make love to one another. I'm not bothering anyone. *Leave me be.*"

The blond kicked me in the abdomen. My body thudded against the ground, my involuntary groan fading into a low whimper.

"That's where you're wrong," he said. "Your kind's bloody existence bothers me. You poison dreams, melt flesh, make men incapable of love, and have ruined countless lives. If it weren't for vermin like you, I'd still be with my wife and children."

The very Nature he hated so much brewed within me. "What do Blackhearts have to do with your wife and children?" I spat. I was sick of being blamed for everything, even by other Dark Natured. I had yet to see his palms, but I'd bet they were marked in stone.

He reached down, gripping my hair and yanking me to my feet. I yelped as he brought his mouth to my ear. "My wife is Natureless. My children, too, and now she's likely remarried to afford them, all because I was forced into these damned walls," he growled, his breath hot on my face. "I'll never see the love of my life again, and it's all because of a Blackheart like *you*."

"Edmund? Let go of her," an unfamiliar voice said.

He released his grip immediately, backing away as I caught myself against the wall.

I took slow, intentional breaths as a man with short brown hair and a neatly trimmed beard approached. He stopped a polite distance away, examining me.

"It's bad business to attack a woman in the middle of the street, is it not?" he questioned, his gentle scold surely meant for children, not men.

"She's a Blackheart," the blond answered defensively, shifting his gaze and pointing at me. One quick glance at his palm was all it took to confirm my suspicion. The grey, rough texture couldn't mean anything else. Perhaps if we were outside of the Waywards, he would have sent a rock soaring into my skull instead of a foot to my stomach.

The well-dressed man tightened his jaw, his lips falling into a flat line. "And I'm a Nightcastor. Go make yourself useful elsewhere before I decide to never pay you another copper."

The posse of imbeciles scurried away.

I was alone in the alley with the brunette, both of us silent. His clothes weren't thinning and falling apart like mine. They were a simple yet fresh set of garments. A Pearl dweller.

"I'm sorry. My security does too good of a job sometimes," he laughed.

If he could afford security within the Waywards, he must have been incredibly wealthy prior to being forced into them.

"I'd like to go now."

I didn't care about an apology, and even less, a conversation.

The man was generically handsome, with a youthful face despite the evidence of aging around his kind eyes.

Hands in his pockets, he rocked back on his heels. "Of course. However, I'd love the opportunity to make up for this embarrassing inconvenience. That's my building you're leaning on. Perhaps you might consider returning this evening—if you're available. I'm an excellent host."

"Hm." I was familiar enough with men and their intentions to recognize his tone and the true meaning of the invitation.

But...I did need somewhere "hospitable" to sleep. I hoped to be out of the Waywards after the midwinter celebration. Perhaps, I'd find my escape after Orb Hazy, when many Drakers would be drunk and partying late into the night. That was only a day away. The Pearl would be a perfectly acceptable temporary solution. Lord Ansel would be oh-so-pleased with this joyous turn of events.

"I'll be available," I decided, offering a rare smile.

"I'll be expecting you."

————

Between the heavy workloads of both jobs, the day flew by. I locked up Widow's Way and travelled across town back to the Pearl.

Lord Ansel would not be interrupting my sleep, nor would he be *putting* me anywhere.

It was already past midnight when I knocked on the black door of the two-story building. When the Nightcastor had initially invited me to return that evening, he hadn't specified a time, but I was sure he would answer.

"You're late," he noted, neither happy nor upset. His brown hair was slicked to the side, and his beard was neatly trimmed. Despite the hour, he was fully dressed down to his shoes.

He'd waited for me.

"Do you want me to leave?"

"No, of course not."

I smiled. An easy win.

As I'd suspected, my late arrival meant he didn't have the time to torture me through hours of small talk before inviting me to his bedroom.

————

The fuzzy light of dawn streamed in from the circular window as I lay awake.

A soft snore rumbled behind me in symphony with the crackling fireplace across the room. It was otherwise quiet, including the streets outside. Perhaps this side of town didn't bother or need to wake early, or perhaps it was because of the midwinter holiday. Many of us were excused from work for the occasion, a gift we were expected to be grateful for. We'd also be expected to work twice as fast upon our return.

I sat up. The room wasn't bad, especially for the Waywards. In fact, it was nicer than anything I'd lived in outside of the walls, though that wasn't saying much.

My mother always moved us around to wherever was cheaper, or wherever a man would let us stay if she warmed his bed. They were never noble nor kind for longer than it would take to lure her in. As soon as she felt safe and settled, they'd change, and always for the worse. I'd learned as a young girl that a man's pants' button would open long before his heart would.

It was ironic to think of, as I too lay beside a nameless stranger simply to survive.

The tidy room had high ceilings, a few paintings on black walls, a dark wooden bed frame, and a custom fireplace with markings of the moon and black wisps like shadows along the mantle. Not too far away from the bed was a rug.

I hadn't seen a rug since before the 'Wards.

I stroked the heavy grey blanket covering my bare chest, appreciating its value.

The Nightcastor snored peacefully. How wealthy was he before the Waywards, and how much of his wealth had dwindled since being forced to live here? Had it dwindled at all?

Just because he was within the walls didn't mean his business had to be. How many Drakers were smuggling coppers in and out? King Clarke couldn't be paying them well enough for loyalty to matter.

The calm room was only interesting to stare at for so long. My stomach grumbled as boredom settled in.

"I'm leaving," I announced plainly. The warmth emitting from the fireplace was difficult to give up, but it was time to go. While I was free of tailor house duty for the day, there were other things to do before the celebratory game at sunset.

The Nightcastor inhaled a startled breath, rolled over and mumbled, "Very well then."

A brief, awkward moment passed as we both dressed and he escorted me out of the attractive apartment.

As the morning chill prickled my neck, I almost regretted my departure. He was no prize in bed. No, the bed *was* the prize. Comfortable, warm, with real pillows and clean-enough linens. I thought about doubling back.

The night was over, though, and he would fade into yet another indistinct memory.

Thankfully, one part of my daily routine felt normal. I pushed through the creaking door of my favorite establishment, and the sight of Trista behind the counter, water already steaming, filled me with comfort.

"Well! It's nearly an appropriate hour to be awake. Where have you been this morning?" she beamed.

"I had a further walk today..." I began, a grin sliding across my face, "And I may have boffed a Pearl dweller."

Trista perked up, ravenous for any gossip, per usual. Especially mine. "How was it?"

I propped my elbows on the counter. "The man? Okay. The bed? Amazing. The best few hours of sleep I've had in a while. How can they afford to live in such luxury even after being stuck here?"

She idled on my question for a moment. "Old money lasts, and these lousy Drakers work for whoever pays the most. Wouldn't surprise me if they were doing business with people on the outside, but who knows? Why do you care?"

I shrugged. "I want a bed like that."

"Wed one of those Pearl boys and I'm telling you, you'll have it."

"Ah, of course," I joked. As if they would marry a Black-heart to begin with, much less me. While there was nothing I'd love more than to be rich, have babies, and drink tea, I was self-aware. It was not in the cards, nor would I want to bring children into the Waywards.

———

I helped Trista ready her shop for the holiday crowd late into the afternoon. We prepared treats and adorned the windows with strings of dried flower petals, a reminder of all that had died since spring.

Aside from Luna's absence, the Waywards felt slightly less grim than it had since the Sapphire attack, with an array of homemade decorations and children tossing bean-filled socks in the streets. Customers happily filled the seats of Trista's shop, and no one dared mention Arielle.

The midwinter holiday wasn't the time for grievances and disputes.

I waited all day for the sun to set, anticipating the game of Orb Hazy. Luna's betrayal stung now more than ever as I went alone. Despite her absence, I'd never miss the one night a year we were allowed to watch a group of Dark Natured intentionally use their Nature.

The Drakers on duty throughout the Waywards were more relaxed than usual—almost casual. Some mucked about in groups, laughing with one another and already making bets on which team would rise, and who would fall.

I'd yet to see any Witchlords on my walk. No black cloaks or auras of light magic. Just the community in a buzz.

As I weaved through the crowded, narrow streets, I rubbed my hands together, occasionally glancing up at the stars. Fate, or whatever was out there watching, had given us a clear night for the celebration.

It was unclear whether King Clarke was aware of the Orb Hazy tradition, but the Witchlords hosted the game every year as a reward and a reminder. We were caged for a reason. Because we were dangerous. The game refreshed everyone's memory, through orbs and bloodshed.

While most of the Waywards was a cramped shithole, there was one area clear of buildings that allowed space for the game. The only stretch of grass, tucked away in the farthest corner from the gates, with wooded land nestled at the bottom of the hill. If it weren't for the slope, they would have built over it by now.

Towering behind the trees in the clearing below was the obsidian wall. Three times as tall as any of the buildings and shimmering like a threat. A glowing cage meant to protect the rest of the world from us.

It's just a wall.

From my seat at the top of the hill, the clearing was practically a domed arena. We could see everything below.

All around, crowds of Dark Natured gathered with ales and eager eyes. Drakers were scattered about, some wearing masks and others drinking with their faces on display.

Three Witchlords stood in the middle of the makeshift arena, all dressed warmly in layers of black and talking amongst themselves. Preparing.

Four were absent, including Lord Ansel.

An uncomfortable wave of disappointment simmered through my chest. I'd wanted to know who he would pick and what his team's strategy would be. He didn't act like the other Witchlords, and he probably wouldn't play by the same rules, either.

The crowd continued to grow. It was my first time not being intoxicated for the event. Funny how much more I noticed when alone and stone cold sober.

Like how relaxed the weaker Dark Natured were. They stood casually, excited to watch without fear of being picked. The strong and large gathered with menacing patience, wishing all year to be chosen.

One of the Witchlords had already cast a golden orb of light in the sky above the arena, offering a glow of visibility. All three were Lyonhearts.

Light Natured. Better than us.

"But not him," I mumbled as a tall figure walked onto the field.

Lord Ansel reached the center, falling into conversation with the other Witchlords. I hadn't forgotten about the cloud blanket he'd offered me, or his electric touch when he'd checked for uses of my Nature.

The orb above the field suddenly pulsed, followed by a ring of light falling over the crowd.

"It's time to begin, Waywards!" Lord Dronis boomed with a smile.

CHAPTER 8

DREADFULLY DEADLY

"Vitalis Depletion, what the unlearned so fondly call burnout, is the body's rather dramatic protest when one's Nature is wrung past reason. It often announces itself with nausea, soon followed by headaches, trembling, and a breath that feels borrowed."

— *HENVRI JOYE, HIGH HEALER*

EVEN BEFORE WE LOST OUR FREEDOM, IT HAD BEEN taboo to use our Natures, for generations. The Dark Natured were assumed to be dirty, poor, and of terrible character. I never bothered with my Nature because of the sickness, but there were plenty of people dying for a chance to be reunited with theirs without consequence. They itched for the opportunity to release the darkness that idled beneath their skin.

The four Witchlords stood in their daunting cloaks, gazing up at the roaring crowds, subtly casting their attention to different sections as they surveyed the options for their teams.

Brutish Blackhearts, Nightcastors, Stonesenders, and Flamecastors stalked up and down the sidelines, chugging beers and rousing their spirits. Through every laugh, chant, and squeal, I sat still on the grass, knees to my chest.

Lord Ansel's eyes searched the crowd, sliding from the left until they landed on me. I swallowed as he tilted his head from across the field.

Did he know where I had found suitable sleeping arrangements? Did he bear a grievance with it?

The silent battle lasted all but a moment before a grubby little green fuck yelled from behind me, "Look at yee! Eeeeee-LOR-AH! Out of the tavern! So so prit-tee! It pains me eyes to look at yer stuns!"

I groaned. "What do you want, Charles?"

He boldly squeezed my shoulder with a slender hand. "A chance! Stop be'in a bitch! A bitchy witch!"

I smacked his piss-scented grubber away, baring my teeth.

"Don't touch things that do not belong to you."

"I touch where I want!" he yipped, reaching fast and squeezing my breast.

Mind-blinding rage surged within me as I caught his fleeing wrist. I twisted it low to the ground, his wavering joint threatening to snap. I had little left to lose, and suddenly, murdering Charles in front of the Witchlords didn't seem like such a terrible crime.

His warted nose crinkled, face melting into a spiteful frown. "Nobody else will want yous! And it hertz nothin ta do with ya bein a Blackheart!" he spat, yanking out of my grasp. Fury churned in my veins, begging me to wipe him from his miserable existen—

A pinch of lightning zapped my side. Down the field, Lord Ansel was watching. Warning me to stop.

Fuck Lord Ansel. I snapped my attention back to Charles. "The next time I see that grimy, vile-odored, shitstick of a finger, I promise you will lose it."

He bounced off the ground with his fists clenched. "Nobody! Nobody, nobody, nobody will want EEEELorAh!" he chanted, giving me one last ridiculous pout before stomping off into the crowd.

I stared out at the field, pushing every nasty feeling deep down, leaving an empty void.

Lord Ansel towered next to the other Witchlords, his silky hair framing his face. Lord Dronis strolled beside him, his demeanor relaxed, per usual. Luxurious braids hung from the top of his head, while his smooth brown skin glowed under the golden orb. Lord Dayire and Lord Jaysel came next, determination and excitement visible in their steps.

How early in the winter did they begin scoping out who they would choose for their teams? Or had they waited until the night of the event?

The orb above flickered from a bright beam to a fluttering, warm glow.

"Waywards! It is *your* holiday." Lord Dronis thundered over the drunken audience. "Most of you have behaved properly thus far this winter and made it another year in this thriving community. You have aided your kingdom in the war to come against the Sapphires, and with that, this midwinter game is your reward."

Claps, squeals, whistles, and chants of violent affection raged through the crowd. I remained silent, holding my arms around my bouncing knee.

Lord Dayire was next to step forward. The warm glow radiating over the field was complementary to his short red hair, reminiscent of autumn. He was probably the one casting the orb, not that it mattered. None of the Witchlords appeared drained or bothered at all to wield their Nature in that way.

I wouldn't know where to begin with casting a dark orb.

"Twelve of you get to play! As we've seen in previous years, this can be a dangerous game," Lord Dayire announced. "I believe it serves as a reminder of *why* you are in here, but it's all in good fun. If you want to watch, then you have volunteered. Leave now if you have no interest in being chosen."

The rule was not a new one, nor one that swayed the eager audience. No one appeared remotely concerned. Surrounding me were plenty of Dark Natured with relatively normal lives, dressed in their warm garments and half-drunken smiles.

Beck poked his head next to mine, sneaking up with expert execution.

"Oh, for Fate's sake," I choked. I hadn't seen the Nightcastor in weeks. He must have moved on to other taverns in his rotation.

Beck grinned, wrapping an arm over my shoulder, his curls tickling the side of my face.

"Ah, my favorite Blackheart. Did you hear that Arielle is alive?" he whispered.

I sighed. It was unfortunate that I was the one with incorrect gossip the last time we spoke. I nodded in defeat.

He clicked his tongue. "You need better informants." With

a parting pat on the head, he vanished like a shadow caught in sunlight.

My stomach fluttered. He'd just used his Nature. Casually, too. If the Witchlords or a Draker caught him—

Lord Dayire continued, "Rules are simple enough, even for your kind. This is a game of Orb Hazy. Each team will be given an orb made by their Witchlord. You will protect yours and try to capture the opposing team's. The first team to bring an opponent's orb back to their base wins."

"*What do the winners get this year?*" a voice yelled out.

Lord Ansel looked less than thrilled with the interruption, or maybe the game entirely. With his hands in the pockets of his cloak, he stood stone faced and waiting.

"The winning team will receive gold, enough to buy a spot in the Pearl or drink themselves to the grave through the next two winters," Lord Dayire beamed. "Now, who's ready?"

Mother of Moons. The game would be dreadfully deadly, all for a monetary prize.

The crowd went feral with excitement. People were already making plans with money they didn't have yet and placing bets on exactly how much the prize would be.

My stomach rumbled. I, too, wondered what I would do with so much gold to spend. Probably buy food, warm clothes, and a blanket. If it were truly an extraordinary amount like they'd said, I'd get a new apartment.

It was time for the Witchlords to pick their teams. One at a time, each received a turn to choose a Dark Natured.

For the first round, two of the Witchlords picked Flamecastors, while another picked a Stonesender. None of their choices mattered to me.

Ansel's did.

"Beckham Stroudwick. Nightcastor."

An uncontainable gasp escaped me.

That nosy, slender Nightcastor was being sent into the arena to die. Beck stood with a group of other Nightcastors, showing no signs of excitement or nervousness. He simply handed off his ale to a friend and walked down with a shrug, ready to play.

"Oh, this is something I have to see," one of his fellow Nightcastors giggled. That had to be a good sign. Maybe Beck would do well.

Lord Dronis chose an athletically built Blackheart for the second round, while Lords Dayire and Jaysel chose another Flamecastor and Stonesender. No surprise there.

When they were done making their picks, my eyes shot to Lord Ansel. I wasn't sure if it was his ridiculous height or striking gaze as he scanned the crowd that made it so hard to look away. His eyes landed on my section.

Oh, don't pick me.

"Charles Molde. Imp." Lord Ansel's voice was flat, as if annoyed with his own decision.

I burst into laughter as a very shocked Charles froze in place. He had been sneaking his way closer, almost touching me once more. There were tears in my eyes by the time he'd trudged his way onto the field. I said a silent prayer for Beck, but I was beyond delighted that my archnemesis would be participating in the game. I needed this.

Lord Ansel's team had no chance of victory but every opportunity to provide entertainment. It was comical. The sight of Beck and Charles next to the Dreamsoul, while sizable

Dark Natured tributes maintained their posture and anticipation behind the other Witchlords.

Lord Ansel's status as the newest Witchlord was becoming painfully obvious, as Imps were never picked for the game. Especially not the drunk ones.

The process continued. Two more Stonesenders and a Nightcastor were picked before it was finally Lord Ansel's last turn.

The ground rumbled as the Dark Natured drummed their feet on the ground and hands on their thighs, the beat building with every second.

Lord Ansel cleared his throat, and silence fell.

"Elora Amona. Blackheart."

No.

No.

Lord Ansel hated me. This was my punishment.

CHAPTER 9

FOOD, WARM CLOTHES, BLANKET

"Witchlords must be treated with the utmost reverence. The sacrifice they pay to keep the common lands safe is immeasurable. No wives. No children. How could there be? They are confined within the walls as are the vermin."

— *MARKER DANE, LORD OF LAWSHIP*

STONE FACED, I STOOD ON THE FIELD. VIBRATIONS OF chatter above numbed my mind. Beck and Charles were next to me, deadly silent.

It was supposed to be a reprieve to watch the game and have some drinks afterwards. Never did I imagine I would be participating. The deadliest Dark Natured I knew were on the opposing teams, murder in their eyes. They would kill for a chance to release their Nature, but they would *slaughter* everything in their path for gold.

Beck was the only hope we had, realistically speaking.

Maybe he could sneak his way to another team's base and take their orb? If he were able to hold his shadows for long enough, he would be near impossible to catch. Charles and I could stay and protect our orb, or at least attempt to.

Strategizing for this game was insanity. I just needed to survive, and preferably avoid injury. I wouldn't last the rest of winter if I couldn't work. Trying to win would get me killed.

But what if it could also save me? *Food, warm clothes, blankets.*

Lord Ansel leisurely guided us to our assigned base, his broad shoulders relaxed and hands still in his pockets.

He did this. For whatever reason, he thought it would be amusing for us to get absolutely demolished. Or maybe he wanted *me* dead. Perhaps for using my Nature, or potentially, my attitude.

"Lovely little team we have, huh?" Beck mused. Charles had already gone through several stages of grief and anger, finally settling on exuding a gag-inducing display of confidence at being chosen.

"Of course er team is lovely! I werz picked! I am the best!"

I was ready to kick him in the back of his bald green head.

"You three will win," Lord Ansel ordered as we reached our base, marked with a Silver Circle painted on the grass. It was on the far side of the field, with one tree blocking the crowd from a full visual of us.

"How does one suppose we do that? Hm, Witchlord?" Beck cooed with a feline smile.

"Don't lose."

My veins throbbed, the darkness inside eager to be released. I shoved away the urge. I would find a way to survive without using my Nature. Vomiting all over myself again was not an option.

"Charles and I stay here, while Beck goes to retrieve an orb," I said. "Then we'll be done with this."

Lord Ansel's eyes twinkled. "Is that the best idea you have, Blackheart?"

My best idea was to smack that twinkle right into oblivion, but it would be logistically difficult at the moment, since his parents must have descended from giants.

"It's the only idea I've heard," I shot back, crossing my arms. Waiting to hear anything better.

"Charles stays here. Beck will protect what needs to be protected. Blackheart, *you* go get the orb," Lord Ansel declared.

Beck opened his mouth, but ultimately closed it.

"Do you wish for me to die, my lord?" I whispered. How was I supposed to steal an orb from someone's hands? It was a game to him, but it was *our* lives. Could he be so offended about me not wanting to sleep in his home?

"You are only incapable of what you believe to be impossible. Gather yourselves," Lord Ansel said, catching a swarming insect between two fingers and zapping it with a lightning touch.

My stomach churned. Would Lord Ansel bet against his own team?

As the rest of them moved to the center of our base, I stood frozen in place.

Lord Ansel turned around.

"Eeeee-lor-ah is scared! Scared for game! Scared for game!" Charles jeered. Beck smacked him in the back of his empty head. The Imp scowled.

Lord Ansel's gaze darkened as he strode towards me. My throat became tight as he seized me by the collar of my shirt, leaning down and pulling me close enough that my ear hovered just below his mouth.

"*Don't be scared*, Blackheart. They're watching you," he whispered sharply. It felt more like a threat than any sort of encouragement. He pulled away, locking his eyes with mine. It was cruel for them to be such a beautiful, light blue.

It didn't matter that he'd offered me warmth that night. It didn't matter that he'd told me of Charles' dream or offered me a place to stay. He *chose* to be a Witchlord. I was sentenced to life in this prison, and he enforced that of his own volition.

Lord Ansel could do so much good with his Nature, especially with how well he was able to wield it, and yet *he chose this.*

"I'm not scared," I lied, shouldering myself out of his grip.

My fists curled as I entered the base. Maybe I was afraid, but that did not mean my opponents should feel safe.

I am a Blackheart. I am dangerous.

As we waited for the game to officially begin, I scanned the bits of the field that were actually visible. There were no indicators of where the other two bases were, but the arena was only so big, with only so many trees and hills to hide behind. Finding them wouldn't be the challenge.

Lord Ansel created our team's orb with ease, a storm tapped inside of a light blue sphere the size of my palm. It was remarkably different from others I had seen in the past. A Dreamsoul's, while the other teams would have signature balls of light from the Lyonheart Witchlords.

"It's not uh... er—heavy!" Charles marveled, grasping the orb. The king and his council would never approve, but I skipped the prayer to Fate and instead sent one to the Mother of Moons that Charles wouldn't lose our orb. He was sneaky when he wanted to be, and a pain in the ass. Hopefully, he'd use those skills for good.

"Remember, don't lose," was the last bit of shitty guidance from Lord Ansel as he left us at our base.

My chest ached. I wasn't ready.

Hardly a minute later, a loud horn echoed through the field.

Begin.

Charles gripped the storm orb tightly between his long, warted fingers, and gave us a promising nod. Beck wasted no time moving, trusting me to follow. Sighing, I reluctantly left Charles to guard our base and hurried to catch up.

The warm light above dimmed to a deep blue, while fog rapidly spread across the field.

"Splendid," Beck mumbled. It wouldn't be easy to navigate. The Witchlords had made sure of that.

"Don't poison me when I touch you," Beck warned. "I'm going to guide us."

If only he knew I was more afraid of using my Nature than he was of feeling its wrath. I nodded, letting him grab my wrist.

We sprinted through the fog. My heart pounded in my chest as I spent every second anticipating running into an opponent.

As we traversed the field, the roar of the crowd fell away, almost as if muted. Beck's nature took over, shadowing us. Our footsteps made no sound. Our clothes, devoid of any rustling.

It was only for a moment, but he'd still used his nature far longer than I could have.

I panted as I leaned my back against a tree. Beck hooked an arm around my shoulder and held a finger to his lips.

Lyander, a Stonesender, was just ahead. He wore a dark blue shirt and had spiky brown hair that pointed towards the rapidly darkening sky. As he snuck up to invade a base, his steps were sly enough not to attract the attention of the brutish Blackheart who guarded it.

I knew him, too. Aeri. Neither of them had any idea that Beck and I were watching.

"Keep an eye on them. I'll be back after finding the other bases," Beck said into my ear. He was gone faster than a penniless father.

Lyander charged towards the brute when he wasn't looking. As Aeri turned his head, Lyander's hands released a burst of pebbles directed at the orb in the Blackheart's grasp.

It was either a friendly approach, a warning, or a lack of ability. Nevertheless, the orb was knocked from Aeri's grip and sent rolling down the hill. He let out a guttural growl that promised no less than a brawl.

The orb was for taking, and I had empty hands.

Aeri ran at Lyander, muscles rippling and veins bulging. Lyander was ready, his arms shaking as rocks exploded from his palms, building a barrier between them. The Blackheart hardly slowed down, pushing right through the wall until his fist connected with Lyander's pale cheek.

Mother of Moons.

Their attention was focused on killing each other rather than the glowing, pulsating orb in the grass. Waiting for me. I bolted before I could change my mind.

I'd moved approximately ten feet before making the mistake

of glancing back. Lyander stood over Aeri's body, suffocating the Blackheart on a necklace of rocks as he clawed at his throat.

Then Lyander spotted me, murder in his eyes.

My stomach fell through my ass as he realized where the orb was.

"Don't be scared," Lord Ansel had said. Yeah, well, he wasn't the one out here. Fear kept one foot in front of the other as I swept up the orb and ran straight into the fog. Through the blur, it seemed to separate, making a path for me and swallowing the world behind.

Looking back was not an option, and there was no use in worrying about where I was going. The only footsteps I heard were my own. It was as if Lyander had given up. But that couldn't be possible—

"Where are you going?" Beck asked, running up next to me.

"Where were you?" I rasped, trying to hand off the orb. He refused to take it.

"Doing my part. Sucks though, I liked Lyander." Beck tugged my arm, pulling me behind another tree. He closed his eyes, as if he could barely stand to use his Nature any longer, yet I felt our presence once again become silent.

I swallowed as the realization hit: *he'd killed Lyander.*

Beck shadowed us from a passing Flamecastor. She stumbled a little, radiating with heat, and her bloody leg slowing her down.

The Flamecastor stopped and turned around again, a fiery silhouette in the fog.

She was lost.

Beck, Fate bless him, managed to shadow us the entire time.

His eyes remained closed, squeezing tight every few seconds. After a moment, she finally trailed off.

Wasting no time, we ran. We had an orb. All we had to do was get it to our base. I held it, attempting to mask the glow between my hands while following Beck.

We might win this. *Food, warm clothes, blankets.*

Without warning, the light above the field brightened to a white glow resembling the sun, and the fog vanished. We could see everything, which meant everyone could see us, standing in the middle of the field like prey.

Lord Ansel stood on the sidelines, directly in my path. "Don't be scared," he mouthed.

That did not help.

The injured Flamecastor and a grinning Stonesender set their sights on the orb in my hands.

"Elora!" someone roared from the sidelines. I knew that voice like I knew a hangover. I whipped around, my body tensing as a ball of flames hurtled towards my head. Fear struck me with its icy touch. I was frozen in place, my own instincts failing me. I couldn't act. Couldn't think.

"Move!" Riven shouted, voice surging over the crazed crowd.

Beck rammed into me, knocking us both to the hard ground. I held tight to the orb as if my life depended on it.

As quickly as he'd pushed me to dodge the blow, Beck pulled me back up. "Run," he ordered.

I bolted.

Our base was clear ahead, but no sign of Charles.

Was he hiding somewhere with the orb? Was he dead?

The Flamecastor ran on her injured leg, her fiery glow only

brightening as she picked up her pace. Her brown hair flowed like an enemy flag running into battle.

Crashing into me, we slammed into the ground, toppling over one another.

I winced at the impact, my shoulder screaming as it took the brunt of the fall, just as it had when I'd fallen down the stairs.

"Useless Blackheart," she spat as she ripped the orb away.

I strained to sit up, panting and cursing as she ran off.

Food. Warm clothes. Blankets.

There was no option I could live with except forcing myself up. The pain in my shoulder cried out in obliterating agony, as fragile as cloth right before tearing. I closed my eyes, embracing a moment of darkness.

One, two, three.

I flung my eyes open.

Beck was already chasing the Flamecastor. She cried out for help as he neared. He didn't strike me as the type to fuck around about gold.

Then she halted, giving up entirely on running. Screaming, the Flamecastor barreled a flaming ball towards him.

Beck's face flashed with panic. He had no time to block it.

"No!" I screeched, reaching out as if I somehow could.

A splash of violet and black poison snatched the flames midair, devouring them. The poison fell to the ground and sizzled into nothing.

I lifted my hand in awe. I'd done that. I'd used my *Nature*.

In immediate retaliation, Beck landed a solid kick to the Flamecastor's stomach, sending the orb falling. The audience roared with excitement as I grabbed it. A fight had broken out across the field between a few other teams, and we only had so much time left.

Food. Warm clothes. Blankets.

Beck and the Flamecastor attacked each other with fists and elbows, both too weak to use their Nature again. *Thank fuck.*

I felt it too. The dizziness and nausea. I *hated* it.

The crowd's mania rose louder as I neared the base, and Charles poked his head out from behind the tree, grinning with our storm orb. He was still alive.

Beck yelled out in pain. I glanced back. The Flamecastor was on top of him, her hands around his neck. I could end this. I was so close. Our base, where Charles bounced around, was just ahead.

"Eeee-Lorah! You owe me a kiss soon! I know we-r ya stay!" Charles shouted.

What made him think I would ever let him touch me again? My blood boiled, legs and shoulder burning. I was closing the distance, victory dangerously close.

Food, warm clothes, blankets.

"Get her!" someone shouted.

A world-spinning crack pounded against the back of my head, propelling me down. The echoing pain rang out before I hit the ground.

I blinked, my vision blurry. A rock laid next to my head.

The orb had fallen just out of arm's reach. I tried to force myself up, but my body betrayed me, beginning to shake.

Food. Warm clothes. Blankets.

A Stonesender stalked towards me. He knew he had won.

My head throbbed, and a warm trickle ran down my neck. I pressed my hand to the wound.

A screech cut through the air, the Stonesender's confidence fading. He stopped in his tracks, petrified at whatever was happening. I moaned, finally sitting up.

Beck had a wad of the Flamecastor's hair in his grasp, yanking her head to his chest. "Sorry," he said breathlessly before snapping her neck in a swift motion. She fell to the ground, just as easily as the fly caught between Lord Ansel's fingers had.

Wiping the crimson trail from his nose, Beck grinned at the Stonesender. "Your turn," he said, shadows clouding his eyes.

Beck was teetering on the edge of burnout. He couldn't do this on his own. My injuries weren't ideal, but I was plenty used to pain.

I took three intentional breaths before hauling myself up with trembling arms. If there really was a monster within me, it had best keep me fucking moving. My head was spinning.

Charles was still alive at the base, hopping around and protecting our orb. "Eeeee-Lorahhhhhhh! KISS KISS KISS—"

"Shut the fuck up!" I screamed.

As if the orb heard me, it struck the Imp with an electric bolt. His green body dropped to the ground, smoke emitting from his hands and feet. Lifeless.

Our orb had electrocuted him.

Beck charged the Stonesender as he ran towards me, *towards the orb*. I flung myself on top of it, using my body as a shield. The Stonesender clawed at my shoulders, pulling me like a wild animal fighting for food.

"I'll kill you!" he screamed with crazed desperation. He knew the value of this victory. He knew how horrible these winters were. "You wretched bitch! Let go!"

I held on, squeezing my eyes shut just as he punched the back of my head. I choked back a cry. The impact of his fist was somehow worse than the rock. It was all I could do to fight against the darkness at the edges of my vision.

Then everything stopped.

There was no more pulling and punching. I blinked against wet eyes, the light of the arena nearly impossible to bear. An icy shiver ran down my spine, a reminder that I was still very much alive.

Beck landed a tooth-knocking hit into the Stonesender's face as the two of them brawled next to me. Across the field, another team ran with the third orb to another base. I had to move.

Get up, dammit, I begged my body.

A bone snapped. I could not force myself to look to see if it was Beck's or the Stonesender's. I heaved myself up and stumbled forward with the orb, limping as I counted my steps.

One, two, three,

Someone belched and gagged behind me, likely vomiting. Maybe even burning out.

Four, five,

A woman's voice screamed at an octave I didn't know was possible. The smell of melting flesh permeated the air.

Six, seven, eight,

The line was so close.

Nine, ten.

I cried out as I fell to the base.

A horn sounded, and the Waywards roared with cheers. The world became so loud, the thoughts in my head faded into the distance.

I lay in the grass, Charles' body a few feet away. Had Lord Ansel done that? Or was Charles just that stupid?

The spectators were a howling beast above, but I couldn't move, much less give them a victorious show of pride.

"What are you doing on the ground? We won," a slick voice said, smiling proudly over me. Beck was bloodied and dirty, but it could've been much worse.

"You're not dead," I whispered, examining his brown eyes.

"Of course not. You, though, look ready to join Charles," he said, extending a hand.

I took it, grimacing as I stood. My head was pounding.

The partying had already begun and would go on all night. How many people had bet on us losing? How much money had been made tonight? Gazing across the field, I counted the cost of the victory. At least five lives, maybe more. They'd died for this. Was it worth it?

While winning was a complete shock, I was in more disbelief that I'd used my Nature to smother a flame.

The Witchlords gathered once more, talking amongst themselves, hashing out coins.

How much had I actually earned? I prayed it was enough for a blanket, a fresh loaf of bread, and a warmer sweater. *That* would be a dream.

Lord Ansel took long strides across the field, his cloak billowing behind him.

I swallowed as he approached, motioning to Charles' body. "Did you kill him?"

Whether or not I was out of line for confronting him mattered no longer. I wasn't upset that Charles was dead, but I needed to know if the Witchlord would kill someone on his team.

"Would you like it if I did?"

"Answer the question."

Lord Ansel shrugged. "The Imp shouldn't have been careless."

He had no morals, not that I should have expected much from a Witchlord.

Beck cut in. "My prize, Witchlord," he demanded, holding his hand out.

"Of course." Lord Ansel plopped a small black bag in his palm, clinking from its weight. It was full of enough gold to survive months in the Waywards if spent wisely.

Beck gave me a friendly nod, stuffed the pouch into his pocket, and left without another word.

Lord Ansel's eyes slid to me. "Do you have anything specific you'd like? From outside the walls?"

I was still in shock that I had gold to spend at all, or that I was coherent enough to have a conversation. Of course, there were things I wanted.

"I desire food, warmer clothes, a blanket, and more immediately, I need a drink."

Lord Ansel nodded, tossing me my gold while casually surveying the field.

Tucking the prize money into my threadbare pocket, I brushed myself off and crouched next to Charles. Or, specifically, his fingers.

I'd promised he would lose one.

"Do you have a knife?" I blurted.

Pulling a folded blade out, Lord Ansel tossed it my way

without question. The game was supposed to be a reminder, but to me, this finger was the reminder. I severed it without a second thought.

With the green trophy in my pocket and Lord Ansel's knife returned, I crossed the field to the rest of the Waywards. I needed food. My already aching stomach was even more unsettled after using my Nature, and I had a Nightcastor waiting in bed for me in the Pearl.

The excitement of winning almost made me forget about my injuries. I gently tapped the wound on the back of my head and looked at my fingers. There was no more blood. The rest of my body would take days, maybe weeks, to heal. I could live with that.

There was still celebrating to do.

Chapter 10

The Draker

"Ah, midwinter. Trust them to make even a celebration smell of death."

— *Jon Harvington, Golden Scholar of Lyonscliff*

I wasn't sure what was worse—the deep pain in my shoulder or the massive hangover. Even more dismally, there was an abhorrent pounding on the door to the posh apartment.

I sat up. The Nightcastor had been heavily in his cups just hours before, and snored away next to me.

It couldn't be morning. The partying outside was still louder than a brothel on payday. The midwinter celebration would go on all night: the music, the drinking, and the socializing.

The knocking continued. If I woke the Nightcastor, he

might've dealt with whoever was at the door, but he also might've tried to bed me again, and I was in no mood.

I stood up and threw on a loose grey shirt that had been strewn about the floor. Passing the crackling fireplace and ridiculously large living room, I opened the heavy front door.

"Riven?"

His warm skin was unusually pale, and eyes nearly glowed in the moonlight. He was not in his usual Draker armor and mask, either. Instead, he wore black mercenary leathers with a blade strapped to his side.

"Come with me," he said, deathly soft.

"What?" My stomach churned. Had Luna been found? Was she in the burn pile?

"You are to appear before the king."

I tilted my head.

"Are you drunk? Is this a cruel joke? Because I don't think this is funny, and I'd like to go back to sleep."

"I don't drink." His jaw tensed as his eyes roved over my lack of clothing, as if analyzing the conditions under which I was allowed to stay in this apartment.

Maybe he'd watched me come here and assumed I'd taken up the same line of work as Luna. Whatever his reasons, they had nothing to do with the king. I would believe Riven was here to bed another Blackheart before I'd think the king knew my name.

"I'm not Luna. While tempting, I have no interest in going anywhere with you. Goodnight, Riven."

I went to close the door, only for it to be caught swiftly by his hand. He easily pushed it back open and let himself in.

"I don't need your compliments," he hissed, firmly shutting the door behind him.

"Oh, fuck off. You can't be here. The homeowner is in the bedroom!"

He gestured with his head at my lack of pants.

"I'm sure he is. Now gather your things. The king is waiting."

My mouth opened, ready to start another argument, but his features were cold.

It was no jest. The king had requested me.

Was it because I'd won Orb Hazy? Had Ansel reported me for using my Nature?

"Why does the king want to see me?" I asked softly.

"You'll have to ask him yourself."

CHAPTER 11

LYONSREACH

"Little is known about the origin of the Sapphires, but we do know they come from the west. They conquer not for glory, but to drain."

— *CAPTAIN OF THE KING'S GUARD*

RIVEN MADE HIMSELF COMFORTABLE ON THE COUCH while I quietly gathered my things upstairs. It was easy considering I only had my clothes, some gold, and my cyanotic, green trophy.

Another knock thudded downstairs. I snapped my head around.

The homeowner still drunkenly snored like a hog as I tugged my boots on. I prayed it wasn't Pearl security—or worse —an intruder attempting to take my gold.

I rushed down the stairs, passing by Riven, who sat silently in the darkest corner of the living room. He watched from the shadows, waiting for me to open the door. If it were a thief, at least Riven was here.

I exhaled and twisted the knob.

My eyes widened at Lord Ansel towering in the doorway, holding a black pack with braided straps.

"For Fate's sake. What do *you* want?"

He leaned back. "Have I offended you, Blackheart?"

He truly had no idea that the king had summoned me, nor did he know that Riven lurked within the residence.

"It's late."

He narrowed his eyes, noticing I was fully dressed, down to my boots. "It is. I figured you would still be celebrating. Heard I might find you here. I brought the things you requested."

He dropped the bag at my feet.

Shocked into silence, I swallowed, unsure of what to say about being *given* something. "You didn't have to do that."

"You earned me quite a bit of gold tonight, so consider it a thank you." He glanced at my boots. "Heading somewhere?"

Riven slowly mouthed 'no'.

The Draker wanted me to lie to the Witchlord? That could be just as dangerous as trying to avoid the king. I carefully picked at the skin on my thumb. Riven had always proven to be different—better than the other Drakers and Witchlords. I hardly knew Lord Ansel.

"I just got in for the night. I was actually about to go to bed."

Lord Ansel stepped back, full lips falling into a flat line. "You're a terrible liar. Goodnight, Elora."

Something about a Witchlord saying my name and not simply calling me a Blackheart or an inkweed left me stunned.

The door remained open as he took to the streets on foot, not bothering to use his clouded mist to travel.

My face stung with embarrassment as I stared at the gifted bag resting at my feet.

I turned toward Riven. "Why doesn't the Witchlord know we're going to see the king?"

He leaned forward, elbows on his knees. "It's not his business."

If even the Witchlords didn't know, then it was surely bad news. Though if it really were the king's orders, I had no choice.

Reluctantly, I left the comfort of the Pearl, following Riven through alleyways and unpopulated streets. Practically dragging my feet in silence until he brought us to an abrupt stop.

"Put this over your head," he instructed, holding out a black hood.

"Have you lost your mind?"

"Have you got one? Do you want the entire 'Wards talking about you the way they do Arielle?" His jaw ticked, the hood still waiting in his fist.

He had a point. If I were returning, I didn't want to be labeled mad. "How am I supposed to see anything with it on?"

"You're not." He tried to hand it to me again. "You'll survive this. I promise."

The Oathkeeper.

Luna had loved to talk about his famed reputation with the king and other Drakers.

Oathkeeper or not, I found it hard to believe that the king would want to see me for any benevolent reason.

Fear rapidly outweighed any trust I had in Riven. I turned on my heel and bolted back down the alley.

Riven followed, yanking me by the braided strap of my bag.

I yelped before a gloved hand covered my mouth. His harsh eyes scolded me, a wisp of brown hair falling on his forehead. It was as if a small piece of Riven refused to be tucked neatly into place like the rest of him. He removed his hand and pushed the hair back.

I groaned. "Swear that I'll make it out of the castle alive *and* not go mad."

"I swear," he promised, eyes locked on mine.

I felt the soft hood. "You only get my trust once."

"That's all I need," he said with certainty.

For better or worse, I placed my life in his hands. He put the hood over my head and a gloved hand on the back of my arm, guiding me towards the Northern Wayward's gate.

The blinding darkness wasn't scary, but trusting a man was.

The rowdy festivities continued, voices and commotion growing louder and the air sour as we passed taverns. My new bag bounced against my back as we walked. It wasn't too heavy, but certainly not empty. I'd yet to have the chance to even look through what Lord Ansel had given me.

"Dronis," Riven said casually as we came to a stop.

"You're late," the Witchlord replied, his voice deeper than most.

My body tensed. Lord Ansel was kept from knowing that the king had requested me, but Lord Dronis was privy to such information?

"Apologies."

A slow whine followed a click as the gate creaked open.

Riven pulled me forward once more, but we only made it a few feet before being stopped.

"Wait—"

Lord Dronis's voice was so close.

"Yes?" Riven asked sharply.

"May the Mother guide you well."

I stilled, exhaling shakily into the hood. The Witchlords enforced that we follow the church of Fate, with no exemptions or mercy for those found worshipping another. For Lord Dronis to say such a thing out loud was heresy.

A distant commotion caught my attention. It was hard to make out, but it was certainly something I'd never heard before. It wasn't coming from within the Waywards, but beyond. The darkness under my hood made the sound feel intimidatingly closer, like a march.

"You as well, Brother," Riven said as he tugged my arm.

His pace quickened to a jog while I followed, blind as could be. We were out of the Waywards. The moment would have felt liberating if I could have seen it for myself.

The marching became louder, followed by other unfamiliar sounds. Were they wagons? There was clinking, too. We slowed and started an uphill trudge, my shoulders bumping into tree trunks every so often.

Then there was a huff. Not from Riven, but an animal?

He pulled the hood off my head, revealing a horse standing in the moonlit woods. There was no jail wagon and no rope to tie my hands. The black stallion waited patiently, coat shining and mane swaying gently in the wind.

The bizarre sound was getting closer, but I could hardly see through the woodline.

"What is that?"

Riven strapped a pack to the stallion before stretching his hand out, motioning for me to give him my bag. I complied, dropping it off my shoulder and tossing it in his direction.

"Not our concern."

It certainly *sounded* concerning, like a million stomps, working their way toward us.

Riven remained unbothered, helping me onto the horse and then sitting in front of me.

"Don't fall," he said before setting off for the capital.

As we rode, I kept my eyes peeled for any sign of Luna.

The majority of the ride was through the woods. A couple of hours passed before Lyonsreach—the famed castle carved into the top of a cliff—peaked over the trees. It sat above the wintry capital of Lyonscliff, which was beautiful from a distance but a notoriously annoying climb.

The black stallion picked up speed, racing along the cobblestone path.

My muscles tightened as I neared the entrance to Lyonsreach. It hadn't even been twelve hours since I'd won Orb Hazy, my body still aching from head to toe.

The massive grey and gold structure was only steps away from where we dismounted. Riven guided me through a secluded entrance. Strangely, no guards stood waiting, nor stableboys around to gather the steed.

Late as the hour was, the castle hallway was eerily quiet, especially compared to the celebration in the Waywards. Bulbed lanterns trailed along the elegant cream and gold walls, dimly lighting the stone walkway. Riven led me up a stairwell, around and around, until we finally entered a new floor.

Dread set in.

I no longer cared to know why the king would want to see me. I wanted to disappear, hide, melt into a puddle.

Riven stopped in front of an ivory door, elaborately carved with flowers and the sun in a soft pink. It was more artistically elegant than any I had ever seen.

Before opening it, he turned to me. "Promise me that regardless of your conversation with the king, you will not lose trust in me."

I lifted my chin. "You said nothing bad would happen."

"You will leave this castle alive and sane. That is my promise to you."

I sighed. "Can we please get this over with before my heart succumbs to an explosion?"

Riven nodded and opened the door, gesturing for me to enter first. I couldn't calm the shaking in my legs or the churning in my stomach as I took slow steps forward into a bedroom.

White and pink stained glass windows overlooked the capital of Lyonscliff. To my right was a white and gold bed, and in it lay little Princess Clayvarie.

Oh shit.

I stepped back.

The princess was as still as death, her golden hair like silk over the light covers. Her skin was almost as white as her night-gown, but her veins were dark as night. Her face looked towards the ceiling, eyes open and clouded over entirely black.

The *incident* had happened on her fifth birthday. Soon, she'd be nine. For almost four summers she had been trapped in a nightmare.

Chills ran down my spine.

Shackles chained her dainty wrists to the bed. She did not react to our arrival, as if sleeping with her eyes open. Forever stuck—forever *trapped*.

Steps came from the balcony until a man stood in the doorway.

The king.

"Your Grace," Riven said, bowing.

I was still, like a small bird caught in a lion's den.

Though the king was young, he looked *aged*. His crown shone on top of brown, disheveled hair, but there was no light in his eyes. He did not acknowledge Riven, but nodded at me curiously, studying my face. I wasn't sure if I should attempt a curtsy or fling myself out of the window.

"No such formalities are necessary, Sir Riven." His voice wasn't booming or deep like I'd imagined. It was calm and quiet. Dark circles shadowed his tired eyes. Wouldn't he of all people have time for sleep?

His mouth opened slightly, then closed, words failing him.

Riven cleared his throat. "I have brought—"

"Elora," King Clarke interrupted.

The breeze coming in didn't help the sweat gathering in my palms. The King of Drakington and the Castivian territory knew my name and had said it himself.

I was speechless.

The king walked over to Princess Clayvarie's bed, brushing his hand over her forehead, sorrow filling his sunken eyes.

Guilt ripped through me for a crime I had not committed.

King Clarke coughed, blood dripping from his nose. He hastily pulled out a black handkerchief, dabbing it away.

He should have resented me. Should have wanted me dead for being there, in her room, after what a Blackheart had done to her. But when the king looked up at me, it was not with hate. It was with shame.

"Come with me, Elora," King Clarke said, motioning his head towards the open balcony.

Heart thundering, I turned to Riven as if he could save me. He offered an encouraging nod. He'd promised I would be okay, and I had no choice but to believe it.

I followed the king outside.

He gestured for me to sit, and so I did, the frosty wind whipping my hair. He sat with his shoulders curled forward and his lips in a flat line. "Are you cold?"

I was always cold, but it was winter, and there was nothing to be done about it. I tried my best to answer properly. "It is cold outside, Your Grace." Speaking with such formality was embarrassing. Trista would have cackled to witness it.

Clarke wore simple clothes for a king, a plain white dress shirt and tan pants. I looked like an alley rat in my layered black rags that became looser every winter. I had only bathed because the Nightcastor from the Pearl had required it. Before that, it was only soap and wet rags while standing in the backroom of the tavern.

The king raised his hand, golden light pouring from it. With his Nature, he heated the terrace, making the surrounding air perfectly comfortable.

King Clarke was a Lyonheart, like Lord Dronis, but with royal blood. For the heat alone, I wished so badly to be Lyonhearted.

He offered me a gentle smile. His kindness felt off, as if

something terrible was going to happen as soon as I accepted it to be genuine. He removed his crown and plopped it onto a short, gilded table.

"What is your life like in the Waywards?"

I shifted awkwardly. He had me brought all this way to ask about *the cage?*

I took a deep breath, attempting to formulate an appropriate response that did not include 'fucking' and 'terrible'.

He lay back on his lounge chair, propping his feet atop a beige pillow. "Speak freely, please," he added.

Well, if the king wished it to be frank, he could have it his way. "It's a shithole."

His face twitched with pain, and then disappointment. "And before that?"

I held my hands together in my lap. "Before what?"

His Nature swirled around me, like a bright shimmer painting the air. "What was your life like before the Waywards?"

When I was twelve, my mother ran off with a man, leaving me to fend for myself. She'd told me many times that my father and brothers left us because she and I were Blackhearts, but I was fairly certain she'd been the one to leave. Then, when I was seventeen, a Natureless boy I liked took my maidenhead but refused to marry me because of my Nature. Beyond that, I had worked almost every single day of my life.

"Also terrible."

"Tell me about it. The beginning to now."

The past twenty-three winters of misery were not worthy of being discussed with the King of Drakington and the Castivian territory.

I straightened. "Your Grace, is there something I have done?

Or something you need? I'm sure my life story is of no genuine interest to you."

"My name is Clarke, not Grace, and if you have not already heard, I am sick and dying. So please, tell me about before the Waywards, and after."

It took everything in me not to gape. No one would ever believe this had happened.

I sighed and began telling him every pathetic detail. After all, he'd asked for it, and no one else ever would.

Before long, I was lounging in my chair as well, facing the star-scattered sky and telling the king more than he probably wanted to know. I talked about my mother first, then about how I'd wanted to be an actress at one point, and travel. I mentioned every bully I had encountered in childhood and afterward. I told him my favorite animal was a bladebreather, even though I had never seen one myself. If I ever got the chance to fly on one, I would be okay dying right after. I talked about Luna, and how she had broken my heart worse than any man could when she ran away. I told him about how I loved fashion but hated sewing, and how I hated drinking but loved being drunk.

"That's a bad habit, you know," he said.

I nodded, turning to face him. "Oh, I know."

He told me about his life as well.

He told me how he loved mathematics now, but when he was younger, he hated it. He told me how his childhood had been spent learning swordsmanship and that he and his bastard brother bonded over it. He wished his brother never had to leave Drakington, but he was proud of him for taking the traditionally passed down spot of Keeper of the Bastard Kingdom.

Clarke hated courting and had not wanted to take a wife for the longest time. When he found Lady Delaina of Jadehill, he was relieved. He discussed marriage and how making an heir had been a difficult and, at times, devastating process for his wife. He spoke of Princess Clayvarie's birth as if it were the best day of his life. He didn't bring up the day she was poisoned and didn't talk about creating the Waywards or the looming war with the Sapphires. The entire interaction was surreal. It was as if I was catching up with an old friend, not talking to a stranger, much less the *king*.

"You would like my brother, Xavian," King Clarke added.

My arms rested behind my head. The night sky above was so relaxing that I did not want to ever look away. I had never known much about the Lord of the Bastard Kingdom, just that he ruled Clarke's second kingdom with much more leniency than Drakington.

"Why's that?" My voice was a soft chime, like I was in a dream.

"Because he's a lot like you."

I wasn't sure if I would like someone like me.

"Your Grace," Riven interrupted, stepping out onto the balcony.

I sat up, but King Clarke did not.

"I know," the king said softly. He pulled his handkerchief out, wiping away the blood that trickled from his nose once more.

He was a Lyonheart with a historically strong bloodline. If he were truly unable to heal himself, his condition must have been awful.

"Elora, I have one more story to tell you."

As the king spoke, Riven refused to look at me. Instead, he faced the city, tension sinking into his brows.

My heart sank.

"About?" I asked quietly.

"My brother."

Xavian Steele, the Lord of Castivian.

Drakington had claimed the second kingdom generations ago, always passing the title down to royal bastards. The tradition started when a king's bastard discovered the Castivian territory, claiming it for his father. The king named his bastard Lord and Keeper of Castivian, allowing the lands to be ruled in their own way, as long as they paid their taxes and kept their loyalty to the mother kingdom. From what I'd heard, the land itself was massive, just across the Sea of Blades.

I was relieved to know it was just another story about his brother.

"I'd love to hear it," I said, relaxing back in my chair.

Riven walked away.

"I was the only legitimate heir born during my father's reign. They say he didn't spend enough time in the bedroom with my mother because he was utterly in love with his mistress. I was ten when she became with child, and my mother despised her for it. My father didn't care what she or the council had to say. He doted on his mistress in the castle during her entire pregnancy. I liked her a lot. She was kind and made my father, who was a stern man, laugh."

"That was Xavian Steele's mother?" I cut in.

He gave me a hard look, but continued. "Yes. I remember the night her labors began. I was elated to have a sibling, bastard or not. I snuck into the crowded room, watching from the corner as my father stayed with her the entire time. It wasn't proper for a king, but he loved her. He vowed to raise the bastard as his own, in the castle for all to see until he was old enough to claim his place in Castivian."

"And that's what he did? You and Lord Xavian grew up together here?"

Dustings of snow sprinkled from the sky, though never reached my face as his Lyonheart magic swirled around like a shield.

King Clarke certainly did not like when I interrupted his story, as he paused again before continuing.

"Xavian did grow up here, yes. Anyhow, I watched from the corner as he was born, pink and wailing. Natureless and pure. 'A strong boy,' they'd promised he would be."

"Well, that was a cute story," I said, finally at ease.

"And then there was a second child born."

My heart skipped a beat. I sat up. The king was telling me something *no one* knew.

He did not allow me to interrupt again. "This one didn't cry, and was so much smaller than the first, they wondered if the babe would even live."

"Did it?"

He swallowed. "You did."

PART 2

CHAPTER 12

THE KING'S MARK

"They call it a blessing, the King's Mark. But to those who know of the Crown's darker dealings, it is proof of the Lyons' own trespass."

— *LYONSBLOOD LEGENDS AND MORE, BY*
KADE GREER

MY ENTIRE EXISTENCE SHATTERED.

Clarke carried on as if it were any other tale.

"If my father knew your mother was a Blackheart, he never let on. When you were born, eyes dark as night, poison seeped out of your tiny fingers." He paused for a moment. "The handmaidens tried their best to soothe you. My father was petrified when the first one dropped dead."

Clarke coughed, choking on his words and shaking his head. "I didn't understand at the time. My father was so in love one moment, but the next he was yelling, 'Save the boy. Get the

Blackhearts out of my sight'. I stayed hidden while they forced your mother out of bed, begging to stay with both children. My father—*our* father's order did not waver. You and your mother were sent into the streets."

My hands twitched, torturous pain cutting through my soul and identity, but even more so, my heart, black as it may be.

"Is this some sick joke? To punish me for being a Blackheart? To make me sound mad when I go back to the Waywards?" The first tear rolled down my face. I hadn't been upset enough to truly cry since my mother left.

To think of her, the woman who was kind when she did not have to be, and always brave when no one asked her to be, being thrown to the streets minutes after her labor...

I was going to vomit.

"You are not Elora Amona, and have never been. You are Lady Elorengail Steele, sister to King Clarke of Drakington, and twin to Lord Xavian Steele, Keeper of Castivian, and you will never return to the Waywards. I cannot protect you there anymore. The Sapphire attack proved that, and still they are not your greatest enemy."

I shot to my feet, backing away. I had spent twenty-three winters not privy to my own name.

"Protect me? You knew who I was all these years, but still left me in a cage! You say you want to know what it's been like? We're starving! Freezing! We have no medicine! No healers!"

"The council has not made it easy to protect the Dark Natured."

"You are a spineless coward!" I spat. The king of all people, blaming the goddamn council for a decision he had made.

Clarke sat up, grimacing and hollow. "Perhaps I have been. Perhaps I should have done more. But you do not yet understand the pressure of the world's opinions on your shoulders. The council and my own wife called for the eradication of the Dark Natured, but I saw you as my people. I thought I could appease everyone without so much death. I was wrong. I'm sorry that I have not been a good brother to you."

I clenched my fist, explosive rage building from my core.

"That's all you have to say? That you're *sorry*?" Hot tears raced down my cheeks. He had been so kind, so easy to talk to. But twenty-three winters of hardship while he lived in luxury were not forgivable.

He coughed again, forcing out his words. "I have something to give you."

"I want nothing from you."

Riven cleared his throat. "Your Grace, there are reports of Sapphires."

Clarke sighed, as if he already knew. "Elora, I'm sending you to Castivian."

"Oh, so I can meet my other piece of shit brother? No. Put me back in the Waywards. Eat your guilt, *King*."

"Rest assured, I will die drowning in the guilt of my failures," he raised his voice for the first time. Then he stood, pulling a letter out from behind his pillow.

"I have no interest in whatever that is."

I did not have much in this cruel life, but dammit, I had my dignity, and not even a king could buy it.

Riven gave me a longing glance. A plea to listen. With my lips in a tight frown, I grandly gestured for Clarke to say his piece.

"They say I have little time left, and while I cannot change the past, there is one thing I can still do. For you, for Xavian, for the Dark Natured."

For the Dark Natured.

He raised the letter, sealed with the golden falcon emblem. "This," he said, "is the deed to Castivian. Signed by me, to release the bastard kingdom from Drakington's rule. Get this to our brother, and the Dark Natured will have somewhere to seek refuge. The council has made it impossible for me to pass any last-minute laws here, but they cannot stop what has already been done once this is in Xavian's hands."

"Your wife is to be queen here, is she not?" I argued. "Would she not do as you wish if you want the Dark Natured to be free?"

"I'm afraid not." He coughed, glancing back into the room at the poisoned princess. *My niece.*

It was that simple. Queen Delaina would never forgive the Dark Natured.

"You're telling me that I am of royal lineage, twin to Lord Xavian Steele, and I'm supposed to travel across the Sea of Blades to deliver a deed to make him king of his lands, so that the Dark Natured have somewhere to flee?" I asked matter-of-factly.

"If the deed is not delivered, the council will seize his lands and demand that the free Dark Natured be executed. Xavian is not the type to obey such an order. If Castivian is declared its own kingdom, the council and the queen cannot touch those lands. It is all I can do with what little time I have left to protect you both."

All he could do? "You're the king!"

"One they already consider dead."

The pounding of marching steps grew nearer. It was still dark, nothing visible except the snow-capped buildings across the capital.

"What is that sound?" I gritted out. Someone had to know, if anyone, the *king* should.

A horn blared. Once. Twice.

"*Sapphires!*" a voice yelled from somewhere below.

"They're storming the capital," Riven said, reaching for his sword.

Clarke did not cower. "In this, you will find the deeds to Castivian and Moonhill. It's a newly developing hold in Castivian. A home for you, and if you're able to bring the Dark Natured over one day, you'll have the land for them."

Fire. There were flames below as the Sapphires entered the capital, flames engulfing buildings at the bottom of the hill.

"Elora, we must go if I am to keep my promise to you," Riven warned, eyes darting to the approaching army.

My heart raced. Leaving my brother here didn't feel right. Learning that the king was my half-brother didn't feel real.

Clarke held the letter out. "Go. Our bloodline and the Dark Natured are depending on it. Sir Riven will escort you there. Don't let anyone take this from you."

Our bloodline.

Castivian becoming its own kingdom would mean my twin would be the first king. It would be *our* blood upon which the royal line was built. Clarke's ended here in Drakington.

Everyone knew his heir was never going to wake.

Another horn sounded, and screams suffocated the streets as Drakers and Sapphires met each other's blades.

"You will need one more thing if your lineage is to be believed," Clarke said.

I wasn't ready. My throat was tight, dizziness setting in. I needed a minute to process. "I'm not sure *I* believe—"

Clarke grabbed my forearm with surprising strength, pressing his palm, his *Nature* searing my skin. I gasped and yanked my arm away.

"I hope it was painless," Clarke said.

I held my hand skyward, eyes widening at what had been left on my skin.

The King's Mark.

It could only be used once per king, and most saved it for their children. There were many rumours of what a King's Mark could do, from enhancing your Nature to bringing good luck. One thing was for certain, though: a King's Mark could only be passed to someone in his own bloodline.

Just like in the tales, it was a golden outline of the sun, sparkling on my skin.

Clarke held the sealed letter out. "Leave," he urged. "Go to Castivian. Find Xavian."

Riven marched over, snatching the letter from Clarke and grabbing me by the arm. "Welcome to being an heir," he said, pulling me towards the exit.

I resisted, but he did not flinch, my feet dragging along the floor.

"Wait!"

I still had questions.

Clarke watched with solemn eyes as Riven pulled me through Clayvarie's room.

"Please, wait!" I screamed.

"We cannot," Riven argued.

Clarke began to close the balcony door. "Goodbye, Elorengail."

He pulled the doors shut.

That was it. There was no going back. No more answers. No more stories.

Riven held my arm as he led us back down the stairs and out the door, his horse still waiting as flames and golden sparks of Lyonheart Nature painted the smoky skies.

"Get on," he ordered.

I couldn't do this. Not this fast. It felt hard to breathe. The air was escaping too quickly. I ran along the side of the castle, desperate to find somewhere to be alone, for just a moment.

An explosive rumble shook the ground. Across the city, the clock tower was in flames, as if the Sapphires were here to stop time itself. The poison within me swirled, teasing me. Calling to me.

Riven cursed as another explosion sent clouds of smoke billowing into the horizon.

A high-pitched *whoosh* flew past my head, knocking into the side of the castle. An arrow.

Riven sprang forward, yanking me off the ground and throwing me onto the horse with ease. I scrambled to jump down, but he was already behind me.

"I fucking dare you to get off this horse," he hissed in my ear, grabbing the reins.

Another arrow soared overhead. Thunder rumbled, and a lightning bolt struck in the distance.

We took off, belting down the clean stone streets for the woodline. We passed companies of Drakers moving through the capital, hunting for Sapphires while citizens peeked out their windows. This could have been the last time I saw the capital or anyone Drakish. Too much was happening too fast.

"I *need* to be alone," I gritted out, grabbing the reins. Riven braced me between his arms, his chest locked against my back. The horse reeled as I pulled and leaned my body weight towards the castle.

Riven yanked the reins from my grasp, whipping us back toward the woods.

If he wanted the reins so badly, he could have them. I pushed away from Riven's hold and threw myself off the stallion. I hit the ground, the pain laughable in the wake of everything else I had been through in the last few days. Anger rose like bile in my chest as I forced myself up, heaving through the heartache.

Riven quickly made his way back to me. "Move!"

A buzzing sound came flying toward me, piercing directly through my thigh.

CHAPTER 13

THE BEST GIFT

"In the wake of this week's treacherous Sapphire assault upon the Northern Wayward's, several prisoners have fled their chains. The Crown Council claims its finest hunters now ride to reclaim what was lost."

— *EXCERPT FROM THE LYONSCLIFF PRESS,*
MOST RECENT ISSUE

I DREAMT OF NOTHING BUT DARKNESS.

When I woke, I found myself on horseback, my head leaning into Riven's shoulder. Dark fabric tied us together as my weight leaned back into his muscular chest. It was bright out, with nothing but trees surrounding us.

"Why am I tied to you?" I groaned, pointing to the band that held me.

"Holding onto you grew tiresome," he grumbled.

I stared down. A white cloth was wrapped around my thigh, caked with dried blood, but no arrow.

It had been real. Everything was real. I gasped, panic surfacing again.

Riven gripped me. "Stop it," he growled.

"Tell me what happened!"

I needed to get off the horse, to stop moving.

"To you? You got yourself shot with an arrow. To the Sapphire who shot you? I broke the hand that held the bow, and my blade claimed the one that released the arrow. Everyone else? Captured or free. Only time will tell."

As flattering as it was that he'd made a handless man out of my attacker, I had no interest in being tied to him on horseback. I reached down and ripped the band, releasing myself so I could at least stretch my torso while I simmered in my dread.

"I *liked* that sheet," Riven muttered.

I turned to face him as he tossed the ripped fabric to the ground.

"I wasn't aware you'd brought your *bedding*."

"Now you'll have to share yours."

My cheeks flushed. "I'll share my bedding with a Draker the day Queen Delaina shares hers with a Blackheart." I didn't even have bedding. I had nothing except my bag, a deed to Castivian, and the King's Mark.

I had been unconscious long enough for the Sapphire attack to either be over, or so far behind us that only the wintry wind rustling the trees could be heard. If I didn't know better, I'd have thought Riven managed to sleep at some point as well. He was alert and put together, as if he would not be caught dead looking out of order. The same could not be said for me.

I leaned forward, giving my best attempt to relieve the tension. The morning sun was just peeking through the trees. With every stretch, my body ached with protest.

"Do you need me to crack your back?" Riven asked.

"On horseback?"

He pulled the reins to a halt and hopped down. He didn't bother to stretch his legs or show any sign that he had been riding all night.

"His name is Kostini," Riven said, referring to the horse.

I stroked Kostini's dark mane, and the horse snorted. I supposed he was grateful for a break, too. One leg after the next, I clumsily swung off, planting my feet on the ground. A shattering pain shot through my injured thigh.

Riven pulled our packs down with ease, tossing them next to a tree. I leaned down, giving a piss-poor attempt to touch my toes, and was instead met with another shooting pain that sent me back upward.

Riven shook his head. "Cross your arms over your chest."

Desperate for relief, I obeyed. He stood behind me, wrapping his arms over mine and lifting me off the ground with a tight squeeze. Cracks rippled down my spine like an avalanche. I sighed as he lowered me back down.

"Thank you."

He reached inside his pack and pulled out a smoke. Lighting a match, he picked a tree to lean against.

"But you don't drink?" I asked.

He kept his head against the bark, eyes aimed at the canopy of forest above. "Does this look like a drink?"

"Looks like a vice, no different."

Riven's weapons were strapped along his chest and the sides

of his black leathers. The longer I looked, the more steel I noticed tucked in various places.

I probably appeared ridiculous in comparison, wearing two layers of loose, black pants and a dark sweater that had seen better days. I thanked Fate it wasn't the worst cold I had ever experienced, as we'd surely be spending the entirety of the day outside.

"Kostini needs rest, I assume?" I asked.

Riven lifted his head in pained annoyance as he took a break from his smoke.

"That's rather presumptuous, even for you."

Kostini *snorted* as if he understood, yanking his head forward.

I crossed my arms. I had never been rushed by a horse before.

"He'll let us know when he needs rest."

Riven offered me a piece of dry bread and a sip of water from a capped jug before we saddled back up. I rode behind Riven this time, silently drowning out the thoughts of the last few days.

By the time Kostini stopped on his own, the sun was low on the horizon behind us. We had found an easier trail, and there were no signs of anyone following. We'd been traveling through the Eastern Woods to get to the coast. I knew they were barren, but these lands were eerie. Being the height of winter, there weren't even birds singing or crickets chirping.

As soon as we pulled our bags off, Kostini promptly plopped down with a thud. Riven fed and watered the steed with what he could. He removed his light armor and top layer, revealing a plain black undershirt. Tattoos of flames, swords, and other symbols almost entirely covered his arms. Scars filled the empty spaces, old and fading to white.

He repacked his bag and strapped a bow to his back while I sat against a tree. Blood, black as night, seeped through the wrap on my thigh. Riven offered me our last bandage.

I declined. The wound would need washing soon.

"Stay here and keep watch over our things. I won't be long."

I stared out into the forest. "Do you think there are Sapphires out here?"

Riven rubbed his hand along the side of his jaw. "We need food either way."

I sat quietly as he ventured to find something edible. Riven and I had shared so few words throughout the day that being left alone didn't feel much different. In fact, I appreciated it, even praying that I was truly alone, and not soon to be attacked by Sapphires.

Back against the tree, I listened for any sign of unwanted company.

If Clarke had been worried about the deed's safety *and* Riven didn't want Lord Ansel to know I was leaving, it was fair to assume I must not be seen by even the Drakers, regardless of whether the king himself had released me.

Riven was the only exception.

Not even my existence was lawful on these wretched lands. It did not matter that I was born here, in the castle no less. It did not matter that I'd spent countless hours of my life sewing the very clothes that Drakers wore beneath their armor to keep from freezing their asses off. I was born with blood deemed dark, and if I were to be discovered, I would be punished. Likely with my life.

Being outside of the Wayward's walls did not feel as warm and fuzzy as I'd dreamt it would. It felt dangerous.

It did not take being the golden scholar of Lyonscliff to know that in order to overcome danger, you must become it. Being injured did me no good. I had to find a healer soon, or the puncture to my thigh may be the end of my freedom, and the rest of the Dark Natured with it.

Why couldn't Clarke have done this years ago? Before the Waywards? Why wait until his dying days?

Kostini slept soundly a few feet away while I waited, and waited, and waited, and *waited* for Riven to return.

Many hours passed, leaving the faintest moonlight coming through the canopy. No fire, no food, and more concerningly, no Riven. My teeth chattered, rivaling the wind howling against loose tree limbs. Had he not said that he wouldn't be long?

I braced myself as I stood, cursing at the pain.

A gust of winter's wrath blew against me, and a sharp chill raced through me. Riven was out there somewhere with only his undershirt on.

I pulled over the pack Lord Ansel had given me, hoping there was food inside. As I opened the top flap, the aroma of pumpkin embraced me. My stomach rumbled, and I dug through the bag, grabbing the source of the smell—a muffin wrapped in crunchy brown parchment paper. I took a healthy bite, closing my eyes as vanilla, pumpkin, and sugar melted against my tongue.

It was large enough that I only ate half, not used to filling my stomach beyond need, which was fine. I would surely want the rest later. I peeked back into the bag and pulled out a black garment. It was a sweater, thick and softer than the one I had been wearing, with no holes or stains.

I put it on immediately. It was new. No one had ever worn it except for *me*.

There was more inside. At the bottom, folded up neatly, was a dark-heather blanket. I pulled it out eagerly, letting it unravel. Falling from the folds of the blanket was a little black orb, landing straight in my lap. Picking it up gently, I held the light weight of it in my hand.

I tapped the orb, and it stirred to life, emitting a calm, blue glow. The blanket buzzed, soft flashes of lightning bouncing within it.

It was warm—*unnaturally* warm. Lord Ansel had imbued the blanket with his own Nature.

I took in the sight of the bag with the braided straps, the glowing orb, my new sweater, the half of a muffin I had left, and the blanket. They were the best gifts I had ever received. And they had come from a Witchlord.

None of it would go to waste. The orb would be especially useful in the darkness.

Now, where the hell was Riven?

CHAPTER 14

KOSTINI

"Drakers endure the harshest of disciplines. Hunt, blade, and their defiance against Dark Nature. Without it, they would surely fall."

— *A HISTORY OF DEFENSE, AUTHOR UNKNOWN*

MY OLD SWEATER WAS RATTY ENOUGH TO TEAR A strip off to wrap around my wrist. Next, I gathered the upper half of my hair, securing it in a loose bun. I tore another strip from my sweater to wrap around the orb and attach it to my waist.

Kostini woke, shuffling to his tall stance. He whined abruptly, rushing me once again.

"I hope you had a good nap," I mumbled, loading Riven's bag first, then mine. Getting onto the damn horse by myself was going to be an obstacle. My thigh throbbed just standing, much less climbing.

Accepting that it would suck, I gave my best attempt to mount. Breathing like a mating boar, I pulled myself high enough to swing my bad leg around and plopped in the saddle. I let a string of curse words fly before I regained my composure.

I gathered the reins cautiously, unsure of exactly where to go.

Kostini did not share the same indecision. He took off.

Soaring through the woods, we were guided by nothing but the glow of the orb. We went completely off trail, weaving between trees and leaping over ditches. My long hair bounced behind me, the wild breeze kissing my face.

The breeze. Oh, how I had missed its true nature while within the walls. I didn't care if the skin on my chest, legs, and fingers pricked at the temperature. I was riding horseback, on the run to Castivian, but free.

Free.

"We're free," I said to Kostini. He neighed and pushed faster, riding through the night. I laughed and said it over and over and over again. *I'm free. I'm free. I'm free.*

My orb began to flash gently, dimming. I tapped it, urging it to brighten. But it went dark, leaving only moonlight and the stars above. Kostini stopped and backed up a few steps.

The silence surrounding us suddenly felt very loud. I surveyed for threats. What would I even do if there were any? I had no weapons or training.

Nothing good ever came from using my Nature. I would use my fist before it came to trying that again. Vomiting in front of the Sapphire had taught me enough of a lesson.

I tried urging Kostini to push further, but he refused.

"Fine," I said. The orb and the horse were evidently in charge. Perhaps I'd consider the orb a Witchlord and Kostini a Draker.

"I suppose an orb like you *did* kill an Imp. Perhaps you could be a Witchlord," I chuckled, tapping the orb again. It glowed dimly in response. It had a sense of humor.

Thankful to have a light again, I dismounted.

Kostini whinnied and scratched at the ground.

I took the bags with me. Riven's was heavy on my back, while mine annoyingly hung off my good shoulder. I made it about ten feet before hitting what felt like a wall.

I stepped back and tapped the orb, urging it to produce more light. It flashed defiantly, as if telling me to stop. I placed my hand out into the air, and there it was again—the feeling of a wall. Either it was completely invisible, or I was losing my mind. I laid my hand flat against it, walking slowly to the right, feeling for an end.

Suddenly, a hand grabbed me, yanking me through.

CHAPTER 15

THE VODKA, AND THEN THE RANSOM

"A midwinter rose has bloomed. Prepare accordingly."

— *ANONYMOUS CORRESPONDENCE FROM LYONSREACH TO LORD XAVIAN STEELE*

I BARELY CAUGHT MYSELF BEFORE TRIPPING ONTO THE ground.

"Mother of fucking Moons," I cursed. I lifted my chin, taking in the surprising sight of a golden manor. Floating throughout the air were fiery bulbs of crackling lights, like enchanted lanterns patrolling the sky.

"Hello," a young woman said from my right. She smiled, tilting her head curiously.

A thick silver braid fell to her waist, swaying against a strappy sheer gown that hugged her narrow frame. Her skin was icy pale, and her eyes a light green. She was the last thing I expected someone living out in the deep woods to look like.

Kostini stood behind me, yet it was obvious he could not see me, nor the manor. It was masked entirely.

This was blood magic.

Shit.

Other women of all colors and sizes lurked outside the estate, doing a terrible job of discreetly eavesdropping and all wearing equally revealing gowns.

There were no men in sight. On a typical day, I'd be thanking the heavens. But no men meant no sign of Riven either, and I needed his help if I was ever going to make it to Castivian.

"Don't worry, Elora, we'll retrieve your horse," the woman said, boldly grabbing my hand.

My hand, a *Blackheart's* hand. This woman was either entirely unafraid or painfully unaware. How did she know my name?

I pulled away. "I can get my own horse just fine."

Her face fell as she drew her own hands back, as if her feelings were hurt.

Blood magic was the only logical explanation for the illusion hiding the manor. Yet, she did not act like a Sapphire at all, and she certainly did not look like any of the Sapphires that had attacked the Waywards. There was no sign of power or the hunger for it in her gaze. She looked broken more than anything.

"It's very late. You're welcome to join us. Sir Riven is inside too, if that's why you've come."

My lips pressed into a flat line.

"Show me to him."

He'd said he was going to hunt for dinner.

He was a *liar*.

The woman guided us through a well-kept garden of various white flowers. She was petite, only slightly taller than I, with slender limbs and a slight slouch as she walked.

"Are you a warrior?" she asked awkwardly.

I had never been asked anything like that before. With no notable muscle on my body, it was blatantly obvious I was not. I couldn't even lift a sword properly.

"No," I said.

"Oh."

"Why?"

She shook her head. "I just thought you might be. Anyway, the master of the house will want to meet you before we show you to the guest room."

I was not expecting to be hosted through the night.

"Does a lord live here?" I inquired cautiously.

"No, just a master. We're all titleless here. My name is Sitara."

She padded up the shimmering steps before twisting the golden doorknob and leading me inside.

Life-size sculptures of bodies were displayed around the seating area. Lavish weapons hung on gilded walls beside at least a dozen paintings, all of different women.

Everything was too formal and over the top. The white and gold couches were unrealistically pristine, and the chandeliers overly shiny. Too polished to be real.

"Zain, your company is here," Sitara chimed. We waited a moment in silence.

She had claimed Riven was here, but could I trust her word? There were plenty of weapons on the wall I could grab, and while the swords would be too heavy, there was a slender stone club no bigger than my forearm. It was entirely out of place.

The club's long wooden handle was black, with a thin silver material spiraling to the top. The end held a flat stone, the silver securing it in the shape of an 'X'. Embedded in the middle of the stone was a round, dazzling, violet gem.

It was a beautiful, dangerous weapon.

"Elora... of Blackheart," a charming voice purred.

I turned away from the stone club, finding a strikingly handsome man with champagne skin and scarlet hair tied into a loose bun. He wore a fitted black dress shirt with his sleeves rolled up his forearms, and a pair of tan trousers. He did not look like a Sapphire either. Feline-like curiosity swirled in his eyes as a smile crept across his lips.

"And you are?" I asked, still standing near enough to the stone club to grab it if needed. Its violet gem sparkled in my mind, calling to me.

The man ambled over to a glass cart, which was well stocked with high-end liquors. We never had the luxury of experiencing these in the Waywards.

Riven swore he did not drink.

"I'm known as the Warlock of the Western Woods. You may call me Zain, if that is to your liking," he said, swirling a freshly poured drink.

He flashed a quick smile before pouring a second glass.

I didn't bother returning the gesture. 'Warlock' was an unusual term. The only Warlocks I'd ever heard of were ones used long ago to defend heretic kings prior to the Lyonaire reign. My *family's* reign.

My stomach churned.

Riven entered the far side of the room, escorted by several women, all wearing sheer gowns. He narrowed his eyes, jaw tight.

Zain's face lit up. "Your friend was so concerned about returning to you, I had to meet you myself."

I did not like the sound of that at all, and judging by how pissed Riven looked, it was safe to say he shared the sentiment.

"Care for a drink?" the self-proclaimed Warlock offered, strolling towards me. Fury danced in Riven's eyes, but he stood still in front of the door.

"I'm actually rather tired, and we need rest. It's been a shit day," I said.

Zain downed his drink in one long gulp, then started on the one he'd made for me. When he finished both, he shook his head.

"Very well. Do you wish to hear the ransom price for your friend now, or after you've slept?"

I took a step back, eyes darting to Riven. Every time he tried to step forward, an invisible force stopped him.

He was paralyzed by magic. We had walked right into a trap.

"Interesting for you to think I need him more than I need gold," I said coolly.

"The ransom doesn't include gold. Please, take a seat." He waved me to the white couch across from him, entirely calm.

I could be unbothered, too. I strode over, settling down on the couch like I'd bought it myself. The orb at my hip glowed faintly.

Deceptively beautiful and stoic, the Warlock swirled

another drink. "There is a cost for me to live in such luxury, as I'm sure you know."

I didn't know shit about living in luxury, actually. Glancing around the gaudy room of golds, whites, and occasional silver, I wasn't sure I liked luxurious things.

"This is all blood magic. You're a Sapphire, living on Drakington lands. If your request is my blood, I'm afraid we won't be making any deals tonight," I said, tracing my finger along the curve of my orb.

Zain chuckled.

Riven's brows pulled together, tattoos rippling as he flexed his arms, trying to break free of the invisible chains.

The Warlock wiped a dribble of liquor from his chin. "I am no Sapphire, and I have nothing to do with that reckless cult. As I've told you, I'm a Warlock. The last one in Drakington, no less." He snapped his fingers at Sitara. She came quickly to grab the empty glasses from him before hurrying to refill them.

She had referred to him as the master, but I'd hoped it was more title than truth.

Grimacing, I crossed my arms. I didn't escape one cage to be placed into another. Moreover, Riven was the only one of us who knew how to wield a sword, and if I lost him, I might never make it to Castivian. Walking back up to the gates of the Waywards, knowing I'd doomed everyone in them wasn't an option either. The deed had to be delivered. Too many lives depended on it for this wanna-be-lord to be wasting my time.

I kicked my feet up onto a glossy rock coffee table. "So you're a blood-drinking Warlock? Not to be confused with Sapphires, who do the same thing, but are more successful. Is that right?" I asked.

He smiled, lifting his glass. "Never blood, only vodka." Sipping again, he gestured with his free hand to the bar cart in testimony.

"Takes the entire cart to satisfy you?"

Sitara placed an entire tray of full glasses in front of him, dangerously close to my boots. The poison within me marveled. What reaction might I get if I were to kick the entire tray? Glass would shatter. Someone would need to clean it up. All the attention in the room would be on me—bad attention, but attention no less.

Stop it, I snapped at myself.

When I was a child, it was more difficult to control my unwanted thoughts. Sometimes I would misbehave, knowing I would be in trouble. A lonely child who sought punishment. Any attention was better than none at all.

Zain shrugged. A piece of flaming red hair fell from his bun and brushed over his brow, just like the frizzy curls on Trista's head. I wish I had said goodbye to her. Hopefully, I would see her again on the other side of the Sea of Blades.

He chugged down another two glasses. "Unfortunately, it has little effect on me these days. I drink for the flavor."

"You drink straight vodka for the flavor? Sounds dangerous."

Zain nodded, looking over his glass with a sly grin. "I have a taste for dangerous things. Perhaps I'll have an appetite for you, too."

My treasonous cheeks may have flushed, but my sane stomach coiled. I sank further into the couch, wincing as a sharp pain shot down my leg. Riven's eyes bulged. My thigh needed to be healed, or at least redressed.

Zain chuckled and downed another glass. "I have a deal for you, Elora of Blackheart. Are you in any mood for business, or shall we wait until morning?"

Business. A business meeting in the middle of the night while my friend—kind of—was bound by the Warlock's magic.

"Oh, go on with it," I droned.

Sitara flinched at my tone, timidly checking Zain's reaction as if she were afraid for me. He was quiet of course, as his mouth was filled with liquor, not that I particularly cared whether he liked my tone or not.

I had little to lose, and even less patience.

Zain leaned forward. "I will heal you, as it appears you're injured. I'll also release Sir Riven. You just have to do one little thing for me."

I blinked, waiting and restless.

He grinned. "Well, you see, Elora. I've never had the chance to lie with a Blackheart, and that is precisely how I absorb my magic. No 'blood' nonsense. I've mastered the abilities of nearly all Natures through the act, and other illusion magics as well. I just need to collect a Blackheart, and how lucky we are to meet."

A feral snarl sounded from across the room.

Riven broke free, charging for Zain. The Warlock's eyes flared wide before he lifted a hand, blasting his power through the room. Riven smacked into a transparent wall, nearly knocking him down. He regained his balance and tried charging again, but the magic held him. He punched the barrier with a hit that could probably kill most men. He didn't stop at one. He reared his arm back and slammed his fist again and again and again. Red smeared across the barrier as his knuckles cracked open, slam after slam after slam.

"I'll break every bone in your body," Riven barked, shooting Zain a glare sharper than any of the blades mounted to the wall.

Zain lifted his hand again, silencing Riven with magic.

The back of my neck felt warm. Perhaps I should have accepted that drink.

"What will happen to me if I do it? The act?" I asked.

The Warlock's eyes twinkled. "You'll be weak for a bit, but will regain your strength. I do need to drain a considerable amount in order to retain it for my lifetime, which should be very long after this. I will be the most skilled Warlock in history, thanks to you."

I glanced around at the paintings on the walls. They were all women of different Natures.

"Did you paint these?"

He smiled proudly. "Yes."

"And will you be painting me next if I accept?"

"Yes."

The portraits were each sultry and provocative. Had he painted them from memory, or made the women pose for him?

"You swear on your life that no harm will come to me or Sir Riven? And that you will release us promptly after?"

Zain's skin shimmered beneath the chandelier. "Of course. I'll even fix your injuries before you fulfill your end of the deal, so you can rest assured I'm trustworthy. How does that sound?"

"Deal."

CHAPTER 16

A PROPER BED

"Warlocks are equally as lustful as they are wicked."

— *A HISTORY OF HERETICS, BY COLESON JAMES*

ZAIN PREFERRED I REST AND BATHE BEFORE receiving his new Nature source, and I wasn't in any position to deny a bath or sleep.

He'd gently handled my thigh, using Lyonheart magic to heal me before sending me off with Sitara. She guided me to a guest room for the night, which was simple, but more than enough.

I lay in the bed, full of white linens and more pillows than I had things to do with. As much as I wanted to enjoy the luxury, I couldn't help but think of Riven in the invisible box, and Clarke—slowly dying.

And my twin, Xavian Steele. Did he even know I existed, or was he just as guilty as Clarke?

He couldn't be the worst person in the world. He allowed the Dark Natured to live free in Castivian. Thousands of people across the sea with dark blood had jobs, families, and lives. That would all be taken away if I didn't get the deed to him in time.

My chest ached as memories kept forcing their way in. Trista and our morning tea. Luna and I cuddled up on our raggedy couch. Beck, and how he'd saved me more than once, never asking for anything in return.

I sighed, turning over and clutching a pillow. I would've killed to lie in a proper bed two days prior. I would've pleaded for a warm bath like the one I'd indulged in before flopping onto the mattress.

While it was nice to be clean and warm, fear masked the relief of comfort.

I moaned, getting up and walking across the small room to where my bag was lying on the floor. I pulled out my new grey blanket before crawling back into bed.

It smelled of winter and pine, and I held it as I fell asleep, dreaming of nothing but the abyss.

———

By the time morning came and Sitara knocked on my door, I was already awake and had made the bed twice out of boredom.

"Good morning, Elora. I have something for you to wear later," she said, closing the silver door behind her and smiling politely. In her hands was a small white box. She handed it to me with her eyes facing downward.

I opened the box, jaw dropping at the contents. Inside were lacy black undergarments, which certainly didn't seem necessary for a business transaction.

Sitara insisted the attire was required.

I closed the box and tossed it onto the bed. "May I speak freely with you?"

She checked outside the door for listeners, then quietly closed it again and nodded.

"Is this manor a prison?"

I'd been looking out the windows all morning, watching Sitara walk around and tend to the gardens. No one appeared happy or free.

Sitara was hesitant, her head down before finally coming up with an answer. "Yes. But if a bird is caged long enough, it can make it a home." I'd been caged for years, but never once thought of the Waywards, or anywhere, truthfully, as my home.

"Do you think the bird forgets how to fly?" I asked.

She stared out the window at the garden and woods beyond it.

"No. I think they long for the sky."

"Why are you here?"

"I've been here for years. We all have. Zain wanted our village because it's closest to the river. In the middle of the night, he used his sorcery to transform our village into this mansion. All of us have been bound by his magic since."

I stood beside her, noting every single woman—prisoner outside. "What of the children? The men?"

She was quiet long enough that it was clear I did not want the answer.

"I'm sorry." It was all I could offer, and I was ashamed of it.

She tried to smile. "It's alright. A warrior will come."

There was no trace of sadness, but something else. Hope. Riven was a warrior and had come, but Zain had just as quickly seized him.

I would do something for her after I delivered the deed. If Xavian Steele were truly my twin, then he would be a king soon enough. Not a bastard, but a *king*. The first of Castivian. If I genuinely had a drop of royal blood in me, I would use it to help her.

To my surprise, Sitara gifted me a necklace. It was a simple silver chain with a small, violet pendant, similar to the stone club I adored. "It enhances your Nature, for the act," she explained before helping me clasp it and leaving me with instructions to wait until Zain summoned me.

I waited, with nothing to do but observe the pretty women walking around the courtyard, trimming the flowers. They were little birds, tending to their cage. I hated it, and I bet Riven did too.

By the time I was fed and summoned, it was dark. An entire day had gone by, and Castivian was no closer.

I changed into the skimpy undergarments that were 'required' while Sitara waited outside the room. Did they expect me to walk through the manor nearly bare?

The sheer gowns the women wore weren't far off in measures of modesty. If they could endure it, I supposed I could too.

I opened the door, wearing nothing but scraps of lace and the violet necklace.

Sitara was pleased that I'd followed all instructions and led me down several annoyingly extravagant hallways to the Warlock's room. The gold wallpaper, sculptures, and paintings were all so *ugly*. Nothing but a sign of wealth.

At the end of the longest hallway were grandiose double doors that reached the high ceiling. They opened on their own, surely controlled by Zain's magic. The marble floors were cold beneath my bare feet. Sitara patted my shoulder, then she was gone.

A deal was a deal.

CHAPTER 17

THE ACT

"Pray for your king this sickness season."

— *HENVRI JOYE, HIGH HEALER*

ZAIN GREETED ME AND GRABBED MY HAND, LEADING me into his lavish chambers. His bed was at least five times the size of any I had ever seen, filled with luxurious black blankets and fluffy fur pillows. He stood with his back against the edge of the bed and a glass of vodka in hand.

"I must say, Elora, you clean up nicely." The devilish amusement on his face was nothing short of sinister.

With slow steps, I approached the Warlock, doing my best to keep my forearm turned inward to hide the King's Mark. If he were to realize I had a greater value, I might never get to leave.

"You think so?" I teased. My heart thumped so hard I thought it might explode.

"I think—" he began, boring into my eyes.

"You think nothing."

Looking down at his lips, I pushed him onto the bed before he could mutter another word, sending his glass falling to the floor.

He tried to sit back up, but was met by my hand at his lower abdomen. I pulled the stupid lace garment over my head and climbed on top of the Warlock. He was beautiful, with blazing red hair and a chiseled, shimmering physique.

Perhaps he was an illusion too. A pretty package to hide the stolen Nature lurking beneath his skin.

Straddling his lap, I leaned over to meet his face. His mouth twitched into a smile a moment before our lips met.

I softly opened my mouth as the Warlock sat up, holding me against him. He was warm and tasted of vodka and cigars. Reaching my hands around him, I dragged my fingers across his back before pulling off his shirt.

Pressing his hands against my hips, my chest met his as he kissed and bit at my neck. I ran one hand through his hair while reaching the other for his trousers. In a frenzy, he flipped us over and yanked me to the edge of the mattress. He snapped his fingers, and the rest of his clothes were gone. He stood at the end of the bed, scanning my body ravenously.

The Warlock placed his hands delicately on my thighs as he beheld me, his first Blackheart.

He slowly caressed my leg as he brought his face below my navel. I tugged at his hair, draping my legs over his broad shoulders as he began to feast. He inserted his fingers inside me in a rapid motion. I didn't need to count the paintings on the walls to know he was experienced.

I moaned softly, letting him toy with me. There was no harm in enjoying it. Within a few moments, I was pulling Zain onto the bed and pushing him onto his back again. He traced my spine with his finger as I found my place on top. I grabbed his length, fit for a Warlock, positioning it teasingly before slowly sliding down, enjoying the surprise in his eyes.

"Oh, *fuck*," he moaned.

Seated to the hilt, I ground against him, leaning in playfully to grab his neck. He pulled my hair, reminding me who was in charge.

I placed my hand around the necklace Sitara had given me before focusing back on the Warlock. His eyes disappeared with every roll of my hips. He was easily the most striking man I'd ever lain with, possibly even the best altogether. I leaned over to kiss him again.

For Sitara.

I took him as deep as possible, pressing my mouth to his.

My Nature exploded from my core. Dark, hot poison flooded between my thighs and erupted from my throat and into his.

His eyes flew open as he desperately tried to push me off, but I squeezed my thighs tighter.

I am inescapable.

My Nature worked through his skin quickly, choking him and infesting his groin and mouth. He raised a palm to his neck, trying to heal himself. I grabbed his wrist, pressing every bit of poison I could summon into his flesh, my darkness entirely swallowing his light.

Necrosis spread like wildfire around Zain's lips and crotch. He clawed at his throat, unable to speak. I climbed off of him, taking in the view of his naked body as it wilted. He gazed at me with pleading eyes, as if he could not understand why.

I knelt by his side, leaning in close enough to ensure I was heard and understood clearly by the fading Warlock.

"Caged birds do not forget how to fly," I said.

His eyes bulged one final time in protest, his body flailing until it was completely overrun with venom.

My venom. My *Nature.*

I did not spare him another glance as I stood. He was nothing but rotting flesh and a bad memory.

The ugly walls of gold and black cracked, melting away and transforming into something else entirely. I did not cower or run as the cage crumbled.

The illusion dissipated. Instead of a luxurious bed, Zain's lifeless body lay on dirt. We weren't inside a manor at all. We were surrounded by a woodland village, filled with humble, earthy cottages. The women from the gardens were scattered around, no longer wearing sheer gowns but all sorts of sweaters, dresses, and outfits more fitted to their liking.

I stood in the middle of the village, exposed and naked, with black poison running down my legs and dripping from my mouth.

Everyone stared. Both shock and fright were painted across their gazes.

Sitara and Riven stood out among the villagers. Sitara's silver hair was now a beautiful brown, and her pale green, watering eyes were full of light.

Riven was completely still, eyes softening as he registered where we were and what I had done.

I did not cower as they took in my bare body. I displayed my Nature and all that came with it.

"Warrior," Sitara declared.

The women gathered in closer, seeing the dead Warlock for themselves.

One by one, they all repeated after Sitara.

"Warrior. Warrior. Warrior."

But I was no warrior. I was just a bird.

CHAPTER 18

OH, TO BE LIGHT NATURED

"She did not escape. The girl who won the midwinter game was hunted and put down. Their kind are but thieves and killers. I will not waste the Crown's hand in chasing corpses."

— *WITCHLORD DRONIS LYFIRE, AS OVERHEARD BY A DRAKER BOUND FOR LYONSCLIFF*

COVERED WITH NOTHING OTHER THAN A FOREST green blanket, I spewed the contents of my stomach into a bucket. I sat on a wooden stool in the village sickhouse, sweat running down my back and legs shaking. The woodland villagers were maternal in their attempts to soothe me with cool rags and herbal teas that reminded me of Trista.

I hurled again.

An older woman stood with her weathered hands on her

wide hips, grasping a rag and frowning. "I've never seen a Black-heart get so sick."

Gripping the bucket, I raised my head, dry heaving and sweating. "Always glad to impress."

The woman clicked her tongue and strode off, her salt and pepper bun bouncing behind her.

Riven was somewhere with Kostini. The healers had shooed him off before we'd had a chance to speak. In truth, I was thankful for the space. So many questions had surfaced in my mind over the last few hours, I wasn't sure where I would even begin.

In my short time with the healers, I'd learned the village was hundreds of years old. Everyone was Natureless or Lyonhearted. No Blackhearts and no Dark Natured, though that was no surprise.

Sitara assured me no one in the village would report me to Drakers. The nearest town was hours away anyhow.

The older woman barged back into the room with an armful of towels. "A bath will do you some good," she said as she crouched at my feet. "It's a communal space, so we've got to get your Nature cleaned up first. I'll need to wipe it off."

I raised a brow.

"Oh, don't be shy now, girl."

With the bucket in my lap and occasional breaks for my sickness, the healer wiped away the black streaks. Evidence that I had truly killed a man. She changed towels frequently and was extra careful not to get any on her skin.

The woman worked consistently until she got to my arm.

"Is this what I think it is?" she rasped, gripping my wrist.

After what happened to Zain, I prayed I could trust her not to harm me if I told the truth.

"Yes."

She ran her finger over the golden mark, as if she couldn't believe her own eyes. "You are a Lyonaire. This is the King's Mark."

By blood? Yes. By name? I wasn't sure anymore. Was I Elora Amona, or Elorengail Lyonaire? Or the royal bastard name of Steele? Or all three?

"I have something extremely important to deliver on behalf of the king. It's the only reason he gave me his mark."

She narrowed her eyes, but didn't push further. Quietly, she finished cleaning my Nature, and afterwards handed me a new towel to cover myself.

With a labored huff, she stepped back and pursed her lips. "Don't spring a leak."

That was the least of my concerns. "I have no interest in ever using my Nature again after this."

Killing Zain was a special occasion.

She chuckled. "As if a Blackheart could resist for long. Get to the river, girl. You've earned your bath."

I grinned and thanked her. My stomach was settled enough that I had faith my bath wouldn't be ruined by further hurling.

Barefoot and wrapped in a brown towel, I left the quaint sickhouse to find Sitara and a few others waiting, excitement in their eyes, and all wrapped in similar towels. They urged me to follow. I nodded and trailed the group as we practically ran through the woodland village.

Downhill at the far end a secluded bathing spot, surrounded by high-reaching, snow-capped trees.

The air was painfully cold, and I wasn't sure I wanted to find out how the water would feel. By the frosty bank, the women dropped their towels with no interest in waiting for the rest of us. Sitara and a few others had signature sun markings on their backs. Lyonheart indicators. They were proud to wear such a symbol, as they should be.

Sitara beamed as she entered the water. A faint glow shone throughout the river, coming from her and the other Lyonheart's palms—Light Nature.

They heated the water, just as Lord Dronis had heated his sword and Clarke heated the terrace. *Oh, to be Light Natured.*

"You will be warmer in the water, Elora!" Sitara chimed.

I dropped my towel and hurried in. She wasn't lying; it wasn't chilled in the slightest. I lowered myself into the river until I could hardly reach the bottom. The water was just like the cloud Lord Ansel had wrapped me in, warm and embracing.

The other women washed themselves and played like young girls, giggling, gossiping, and making plans. I held on to the moment, letting it linger and basking in their joy as if it were my own.

But it wasn't. As they danced and laughed amongst each other, I ventured further out to a more isolated spot.

The water was still warm. Snow flurries gradually fell, melting on my cheeks like butter. I inhaled slowly, soaking in the peace. This felt like freedom. Everyone in the Waywards deserved *this*.

Where the bank rose, a fallen tree lay above the river, creating a bridge. I swam under it. Sounds of splashing came from the near distance, in the opposite direction of the women.

I stopped, gripping the wall of the tree trunk and peering carefully around it. The bridge must have marked where the bathing section was, because past it, Riven sat on the water's edge, shirtless and washing his clothes.

Kostini drank while the Draker rang out a black shirt, setting it on top of his bag and moving onto the next article of clothing. I'd seen Riven shirtless the day of the Sapphire attack in the apartment. Tattoos covered his arms and chest, but I hadn't noticed the one well below his navel. It said something indistinguishable. I squinted—

Kostini neighed abruptly, raising his head at me.

Shit.

I hid behind the curved tree, covering my mouth with my hand.

"Who's there?" Riven called out.

I didn't move. Didn't speak. If I stayed put, he would assume it was a natural sound from the river and nothing more. I could leave him to wash his clothes, and when he was gone, I would finish bathing.

There was a shuffling of clothes accompanied by small splashes. My heart thundered as I tried to make out where Riven was without looking for myself.

Another splash, but closer. If I moved, Riven would see me.

With my back pressed against the tree, the river rippled against my side.

Then Riven jumped around the corner, nailing the back of my head to the trunk with a blade at my throat.

Both of our eyes widened as we stood chest-high in the water, his forearm braced against my collarbone.

He lowered the knife. "You're supposed to be with the healer."

I sank my body further into the water. "I'm bathing!" I hissed.

He scoffed and looked down at himself. "No, *we* are bathing, evidently."

"I did not ask you to get in!"

"You were silent when I asked who was there. That was practically an invitation, was it not?"

My face heated, brain scrambling to properly formulate an answer. "Just go back to washing your clothes."

He tilted his head, jaw flexing. "Ah. You *were* watching me."

"I saw you. Not watched. There's a difference." Light snow melted onto his broad shoulders, and it took everything in me not to glance down and read his tattoo.

The sun caught the chestnut sparks in his dark hair as he moved away, flicking his knife between his fingers. "The next time you want a show, let me know I'll be performing."

As if I'd seek him out in that way after he'd been with Luna. I held my arms over my chest, preserving the last bit of modesty I could. "A show won't be necessary, but I do need some answers. Why did you go to the Warlock's mansion? And when did you know I was King Clarke's sister?"

He stopped flicking the knife. "Well," he began as he reached for the tree hanging over us. He pulled himself up with ease, muscles rippling down his abdomen before sitting on a sturdy branch. I thanked Fate he was wearing shorts and not naked, as I unfortunately was.

"I'd heard the Warlock had a portal. I was hoping we could

take a shortcut to Castivian. As for being the king's sister, I've known for three years."

"The entire time you've known me? And you said nothing?"

"You didn't ask."

"How the hell would I know to ask?" I steadied my breathing. I'd promised the healer I wouldn't spring a leak.

He flicked the knife again, like it was a game. "It wasn't my job to tell you. I had an oath to keep an eye on you until told otherwise, and I've kept it."

Oathkeeper.

"What about Luna?" Was I an idiot to have thought he was in love with her? I'd even felt sorry for him when her eyes wandered.

"What about her?"

He said it as if she were insignificant. As if he'd already forgotten her.

"She was your lover!"

He forced a laugh, head tilted down and dimple peeping. "If she was my lover, then Zain was yours."

He couldn't be serious.

"You can try to make sense of things that are of little importance," he said, sighing. "Or you can accept that you have a greater purpose."

I took a calming breath, trying not to kill a second man in less than twelve hours. My anger only rose.

"Don't you feel guilty?" I asked. "For being a Draker? For locking innocent people away and beating us if we misbehaved? Killing us? Does knowing you're delivering me help you sleep?"

His eyes narrowed, jaw ticking.

"I fucked Luna because she liked to fuck. I became a Draker because I wanted to serve my kingdom. I worked in the Waywards because I swore an oath to my king to keep his sister safe, even if she's an irritating, difficult, craven woman who thinks she will best me in the game of fucks to give. If you're so bothered that I would accept a courtesan's advances, I suggest you stop asking questions, as I don't think you'll like the answers. My last oath to the king is delivering you and that deed to Castivian, and I intend on keeping it."

I didn't know what to say. I had never heard him speak so much.

He hopped down, splashing back into the water. "Our interests align. Don't make an enemy of me, Elora."

My frown tugged to the side. "That's an interesting invitation for friendship, considering you do not care for my company."

He glanced back at me. "Haven't you made enough assumptions for one day?"

With his knife clean and hair wet, he left me speechless, wading back to his clothes and Kostini.

Traveling to Castivian with Riven might be the death of me long before any Sapphires or Drakers.

I swam back to the growing group of bathing women and gave myself a proper cleaning. I had worried I might regret killing a man, especially mid-fuck, but the smiles on the women's faces made it impossible. Sitara twirled in the water, light beaming from her fingertips and trickling from her sun marking. The girls around her cheered, giggling as her Nature warmed the water despite the increasing snowfall.

Killing Zain was worth it.

Hopefully, leaving Drakington behind would be worth it, too.

CHAPTER 19

TAKE ME WITH YOU

"Saffron's whereabouts remain unknown, though his men have been sighted both eastward and west. Their aim remains unclear, but it will not be peace."

— *CAPTAIN OF THE KING'S GUARD*

SITARA CLAIMED THE WOODLAND VILLAGE LOOKED untouched, like it had been frozen in time all those years.

At least one good thing had happened since leaving the capital.

With the gold I had earned from capturing the orb, I planned to visit three shops Sitara recommended. None were exactly back up and running yet, but she insisted the owners would be thrilled to help me, and I'd rather give business to these women than anyone else.

The first stop was a tailor. A plump woman with dark skin and pale spots scattered along her body greeted me ecstatically, clearly expecting me. Pulling me into her shop, she placed me on a tree stump in front of a silver mirror.

I looked terrible.

My dark hair was unruly after being washed in the river, and although my sweater was new, it was very plain.

My sharp and narrow features had once again fallen into a resting face of misery. Usually Luna reminded me to soften my expression. Now I had to start reminding myself.

"What can I make for you?" the woman asked, poking her head up behind me. She was elegant, wearing an emerald green gown with intricate black lace. Her hair was braided from the roots, falling down into curls. She was gorgeous.

I had no reason in my life to be gorgeous.

"I'm leaving in the morning. I want something warm, maybe a cloak to go over what I have? Black is suitable, if you have the time."

She eyed my outfit while nodding and rubbing her chin. "I'll see what I can do."

By the time she was done taking my measurements, she offered me three pastries and sent me on my way with a loaf of bread as well.

She probably thought I was wasting away. The food in the Waywards hadn't been enjoyable beyond a means for survival. I wasn't muscular at all, more so a frame of whatever fat my body could hold on to and an enclosure for the darkness inside of me.

Next, I stopped by a feed store to secure treats for Kostini, but the third stop was by far the most daunting.

A weapons shop.

I prayed to the Mother that the stone club I so heavily

admired was inside and not just part of Zain's twisted illusion. It hadn't been gold and ugly like everything else. It was unique.

I reached into my pocket, feeling the weight of my remaining coin. I didn't know much about the price of such things, but it should have been enough.

Inside the stone shop, a woman, blonde and petite, cleaned a blade. She smiled and set the sword on the counter. "My wife said you'd be stopping by."

"Your wife?"

She pointed to a crocheted sun on the wall. "Sitara. Are you looking for a sword?"

She pushed her shoulder-length curls away from her face and gestured to the edged blades.

I half-heartedly smiled. "No, a club that was on the Warlock's display. It had a thin black handle with a flat stone at the end and a violet gem in the center. Do you know where I might find it? I can pay for it."

I hadn't been able to say that in a long time.

"It's interesting you want that one," she said as she crouched down, rummaging behind the counter.

I lifted onto my toes, but couldn't see what she was grabbing. "Why is that?"

She popped back up. "Because it was left here by a Blackheart."

Sitara's wife dropped a narrow black box on the counter. The casing had a silver outline of a bladebreather on top, all four of its legs visible, with grand feathered wings and scales lining its body. The box was still closed, but the stone club called to me, its energy singing through the walls of its enclosure.

Sitara's wife sighed. "Her name was Viviana. She loved this thing. I was surprised she left it behind." She opened the lid, revealing the unique weapon.

"I don't want to take it from someone else," I said. Even if it were perfect, it wouldn't feel right.

She slid the box closer. "She's not coming back. It's been many years since anyone has heard from Viviana. She would want it to go to another Blackheart."

Take me with you, the club seemed to say as the violet gem glimmered against the soft light from the window.

"How much do you want for it?" I pulled my coin pouch out of my sagging pocket, setting it on the counter.

"It is not mine to sell. Consider it a gift from your own kind. Viviana would want that."

Her eyes softened, lips tight. If she was certain that Viviana would want me to have it, then who was I to refuse?

"Thank you."

"Thank *you,* for what you did for all of us," she said.

Three years in the Waywards had made it difficult to accept kindness. Operating like a normal person seemed impossible.

I cleared my throat. "Your village and Sitara have been so generous. I'm sorry, I didn't catch your name."

"Jayzen. There's no need to thank me or anyone else. We are women; we help one another."

———

That night, Sitara and Jayzen hosted me in their home. They served mushroom soup and discussed the surrounding towns, including the easiest routes to any ports within a few weeks' travel.

After being imprisoned for years, they weren't sure which areas were safe for the Dark Natured, if any. I didn't expect otherwise.

After finishing dinner, they wished me a good night, blowing out a candle in the quaint living room as I curled up on the couch. Sitara's cottage was full of quilted items, but I used my charmed blanket instead. Its softness and essence of pine were the only things that felt consistent in the past two days, and for that, I was thankful.

I had no idea where Riven slept, but I honestly didn't care. Hopefully Kostini hogged whatever fire they had, and Riven was unable to find a patch of grass dry enough to sleep on comfortably. I had yet to wrap my head around what he'd said about Luna, or what she'd told him when she left the Waywards, and left me behind to die.

My mind wove dark thoughts in circles until I eventually fell asleep.

———

I woke with the rising of the sun. Sitara was up early, too, and had prepared travel packs of baked goods for Riven and me. On the doorstep was a package from the tailor, with a small note that read:

For a warrior.

"Oh, you must put it on," Sitara urged.

I plopped down on the couch before opening the package. Inside were *two* identical sets of clothes.

Black pants, which fit me like a glove, and a pair of matching tops with silver thread lacing down the bodice like a loose corset. It was simple, but pretty. At the bottom of the package was a cloak—Mother of Moons, the *cloak*.

It was velvet for Fate's sake.

Soft, black, and lined in silver thread, the cloak was ankle-length and thicker than a quilt.

"Oh, she did good," Sitara said in awe.

And that she had. It was fit for royalty, which I certainly was not. Well, not exactly. Nonetheless, I loved the clothes. Trista would have loved them too.

Jayzen had the stone club ready and gave me a black holster to keep it hanging at my side. I tied my orb on the other hip and threw my pack on. Sitara braided the top half of my hair on each side, where they met together at the back of my head in a conjoined braid that laid on top of my curls.

It was a bittersweet goodbye, but my time in the woodland village would be looked back on fondly.

Meeting Riven outside, I hopped onto Kostini without so much as a good morning.

He turned his head back, side-eyeing me. "Ready?"

I smiled at Sitara and Jayzen, pulling my hood up. "Ready."

———

We passed several villages without stopping, the snow falling on and off. Riven hardly said a word.

As the sun lowered, the night wind brutally traced goosebumps along my hands. I had plenty of gold to get a room, but Riven insisted on staying in the woods.

No comfy bed. No roof to block the snow nor fireplace. No wall between the Oathkeeper and me.

Riven began setting up camp, not bothering to ask for help.

"I'll go find firewood," I said.

He glanced up from where he sat, unpacking Sitara's meat pie. "I'd rather do it myself," he said, taking a bite and nodding approvingly at the taste.

"Then what do you want me to do?"

"Stay alive." There was a crumb under his lip, and as his thumb slid across his mouth to wipe it away, my core heated in the most despicable way.

I grimaced. "I'll get the firewood."

"Make sure it's dry."

Being dry would be nice.

I ignored him, venturing out to find the stupid wood—*dry wood,* as he had so helpfully pointed out. Riven must have believed me to be an idiot. Of course, the firewood needed to be dry. With the snow sticking to the ground, it would be difficult to find ideal pieces, but certainly not impossible.

Or so I thought.

Every piece was drenched, and after more than ten minutes of failure, I sought better options. There was a town in the distance, lit up just through the treeline.

I tapped my orb, awakening it. It glowed softly, like its attention was elsewhere. I tapped it a second time and it reluctantly brightened. Riven would have a fit if he knew I was going into town, but snow-covered bark wasn't going to get us anywhere but dead.

As the sky darkened, I hurried through the woods,

following my orb and the distant lantern lights. It was nice to be on my feet, though even better to be headed towards civilization.

Finally, through the woodline, I tapped my orb off. Cackling came from the back of an establishment, probably a brothel or tavern. I scanned the area for firewood.

"You have pretty eyes, Blackheart."

A trio of blue-cloaked strangers stalked towards me: one woman and two men. Three sets of crimson eyes.

Sapphires.

CHAPTER 20

A NAME FOR A NAME

"Sapphire's eyes do not burn crimson by nature. It is nothing but a stain of taken blood. The color wanes, but their thirst is unending."

— HENVRI JOYE, HIGH HEALER

OH, FOR FUCK'S SAKE.

I couldn't call for help. Any nearby Drakers would just as soon kill me themselves. Instead, I pulled the stone club out of the holster, holding it tight with both hands.

The Sapphire on the right scoffed. "Are you going to whack me with a bejeweled hammer?" His hair matched the shining moon.

"If you come close enough, I might," I said, white knuckled and knees bent.

The two men charged forward. I hesitated a second too long

before snarling and swinging the club, my Nature rippling through me.

Drawing on my Nature, the club released a wave of power towards the white-haired Sapphire. He roared in pain as the poison grazed his arm, tearing through his cloak and eating through his skin.

Mother of Moons. I hadn't meant to use my Nature.

The Sapphire growled in pain. "I should *beat you* with that twig of a wand."

He didn't know its proper name, but I finally did. Singer. Because she played by her own tune.

The other man, dark-haired and hefty, seethed as he set his sights on me.

My traitorous stomach whined—a warning. I was going to vomit.

For the love of Fate.

Beck wasn't here to save me this time, and Riven had no idea where I was. If the club took matters into its own hands again, I would be hurling long before they feasted on my blood.

As the dark-haired Sapphire lunged, I swung Singer with both hands, landing a blow to the top of his head. It didn't land as hard as I would have liked, but it staggered him long enough for me to bolt.

Back into the woods, my orb flashed on, guiding me as I leapt over fallen trees and crunched through snow as fast as my legs could carry me.

Riven was going to be pissed. He might not even help me get to Castivian anymore. We couldn't make it a single day without trouble. How were we supposed to get to a kingdom across the sea?

I slipped, my knees slamming into the wet ground. Snow soaked through my pants.

My *new* pants.

The orb flickered rapidly. Maybe it was mirroring my emotions because my heart was also pounding.

Black stains painted the snow as I pushed myself up, staggering frantically over another log.

I wasn't fast enough.

A thick rope wrapped around my body, yanking me backwards over the log. I fell, hitting the back of my head on a rock.

I tried to sit back up, wincing as pain flooded my senses, a shitty reminder of the midwinter celebration. This was somehow worse.

The burly one crouched next to me. "Doesn't feel good getting hit in the head, does it?" he gritted through his teeth.

My nostrils flared. "Ask yourself, dumbass."

With Singer in my right hand and the man at my left, I shifted and swung, this time letting the weapon take what it wanted from me.

The violet gem glowed as it made contact with his face, a burst of Nature going through him like an arrow. It was a clean blow, the club sliding through his face like warm cheese. He fell over, lifeless. Poison pooled out of a palm-sized hole in his cheek.

The white-haired asshole caught up, but I was far too weak to even attempt to stand. His boots crunched closer, his cloak swaying.

I tilted my head skyward as he towered over me. His cloak was scorched where my Nature had taken a toll on his arm.

"You're dangerous, Blackheart."

He looked at me like I was the first person he'd seen in a long time.

He must have been Fate's favorite to craft. His hair as white as the snow, brows dark as night, and skin smooth as silk. He probably hadn't spent a day of his life unnoticed.

"You look like your mother fucked a troll," I mumbled, my nausea demanding release. Just before the darkness pulled me away, I spewed all over his snow-covered boots.

―――――

Lightning zapped my hip, jolting me awake. My eyes drifted open. The orb zapped me again.

"Stop that," I hissed.

Now I was talking to an orb.

The surface beneath me was harder than the ground had been. Facing the dark sky, I rolled over and nearly pissed myself.

I was suspended in the air on a wooden platform, held up in a tree by a net.

Just like an animal, I was in yet another cage.

I crawled to the edge of the platform and poked my fingers through the holes of the net.

Below me was an entire camp of busy Sapphires. It had snowed a lot more, but other than that, we could have been anywhere.

I sat up, sucking in a breath and reaching for my pockets. My gold was gone, and so was Singer. My heart sank. I'd lost her.

A glimmer caught my eye. Hanging from the next tree over, on its own platform, was Singer.

These bastards had put my club in its own net. I smiled. Singer must have really startled them.

Idling below, the white-haired Sapphire looked up at me. Someone had wrapped his injured arm, and he now wore a dark navy tunic instead of a blue cloak. The flames reflected in his red-rimmed eyes.

"Can I cut you down, or are you going to misbehave?" he asked, nudging a log further into the fire with his boot. His hair was tied away from his face in a knot, revealing the true grey of his eyes.

"You must be thirsty if you want to release me." I would throw myself into the flames before I let him use my blood against my own kind.

He considered this. "Not yet. What's your name, Blackheart?"

I ignored him. If I could keep one thing for myself, it would be my name. He didn't get that part of me.

He held a vial in his hand, swishing around the crimson contents.

"I'll make a deal with you. One I think you'll be interested in." He didn't bother looking up at me anymore. The rest of the camp attended to their own business, talking amongst themselves and cleaning weapons.

"I'm done making deals."

"Ah, but you've yet to hear mine."

I scoffed. "You've already taken from me. Any deal would be unfair, as you owe *me*."

"You killed one of my men, and I spared your life. I'd say that makes us even." He kicked another log into the fire.

"I don't care what you say. Have you considered that, Sapphire?"

That got his attention. He chewed his bottom lip in contemplation until finally grinning. "A name for a name then?"

I ignored him. I would already have a terrible time forgetting his face.

"Mine is Payn," he said. "Your turn."

I laughed. "Pain? Your mother must have *truly* bedded a troll. Were you named after the horrid experience?"

His menacing red eyes narrowed. He was angry.

Good.

"Dangerous and a sharp tongue. I'm impressed. Though your manners are lacking. If you're set on keeping your name, fine. I'm only seeking one Blackheart, and any information from you would be valuable."

I would not waste even my dying breath on helping a Sapphire. "I have no need for manners, and I have no loyalty to you."

He paced, taking contemplative steps. "Loyalty is a tricky thing, you know, because you have to choose. Who should you be loyal to? My advice would be, the person who can set you free."

"I don't know where anyone is. I don't know where *I* am. Even if I did know, I would die before telling *you*," I spat, crossing my arms.

If there was one thing Blackhearts had in common with the Sapphires, it was being hated by everyone. I knew that, but evidently Payn did not.

Uncapping the vial, he drank its contents. After finishing, he tossed the empty container and walked off.

Artwork by Ashley Griggs

I sat on the platform all night, watching the Sapphires interact with one another. I was suspended too close to the fire. Even if I found a way to cut myself down, I would fall right into it. If I used my Nature, I could maybe kill two of them before the rest swarmed me.

Riven had probably already accepted that I'd run away or was dead. How long would it be before he would be on the ship to Castivian, sailing away to deliver the deed himself? I thanked the Mother that at least he *had* the deed. There was still a chance for the Dark Natured.

It was disappointing to die having never met Xavian.

My twin's name was spoken just as he crossed my mind.

Sapphires below gossiped around the fire. "I hear the bastard is making his own alliances. Xavian Steele knows war is coming for him if he insists on being an inkweed lover."

Another one grunted. "Ole' Clarke will die soon enough. Drakington will be easy to take once he does. The bastard is young yet. I'm sure Saffron could strike a deal with him for his lands. I'd like to go home to my wife at some point, so the easier this is, the better."

Saffron was mad if he thought he would be given two more kingdoms and the Dark Natured to feed off of without a fight.

"Castivian doesn't have the resources to supply a war," another one added.

"If I were Xavian Steele, I wouldn't bother fighting it. I'd keep my position, pay my taxes, and send the Dark Natured on their way. Better yet, I'd fuck Delaina too. She liked his brother enough."

I gagged.

They changed the subject to their own kingdom and politicians, which was dreadfully dull. I counted the stars to fall asleep, net swaying in the breeze.

The next day was the same. For hours, I was left hanging. No food. No water. Nowhere to relieve myself.

I held it as long as I could, until I finally pulled my pants down to piss off the corner. I prayed it landed on someone walking by.

As the thundering sky darkened, not even the stars accompanied me. The wind whipped, and lightning struck in the distance. Judging by the thick clouds rolling in and the wavering temperature, it was going to hail.

I was fucked.

Ice storms this time of year were lethal, and I had nothing to cover my head or any other part of my body. Down below, the fire fought against gusts of wind, slowly dying with no Sapphires bothering to tend to it.

Cutting myself down was the only option, though I'd likely die from the fall. Death by impact couldn't be much worse than being stoned by ice.

Thunder boomed once more in warning. The storm had arrived.

I stood on the wobbly platform, gaining my balance.

Most of the Sapphires below retreated to their tents. No one paid me any attention.

I took a deep breath and grabbed onto the side of the net. The shift caused the tree limb to sag, rocking me to the side. I held on, praying I could pull this off. Once it stilled, I carefully pulled myself to the top, where the net was secured to the tree.

Reaching through a hole in the net, I tugged on the knot. It was thick. I would need a knife, which I most definitely did not have.

Placing my hand over the knot, I used the next best thing. I gently released my Nature. As soon as it trickled out, I cut off the release. Poison ate away at the knot, bubbling and popping threads.

"Do you wish to die?" a brooding voice yelled out as heavy footsteps ran towards me. I didn't care to look. There was nothing they could do. If the fall killed me, then so be it. I would not be waiting for my blood to be drained, nor would I ever be giving up any information.

I would break the cage.

Thread by thread, the rope sizzled away until the net released. I fell, facing the vengeful sky. Death was a mere second away; my only regrets were not being able to see the moon once more, to say goodbye to my friends, and never having the chance to meet my twin.

A roar of magic captured me, obliterating the pieces of falling net.

Instead of on the ground, I landed in firm hands that tightened around my shoulder and legs.

Only a few inches from my face were red eyes full of regret.

It was Payn.

"Get your hands off of me!" I yelled, pushing myself out of his arms. Hoping my Nature burned him again.

"Don't act like a child," he seethed.

"A *child*? You left me hanging in a tree for two days! If you're going to kill me, *do it*. I'm not going into another cage."

"Who said anything about killing you?" he asked rigidly, lowering his face until we were nearly nose to nose. "I'm looking for one person. You tell me what you know about her, and I'll let you go."

"*Who?*" I snarled.

My social circle was about the circumference of my pinky finger, but that didn't mean I couldn't lie.

"A Blackheart from the Northern Waywards. Her name is

Elorengail Steele, but she goes by Elora Amona. Do you know her?"

My body stiffened. That was quite possibly the worst thing he could've said.

"I knew it was you," he said, wonder lacing his tone.

Fuck.

Thunder shook the ground, beating through the sky almost as loud as my heart in my chest.

"Follow me to shelter, *Elorengail.*" My name slid off his tongue as if it were special, like he'd been waiting his entire life to speak to me.

If I ran, I wouldn't survive the storm, nor would I receive any answers. How did he know about me or where to find me? And worse, what was he planning to *do* with me?

I was forced to walk in front of him through the camp until we reached a regal blue tent. Another Sapphire stood by the entrance, ushering us inside.

Never in my life did I think I would voluntarily walk into a Sapphire's tent. Inside was a bed layered with fur blankets and red pillows. To my left was a long brown table scattered with documents.

Across the room sat a woman, the same one who had been in the original trio that attacked me. She lounged back, only briefly glancing up from her book.

Another Sapphire gathered up the papers, removing them before I was instructed to sit.

I skeptically did as I was told, keeping my eyes on Payn. He sat across from me, leaning back and spinning a ring on the table. He must not have drunk a satisfactory amount of blood to save me from falling, or it had taken a great deal of blood magic. The red in his eyes faded to a watery grey.

"I'm afraid I can't let you go," he announced.

While not the news I hoped to hear, I'd figured that was the case since the moment he tied me up in a tree.

"How do you know my name?" I pushed.

He sighed, stopping the spinning ring and flattening it on the table.

"Let's start fresh, shall we? I am Prince Payn Vikesh, son of Saffron the Blood Bather, and Heir to Lestivia. Now, it's your turn."

Mother of Moons, I was sitting across from the mad conqueror's son.

I cleared my throat. "I'm Elora Amona, daughter of a dead man."

He smirked and shook his head. "No, you are Elorengail Steele, of Blackheart. Daughter of King Ashton, and an heiress to the Bastard Kingdom of Castivian. Have you not spent enough of your life belittled? Must you cast your own shadow?"

He tilted his head. "Your brother is looking for you, too."

I stared at the table, heart racing. If he were telling the truth, then Xavian *knew* I existed. Had he known his whole life?

Payn shifted his weight. "War is a complicated thing, love. My father is well-practiced, which is why it's dangerous for everyone if I let you go."

I shook my head, staying silent.

"My father wants Castivian, and he will wage a war if he must. Your bastard of a brother has turned away any offers that have come his way for a peaceful surrender. But my father thinks he'll reconsider once we're married."

"Pardon?" I sat up straight.

He spun the ring again. "Marriages are an alliance, get used to it, Princess." He looked at me with understanding, like he, too, had been in my seat, learning his fate of marriage.

The midnight-haired woman across the room peeked up from her book, face twisted and red eyes simmering. I glanced back at Payn. She was jealous. He meant something to her.

I'd never experienced someone who was so clearly wanted, wanting me. I was ashamed of the rush in my dark veins at the thought.

"King Clarke doesn't have a sister," I said. "Everyone knows Xavian Steele is his only bastard sibling."

He leaned forward, the ring still rapidly spinning on the table. "Have you always been a liar? Or is it a recent development?"

He didn't give me a chance to respond before pushing forward. "Or maybe you have no idea yourself. Have you noticed any special treatment in recent months? Or even before that?"

Riven. Lord Ansel. The Nightcastor in the Pearl. Did all of them know? Either way, it was not something a Sapphire should know.

"I'm a Blackheart, if you haven't noticed. People treat us like shit." That was the truth.

His eyes rose to meet mine in defiance. "I wouldn't."

The smack of a book slamming cut through the rigid tension. The dark-haired woman seethed in her seat, poorly pretending to pick a new book to read.

He either didn't know she existed or didn't care enough to spare her from this conversation.

Hail drummed against the tent. Not even a dip or dent as thuds of ice pounded on the roof and slid off the sides. It was the one time I was thankful for blood magic.

"I don't know Xavian Steele. I have no interest in your kingdom or its problems. In fact, I hope Lestivia caves in and takes your father with it. And lastly, I would never marry you, *Sapphire*."

"I thought we were on a first name basis now?"

"You thought wrong."

"I see," he said, looking at his entourage. He waved his hand, dismissing them. The woman slammed her book shut once more and was the first to leave.

Once it was just me, the blood prince, and the sound of hail, he left his seat and moved to the chair beside me.

He was so close, I could kill him. I wouldn't survive another five minutes after that, but I could end his life. But that would not end the war; it would probably make it worse.

Payn's gentle hand steered my face towards his.

"Understand this," he began. I swallowed, unable to look away from eyes full of fear and warning. "War is no place for pretty things."

Leaning into his hold, I whispered, "It's a good thing you're ugly."

Amusement tugged at the corner of his mouth. "That woodland village was pleasant, wasn't it?" he taunted.

My face fell. The Sapphires left a trail of destruction everywhere they went.

He traced his thumb along my jawline. "I did not care for

Zain touching you. I was going to handle him myself, but you were so intriguing to watch. Beautifully done, really."

My hands shook. The village. Sitara.

"What did you do?" I asked breathlessly.

"War is no place for my girl. If I let you leave, every village you come across will be burned and drained just like the last. So many lives lost, just for you."

"No..."

They were dead. Every single woman I'd saved—freed from their cage, just to be slaughtered. A warm tear rolled down my face, hitting the floor like black ink.

His lips tightened. If I hadn't already been certain he was the worst person I'd ever met, I'd think there was remorse in his eyes.

"Don't cry." He wiped the tear away. No gloves. No fear.

I waited for the poison to burn his finger, but it never did. He leaned back, observing my Nature on his finger before licking it clean off.

"When I found out my betrothed was a Blackheart, I began preparing. Do you know how terrible it was to work up an immunity to you?"

"I burned your arm," I fumed.

"No, you didn't. That wicked wand did. I'm the only man alive who's immune to you."

"Is that a challenge?"

He would die for what he did to the woodland village, and every person in this camp would fall with him.

The hail stopped, and as it did, a new commotion erupted outside. The pounding of steps, yelling, horses neighing, and weapons clanging.

"Stay here," Payn ordered, opening a chest and grabbing a vial of blood before rushing outside.

Stay in the tent? Absolutely not.

I immediately got up, opening the same chest hoping to find a blade. The entire damn thing was filled to the brim with identical vials.

Fuck this place, and fuck the Sapphires. I kicked the chest over, busting every single one. Blood spilled as glass shattered, my heart breaking along with it, knowing the source of the blood.

I crossed the tent, tearing open a blue pack in the corner. Clothes. Wraps. Nothing useful.

Footsteps entered the tent. I turned to face the dark-haired woman.

With a blade in her hand, embedded with blue sapphires, her eyes burned with ferocious resentment.

"*You* will not be marrying Payn." She jabbed her dagger at me with every word.

"No, I will not."

The blood prince may have been immune to me, but she wasn't.

I launched my Nature across the tent. Violet and black splashed onto her skin. She dropped to her knees as it covered her, eating away at her twisted face. Her screams were short-lived before the dead silence.

I stalked over, kicking another chest of vials and picking up her dagger.

Damn them all.

Outside, horses stormed through the camp, their violent

riders masked with dark hoods and falcon emblems on their chest plates—Drakers.

Bodies and clumps of hail were scattered along the ground. The Sapphires attempted to fight back with blades, but the blood wielders had no warning or time to fuel. Every single dead body wore a blue cloak, none of them with white hair, and no sign of Prince Payn.

As the Drakers swarmed the Sapphires, I'd never been more thankful for the Natureless soldiers in my life. I could run as fast and far as possible before either side noticed me.

I just needed to do one thing first.

Singer was still hanging from a tree, and thanks to Payn's admirer, I had a blade to cut the club down. I ran through the camp, keeping to the outskirts and ducking behind tents, leaving the blue and black cloaks to kill each other. Just ahead, the campfire still managed to burn.

I halted, hiding behind a tree. I was so close, but I would have had to insert myself into the fight.

In the center of the chaos was a flaming sword, held by a maskless man with impeccable braids.

Lord Dronis, of all people. The Lyonhearted Witchlord slammed his hand, beaming with a bright light, over a Sapphire's face. His victim screamed relentlessly, blinded. Lord Dronis let go, turned, and sliced through another blue cloak, setting the Sapphire ablaze.

The king's favorite Draker plowed through bodies on horseback, reloading a crossbow. He was the only one without the falcon armor, still wearing his black leathers.

Riven had come for me.

I went to move from behind the tree, but my arm was

firmly pulled back by a fuming, white-haired prince. He forced me to face him, his shaking breath brushing my nose. His nostrils flared, eyes burning with rage.

"You killed Vyra? Another one of my people? *Your* future people?"

I tried pulling away, but Payn held firm.

"Tell me! Did you kill her?" he yelled.

I swallowed. "Yes."

His eyes softened, and shoulders anchored. He let go of my arm, refusing to look at me as his jaw wavered. He reached into the pocket of his cloak, pulling out a vial of blood.

"You will regret this," he said before tipping the vial to his mouth.

I held the dagger firm, wishing it was Singer instead. *He* was the one who had attacked and kidnapped me. *Vyra* was the one who came into the tent, blade drawn. I did not seek her out.

An arrow came spearing toward Payn's head, but faster than my brain could comprehend, he caught it with his *hand*. The blood prince looked at the gold and black arrow, unimpressed, and dropped it to the ground.

By the fire, Riven was no longer on horseback but walking toward us, unsheathing his sword.

Payn slid his attention back to me, eyes glowing red. "You will learn what it means to be an heir, and when we bleed the same, I promise I will not be the first to bleed dry."

With that, he vanished, most of the camp disappearing with him.

Singer fell from the tree, hitting the ground gracefully. Even the dagger in my hand was gone.

He took it all except for Singer, the Drakers, and me.

I sighed with the weight of my entire body, letting the reality of the past few days hit me. I had expected to be dead by now. I was dirty, hungry, and bone tired. I hadn't had a proper shit in days, and had just killed a woman over a man.

Riven closed the distance between us, sheathing his sword.

Sitara was dead. Everyone from the village was dead. The blood prince hated me. I could barely breathe.

Riven looked ready to scold me, or maybe worse. But how could I care?

Luna was probably dead. Clarke would be dead any day now. If I failed to get the deed to Castivian, all of the Dark Natured would be dead. I hadn't even saved the women in the woodland village; I had doomed them.

I dropped to my knees, covering my ears. Trying to block out the names pounding in my mind.

Sitara, Luna, Trista, Jayzen, Mom—the list went on, each crashing into me like a wave.

My body trembled, but not out of anger or sorrow. It was so much worse.

Riven crouched next to me, placing a gentle hand on my back. Blocking me from the other Drakers. "Elora..."

"What?" I croaked.

He stood me up and pulled my face to his warm chest. He held the back of my head, smoothing my hair down.

Riven had never hugged me before. His body shielded me from the rest of the world as I breathed in and out, each breath heavier than the last.

The Drakers were gathering with Lord Dronis, not bothering to look our way. It struck me that I was a Blackheart outside of the Waywards.

I backed away from Riven's embrace, brushing myself off. "Why are these Drakers not attacking me?"

"Not everyone hates the Dark Natured."

Many of them were removing their hoods for their briefing —smiling even, at their victory.

"Are these rebels?" I asked.

Riven wiped the sweat from his neck. "They call them Rogue Drakers."

I never imagined there would be Natureless people fighting for people like me. If loyalists were to catch them, they would all be branded traitors and burned.

"Will Queen Delaina truly start a war? Just to outlaw the Dark Natured in Castivian, too?" I asked.

There was already the threat of Sapphires, now probably worse than ever.

Riven straightened. "Yes."

Clarke was the only thing standing in the way of a war between the three kingdoms. His time was running out, and so was mine.

CHAPTER 21

THE WORST BARD IN ALL OF CASTIVIAN

"Word reaches us that His Majesty has not left his chambers in days. Bend the knee to Fate, and offer prayer for the King and his daughter. Sickness walks the palace halls."

— *THE LYONSCLIFF PRESS*

LORD DRONIS AND THE ROGUE DRAKERS STAYED long enough to debrief then departed soon after. We weren't far behind, as Riven decided we needed to travel east before the Sapphires could return.

It was possible Prince Payn would come back, but it didn't seem likely. Not with the way he'd looked at me when he left, like he wanted nothing to do with me.

Mission accomplished.

Lord Dronis had given Riven an updated map with a path marked to a long-abandoned port. A ship sailing for Castivian would be docked there within a week, supposedly sent by Xavian Steele himself and welcoming any of the Dark Natured.

Riven had also been given two updates.

The good news was that while Lyonscliff had faced damages, Clarke and the Drakers stationed there were able to fend off the Sapphires.

The bad news was that the Northern Waywards had been attacked again, and groups of Dark Natured had escaped the gates, more afraid of being drained by Sapphires than punished by Drakers.

There wasn't much that Lord Dronis and the Rogue Drakers could do for the escapees, except ensure a map landed in their hands. After that, it was up to them to survive. Hopefully, the rumors of a safe ship were true, and the information didn't find its way into the wrong hands.

"Lord Xavian Steele will need every resource for the storm that's coming," Lord Dronis had said before leaving.

On the back of Kostini, we trekked through a dense, snow-packed trail that grew more treacherous as the day went on. A burst of cold air slapped my face, and I pulled my hood up, bracing against the brutal winds. Riven did not bother using a cloak, and never complained either. If anything, he leaned his torso to take the brunt of the gusts.

"We'll have to stay somewhere tonight," Riven murmured, unfolding the map.

I peered over his broad shoulder. We were close to the small town of Wellsburrow, only an hour or less of travel. We would get to sleep indoors, probably even in a bed. There might be warm food and Gods, I could go for an ale, but—

"Payn stole my gold," I reminded Riven.

He closed the map and passed it back to me. "I'll pay for the room."

I slowly nodded, snuggling my arms inside my cloak. Was I wearing the last piece of clothing the woodland tailor had made?

It wasn't long before my feet were planted in the quaint hamlet of Wellsburrow. The frigid wind whipped at my hair, numbing my nose.

Riven set Kostini up in a stall while I waited against the wooden frame of the stable door. He refused to let me wait inside the inn for him, as a few minutes of warmth were not worth the potential consequences. Every time that he reminded me I was a liability, I complained. And each time, he did not care.

"If anyone asks," he began as he laid a jacket over Kostini's back. "You are my Natureless wife, and we are traveling to the coast to purchase new land. Simple enough?"

I scoffed. "Why can't I be your sister?"

"Do you not have enough new brothers for one week?" He passed by me and out of the stall.

I shrugged. "I mean, what's one more?"

"I'll be whatever you want me to be, Elora."

My cheeks flushed. What did he mean by *that*? Or was he just too tired to argue with me?

The tavern was a warm sanctuary of quiet patrons and barmaids serving ale. It was early enough that no one was belligerent, nor had a bard begun playing yet, though there was a chair and several instruments prepared in the corner.

As a hefty brunette filled a slouching patron's glass, I almost missed slinging ale myself. This inn was larger than Widow's Way, with at least fifteen wooden tables and two sets of stairs leading to the second level with rooms for rent.

After Riven paid, I followed him up the steps, resisting the urge to make eye contact with anyone. Imitating the pure picture of a lady, I kept my arms free as Riven carried our things to the room. I'd gone entirely unnoticed, which was humbling but preferred.

He slid a metal key into the lock, turned it, and swung the door open.

I perked up at the impressive room. The bed was pushed against a snow-frosted window, neatly made with clean blue quilts. On the wall was a fireplace. Riven dropped our packs in a corner before plucking a match off the mantel and starting the fire.

I could sleep right by it if I wanted to, or in the bed, and I didn't have to have a man's seed inside of me to earn it. I exhaled with the weight of relief and exhaustion.

Riven stoked the flame, narrowing his dark brows from across the room. "What?"

Had I been staring? Or quiet for too long?

In truth, I was excited. Riven and I were grown enough to share the bed without it being strange. There were times on horrid winter nights that Trista, Luna, and I had all huddled up in Trista's bed together, and that one was much more narrow. Maybe in the morning I could offer to help with kitchen work in return for a meal from the tavern. I didn't need Riven paying my way; the room was already enough.

"This looks wonderful," I finally said, spotting a hook on the wall and sliding my cloak off. I hung it while smiling, knowing it would not be lying on the floor all night long.

Maybe in Castivian, I would have a similar room to keep for myself, and more clothes to hang in the evenings.

Riven's face twisted. "This wasn't expensive."

"Does it need to be expensive in order to be nice?"

He shook his head. "No. Sorry."

I broke eye contact first, not acknowledging the unexpected apology. Usually I was the one giving those.

The bed called to me after the horribly long day, but a bard had arrived at the tavern at last. As he screeched out his first song, I was worried my ears might begin to bleed.

Riven grimaced, his frown deepening with each note until he stormed to the door. "I'll be back."

The fire crackled and popped as the door closed behind him.

My thighs ached. Nothing sounded better than taking a seat.

The bed was pleasantly soft as I crawled across the blue and white quilts. Outside the window, the world was a charcoal, snowy blur. Just being inside the inn, sitting on a bed in a room with a fireplace, was a luxury beyond what I had ever considered in the Waywards.

What if I didn't deserve it?

Riven swung the door open, returning with an entire bottle of dark liquor in hand. He shook his head in agitation and closed the door firmly behind him as if it could block the screeching bard out.

"An entire bottle?" I exclaimed as he took the first chug, drinking long enough to burn a hole through his stomach.

He'd claimed not that long ago that he didn't drink.

He held up the bottle. "It's for you too, unless you'll be enduring this sober."

The last time I had split a bottle was with Luna after she'd had a fight with another Draker she fancied at the time. There had been so many men to drink over in the past three years, but there were celebratory times, too. Like when we finally saved up enough for our apartment and didn't have to huddle together in an alley at night anymore. We'd just barely survived our first winter in the 'Wards.

I held my arm out, and he passed the bottle. I took a healthy swig, trying to forget every shitty thing that had happened since Princess Clayvarie was poisoned. I must have drank for too long, because when I released the bottle from my lips, Riven's eyes were wide.

He fought back a smile. "Should I get two?"

I choked on a laugh, covering my mouth with my arm before passing the bottle back.

"You might have to. The music *is* terrible," I said. Riven had always been so serious and typically short with me. It was almost embarrassing to enjoy a conversation with him.

He drank again, quickly swallowing. "Terrible is not the right word. It's sickening."

"Sickening?" I jested.

"If I have to drink myself sick to listen to it, then absolutely. It's sickening."

I laughed at the ridiculousness. Outside, the snowstorm was picking up, and the wind roared in siren whistles against the windowpane.

Then Riven was taking off his overshirt for the night, folding it and placing it neatly into his pack. He was so particular in the way he did things.

As he looked down, sorting through his belongings, that rebellious, little curl fell in his face—the one that reminded me he could not always be perfect.

Did it remind him as well?

The mysterious tattoo at his beltline just barely showed before his black undershirt fell back down over his abs, too fast to read. Only the markings along his arms remained visible.

I wanted to know what it said, but not bad enough to find out for myself in a bedding manner, even if he *was* painfully attractive when annoyed by bard music. I wouldn't cross that line. Not with him.

But just how good was it if Luna never charged him—?

I'd already drank too much.

"Here," I said, holding out the bottle. There wasn't much left, but I didn't need another drop.

I got up to grab my blanket out of my pack and crawled back into bed, scooting all the way over until I was up against the windowpane, leaving plenty of room.

He finished off the bottle and stoked the fire before sitting on the floor in front of it, forearms relaxing over his knees.

"Goodnight, Elora. Sleep well."

I promptly sat up. "Are you sleeping on the floor?"

"Yes."

He'd paid for the room. If we weren't sharing the bed, I surely did not deserve it on my own.

"I didn't consider that you wouldn't want to share with me, I'll take the floor," I said. "I like fire anyway."

He shook his head. "You almost managed an entire day without assumptions."

"It's not an assumption if you just *said* you were sleeping on the floor." I hopped off the bed and sat by the fire with my legs crossed.

The reflection of flames danced in Riven's eyes.

I'd slept on plenty of floors. At least this one was warm. The bed wasn't worth being indebted to him.

"Elora."

I slid my eyes to his. "What?"

"Sleep in the bed—"

"No."

"With me."

My shoulders went rigid. "I don't want you to share with me if that's not what you want—"

He shushed me, the evidence of alcohol flashing in his glassy eyes. "You don't know what I want," he said quietly.

"What do you want?" My words were so quiet that I wasn't sure if I'd actually said them out loud.

He opened his mouth to speak, then closed it, shaking his head. "I want you to get in bed. We have a long day tomorrow."

The hour *was* becoming late, and I was too tired to argue any further. I had already embarrassed myself enough.

I crawled back into bed, scooting all the way back to my spot. Just as I closed my eyes, Riven eased into bed behind me, his warmth so close that the hairs on the back of my neck stood. I squeezed my eyes tighter.

What if I pressed into him? Would he want that?

No. He'd tried to sleep on the fucking floor. He was only in the bed because I'd said something.

————

I woke early to frosted light shining on my face. I snuggled into my blanket.

As I lay on my side, I stretched my arms down, back arching until a hand gripped my waist, tugging me backward.

I inhaled sharply, snapping my eyes open.

His soft snores were steady. I stayed deathly still. The least awkward way out of this situation was to pretend to be asleep, and when he woke, he could break contact and we'd go on about our day like it never happened.

I closed my eyes, doing such a great job at pretending to sleep that I actually dozed off, secured in Riven's embrace.

When I woke again, he was dressed and aggravated. I rubbed my eyes, groggily sitting up.

"We'll be staying another night," he groaned.

Well, good morning to him, too.

Riven's jaw was tense as he stared past me out the window.

The snow had piled up overnight to the point that the door downstairs would be stuck. We were trapped in until it could be cleared away.

With impeccably horrible timing, the bard's raking voice burst through the stillness, singing from just outside our door.

Steam practically rolled out of Riven's ears as he whipped his head toward the sound, knuckles paling.

The bard hit a horrendously high note, sending Riven reeling and snatching his pack up. "I've changed my mind. We will not be staying."

We needed to leave anyway; our time was limited. I enjoyed my last moment of comfort in bed for the foreseeable future, then silently gathered my things.

It was disappointing to leave, even if it was for the best. Under those sheets with the fire going, I truly slept for the first time in forever. I hadn't woken up on a piss-soaked platform hanging in the air, or in a twisted Warlock's manor.

I had woken up next to Riven. Maybe this priceless feeling was the reason Luna had never charged him.

He crouched on the bed, propping the window open. Then, one by one, he tossed our bags outside onto the ground. With each *plunk*, I winced. Soon that would be my body hitting the ground.

Riven hopped down with ease, landing firmly on his feet. He wore only his leathers and a bow strapped to his back. How the cold didn't bother him enough to wear a cloak, I wasn't sure.

I was fully dressed with Singer on one hip and the orb on the other.

Riven waited below, squinting as the sun shone in his eyes.

My stomach churned. It hadn't looked so bad when Riven did it, but the last person I'd seen jump from a window still haunted me. She was so young, and her baby would never remember—

"Elora?"

"I'm coming," I said.

While it wasn't as graceful an exit as Riven's, I forced myself out the window and landed in the snow, nearly toppling over before he grabbed me.

"Thank you," I mumbled.

Riven led the way to the stables, which were thankfully beneath heavy tree coverage.

While the day's travel would be heinous in this weather, at least we would be making progress.

The Bastard Kingdom was waiting for me, after all.

CHAPTER 22

THE RIVER, THE ARROW, THE FIRE

"It is infrequent that Drakers are awarded the title of Oath-keeper. One must complete an extraordinary amount of quests, never failing at their duty or befalling to harm before they can be considered for such recognition."

— *A HISTORY OF DRAKERS, BY LOUIS GREYSTORM*

KEEPING UP WITH A TRAINED SOLDIER WAS exhausting, and I wasn't even carrying my bag. Kostini trotted along with the packs, while Riven kept his sword at his hip and bow on his back.

I focused on not falling behind.

The terrain was too treacherous for us to weigh Kostini down. I didn't think walking would be so terrible, but I was mistaken.

In some areas, the snow was soft, thoroughly soaking me

from knee to toe. I was thankful for the reprieve of solid ground whenever we found it, but my clothes never had enough time to dry.

"How much farther do you think?" I asked after hours of silence.

The sky was clear, so it was doubtful Riven would be up for an unnecessary inn stay.

He pulled out the map and closed it just as fast. "The ship leaves tomorrow at sunset. We must keep moving."

I squinted as the sun reflected off the white sheet beneath us. "So, no inn?"

He kept walking ahead, perfectly avoiding any rough spots. "No, but you'll have a bed on the boat."

I knew nothing about boats. I had assumed I would sit in a seat like on a wagon the entire way to Castivian.

"I wasn't aware boats had beds."

He slowed, falling into place next to me. "Did you think everyone would sleep on the floor?"

My face fell. "I didn't know there would be floor space."

He *laughed.*

"What?"

He shot me a sideways glance and shook his head. "Nothing."

I smacked him on the arm, which, to my surprise, hurt *me.* "Say it."

"Is that an order?"

Two could play at that game. "Would you take one if it was, *Rogue Draker?*"

"Maybe from you."

I don't know what had possessed me, but even the ice up to

my thighs couldn't stop my face from flushing. I tucked a loose strand of hair back, pulling myself together.

Riven pushed on, picking up his pace and leaving me to fall behind again. He turned to check on me every so often, and when he did, I would catch myself longing for him to walk beside me.

Maybe spending days hanging from a tree had given me brain damage, or perhaps I was ill.

My mind wandered to Luna, and all of the things I would tell her if I ever saw her again. She wasn't one to die. What adventures was she was having outside the walls?

When we finally stopped, it was only for water and for Riven to have a smoke.

My legs ached, but my feet were worse. How was I going to tell Riven I could not keep up like this? How was I supposed to meet my brother, who everyone regarded as a 'great warrior' when I could not even walk a day through snow?

I wanted nothing more than to take off my icy, wet boots and change into something dry.

God, I hated winter.

Riven exhaled a cloud of smoke before flicking the ash and pushing himself away from a tree. My legs had gone numb to the point I wasn't sure I would be able to get back up.

"Ready?" he asked, peering down at me.

"I believe we're only waiting on you."

———

Several arduous hours later, Kostini and Riven were still doing fine. I was not.

The path became a downhill slope through the trees, and while I thought that would be a nice treat, it was the opposite. Keeping my balance was a feat, and my pace continued to drag. Riven slowed some for me, but even the horse easily kept ahead.

Pain may have radiated through me, consuming my weak body, but determination sang louder. I would not stop.

A day of discomfort would not kill me, but failing to make it to Castivian could kill thousands.

With every slippery, miserable movement, I picked which trees to balance against and what patches seemed the safest. Pure willpower took over, and time seemed to go by faster. As we continued down the hill, the snow lessened, and in some areas, the grass showed.

I carelessly stepped on a seemingly clear patch, but it was camouflaged ice.

My ankle rolled, and down the hill I went.

"That's one way to catch up," Riven said, lunging in a failed attempt to stop me.

I cursed and flailed as I slid past him, crashing right into Kostini's legs.

Kostini bucked up in a panic. His hoof came down, crushing the center of my arm.

The crack and my following scream were deafening.

Riven raced down the hill, shooing Kostini back as I gagged in agony, holding my sagging arm as if it would mend the bones back together.

Crouched down, Riven surveyed the injury with a grimace, cursing under his breath. Not daring to touch me.

No matter how little I moved, every shattered piece of my

arm wailed in misery. The King's Mark looked like a melted puddle, unrecognizable. I exhaled sharply through my nose, teeth chattering at the pain.

"I'm going to have to wrap it," Riven said with finality, hopping up to get the pack.

As miserable as it was going to be, I did *not* hike through trenches of snow all day just to miss the ship over a broken bone.

Riven returned with two torn shirts tied together.

I held my wobbly arm out through the fiery pain. It was practically a sack of bones, with no proper structure.

"Just do it," I said bitterly. I would not cower or allow myself to get queasy.

Riven delicately grabbed my arm and pressed it against my body, like it was something he had done before. I squeezed my eyes shut through the roaring pain as he wrapped the fabric, securing the injury.

Pain was no stranger, so through it, I endured. Riven tied a final knot as I gritted my teeth, then finally backed away.

The day had been absolute shit, and I was ready to be done traveling for good.

"Let's just hurry up and get to the port already," I mumbled.

Riven eyed me. "We can take a break first."

It wasn't much of a suggestion, as he was already pulling out a smoke.

I frowned.

"I don't want a break, or to be in this goddamn forest anymore. I don't want *any* of this. All I've ever wanted was a simple life. A home, freedom, children, food. Nothing crazy, but no. I get two shithead brothers who have all of the resources in the world but leave this wretched task to me!"

He took a drag. "Hm."

"What?" I snapped.

He leaned against a tree, tilting his head to the sky and huffing a laugh. His dimple flashed.

"The sister of not one, but two rulers, just wants *comfort*," he said curiously.

It did sound strange when he worded it that way, but Clarke wouldn't be a ruler soon. He would be dead. His wife, Delaina, who sounded more and more like a miserable wretch, would be the ruler of Drakington.

As for Xavian Steele, he had better have something amazing to say after I crossed the Sea of Blades to bring him his deed. Otherwise, he would be no brother to me.

"I want to be done with this."

Riven finished his smoke and offered to help me up, but I didn't want or need it. I pushed on by myself, wincing and cursing as I trudged through the terrain, cradling my broken bone.

We made it less than an hour before Riven motioned for me to stop.

I stilled, carefully waiting. The trees rustled just ahead.

Riven took us another way. I wanted to ask if it would delay our arrival, but I stayed quiet.

A faint whistle flew over our heads.

A gold arrow struck the bark of a tree, narrowly missing us.

"Rogue Drakers?" I whispered.

Riven grabbed his bow. "No. Real Drakers. *Run.*"

"Run *where*?" My heart stammered. "I'll get lost on my own."

Another fast-moving hiss came towards us, and I turned on my heels.

I cried out, collapsing to the ground onto my broken arm.

With rage in his eyes, Riven rushed to my side.

An arrow was lodged in the back of my leg just like before, but this time it had not gone clean through.

"You're worse than a training target," Riven mumbled. "I'm pulling this out. We have to move."

It hadn't felt great going in, but having it come back *out*? Shouldn't he cut it and leave the head in? What if I bled too much?

He yanked it before I could protest.

I shrieked as another arrow flew by our heads. My leg bled onto the virgin sheet of snow.

Riven tossed the broken shaft to the ground. "*Run.*"

Running seemed impossible. Holding my arm, I limped through the frosted trails. Kostini had taken off on his own, spooked by the arrows. Riven stayed back, choosing to fight. Part of me wanted to join him, but I'd already made it this far. I could keep running.

As I turned onto the path, four Drakers were ready for me. Golden masks, hoods, and armor hid their identities, but the golden falcon on their chests represented exactly who they were.

Three had swords, and one, a bow. Was he the shithead responsible for my leg?

He aimed his bow at me and drew it back.

"Yield!"

I couldn't outrun another arrow, but surrendering was just as stupid. We'd come so far already. It couldn't end like this.

An arrow blasted through the archer's neck—a clean, lethal shot. I whipped around and spotted Riven notching another arrow for the remaining three Drakers.

"Go!" he yelled.

Pain or not, I ran in the opposite direction.

Down and down and down the path I ran, letting adrenaline fade the limp away. The blood from my leg left an inky trail, but there was nothing I could do about it.

Swords clashed behind me, but I pushed on towards the sound of moving water ahead—a river.

I hobbled down the bank, reaching the edge only to discover there was no easy way around. I could swim well enough, but there was ice floating through the water, and I only had one working arm. The temperature alone would be unbearable.

Five more Drakers came running down the bank, swords in hand. "Get the Blackheart!" one ordered.

My orb flickered at my waist as I took the first step into the water, my ankles going numb.

"We'll be okay," I promised the orb, as if it were sentient. Maybe I was losing my mind.

By the time the water was up to my waist, Drakers were joining me in the river. They were too fast, and I could barely walk.

Think, think, stupid mind. Please, think.

They were all in the water now, ankle deep and not far behind me.

"*Fuck,* it burns," one of them bitched, splashing and swatting at his skin.

My leg was still bleeding, and while my blood alone wasn't poisonous, black and violet streaks were mixed in, my Nature utilizing the wound as an outlet.

He *had* been burned.

I grinned maniacally, turning towards them. Riven caught up to the bank, running towards the water. I shook my head at him and he stopped, confused.

I looked right at the Drakers, directly where the mask hid each of their eyes.

I smiled. "You're all dead."

My Nature burst from every wound I had, bubbling out of my hands, my leg, even seeping from minor cuts I'd gotten from my run through the woods.

The Drakers scrambled, yelling and pushing one another out of the way as they scrambled back to shore, but it was too late. My poison had infested the water, eating away at their armor and skin.

They screamed. Begging for help. Begging for mercy, but I couldn't be bothered to give a wet fuck. One by one, their bodies sank, the bloody black river taking them prisoner. Dozens of dead fish and plants rose to the surface.

I was in too much shock from the intensity of the icy waters to be nauseous. Riven was running along the shoreline, looking for a safe way across.

Within minutes, the Drakers were nothing more than bodies floating down the river.

As I made it to the other side of the bank, I collapsed, clutching my broken arm.

The sun was setting, and we had nowhere to stay for the night. Even if there was a village close by, I wouldn't make it another step.

I lay on the ground, eyes closed and shivering. My every garment wet and sticking to me.

There was no escaping the cold. It consumed me.

At a familiar whine from Kostini, I opened my eyes. The black stallion nudged my head, as if apologizing for my arm. Of course, Kostini was perfectly fine while I was close to death.

Riven hurried to my side, dropping his pack and flinging his bow to the ground. "You're going to freeze to death," he said quietly.

"Of course I am," I bitterly laughed. I had made it out of the Waywards, just to end up freezing anyway.

He didn't laugh back or comment at all. He was gathering wood and tossing it in a pile. It didn't take long for him to start the fire.

I'm not sure what I expected him to do, but I wasn't prepared for him to kneel at my feet and begin removing my boots. I didn't complain or move, just lay on my side, holding my arm while my body trembled. The river had washed away my Nature. At least I didn't have that mess to worry about.

"Your clothes have to come off," he said. "They're soaked."

"I can't get up to take them off. They'll dry eventually," I mumbled sleepily.

Metal rang at his side as he slid out a dagger. "You won't be alive to see them dry if we wait that long."

I closed my eyes. I just wanted to sleep. Perhaps forever.

Wind tickled my bare leg as Riven carefully sliced my pants from bottom to top.

"They were *new*," I complained quietly, utterly drained.

"I know," he said sympathetically, cutting the other side.

My eyes fluttered as he removed the wet fragments. He was focused and precise, but as he unclipped the orb from my hip, it zapped him.

He pulled his hand away, glaring at it. My orb had never done such a thing.

Riven tossed it to the side and continued working.

With a gentle caress of the blade at my hip, my underwear broke away. My shirt was next, and he maneuvered me with care onto my side before removing the rest.

A chill ran between my thighs as his warm hand slid across my back, pulling the last piece of wet clothing away.

He wasted no time after, taking my blanket out of the pack and laying it out by the fire.

"You can't lie on snow all night," he explained quietly, mostly to himself. Just as quick as he'd set out the blanket, he moved me onto it.

I stared at the fire. Numb. Teeth Chattering.

He shuffled through a bag, tossing things to the ground. Curiosity got the best of me, and as I turned my head, Riven was bare-chested, ripping his own dry shirt into pieces.

"What are you doing?" I asked, glancing at the marks along his tan chest.

"I need to wrap your leg. Don't move."

I did as he said, facing back to the almost useless fire and cringing as he tended to the wound. I hadn't expected him to use his own shirt.

When he was done wrapping my thigh, he crouched, gathering up my wet hair and tying it in the most horrendous bun.

"I'm moving you closer to the fire. You're too cold," he warned before hooking his arms under my bare waist and carrying me closer. I melted into the warmth of his arms against my damp skin. He placed me down with ease, and I was thankful to finally feel the heat of the fire.

He rolled up my cloak and stuffed it under my head like a pillow. "Don't hate me," he said.

"Why would I hate you?"

Down to his black undershorts, he scooted behind me, lying down before throwing his blanket over us.

I suddenly became very aware of my breathing, as I thought it may have stopped.

Careful of my broken bone, he wrapped his arms around me, warming my skin. His touch soothed some aching part deep within me, more vulnerable than any of my physical injuries.

It was impossible not to want more. I wanted—no, I *needed* him closer.

Nudging myself slightly back, he took it as an invitation to readjust, sliding his hand over my bare hip and pulling me close. This time, I was certain he meant to do it.

His unsteady breath on my neck sent shivers down my back, but I wasn't cold anymore.

"I don't hate you," I mumbled.

CHAPTER 23

You're Supposed to be Broken

"No Draker, knight, nor nobleman of this age can contest the skill of Xavian Steele. Bastard though he may be, he is, without question, the finest blade our generation has ever produced."

— *A MODERN HISTORY OF THE REALM, BY JON HARVINGTON*

I WAS NO LONGER ON THE FOREST FLOOR WITH RIVEN. Instead, I strode along an outdoor corridor of a grey building, but it was not me controlling my legs. I had no choice or ability to do anything. I could only watch.

I was locked behind the eyes of another, to where not even my own mind could trick me into believing it was real. It was a dream.

I pushed through towering steel doors and into what

appeared to be a meeting room. Three men sat dripping in wealth at a magnificent black oval table overlooking the ocean beneath the night sky.

Only one cushioned chair was left empty at the head of the table. The body I was trapped in sat, and the four men turned to me attentively.

An older, balding man with spectacles and a hooked nose spoke first. "My lord, I think the Dark Natured are too unpredictable to–"

"I've had enough of your thinking," a voice erupted from my mouth—a man's voice, unyielding.

To my right, a freckled man with cropped red hair grinned delightfully.

To my left was a man with long, sleek black hair. He was perhaps a few winters older than me, wearing a rich emerald green jacket that contrasted with his pale face. His expression was stone cold as he shook his head.

There were no documents on the table, just a space for discussion. No Drakers were present either. The castle could not be in Drakington, because the moonlit ocean was so close.

"Open the brotherhood to *anyone* who will join," my mouth said.

"My lord, Xavian, I—" the older man began.

Xavian?

The one with long, dark hair cut the grumpy one off. "I agree, my lord. We need the numbers for our forces."

"While I'm glad you agree, it was not up for discussion," Xavian's voice said through my mouth, before turning to the one with red hair. "Avan, what is the update on the intruders from earlier? I hear they want me dead?"

Avan nodded. "Oh yes, we've found all but one. I'm sure the straggler will turn up in no time."

Footsteps ran towards the doors, and they swung open. A wild man with frizzy brown hair entered the room, honing in on Xavian.

"Inkweed lover!" the man shouted.

Xavian pulled his arm back in a precise beat, propelling a dagger across the room. It sank directly into the intruder's heart.

"Ah, you found him," Avan said, impressed.

The older man at the table sighed, rubbing a long finger over his deeply wrinkled forehead.

Xavian glanced to his left. "Draven, what updates do you have today?"

"I have gathered a list of possible brides, my lord." Draven's bitter voice was the quietest among them, nearly a hiss.

"My daughter is a perfectly acceptable choice, and she already resides on these lands," the older one began again.

He irritated me, or maybe it was Xavian he was irritating. I couldn't tell the difference anymore.

"She's barren," Xavian said, drumming his fingers on the table.

"How could we possibly know such a thing?" the older man argued, cheeks red.

"I would never buy a sword without testing it first. Next."

When the older man went to speak again, Xavian raised his hand in warning.

Suddenly, my head hurt, my mind became watery and my eyes closed before I shifted back into my own body.

Still, I could not move. I was in the woods, but time had gone backward.

"You need to run," Riven ordered.

The golden arrow was in the tree above us again.

"To where? I'll get lost on my own," I said, just as I had before.

I knew what happened next. The arrow was coming, but I couldn't change anything.

All of it, I was forced to live through again. Riven pulling the arrow out, running through the forest with a blood trail, cradling my broken arm, and then—

Xavian's body drew in a breath, eyes shooting open, and we were at the table again.

"Are you okay?" Avan asked, leaning in.

Xavian stormed out of the room.

Avan and Draven followed behind, close on his heels. "What's happened now?" Draven asked.

"A broken arm, and another damned arrow," Xavian thundered.

Avan caught up on the right, scratching at his lightly freckled face. "Vomit this time too...or?"

Xavian ignored him, pushing through doors leading into a well-lit room with white glowing lights, tables, and a sick cot. Two healers worked inside. Their eyes brightened to see Xavian.

"I need a healer," Xavian ordered. "Maybe both of you."

———

I woke to the sound of Riven packing our things. It wasn't even first light yet, but he was dressed and had laid out dry clothes for me. It was strange to finally have a dream after weeks of not having one. I hoped Riven hadn't heard me talking in my sleep.

Sitting up, I used my blanket to preserve the last bit of modesty I had. The thought of pulling a shirt over my broken arm was more intimidating than most men I had met in my life.

I rubbed my eyes, tensing as I noticed which arm I was using.

"You're supposed to be broken," I whispered.

Riven's boots crunched into the ground as he surveyed the area. "Who are you talking to?"

I gave it an uncertain shake, unable to believe my eyes and unwilling to admit to speaking to a bone. There was no pain, not even when I moved it. I needed to see it beneath the wrap for myself.

"Cut this off of me." The urgency in my voice was sharp. My arm should've been swollen. I shouldn't have been able to move it with ease.

He didn't ask questions as he whipped a blade out and sliced the wrap off in a swift motion.

Riven and I both lost breath at the sight of my arm.

Where cuts and a broken bone had been, there were curved markings like black lightning, curling at the end. It was as if ink had spilled into meandering pathways, reaching halfway down my forearm, leading straight to the King's Mark. I stretched out my fingers, testing the full range of motion. My limb felt new.

Riven stared, tense and bewildered.

"Let me check your leg."

His knife was ready as I lifted the blanket to expose the back of my thigh.

"Tell me what you see," I demanded.

"The wound is gone."

"No scar?"

He braced his hand on my hip, turning me further away, his thumb pressing into the sensitive spot on my side.

He hesitated. "I'm not sure I'd call this a scar."

I turned back. "Why not?"

"Because it looks like the sun. Similar to the King's Mark, but outlined in black instead of gold. It has those same curves as the markings on your arm," he said. "There's not a chance a Lyonheart healed you last night, though."

I covered myself with the blanket. It was warmer out than it had been in days, the snow no longer falling. With any luck, the day would go smoother than yesterday. It had to.

"Maybe it's Zain's magic still lingering in my body," I guessed, rotating my arm and inspecting the markings. Perhaps I still had some leftover, and it just needed hours in my bloodstream to find the wounds. Or perhaps the King's Mark worked a miracle.

Riven didn't seem so convinced, but we had more pressing matters to concern ourselves with than my arm no longer being broken. I feared that if I questioned it too much, the Gods would shatter me again themselves.

———

Kostini carried us fast and steady with Riven gripping the reins, not needing the map anymore. We cleared the woods, and for the first time since leaving Lyonscliff, we found ourselves on a real road. According to Lord Dronis' map, there were no nearby cities. This area had been long abandoned for better farmlands, leaving nothing but a port.

Downhill of a dirt road, the sparkling ocean peeked through at last. My heart tightened at the grey hue of the sea and the embracing smell of salt.

Even better, there was a massive boat, just as Dronis had said there would be.

The black ship was docked in the distance, where small groups of people boarded while others worked. I closed my eyes, saying a prayer to the Mother that traveling to this port would be worth it.

As we rode closer, the design of the flags came into view. There were no Drakington Falcons. Instead, there was the symbol of a beast. The same symbol that had been on Singer's box. A bladebreather. Silver-scaled, with a reptilian head. Its mane was sizable, but of no comparison to its expansive, feathered wings.

At the docking area, there was a grassy patch perfect for dismounting. Riven tied Kostini to a post, bringing only our packs.

"Ready to travel the Sea of Blades?" Riven's tan cheeks were dusted pink from the stiff wind whipping at our faces, his honey eyes twinkling in the sunlight.

I had never been on a ship, but I couldn't be more ready. We didn't know who else would be on it, or what conditions we would have to survive, but I'd survived the Waywards. I'd survived Lyonscliff. I'd survived the Western Woods and the Sapphire camp. I would survive this ship.

Riven must have been thinking the same, because he grasped my hand before brushing his thumb over my skin. "We walk on together, we walk off together." His voice was steady and sure. I looked down at my hand—our hands.

No one had ever held my hand before; always too afraid of my poison. But Riven wasn't scared, or too proud. He didn't see me as a Blackheart. He saw me.

CHAPTER 24

SHADOWS AND GOODBYE

"Bladebreathers are marvelous winged creatures. Yet, even such a beast cannot keep to the sky long without a Natured rider. For flight, it seems, belongs to them both."

— *A GUIDE TO BEASTS AND OTHERWISE, BY DIALOR SNOW*

AS WE APPROACHED THE SHIP, SEVERAL PEOPLE IN black uniforms loaded supplies onto the boat, while others took orders in preparation to set sail. There were even guards. *Castivian* ones. Riven had explained that in Castivian, they had the Brotherhood of Bastards, calling themselves Blademen.

There were no Drakers in sight, only Blademen in their leathers, with swords at their sides, but no hoods or masks. No signs of misery from anyone boarding. No fear.

"Look," Riven said, tilting my chin up with one hand and

pointing to the sky with the other. My jaw opened in awe as the most beautiful creature in existence soared over the ship.

A bladebreather.

Red scales covered its body, and a black feathered tail whipped through the air. On its back, a woman held on with her legs but moved her arms around with ease, shouting out cheerful reports to workers on the deck below.

Her long blonde hair flowed in the wind as sparkling rosy dust followed them through the air, like she was the fuel and the beast was the machine. The woman was curvy, with breasts I was certainly jealous of filling out her white and red dress. Her cheeks were full, like she'd lived a life to smile about and came from a place where she didn't have to fight for food.

I had never been so envious of a person in my entire life.

"Let's hope it doesn't shit on the ship," Riven said. I huffed out a laugh, but my mouth was still ajar in admiration of the woman and the beast.

Eyes on the sky for far too long, I bumped right into the back of Riven as we approached the ticket master, coin in hand.

"No gold necessary," he assured us. His black mustache crinkled with a grin as he waved us on. It seemed too easy. Paranoia spread through me like wildfire. What if this was how they caught the Dark Natured who had escaped? Or what if this ship was setting sail for Lestivia, delivering us right to the Sapphires?

I stood still on the dock while Riven was already halfway up the bridge.

He turned around, locking his eyes on mine. "Together?" he asked softly.

Every fear I had seemed so far away as his gaze melted me.

I nodded. Together it was.

We crossed the windy wooden bridge before stepping onto the busy ship. There were crowds of people aboard, some with luggage and others with nothing but the clothes on their backs. The mixture of tears, laughter, hugs, and celebration was beautiful, chaotic, and overwhelming all at once.

Every moment since leaving the Waywards flashed like lightning before my eyes. I drew in a relieved breath at the sight of my gossipy, tea-loving friend.

"Elora! You made it too!" Trista called through hysterical cackles.

I hurried to embrace her, bumping past a few other groups of somewhat familiar faces.

"I knew you'd gotten out, and I just knew you'd make it, you stubborn girl," she cried into my shoulder. Her blazing red hair was frizzy, and she desperately needed a bath, but so did I.

Arielle cowered behind her, Beck at her side.

It would be a long time before I forgave Arielle for burning my building down, but that didn't matter at the moment. Of course, Beck made it out of the Waywards. Sneaky bastard.

Trista and I squealed like children while Riven kept his distance. I couldn't wait for the first cup of tea that Trista and I could get our hands on. I wanted to hear every story she had to tell. How had she survived when the Sapphires attacked? Were their travels as heinous as mine?

Turning to Arielle, I attempted a smile. Her wild red curls were still there, but something in her eyes was different. Not darkness, but void.

She tilted her head curiously at me. Beck crossed his arms, sizing me up. He noticed the new outfit, the orb at my waist, and Singer at my hip.

"I can't believe any of you are alive," he finally said, a grin spreading across his face.

I scoffed. I should have *known* he'd be here the moment Dronis said there was a ship coming. He survived the games with an intensity that almost had *me* scared of him.

"Did you all travel here together?" I asked.

He shrugged. "Some of the way. I was alone for a bit until I found their group," he motioned to Trista and the others.

Groups.

"Is Luna here?" I asked.

After every ache and tear, it would be worth it. This ship would be our fresh start. We could have our fight and be done with it. I would tell her everything I'd learned, and how I had burned the Blood Prince, killed a Warlock, and been shot not once, but twice. Even if she could be selfish and hurtful, she was my sister. Not by blood, but by choice.

Trista reached for my hand with solemn eyes. "I haven't seen her since the Waywards. I thought she'd be... with you."

I looked at Beck. He shook his head.

Riven squeezed my shoulder. Trista narrowed her eyes at the brief moment of affection. I'd tell her later that it wasn't like that. I was just an oath to him.

I glanced back at the land. It felt wrong leaving Drakington knowing Luna could still be there, but she'd left me first. By crossing the Sea of Blades, I was helping her, whether or not she would ever know. There would be a home for the Dark Natured, even if I had to be shot by a thousand arrows to build it.

———

The voyage began in the evening as planned, and the first night was beyond what I had expected. Riven was right about me having a room on the ship. The bed was made with grey covers and fit from wall to wall, leaving little space to walk around when the door was open. There was no other furniture or private place to relieve myself, but that was fine.

A shared pot was just down the hall, and that was more than I'd had in days. Above the bed was a porthole window that revealed the night sky and noisy waves.

I lay at the foot of the bed, content to watch the blade-breather occasionally pass by.

If anyone on the ship knew I was Xavian Steele's sister, they hadn't treated me differently because of it. The room was the only indicator they might have known.

Riven had his own room as well, though, while Trista and Arielle shared one.

Sleep claimed me early the first night. My body had demanded it. I dreamt of soothing darkness, my mind finally granting me a break. I would have slept an entire day away if thunder hadn't woken me the next afternoon.

Wrapped in my charmed blanket, I peeked out the porthole. The skies churned with hues of deep grey and blue, lightning flashing in the distance.

By the time I dressed and left my room to seek Trista and food, the boat rocked so wildly that I was running back for the pot.

I flew down the wobbly hallway right as Riven opened his door. I had no time to stop, even as he called out to me.

Just as I could not hold it any longer, I gripped both sides of the pot, retching as the ship swayed. Riven placed a hand on my back.

"Are you okay?"

"Don't touch me," I snapped. I heaved again, sweating. Arms shaking.

"Ever?" he asked, lifting his hand off my back.

I didn't have the capability to answer or dwell on what he meant. Instead, I silently begged the Mother to make the sickness stop.

Only once I was certain I had nothing left to expel, I stood, sighing in relief. I was about to apologize for snapping at Riven when a commotion sounded above deck.

The worst scenarios invaded my mind. *A Sapphire attack. Drakers.*

I bolted past Riven, running up the stairs as he followed.

On the deck, the commotion continued to grow.

"She's lost her damn mind!" a man yelled.

I froze.

A group of angry travelers surrounded Arielle. Trista stood nearby, with tears welling in the corners of her eyes and covering her mouth. A body lay on the floor, black poison coating what was left of his skin.

Arielle had killed him, just as she had killed people in the Waywards.

Beck stepped in front of Arielle, blocking her and addressing the growing crowd.

"I think it is best if you all leave for...a few moments, then we'll talk, yes?" he asked, far calmer than I could have been.

There was some protest, but he flicked each of them a coin for their patience, and with that, they scurried off with promises to return. Arielle stood behind him, holding her inky fingertips by her mouth and talking to herself. *Maybe the Waywards did this to her. Maybe we weren't meant to hold our poison in forever.*

Trista's tears ran through the crinkles around her eyes as she walked away.

Arielle hadn't always been violent. She was once a breath of fresh air, always noticed for being fearless and outspoken. Now, she had taken the opportunity of a new life away from the man who lay at their feet.

Riven and I backed away, lingering by a shadowed wall of ropes and hooks as Beck turned back to Arielle. My chest burned, knowing that if she tried to hurt him, I would repay the favor I owed him for saving me in the midwinter games. She could not continue on like this.

I held one of the secured ropes as the ship rocked me further into the wall, partially obscuring my view as Beck grabbed Arielle's slender hand and *kissed it.*

She smiled, the sorrow disappearing from her eyes. He wrapped his arms around her, hugging her in a way that said more than words.

I had been so blind. All that time ago at the tavern, Beck hadn't been nosy for the hell of it. He was in love with Arielle.

As her smile melted away, she tried to hide her face, turning toward the water while holding the ledge of the ship. Beck wasn't deterred in the slightest, slipping his arms lovingly around her from behind and cradling her as they swayed, both staring out at the sea.

What if the mob were to return while they weren't looking?

I couldn't help but walk closer, as if I needed to protect them. I wasn't sure what the solution would be to the Arielle issues, but Beck *loved* her.

He combed her wild curls to the side and kissed her shoulder.

"I'm sorry they did this to you," he said.

"Me too." Her voice was soft, but not sad. It was empty.

She nodded to him as if he'd asked a question. The ship rocked, and I grabbed onto a nearby barrel, narrowly avoiding falling. Riven still stood back in the shadows, his face unreadable.

Beck held Arielle tighter, but she pushed space between them before turning to face him. She pleaded with her eyes, as if a monster was out to get her.

For the first time, Beck's breath was unsteady. His eyes were wild with uncertainty.

There was a silent battle between their stares before he nodded back and met her mouth for a kiss. I should have looked away or gone back to my room, but I could not.

He held her in his embrace as the moment went from dream to nightmare. Fast, thick shadows filled her throat and circled around her body like a storm. I placed my hand to my mouth, holding back tears as he lowered her to the ground. Shadows covered her eyes and blanketed her body. They swarmed into her nose and mouth, and her breathing slowed.

She showed no sign of panic, nor fear. It was Beck who looked afraid as he struggled to conceal the pain, his chest heaving as he wielded his shadows, sending his lover to the darkness she so desired.

My heart shattered.

Beck held Arielle until she was gone, then lovingly closed her eyelids. With unsteady arms, he picked her limp body up, red curls falling like ash. He kissed her forehead for the last time before dropping her over the side of the ship.

At long last, she was free. Not only from the Waywards, but from both her mind and her own Nature.

I scurried off, holding back tears. Trista was going to be a wreck, but I would be there for her, the best I could.

The sail whipped above, and when I glanced up, the blonde woman was perched behind the sail with her beast. If I had been ten steps back, I wouldn't have been able to see them in the darkness. Her and the bladebreather's eyes were glued on Beck, who held the ledge of the ship, cursing at the ocean.

The bladebreather lowered its head, quietly whining and large eyes blinking in wonder.

The woman snuggled into the bladebreather's side, petting his mane. "Bad days always end, as will his," she said.

———

The storm raged on for weeks to follow. I spent most of my time spewing up lunch, having tea with Trista, playing cards with Beck and his friends, or lying in bed watching the blade-breather soar. Its rider kept to the sky, rarely ever on deck.

I thought we would never make it to Castivian.

Then the morning came when I didn't wake up needing the chamber pot. Instead, I woke to the sound of—

"LAND!"

PART 3

CHAPTER 25

EIDEN

"Tell me, are you well, brother?"

— *CORRESPONDENCE FROM LORD XAVIAN STEELE TO LYONSREACH*

THE PORT CITY TWINKLED UNDER THE FIRST LIGHT OF dawn, deep blues and purples filling the skies.

I had expected the Castivian capital to be grim, but I was wrong. Eiden was a mural of a city, even from a distance. A vibrant array of jewel toned buildings with black roofs hugged the coast behind a harbor filled with little boats with glowing bulbs attached to their sails.

Salty winds kissed my face as I braced my hands on the ledge of the ship.

Somewhere out there, my brother was waiting for me.

Was I ready to meet him? I wanted to, yes, but what could we possibly have to say to each other? Where would I live?

What jobs did Castivian have to offer a Blackheart? Did it matter anymore that I was a Blackheart?

"Are you ready?" Riven asked.

The rising sun smeared orange across the water. Soon, the capital city of Eiden would wake to our arrival.

There had always been Dark Natured people in Castivian, ones that never knew the Waywards. Were the people here skilled with their Nature? What did it look like if someone was well practiced with their Dark Nature? Was it dangerous here?

Was I ready?

"I hope so." It was the most honest answer I could give.

Riven leaned on the ledge next to me.

"Are *you* ready?" I asked.

Riven looked out into the distance. "I know I'm ready to get off this ship."

I grinned, but he didn't. He looked almost disappointed.

As we docked, the masses crowded the bridge for departure. I couldn't blame them for being eager, though I'd likely be bruised from the relentless crashing of shoulders.

Riven led the way, shielding me from those who were aggressively desperate to get off first.

At the dock, he went to retrieve Kostini. The animals were last to disembark.

I stood alone with all of my belongings packed away in a bag at my feet, save for the clothes on my body, Singer, and the orb.

Ship bells tolled as waves lapped against the posts below. All sorts of people made their departures and arrivals. They hauled luggage and dreams past fishermen who were out with their nets and buckets, casting lines, while traders unloaded their goods along the docks.

None of the ships in the bay bore the Drakington falcon or the Lestivian swan. Who was Castivian trading with? I had never learned what was beyond the neighboring kingdoms.

Riven led Kostini down the bridge, who greeted me with cheerful neighs and a chipper shoulder sniff. It did not take Riven long to load our few things up before we took off, riding out on dark stone streets into the city.

Some buildings had stained glass, while others had large round windows, revealing families having their morning meals. I tilted my head curiously at the full plates and laughter.

Further down the street, a woman stood outside of a lilac bakery, propping open a door, letting out scents of coffee and rich chocolate.

Some of the homes were like dark cathedrals with colorful flowers displayed in their yards. Others were more humble buildings, but they were well-maintained all the same.

A crimson puddle gathered beneath a bush.

"Why are those roses blue?" I asked. "And why are they... bleeding?" Blood dripped from their petals, staining the grass red. They were the strangest flowers I'd ever seen.

Riven held back a smile. "It's that time of month. When I was a child, I was told it's rude to point out."

I wasn't sure whether or not he was joking, but there were too many things to look at to get caught up on the flora.

We passed inns with colorful paintings on the outside of women with fish-like tails, children in little black uniforms walking in groups while discussing school, street vendors setting up for the day while illuminating their stalls with orbs, and a library stacked four stories high.

I'd always been told that Castivian was an unruly land

where plenty of Dark Natured worked, but the majority of money was sent to Drakington for taxes. Never had I heard that there were still riders for bladebreathers, or even proper cities.

We travelled through the capital until the buildings were behind us, and only grass and rocky patches stretched ahead.

"Is there a castle here?"

"No," Riven answered.

"Where does Xavian live then?"

"The Lord of Castivian and his council's homes are all in the Silver Circle. We're not far."

Riven was rigid, as if he'd taken ten steps back from the friendship I thought we were forming.

I swallowed, palming my orb for distraction until we finally made it to the top of the hill, where there was, in fact, a circle of striking manors.

Each home was dark and hanging onto the edge of the misty, seaside cliff, daring gravity to test its structure's strength. Tall arched windows revealed nothing at the early hour.

"They've already left for the day," Riven mumbled.

"Who?"

"The council."

My face fell. "Where did they go?"

"The House of Sterling. It's not far."

I nervously waited as we rode past grassy, gravel pathways and black stone barracks that were evidently for the Brother-hood of Bastards. Finally, we arrived at our destination.

Long and silver, the stone structure looked more like a fortress than a house, fenced in with a gate made entirely of swords and guarded by a singular Blademan.

Riven dismounted first, then helped me down. The guard

did not wear armor, only black leathers with blades secured in various places, similar to Riven.

As my hands began to shake, I raised them to the straps on my bag.

"We're here to see Lord Xavian Steele," Riven said to the Blademan. "We have a message from the king."

The brunette guard crossed his arms and grinned. "He's in the grand hall. Just finished up an initiation ceremony. You can head in."

The guard didn't bother opening the gate for us, nor did he alert anyone that we were entering. It seemed odd and unsafe for the Lord of Castivian. Nevertheless, I followed Riven through the gate, the stone doors, and finally, inside the House of Sterling.

If I didn't know from Payn that Xavian hated Sapphires, I would think it was blood magic. Murals of haunting battles sprawled across high vaulted ceilings, the array of colors bleeding the stories together. Open windows sat between beautiful spiral grey columns, allowing salty air to flow through the hall.

There were shining stone floors, and carved archways revealing a dining hall, a stunning library, and even a room where women in dresses were having tea. From the outside, this seemed like a place of punishment. Yet the more I discovered, the more it felt like a campus. Riven walked confidently, not surprised in the slightest at anything.

"Have you been here before?" I asked as he turned down another hallway.

"Yes."

He'd never told me.

I swallowed, nervously gripping my bag again as we faced a large black door with silver handles. There were faint sounds of men laughing and swords clashing beyond the door.

"He's in there," Riven said, unenthusiastically.

My heart skipped a beat. "I'm ready."

CHAPTER 26

THE DEED

"No man lies cleaner than a Blademan with orders to keep."

— *LORD DRAVEN WRENAVIA*

RIVEN PULLED THE DOOR OPEN, AND THE ROOM FELL silent.

In front of a silver throne stood three men standing on grey and white marble floors, all wielding swords like they'd been training, only pausing at our interruption.

I stepped forward, face falling as I met eyes eerily similar to my own.

There was no doubt in my mind, from the curly black hair to the dark-brown eyes staring back at me. He was unquestionably my twin.

I also recognized the other two men immediately, but *from my dreams.* Xavian and the redhead wore black leathers, while the one with long, dark hair wore a fancy purple tunic with silver embellishments. In my dreams, their names were Avan and Draven.

A stale silence fell between the five of us as Xavian and I stared at one another. After everything, I had made it to Castivian. I was here and could deliver the deed. I had a twin, and he was right in front of me, and—

"In one piece?" my twin asked, astonished and sheathing his sword. I blinked. He was not like Clarke at all. No bags under his eyes. No soft voice or weakened body. He was built like a warrior, as were his men.

I didn't know what to say.

Riven's lips remained in a flat line.

"Are you Xavian Steele?" I asked, words coming out quieter than I would have preferred. I knew, but needed confirmation.

"Does my reputation precede me?" He stepped forward, eyes flashing with pain as he took in the sight of me, exhausted and half his size.

I had imagined this moment, as he likely had too. It was nothing I could have prepared for. Both of our faces shifted with confusion.

"I have a letter from the king," I said, straightening my posture and rolling up my sleeve to display the glittering gold mark on my forearm.

"I'm aware of the letter, and we will have much to discuss later. You can hand it to Avan or Draven." He gestured to the men behind him.

So those *were* their names. Did the Warlock leave some bizarre magic in me?

I pulled my bag off, walking towards Avan. He seemed more approachable than Draven.

Xavian's thundering voice halted Riven's attempt to follow.

"*You* don't move," Xavian warned him. I was already beside Avan, just beginning to open my bag, but paused at Xavian's order. Riven was my friend, and he needed to know that. I opened my mouth, but a hand was placed on my shoulder.

The red haired one, Avan, shook his head—warning me to let them be.

Riven didn't breathe a word as Xavian stalked across the vaulted room, taking slow, calculated steps.

"Sir Riven, did you swear an oath that you would keep my sister safe?"

The Rogue Draker placed his hands behind his back, lifting his chin fearlessly. "Yes, my lord."

With immeasurable speed, Xavian sent a dagger soaring across the room, pinning Riven's shoulder to the door.

He groaned out in pain.

Avan's arm stopped me as I tried to rush forward.

"It's best you let them fight their own battles," he said under his breath. Draven looked down at me with cold, hawk-like eyes.

"I will have to agree, and know that is not something I do often with Lord Avan," he hissed coolly. My eyes narrowed at both of them.

"Does that feel safe, Sir Riven?" Xavian's voice echoed across the hall.

Riven winced, but didn't dare take the dagger out.

"I tried my best to—" he began as another dagger flew across the room, this time the hilt thudding him in the forehead. The back of his head knocked into the door.

I gasped.

Draven took an annoyed breath. "Sir Riven will be fine," he droned.

I wasn't so convinced. My stomach swirled with poison, my hands tight.

"How does your head feel now? Can you *'try your best'* to explain it?" Xavian mocked.

The Lord of Castivian walked away, reaching behind the silver throne while blood trickled from Riven's shoulder and down the side of his body. I couldn't bear watching him in pain.

An arrow soared into Riven's thigh, pinning him further into the door. He roared as two arms yanked me back, Avan shushing me.

"You will make it worse," Avan whispered.

Xavian stood in the center of the room, bow in hand and head cocked to the side. "You know what I think is really safe?"

Riven shook his head, shamefully looking down, refusing to speak.

Another arrow released, pinning the Draker's opposite thigh to the door.

Then Xavian threw the bow down and stormed across the room to yank the arrow back out.

Riven howled.

"Avan," Xavian chimed with his back to us.

Avan's arm still held me tight. "Yes?"

"Am I forgetting something?"

"The vomit!"

Xavian lifted his head. "Ah yes, the vomit."

His fist slammed into Riven's stomach twice before its contents covered the floor.

I was steaming. Simmering. Close to boiling.

Xavian yanked out the remaining dagger and arrow. Riven fell to the floor, right into his own emesis and blood.

"You best be at training tomorrow morning, since you've forgotten it," Xavian ordered. "Now get the fuck out of my sight."

Bleeding and unwilling to meet my eye, Riven stood and limped out of the great hall.

Xavian Steele wiped the bloody dagger off with his shirt before strapping it back. My brother faced me at last, taking in my rage.

"He's fine." He picked up the bow and tossed it behind his throne.

Avan finally let go. I dropped my bag, crossing the length of the room with my arms stiff at my side until I was standing in front of my brother, Nature swirling inside of me. He crossed his arms.

How dare he torture the only person who'd helped me. How dare Riven let Xavian Steele torment him without putting up a fight.

"You..." I pointed my finger directly in his face. "You are an ungrateful, spoiled *bastard,*" I spat, getting louder with each word.

He frowned at the hurt in my eyes, in my soul. I had crossed an ocean to meet him, and he spent the first moments like *this.* I was disgusted, and he knew. The arrogance was gone from his face, and when he looked as if he may try to speak, I narrowed my eyes, letting him know just how small he was to me.

I gave him one last look of disgust before crossing the room, yanking my bag off the ground and shoving the deed in Avan's freckled hands.

Running down the hallways, I followed the fresh crimson trail, easily catching up to Riven. He walked well for his injuries, and held pressure to his profusely bleeding shoulder.

"Why didn't you fight back?"

He refused to look at me. "Because I deserved it."

He deserved gold and land for bringing me here—for delivering the deed. He deserved gratitude and praise, not assault upon arrival.

"For what?" I stabbed, voice sharp as knives.

He turned the corner, picking up his pace. "I vowed an oath to pay for any injury you endure. I meant it. He has given me my honor back, because without feeling your pain, I would have *none.*"

His honor? He'd already abandoned Drakington. To hell with his honor.

"You're a Rogue Draker, why would you seek honor here?"

He slowed, stepping through a dark wooden door. The same one from my dream. It was so bizarre, having never been to Castivian in my life.

Inside, medicines filled the shelves and several cots were available. The same two healers were there. After a quick look at Riven, they smiled and directed him to a bed.

"Ah shit, Riven, I didn't know you'd be back today!" one of them exclaimed. He wore a black uniform as well, but without weapons.

Back? They knew the Draker by name?

Riven hopped onto a cot, staining the white blankets red.

The other healer laughed, grabbing a pair of shears. "Friend, you've been gone for a while. I see you stopped to say hello to Xavian."

Neither of the men acknowledged me as they cut off clothes and tended to his injuries. They *knew* him.

"I think he missed me," Riven replied jokingly in a Castivi accent, turning his shoulder in to look at the stab wound.

One healer glanced up at me, blond hair falling in front of his eyes. "Are you hurt too?"

"No." Not physically.

They went back to pretending I didn't exist, just like Riven had been pretending to be Drakish this entire time.

No, that was insane. Riven wasn't a liar.

"How do you know each other? When did you have time to visit Castivian?" The words came out so quickly, I wasn't sure he'd caught them all.

Both healers' eyes shot up. They turned to Riven awkwardly.

He *wouldn't* lie to me. He promised I could trust him, and I did—more than anyone.

"You really like to assume things about me, don't you?" was all Riven could offer, settling into his native accent.

He'd never been a real Draker.

Three years in the Waywards, pretending to be someone he was not, faking his voice, sleeping with my friend, and spying on me.

My fingernails dug into my palms. There were no words for the way I felt. It was such a simple thing he could have confessed at any point on the journey. But to leave me blind-sided—to have some ridiculous devotion for Castivian, but not to me...

My reward for crossing the Sea of Blades was nothing but another wound on my heart. No one cared to be honest with me about *a single thing* in my entire life. At least Luna had told me she wanted to leave. She may have been a selfish coward, but she wasn't a liar.

I left the room, ignoring Riven as he called my name.

Avan was waiting in the hall, but I stormed right past him, flicking him off as he called out, too.

I didn't give a shit what any of these men had to say anymore. I was leaving.

I had delivered the stupid deed, doing my part for the Dark Natured. I was free from the Waywards, and free from the curiosity of who my brothers and father might be. I could do whatever I wanted, and that did not include enjoying the company of liars.

Avan wisely did not attempt to follow as I left the House of Sterling. The sea breeze tickled my face and blew my hair. The capital below was beautiful from the plateau, but even more beautiful was the bladebreather soaring above the black rooftops, a sparkling, rosy dust trailing behind.

It was hard to tell from a distance, but I was sure it was the same blonde woman, enjoying being home as her beast flipped its tail happily through the air.

She was truly free.

I strode into the city with resolve. I would never be caged again.

CHAPTER 27

YOU SHOULD COME

"Ah, how I miss Castivian. I was foolish to leave. No Draker
has ever matched a Blademan's...vigor."
Miss Soryl, as heard in passing

IT TOOK ONLY TWO HOURS TO FIND A JOB AS A
barmaid. The pay was twice as much as I earned in the
Waywards, *and* included a furnished room with a small bed and
a single chest.

It took one night to realize Castivian was absolutely
nothing like Drakington.

People of all Natures sat at the wooden tables throughout
Sailor's Tear Tavern, all mingling. People who approached me
didn't care what my Nature was. I was just a person, like them.
Some of the other barmaidens gossiped about me being from
the Waywards, implying I might carry illnesses, but that was
mild compared to the shit I'd heard in Drakington.

No one was *truly* scared of me.

It wasn't until the second night before I understood why.

During the day, Eiden was filled with bustling crowds going about their daily tasks. There were artists, tailors, gem shops, restaurants—and those were just some of the buildings on the same strip where I worked. I had yet to fully explore, but it was beautiful, and full of hope.

But after dark, things became much different.

On the second night, there was a brutal commotion outside my bedroom. I clutched Singer beneath my comforter. A man was mugged and beaten behind the tavern. Right by my window.

When I frantically rose to seek help, Gia, one of my bosses, sat at the bar stirring a drink. She had heavy bags under her eyes, cleavage spilling over her maroon top, and an unlit smoke waiting for her on the counter.

"Don't bother, girl."

Stopping, I pointed urgently to the window.

"Someone outside needs help."

She snorted, tapping her spoon and dropping it next to the cup.

I missed Trista, whom I had yet to find since docking.

"He chose to linger in the streets past bar hours. He knew the risk."

The doors of the tavern were bolted shut. The rest of the girls had already retired to their rooms.

"Go back to bed," she said.

By the third night, it was clear the streets were littered with thieves and crime. There were no Drakers to keep everyone in line.

"Why is it only at night?" I asked Gia.

I had risen to grunting. When I peeked out of my window, a man was dead, with his mouth full of stones—the work of a Stonesender.

"It's an unwritten rule. Lord Xavian Steele expects to wake up to a peaceful city. So, he does."

I frowned. He should be *King* Xavian Steele. He had yet to enact the deed, and last I'd heard, Clarke was still very much alive. Maybe I had travelled all this way for nothing but a new job.

I spent every day wondering why my twin was holding out on declaring Castivian its own kingdom, but I wasn't curious enough to seek him out.

Five days passed before Riven found me.

He stood at the bar as if he were a patron, his hair tousled, tan skin glowing, and eyes locked on mine.

"You don't drink," I said, sizing him up from behind the bar. It was early. The few patrons we had were chatting amongst themselves at tables and playing card games. Business wouldn't pick up until later in the evening.

"I'm not here for refreshments."

"Good. You're not welcome to any."

I turned my back to him, making it three steps before he hopped over the bar, landing in front of me. I glared up at him.

"You promised to trust me," he said.

I choked on a bitter laugh and backed away. "I promised you'd only get one chance with my trust."

"I have never lied to you."

I threw my hands up. "You knew me for three years and didn't tell me my brother was the king, and then you traveled with me across the Sea of Blades and didn't tell me you were returning *home*."

He knew Xavian personally and could have told me about him. He was from Castivian and could have prepared me for what to expect. He could have made me trust him by telling me something no one else in Drakington knew: the truth.

But he didn't.

"I was sworn to secrecy about who your family was. It was not for me to tell. As for not being a Draker, I thought you'd be happy about that."

I crossed my arms. Riven, of all people, was acting like he gave a shit about what I thought of him.

"If you would've told me, then yes. I would've been over-joyed to know that I wasn't crazy for thinking you were different this whole time. I would've been relieved to know that someone who was important to me wasn't a Draker. But you didn't tell me."

His dimple had the audacity to show itself as his eyes softened. He took another step towards me. "Let me make it up to you. We can start fresh. I completed my oath. We're both free."

"No."

"Elora," he said softly. The *way* he said my name was so different from others.

I grabbed the bin that required washing and hauled it to the backroom. Rags and a soapy bucket awaited me. I could get them done before it got busy.

I wanted the distraction; I needed to get *him* out of my head before I considered—

The door behind me opened and closed, then a firm hand gripped my waist, warmth brisking my ear.

Riven's chest pressed against my back, and my breath hitched as his hair brushed the side of my face.

"Enough with the games," he murmured.

Any sense of logic fled my mind. "None of this has ever been a game to me."

The dishes sat waiting, but I no longer had any interest. I turned to face him, and he retreated a step.

"I'm sorry I didn't tell you." His eyes didn't meet mine. They were lower, at my lips, as we stood in the tight, dimly lit backroom. "I'm so sorry," he continued, stepping closer.

I had never truly wanted a man to touch me until this moment.

"You should be sorry," I whispered.

"Let me make it up to you."

As his eyes wandered down, the back of his knuckle grazed my rib cage, skimming the side of my breast like a gentle paint stroke.

I swallowed, trying to regain a thread of dignity, but I was unraveling. "How do you plan on doing that?"

Riven dropped his hand and straightened.

"Let me show you Castivian, and I can train you too."

I groaned, crossing my arms. I wanted to see more of Castivian, and desperately wanted to be able to defend myself, but that didn't mean I wanted to be teased in a washroom.

"You want to spend more time with me—after our travels? And train me?"

His jaw tensed. "Is that a no?"

"Now who's assuming?" I joked.

His eyes flashed with amusement.

My smile fell. We'd traveled so far, had put our lives in

danger countless times, and for what? My brother to do nothing? If he'd used the deed, the entire capital would have been talking about it by now.

"Why hasn't *he* used the deed yet?" I refused to even speak my brother's name.

The Riven who followed me to the washroom faded away. He regained his composure, his face reverting to that of a soldier.

"There's a meeting to discuss that in two weeks."

Two weeks? I'd busted my ass rushing to Castivian, and now they were waiting two weeks?

"Who's the meeting with?" I hadn't been invited, not that I expected to be. My twin had no need for me anymore, and I had no need for him either.

But the rest of the Dark Natured needed him. They needed safe lands, and promises of freedom.

"The council," he answered, sounding like he would rather talk about anything else.

He gave a valiant effort to tame the burning desire in his eyes, and I regretted ever bringing the deed up. It was impossible to imagine a room full of any other men when Riven stood in front of me.

"You should come," Riven added.

I had two weeks to think about the stupid meeting. I did not have two weeks of Riven standing this close, the heat radiating between us. If he wanted to touch me again, I would let him. Just for tonight. Just this once.

Then never again.

He couldn't have this power over me. I couldn't let this need fester.

"Make me."

His eyes darkened. "Say it again," he challenged, closing the distance between us, tracing his fingers along my cheek.

I tilted my chin, looking up at him through my lashes. "Make. Me."

There wasn't a moment to blink before his mouth crashed into mine.

It was the first time I had ever been *truly* kissed in my life.

I ran my hands through the back of his hair as he picked me up, his mouth brushing my jaw, then down my neck.

He knocked the buckets off the table, laying me on my back with his hands firm at my waist, mouth trailing to my chest.

The sun was setting, and hardly any light came through the small window. I wanted to see it all. I wanted this moment burned into my memory. Desperately reaching at my hip, I unclipped my orb and set it beside me on the table. With a slight tap, the room lit up a dim blue.

Riven unbuttoned my pants in a smooth motion before placing warm kisses below my navel. With my back against the table, he only removed his mouth from my body to pull my pants off, then got on his knees, yanking my hips to the edge.

My heart thundered in anticipation, but only for a moment before his face was between my legs, tongue reaching me, unholy and precise. A soft moan escaped my lips embarrassingly quickly.

He looked up, sinful desire lacing his gaze.

He grabbed the inside of my thigh, giving it a playful squeeze before pushing it up and onto the table. With my knee bent, Riven backed his head away. Lustful eyes locked on mine as his finger slid in. Another followed, and I could hardly catch my breath.

Mortifying.

Business in the tavern would soon pick up, and the door to the backroom wasn't even locked.

My legs shook as his tongue toyed with me, pushing me to the edge of more than just the table. I tried to keep quiet, but another traitorous moan came out. Riven's gaze darted up as he circled the spot that had me near release.

"Louder," he demanded.

"People are going to hea—"

He stood up, bringing my face to his, silencing me with a kiss. The tender reprieve was brief before he brought me in his arms and turned me around. He sat on the table, yanking my back to his chest just before his hand reached over, finding its place between my legs.

He did not tire, just slid his opposite hand up my shirt and bit at my neck. Each movement was overwhelming, as was each kiss that dragged along my ear and down my nape.

"I love the noises you make," he murmured, fingers picking up speed.

As if my body answered to him now, and not myself, I shivered—whimpering as I came undone.

"*Fuck.*"

"Let me hear it."

He held my body with one arm as the other finished me, my head tilting back and senses surging. Riven showed no mercy, and by the time my voice quieted, every person in the tavern surely knew his name.

I slid next to him on the table, trying to remember how to be normal.

He hopped up and tossed my pants to me.

"Training grounds, behind the House of Sterling, tomorrow at sunrise." He roved over my body one last time, then shut the door behind him. My shoulders slumped.

If he had done that with just his hand and mouth... I shook my head.

I pulled my pants on and hurried with the dishes. After taking a few breaths, I opened the backroom door.

Gia was waiting for me with her arms crossed. "I sure hope 'Riven' charged you for that service."

I blushed. "I don't know what you're talking about."

"Mhm." Her smile perked up on one side as she tilted her head towards the bar. "Get back to work, *whore*," she teased, eyes crinkling with approval.

I hated to admit it, but I liked Gia. Tired and jaded she may have been, but she was straightforward and genuine. None of the other girls at work really talked to me, as if the Waywards would rub off on them, but Gia did.

The tavern quickly became busy, but all the work in the world could not distract me from thoughts of Riven, and of returning to the House of Sterling.

CHAPTER 28

A PRINCESS WITH NOTHING

"Centuries past, bladebreathers were used to attack ships and conquer. The waters became so saturated with quills, they named it the Sea of Blades."

— *A HISTORY OF HERETICS, BY COLESON JAMES*

I DIDN'T GO.

Riven had fogged my brain of any sense. I had no reason to train. Xavian would be declared king in two weeks, then the Dark Natured would be free to seek refuge in Castivian, and that would be that. The hard days were behind me. I refused to set myself up for any further disappointment by being in my brother's presence.

Leaving Sailor's Tear for the day seemed like the wise choice. Riven wouldn't be able to find me, and I had no desire to be taunted about my absence, nor dragged all the way through the capital to Xavian Steele's doorstep.

The dark stone streets were immaculate compared to the Waywards. The seaside air was pleasant enough that no cloak or long sleeves were necessary. Singer and the orb were at each hip, daring anyone to fuck with me on my day off, training or not.

People of all ages tossed around orbs of Dreamsoul blue, Flamecastor red, Stonesender grey, Nightcastor black, Lyonheart gold, and Blackheart violet. A group of Imps, adorned in expensive fashions, sat on a restaurant patio, enjoying lunch, while a flock of birds fluttered around them, singing a birthday song.

It was all so different. The Waywards were dead, but Castivian was alive.

An artist worked in the window of her shop, sculpting clay and humming a jaunty, unfamiliar tune. Meanwhile, a plump man slid a tray of freshly made bread out of a stone arched opening, stacking the loaves on a display cart.

Potion shops, infusing lessons, botany markets—so many businesses that would have never been allowed in Drakington.

I loved it.

The further I went, the more altitude I gained. I didn't notice until I glanced back and could see the entire seaside city on its slow slope. The ocean gradually came into view as I peered over the black-slate roofs.

Past the bustling businesses was a stretch of sizable residences. The neighborhood was like a kaleidoscope. Vibrant greens, various tones of blue, deep purples, silver, and pops of pink. They all had matching black roofs and doors, with long pointed arches, ribbed vaults, spires, and stained glass windows.

I picked at the skin of my pointer finger. One of those houses could have been mine, but under no circumstances would I beg my brother for charity.

The need to look away from the unattainable homes hit me like a wall of bricks. I swallowed hard, my face tightening. It was all so ridiculous. This land would no longer be a territory of Drakington, but its own kingdom with me as its princess.

A princess with nothing.

I no longer wanted to walk through the city. I just wanted to sleep, with no bizarre dreams or waking up at the break of dawn. To close my eyes, and not have to feel this way, just for a little while.

Shoulders slumped, I turned back towards home, but as I made the first few steps, a shadow soared overhead. I twisted, looking skyward. A bladebreather left a trail of red mist as it flapped its great wings. The blonde woman rode on its back, fearless and free.

My heart drummed in my chest as my legs moved with a mind of their own.

Maybe I was losing it, but I didn't care.

Hitting the outskirts of the city, I chased after the winged beast as if by wild instinct.

The bladebreather passed over the smooth stretch of land at the top of the hill, just ahead of a heavy woodline. There were scattered livestock throughout the plains and a few small buildings. Most of the field was rock and dirt, with scattered patches of tall grass.

Where the hell was the rider going? The opportunity to see more bladebreathers or even potentially get close to one was irresistible. I'd been drawn to paintings and stories of them since I was a child.

This was my opportunity for a future, maybe even my destiny.

I sprinted across the flat terrain.The burning in my chest had long gone, leaving only euphoria as the distant ocean bore witness to me blazing down the wide dirt road.

I pushed harder, running into the woods.

The beast glided over the trees, increasingly difficult to follow through the dense foliage. My steps faltered as I struggled to keep up, desperately searching for the trail or the sound of a beating wing.

"Wait!" I called out, voice hoarse, legs pushing as hard as they could.

Every so often, I passed others along the trail who gave judgmental scowls and mocking stares, but it didn't matter if they thought I was mad. I was far beyond shame.

The green canopy became so thick it blocked my view of the sky entirely, making it impossible to tell which path to take. My desire to press on was hindered, but I fought the part of me that was so ready to give up. The muscles in my legs burned, but the physical pain was nothing compared to the sting I would feel of another disappointment.

Faster. Faster. Faster. Faster—

A person dropped through the trees, boots landing on the ground a few feet ahead. I gasped, trying to stop before I trampled them.

"Mother of Moons!" I yelled, tripping and smacking my palms into the ground, poison involuntarily spraying from them and into the dirt.

Steps approached, but nausea overcame me before I could look up. My hands pressed into the blood and poison-soaked ground as I spewed the contents of my stomach.

My eyes clenched shut—jaw locking tight.

I was so *angry*. So tired of being a Blackheart. My eyes stung with grief as pain flared in my chest.

So tired of being *me*.

"God fucking dammit! I hate this shit," I seethed, trying to gather myself.

"Oh!" a cheerful voice chimed.

I glanced up. The blonde woman stood there, observing me curiously.

"Oh?" I repeated.

She was tall, wearing a practical, ankle-length red dress that fit her large and curvy figure, complemented by a bold ruby necklace. She reached inside the brown bag hanging from her shoulder and pulled out a cloth.

"Here, for your spill." She held it towards me, green eyes bright.

I cautiously took it and glanced around. No sign of the bladebreather, to my utter dismay, though she was definitely the rider.

I cleaned my hands, noting the wipe worked impressively well on my Nature.

"I know you," I said. "You're the woman who escorted our ship from Drakington."

"Yep." The woman brought two fingers to her mouth, letting out a loud whistle.

Descending through the trees, the bladebreather landed with a ground-shaking thud before stretching his neck. He inspected me with huge amber eyes, while his feathered tail whipped back and forth in a feline motion.

Others walking the trail scurried off.

I stayed rooted in place.

His gleaming scales were magnificent up close, and while his wings and teeth were intimidating, they were more majestic than any castle ever would be.

"His name is Zephyros," the blonde woman said.

"But I'm perfectly content being called Zephy," his chipper voice chimed in my head. His mouth did not move when he spoke, yet I knew it was him.

My eyes shot to the woman. "Why can I hear him?"

"Because you're Natured."

No one had ever told me bladebreathers could speak.

The woman placed a hand on Zephy, giving him an encouraging pat.

"And your name?" he asked me.

"Uh, I'm Elora Amona, of Blackheart." I still sat on the ground with my hands planted behind me, in awe of him—of both of them.

The thin straps of her gown displayed soft, rosy arms, and her long, straight hair rustled in the breeze.

"I'm Amzee, Flamecastor. Though, we usually don't lead with that."

It should have been obvious she was a Flamecastor, as they were all marked with a red, glimmering streak. Sometimes with multiple. But usually the marks were across their cheeks or forehead. Amzee's shimmers were perfectly over her eyelids like cosmetics.

Still surrounded by vomit, I tried not to stew in humiliation as I got to my feet and wiped the dirt off my pants.

"You! I want my money back! You're a cheater!" a man yelled from the distance, sprinting in Amzee's direction with a drawn sword.

Her smile didn't falter. In fact, she looked... excited?

The winded man glared at Zephy, his weapon held high and puffy cheeks red. "I'll kill you and your beast too if you don't give me my money!"

Amzee scoffed. "He's just a baby, and sir, we placed a fair bet. Don't be a sore loser," she scolded.

The balding man spat at the ground, wiping back sweaty wisps of hair. "Have it the hard way then," he said, charging her with his blade.

"No!" I screeched. I thought of when a Sapphire targeted Luna.

Amzee did not cower or flinch, but brought her hand to her mouth and blew a sultry kiss.

Flames barreled out from her lips, quickly expanding. The man screeched as it engulfed him.

Zephy coughed, releasing a sharp quill from his throat. It stabbed straight through the man's throat, abruptly ending his suffering.

My jaw dropped. I had never witnessed someone use their Nature in that manner before.

Amzee plopped her bag on top of Zephy's head for safe-keeping and went over to the dead body, its torso still aflame. She grabbed him by the ankles.

"It would be frowned upon to leave him here," she explained with a slight smile.

She dragged him off the trail and into the woodline. Once pleased with the spot, she shook her hand and flexed it a few times, sparks igniting with each movement while she hummed a playful tune.

With both palms out, Amzee torched the body, incinerating it into ash.

When there was nothing left but a charred spot on the grass, she turned to me, spirits still high. "Well! He was totally unpleasant."

Zephy sat happily as Amzee took her bag off his head and slung it over her shoulder.

Typically, such cheerfulness was unnerving, but I wasn't entirely deterred by her. More so, I was envious.

"He was very slow, and kinda mean," Zephy complained.

Amzee shifted her gaze to me. "Now, why were *you* chasing *us*?"

"Curiosity, I think."

"About?"

I picked at the skin on my fingers behind my back.

"About where a bladebreather would go, or where more would be."

It sounded comical, but I had nothing to lose.

"Oh! Easy answer, they live in Moon Hollow. It's pretty close."

There *were* more bladebreathers. While she said they weren't far, the sun would set soon. I needed to head back.

"Where is Moon Hollow?"

She pointed to a crooked sign labeling a trail. "It's in a newly developing area, Moonhill. There aren't people living there yet, or a lord overseeing it. It's pretty unkempt, but the breathers gravitate to it. Without riders, most of them can't go far anyway. Maybe when a lord brings people in, we'll be able to move them around."

Moonhill.

There was no Lord of Moonhill because there was supposed to be a Lady. Clarke had promised me the land as my reward, and I had completely abandoned it.

My heart sank. If that land was intended for riders and their bladebreathers, I surely wasn't qualified to oversee it.

"I hear war is coming," Amzee said. "I visited the House of Sterling today to speak with Lord Xavian Steele about us helping again. I'm told we will be of good use soon, though I fear there aren't many brave enough to face a bladebreather; thus, we are lacking in riders. It sounds like that might interest you. There are many wings waiting."

That caught my attention.

"War with who?"

She shrugged. "Saffron is walking a fine line with Lord Xavian Steele, and I've heard King Clarke is sick. If he dies, who knows what the next ruler will try to do with Castivian? I know Lord Xavian would never give up these lands without a fight. So me and Zephy are prepared."

She had no idea what was truly coming. The Drakington council would be in outrage when Xavian finally became king, and the Blood Prince had already made his father's intentions clear. Was my twin prepared for war against *two* kingdoms?

I needed to speak with him.

CHAPTER 29

A WAYWARD REPUTATION

"Wise men do not venture into Eiden after sunset. For there is no place more unsettling."

— *DREARY NIGHTSONG, THE ONYX SCHOLAR*

AS AMZEE AND ZEPHY FLEW AWAY, I HIKED BACK TO the capital, eyes set on the high-perched Silver Circle.

Through streets lined with proper family homes, I passed by open curtains and dinner parties. My heart beat like a hammer in my chest.

Food, laughter, safety. There were no burn piles, no walls, no Drakers. Life carried on as if thousands of people were not locked in cages across the sea. The people here were ignorant to the circumstances of their own kind. Did they not know, or did they simply not care?

Hesitancy plagued my mind until I no longer hurried

towards Xavian's home. I swung the door to Sailor's Tear Tavern open and fled to my room, avoiding eye contact with Gia.

With my back against the door, I slid down, burying my face in my hands. If only it were enough to block the rest of the world out.

How did I come from the bravest bloodline in the kingdom, only to be born pathetic and indecisive? The pressure to be useful was overwhelming to where I wanted to do nothing at all, but the idea of doing nothing while thousands suffered was ruinous upon my peace.

Yet, every time I tried to help, I messed everything up.

Sitara and her village had been freed from Zain, only to be butchered. Saving Luna from a Sapphire was the last time I'd ever seen her. Gathering firewood from town got me imprisoned for days in an enemy camp. All I did was make things worse.

I could only imagine what everyone else thought of me. I shook my head in my hands, squeezing my eyes tight.

The expectations were too high. I didn't know the right thing to say to Xavian, nor *what* he could possibly say to me that would make up for anything. There were so many people left behind in the Waywards, people I knew and worked with. They were suffering and dying while I sat safe in a vibrant city.

The guilt ravaged me, tearing me apart piece by shattered piece.

I'd yet to check in on Trista, and Luna was probably dead by now. No matter how hard I tried to keep Riven out of my head, he consumed my mind again and again.

I had to stop. I'd already gone too far.

I should have taken Prince Payn up on his offer. At least then I would have been doing something helpful, though it was bold of the Blood Prince to assume my brother would care to surrender on my behalf.

My head spun. The world was closing in, and my days of being nameless were numbered. If I could simply disappear, I would have.

A knock pounded on the door.

I jumped at the vibrations against my back, scowling at the giggles from the other side.

"What?" I growled.

There were several voices, all women. "We're going to play orb-dice. Come out of your room, Waywards girl. Don't you want to join us?"

It was one of my new coworkers who had a clear disdain for me, but I'd yet to remember her name.

"No." There was too much going on in my head to say anything else, and I never wanted to play another game involving an orb after the midwinter celebration.

They didn't bother responding, but chatted amongst themselves.

"I told you, she's a bitch."

"Eh, I think she's just stupid. Gia said she tried to run into the streets after closing one night."

"She's from that Waywards thing. Of course she's dumb."

"Ha! I heard Mister Guzzlesticks and his boys the other day talking about how they couldn't bed a girl with monster eyes like hers. If they want nothing to do with her, perhaps we shouldn't be offended that the monster won't play."

I winced.

"Why does Drakington's errant garbage keep making its way here?"

"Gia, we tried to get it to play! Happy now?"

I did not need Gia's charity, and I was no stranger to hate, but labeling me a monster? A monster would not hide away, sparing dull barmaids from her wrath. They knew nothing about what I was above or beneath. They knew nothing at all.

I had crossed a kingdom and an ocean, just to find out that even beautiful cities could be filled with the same hate that festered in Drakington.

I shot up, swinging my door open. The three women stopped and turned back, surprised—amused even. Snickering in their busty brown dresses. Their hair haggard and teased like a trio of electrocuted trench rats.

The most obnoxious one dared to speak first. "Does the monster not know the common tongue? I thought it said 'no'? Yet now it's out of the room?" She cackled. "Can you read, *Monster*? Do they teach the Drakish such things? I'm truly curious."

Her entourage of slug-bucket bitches laughed themselves to tears.

I knew their hatred well. I was foreign, and the Waywards tended to leave a bitter taste in everyone's mouth.

But *I* was not the Waywards.

She was bold to call me a monster to my face, even bolder to insinuate I could not read.

"Can you?" I hissed. Her eyes widened into saucers as I crossed the room, fists clenched tight. I had done nothing to her, nor the other girls in the tavern for them to treat me like an abomination.

The other two backed away as I came toe to toe with the head wench.

"Oh look, the monster is mad." She laughed before pushing my shoulders, sending me back a step.

My blood boiled as the entire tavern fell silent. She was still smiling, mocking me.

"You're right. I am." I gripped her arm. Her face fell as I twisted it low to my waist. There were no Drakers to stop me, and I would love for someone to make me face the Lord of Castivian for punishment.

The entire tavern stared, but I didn't give a slick *fuck*. I would give them all something to remember about a Drakish Blackheart.

"Let go of me, you Waywards garbage!" she demanded, trying to pull away. I gripped tighter, yanking her arm straight.

I am inescapable.

"I'd recommend not moving." With my opposite hand, I traced a finger along the skin of her forearm. She screamed and thrashed, but I did not budge. It only made my handwriting worse.

Once I released my grip, 'Elora' was crudely written across her forearm, forged in Blackheart poison.

It was enough to burn like hell, but not to kill, hopefully.

She fell to the floor, unfortunately not dead. She screeched at the sight of her arm.

I had no sympathy to offer, only a reminder.

"*That* is my name, should you forget it again."

Customers fled the tavern, as if I would brand every one of them if they stayed long enough.

Gia glared from behind the bar. Her lips a flat line as she slammed a glass on the counter.

"Get out."

I hadn't planned on staying anyway.

Singer beamed at my hip. She wanted a chance to be dangerous, too. If the Castivian nights were as bad as everyone said, she would have her moment. I returned to my room only to cram my few belongings into my bag. My parting gift was a green finger under one of their pillows.

The moon greeted me as I ventured out into the streets, blinded by fury and with no direction.

Everyone else in Castivian seemed to have plans. I passed house parties, taverns, brothels, and even smoking lounges.

As the night went on, I relived every miserable moment of my life while my feet guided me aimlessly.

I thought about my mother leaving. I thought about how easily I let them put me in the Waywards, like some wild animal craving capture. I thought about every man who had once tried to claim my body, as if they were owed a portion of me.

It must have been past closing hours, because as I turned a corner, there was a muffled struggle down a pathway. I pulled out Singer, gripping the handle while the orb illuminated the alley blue.

A hideous man with rust-colored hair shouted at me. "This one is mine, stay back!" He held a smaller man viciously by the collar.

"The land you walk on is *mine*," I seethed.

My poison shot from Singer's gem, smothering the man's face in the blink of an eye. He fell to his knees, crashing to the ground.

The smaller man was grateful to be released, brushing off his stone covered palms and nodding sheepishly before running away, as if I might consider going for him next.

I crouched beside the first man's body.

His chest did not rise or fall, and when I brought my fingers to his neck, there was no flickering beat.

I may have been useless since arriving in Castivian, but I was *not* powerless.

I shamelessly collected every coin from his pockets, the chain around his neck, and an obsidian blade from his hand.

Striding through the night, I searched for the monster they said I was.

Chapter 30

The Tea

"Brother, I have not heard from you in some time. Write soon."

— *Correspondence from Lord Xavian Steele to Lyonsreach*

I propped my elbow on the meeting table. An ocean breeze flowed in between stone columns.

Avan sat at my left, his red hair disheveled. He wore casual Castivian black and tried to hold in a yawn. Draven sat to my right, looking quite the opposite in a plum velvet dress shirt, with his long black hair slicked back.

I knew it was a dream because Riven, of all people, was present, sitting alongside Draven. He wore his uniform with an arsenal strapped to his body while leaning back in his chair.

"Arthur Pos is late. We should start without the old grump," Avan said, spinning a coin on his finger.

"He's *unfortunately* an important asset to this council," Draven droned, a deep frown settling into his face.

The doors opened, and the older man shuffled in, wispy brows low and spectacles on. He wore a burgundy tunic, black pants, and silver rings adorning every finger.

"My lord, you look upset," Arthur said, wrinkles creasing across his forehead as he made his way to his seat.

"I was hoping your tardiness meant you were dead. Now, when is the next ship's departure?"

My voice was not my own; it was Xavian's. I was watching through his eyes.

Arthur Pos did not look surprised by my brother's comment, nor offended. Draven answered, "Tomorrow. Another returns in a week. I hear there are twenty Dark Natured refugees on board."

"Only twenty?"

"Yes, my lord."

Xavian's fingers drummed on the table. The council members held their breath as he contemplated. "If the majority are trapped in the Waywards, then the next group we send needs to retrieve them from within. Is that not obvious?"

Avan rubbed his jaw. Arthur scoffed. "Those who go inside the Waywards do not come out."

"I believe my sister walks on these lands, does she not?" Xavian asked.

Pos's cheeks reddened. "She is an exception. She was given a way—"

"I'll go back."

All eyes turned to Riven.

Avan shook his head. "You've just returned. The Brotherhood has been without its Captain for three years already."

"He knows the Waywards," Dravan offered, nodding with approval.

"These resources are not worth squandering on imprisoned creatures while Saffron ignites wars," Arthur sputtered.

Xavian leaned forward, steepling his fingers. "Creatures?"

"Well, they are simple, and not like us or usefu-"

Riven shot out of his seat, yanked Arthur Pos up by the collar before he could manage a full sentence.

Draven stiffened. "My lord, I implore you to remember that Lord Pos controls our mines. Do not allow the Oathkeeper to behave this way."

Effortlessly, Riven dragged Arthur across the floor to the window overlooking the sea and dangled him over the edge.

"You should have stayed in Drakington! You defiant, hedge-born, *bastard*!"

Arthur squealed like a castrated swine on his way down, landing with a grand splash.

The rest of the council rushed to the window, peering over. He flailed as his head surfaced for air.

Draven glared at Riven, while Avan was thrilled.

"Reschedule our meeting for this evening," Xavian said. "Pos will need time to dry."

He left the meeting room, storming down the stone hallways and entering a courtyard behind the House of Sterling.

Blademen trained while elegantly dressed nobles strolled along casually. A woman with sandy bronze hair wearing a light-blue dress caught Xavian's gaze. She was slightly taller than the other women around her, curvy, and had an element of innocence about her.

She gave him a quick look before strutting back into the House of Sterling, letting the door close behind her.

Xavian moved along, taking a lap around the courtyard while mostly focusing on the training. Nobles rushed to him, their eyes alight by the sight at their lord.

After a few minutes, he exited the courtyard through a side door, and entered a muted stairwell. He crept up the steps before walking down a hallway that appeared... residential?

He opened the door to a feminine bedroom, where dresses were laid along a chaise and an array of powders and cosmetics were scattered on a vanity.

The woman in blue stood against a bedpost, hiding her arms behind her back. From her attractive gown to her freshly pinned-back curls and jewels, it was obvious she was of wealth or nobility.

"How was your meeting?" Her voice was rich and silky, like it too, was expensive.

"None of your concern."

"Of course."

Xavian's eyes practically undressed her from the bottom up as he placed his hands on her waist.

"Did my father—"

He tensed, and she stopped herself, words lingering without an end.

"I have no desire to discuss your father."

She was Arthur Pos' daughter. They shared the same pronounced chin and hooded eyes.

If she was disappointed by Xavian's answer, she hid it well. "What do you desire, my lord?"

"Put your hands on the bed."

Oh, hell no.

No no no no.

I tried forcing myself awake, but my eyes would not open.

As she turned, Xavian gripped her dress and brought his mouth to her ear. "It's a shame that you look better without this." He ripped the fabric straight down the back, corset and all, dropping the garments to the floor. She leaned forward, arching her back, as he brought his face down and—

I gasped and gagged, eyes flying open as I mercifully woke up. I shook the disgusting dream away, orienting myself.

I had spent most of the night searching for trouble, and when the sun finally rose, a port-side alley was the most secluded spot I could find to rest. I was still in the alley, and thankfully not in Arthur Pos' daughter's bedroom.

I rubbed my face. The whole thing was so bizarre. In previous dreams, I'd been unaware of my brother's advisors' names or faces. Yet when I arrived in Castivian, they were real people, as if I'd manifested them myself.

It was like Xavian was in my head somehow, and I wanted him *out* immediately. But if I went to the Silver Circle, demanding for him to get out of my dreams, I would sound entirely deranged.

My stomach rumbled.

This city had an abundance of food options, yet I still hadn't adapted to eating regularly. In truth, I hadn't adjusted to anything about Castivian. I was the only person carrying around something as warm as a cloak, and I couldn't stop looking over my shoulder for Witchlords or Drakers.

I dusted myself off and squinted at the midday sun before setting out. I'd handled two rotten men during the night, leaving me with plenty of coin for simple luxuries. Their weapons were of no use to me, so selling them would be next on my list.

The capital during the day felt so homey, like a dream. Street musicians played enchanted harmonicas and violins, while artists on balconies splashed paint onto canvases, and two women walked out of a quaint restaurant arm in arm before sharing a tongue-swept, parting kiss.

People here were happy.

One day, hopefully, everyone left in the Waywards would experience this.

Silver carriages led by black stallions waited outside of an obsidian theatre, just down the street from a dimly lit violet lounge. Bellows of sweet smoke seeped out, and low music played. I could see myself enjoying both one day.

A familiar laugh stopped me in my tracks. Trista sat at a bar that smelled of fresh fish, her red hair blazing. Cackles and hollers spilled out of the open door.

She caught sight of me, quickly setting her drink down. "Elora! Girl, get in here!"

Finding lunch was no longer a priority.

As I hopped right onto a barstool, she slid me a mug.

"It's late for tea, is it not?" I asked.

Falling back into the familiar routine with Trista was easy, but it was the time and place I wasn't sure about. We usually had tea at her shop on bitter cold mornings. The warm air flowing into the tavern was disgustingly muggy, like a storm was brewing.

"Oh, it's never too late for tea." She wore a strappy grey gown, flowing and unbound compared to the drab sweaters that had swallowed her up in the Waywards. From her sea-salt curls to her smug smile, she looked happy.

After everything that happened, especially with Arielle, I was glad for her.

"Drink!" she urged.

"I suppose I did just wake up."

Both of us sitting on the same side of the bar was strange, but in the spirit of change, I relaxed and took a sip.

It was nowhere near as good as back in the Waywards. In fact, it tasted like dirt coated in the color grey.

I grimaced, placing the mug back on the counter.

Trista snorted, wrinkles tracing her forehead and crinkling around her eyes. "Drink again, please," she laughed, forcing the mug back in my hands.

I warily took another sip.

"How have you been?" I asked, attempting to determine the flavor.

"Since finding out about this new tea—amazing. I feel like I'm seeing life for the first time, Elora. It's all so clear now." She lifted her finger, calling over the server. "Two shots, clear please."

The shots arrived promptly, and went down our throats even faster.

"How have you been? I never see you!" Trista threw her hands up in the air, as if she had just realized this.

How had I been? The world was a spindle of thread from

the tailor house, and I was unraveling with it. With every blink, my surroundings became watery, my mouth drying.

"Trista, what in Fate's name is in this tea?"

She giggled and called for more shots. "They put 'infused' herbs in the tea here. They're splendid. You see the world for what it is, and it's so... beautifully terrible." Tears filled Trista's eyes as her smile dazzled. One by one, her freckles floated right into the air, like specks of dust.

I was so fucked.

Refusing the second shot, I also pushed the tea away, but it was too late.

The bar and everyone within was like a painting, yet I wielded no brush. I was at the maker's mercy, nothing but a drop of ink in the ocean of existence.

"Isn't it magnificent?" Trista mused, finishing my tea off herself.

I felt far away, like I was back within walls. Like I should be at work in the tailor house. I was trapped, an endangered animal waiting to be poached. The Sapphires would come soon. Saffron had not begun his conquest just to end with Lestivia. Prince Payn had warned me. He said I would learn what it meant to be an heir. What did he mean by that? What did it mean to be an heir?

Oh Gods, I was an heir to Castivian.

Trista moved like a ripple in lake water. "What do you think?" she asked.

Was I really an heir? I had the mark, but Xavian had yet to declare himself king. Had I brought the deed for nothing? Was I born for nothing? Was I *nothing*?

"It's terrifying," I mumbled.

At the bar, a man dressed in black caught my eye. I nearly mistook him for Riven, my core heating at the flash of his memory.

I couldn't shake his voice, his mouth, how his hands felt on me. I needed to see him. He needed to know how I felt.

"You'll see the beauty in the horror, just keep drinking," Trista assured me with a clumsy pat on my shoulder.

I shook my head. "I see everything."

Riven was not, and would never be, an option. He was just a man, and I was just another woman to him. Even Luna said he had plenty of others.

"Go see it! Go see it all!" she urged, pointing outside. The rowdy ocean rocked ships in the harbor as dark clouds rolled in.

I *could* see it all.

As I shuffled to get up, she practically pushed me out the door. "See the world, Elora! It's so beautiful!"

Outside, too many people crowded the streets. Too loud. Yet, eerily quiet all the same. Standing still was not an option; my body demanded to move.

I progressed through the city, blinking hard and wiping my eyes—failing to see straight. Time drifted, yet its pace eluded me.

Prince Payn was going to come for this place. I was alone. Luna was probably dead. The people in the Waywards had no way out. I had nowhere to go. My brothers were nobility. My parents abandoned me. I'd abandoned Moonhill. Riven kissed me. I kissed him. Two men died at my hand just last night. I'd lost track of how many lives I'd taken.

Everyone around me was oblivious. War was coming, and

their own kind were already imprisoned across the Sea of Blades. *Why did no one care?*

The sky cracked as lightning split the clouds, and thunder boomed. As the downpour erupted, the streets cleared, everyone running inside. I was the only one left in the rain, wind thrashing through my dark hair. The ocean roared as the storm waged war on the city. I did not seek shelter. I embraced it.

We understood each other, the sky and I. She was capable of setting the entire world on fire, but she spared us, time and time again. The storm was loud, but my thoughts were deafening.

Each step weighed on me, my sorrow threatening to break me from the inside out. I'd been disowned, abandoned, hated, all from the moment I was born. If I dared to reveal that it hurt me, the world would hate me for that too.

"Elora!" a voice called out.

Maybe it was the wind, or perhaps my conscience trying to bring me back from the tea. I looked towards the sky, letting the rain consume me. I was so tired. I had tried for so long to push the storm inside me away. Even here in Castivian I was not good enough. I had never known love, not even from my parents, and I never would, because no one cared to even *know* me.

"Elora!" a man roared again. A firm hand gripped my shoulder. I had no choice but to spin around and face him, my drenched hair flinging to my face.

My brother stood before me, dark curls dripping and brows narrowed, dressed in Brotherhood black with blades strapped across his body.

I was *so* tired.

"You're coming home," he demanded. "This is enough."

His voice was of someone who'd inherited authority and wielded it as naturally as he breathed.

He made the mistake of believing I gave a shit. "I have no home."

Red flushed through his cheeks and ears as his eyes sharpened. "We shared a womb. These lands are your birthright as much as mine. Enough of this wallowing. It's unbecoming of the Lyon's blood."

Xavian's eyes were as dark as mine, which was strange for a Natureless man. Trimmed beard, expensive weapons, a silver chain around his neck—he was put together, even in the rain.

"I don't know you," I snapped, as viscous as I could given the effects of the tea. He'd never cared about me before. There was no need to start now.

Pain flickered in his eyes, so quickly I questioned if it'd actually happened. "I know you better than you think. I have lived through the dreams."

He knew about the dreams?

His voice rose over the storm. "I know you, because I have lived your memories in my sleep. I knew our mother, because I saw her through your eyes. I walked through every home you've lived in. Loathed every person you've hated. You gave me at least one dream a month as a child, and lately, I don't even have to be sleeping to see whatever misfortune you've sent for me to witness. I'm aware of every flaw you have, and trust me, *there are many*. But goddamnit, we've been offered a kingdom, and you will not force me to watch you suffer in my mind while I rule."

I backed away.

If what he said was true, then my mind was exposed, and had been for my entire life.

My dreams weren't dreams at all. They were memories—his memories.

"That's not possible..."

Thunder rumbled above as lightning struck the ocean.

"Ask me anything, something no one else would know about you. Or better yet, how did you learn how to read?"

"What are you talking about?"

His fists curled in aggravated desperation. "When you and mother lived in that awful baker's cellar, hiding away from his wife, how did you learn how to read?"

I hadn't thought about that in ages. Mom hadn't liked the baker much, but he let us stay there for two entire summers before his wife found out. She came at my mother with a knife, and I cried, pleading for mercy.

"I'm not scared of this musty wench," my mother had said, barreling into the baker's wife and knocking them both to the ground. She threw the knife across the room for me to grab. I was only five winters old and wasn't supposed to hold knives yet, but I did that day.

"Fate will punish you for this! He is a fair God, and he will seek justice against you!" the wife screamed. My mother grabbed the woman's face and landed a sloppy wet kiss on her mouth.

"Now your God can drag us both to hell," she laughed wickedly.

"Remember!" Xavian pressed. "How did you learn how to read?"

My eyes fluttered.

Long before we were caught, I grew bored of silently hiding.

Mom was allowed to sneak out at certain hours, but I usually stayed in the cellar, rarely even allowed to speak. The baker brought me wooden trinkets every so often, and my mother taught me to sew, but it made my small fingers hurt, and I pricked myself too often.

There were stacks of books in the cellar, but my mother didn't know how to read.

I wanted to know what those pages said so badly that when I dreamt at night, I felt like I was sitting in a grand library with a teenage boy in front of me, pointing to letters.

"Go over it one more time, just in case," my tiny voice would say in the dreams. I knew it differed from my real voice, but in dreams that was okay.

The teenager smiled softly. "Okay champ. The 'b' makes the buh-buh-buh sound. So, we can make words like B-E-D. Buh-buh-bed. We could also make, b-a-b-y. Buh-buh-baby."

There were dozens of letters drawn out before the teenage boy looked ready to retire from the library.

"Thank you, Clarke. I need to see Lord Elliot now for help with my dream. She might nap soon... I need to send her this memory quickly. She's bad at 'b'."

"She'll get it. Sometimes it takes time."

My eyes shot open, hand grasping at my chest. "You knew!" I heaved. "You *both* knew about me, and you left me there!"

"I was a child."

My eyes burned with tears. "So was I."

He must have sent fewer dreams as we got older, as most nights I only dreamt of darkness. It must have been nice for him to have some lord teach him how to control whatever was causing the dreams. He certainly never sent me that information.

Whether or not he spoke the truth, I was not fit to help rule a kingdom, or to be *known* by anyone, especially a ruler.

That was all he was. This show of him pretending to care was painful, as if I would be stupid enough to believe it. If he knew everything about me, then he knew how badly I'd hurt inside for years, wanting to know my family. He and Clarke had each other, but they never had me.

I pointed my finger like a weapon. "*You* are no brother of mine. You left me to rot, and I hate you for it."

I waited for him to yell or hurt me, as men do when a woman dares to face them with a painful truth. Maybe he would simply walk away and not bother with a last word.

Xavian's features narrowed. "You cannot hate me, because we are the same. Bound in blood and mind, whether you acknowledge it or not."

I laughed, the thunder rolling along with me.

"Then you are wrong to believe you understand me. I hate myself more than people like you could fathom, and it has been that way for many years!" I screamed. "I wonder every day if the reasons I cannot love myself are the same reasons that no one else can love me! So hate me too, if you wish, for not helping you. It won't even scratch the surface!"

It was the truest thing I had ever said, and the hardest to admit. My legs felt like pudding, and my head spun. My own darkness ate at me, feeding on the pain.

His eyes softened.

"It will torment me for the rest of my life that I did not send for you sooner. Our family's actions haunt me. Our separation at birth has plagued me, Elora, and there is nothing you can ever say to me, good or bad, that will remove the stain. Hate me if you must, but I refuse to let you succumb to this drought in your mind as long as I have the hands to carry water to you. You are my sister."

I stared at the ground, focusing on the rain pelting into puddles in a poor attempt to hold back tears.

Xavian sighed. "Don't make me do this alone. We're the only family we have left."

The famed warrior and Keeper of Castivian, Xavian Steele, stood before me, but all he sounded like now was a brother who had failed his sister and was terrified to do the same to his kingdom.

"You have Clarke," I croaked. They had grown up together. They were a true family.

His throat bobbed. "No, I don't."

My stomach knotted. I didn't want to ask.

"He's dead, Elora, and word will travel fast."

I did not expect to care, but as I lifted my head to the sky, it cried with me.

Eyes closed, throat tight, poison rolling down my face.

Xavian and I were the last of the Lyonaire bloodline, aside from little Clayvarie, if she ever woke again.

Queen Delaina would now rule Drakington, and Fate only knew what she had planned for the people living in the Waywards. Time had run out.

"Enough of this mourning. There are things that have to be done at *home*." All evidence of Xavian's sorrow was gone, and returned was the face of an unyielding ruler.

"Are you going to drag me through the streets?" The effects

of the tea hit again as the sky twirled like mud in a bucket of water.

"You're going to walk."

My knees wobbled, eyelids heavy as stone. I couldn't argue anymore, or do anything for that matter. Existing was exhausting enough.

"I can't."

Darkness flashed in and out like the lightning striking in the distance. When my eyes fluttered open again, I was slumped over Xavian's shoulder as he hiked up the hill to the Silver Circle. The rest of the city had avoided the storm, while I'd crashed with it.

I closed my eyes once more. I was so tired.

CHAPTER 31

CHARMING, YET CRUEL

"Nightcastors—conniving tricksters, the lot of them. Trust one, and you deserve what follows."

— *MARKER DANE, LORD OF LAWSHIP*

I WOKE IN A COMFORT I HAD NEVER KNOWN BEFORE. The mattress was soft and plush, my head cushioned by a real pillow. A clean white comforter had been draped over my body.

The bedroom was as grand as Princess Clayvarie's—dark oak bed, intricate violet wallpaper veined with stone, and arched windows facing the dreary skies above the roaring sea and distant capital.

My clothes clung to me, reeking of mildew.

Knock, knock, knock.

I sat up, sliding my eyes across the room. My bag rested in the corner next to a silver armoire.

Knock, knock, knock.

Crossing the expansive space, I snatched up Singer before swinging the door open.

Riven.

The weight in my shoulders dropped as his eyes met mine.

Of course he found me. Who else would have shown up at my door the moment I opened my eyes? It was as if he had listened for the first creak of the bed frame.

"I never showed up for training, or your tour," I began, shame creeping up my chest.

I wasn't sure why I hadn't gone, or why I hadn't just told him I wasn't ready to come back to the House of Sterling.

"It's okay."

"Word must travel fast around here," I said.

Riven stood raffish in his brotherhood uniform, while I needed a bath. The knots from sleeping in rain-soaked hair would be a nightmare to comb out.

He shifted his muscled arms behind him, suddenly at attention. "I've been sent to inform you that your presence is required in the council chambers at the House of Sterling this afternoon, my lady."

The title rolled off his tongue as though I'd been branded a stranger, his words pricking like a rosebush. Charming, yet cruel.

I would've preferred a slap across the face. Depending on the circumstances, I may have even liked it. But this was no game. This was a new line being drawn.

"Is that what I am to you now? Some *lady* you deliver missives to, like a fucking messenger pigeon?"

"Elora," he whispered. *That* was the voice I had begun to

grow fond of. My heart desperately begged to cling to that, to be agreeable and yield, just like I had for men in the past.

But that had only ever left me bedded and broken.

People owed me real conversations and understanding, whether I kissed their ass or not.

My nostrils flared. "Which is it you wish to call me? Lady, like some stranger? Or Elora, like the person you pretended to want?"

He retreated a step, settling back into the cold version of himself—the Oathkeeper.

Pushing him away wasn't my intention. Gods, why could other people operate normally in relationships? My mother had once screamed at me that I was the problem, but I would do anything to be someone worth caring about.

I had not touched another person outside of a mattress in so long, it felt like walking for the first time as I reached for Riven's arm.

He looked at my hand resting on his bicep, then at the bed behind me. "You make it nearly impossible to maintain my honor."

To hell with his honor.

"I don't want it," I said under my breath.

He placed his warm hand over mine, brushing a thumb along my palm, then briefly closed his eyes before letting go.

"I'll return to escort you in an hour," he said, not bothering with my name or a title. Regret spread across his face as he failed to meet my eye.

I closed the door before pressing my back against it and sliding to the floor. I would have preferred for him to yell rather than walk away.

Knock, knock, knock.

I jumped to my feet. I wouldn't give him the chance to walk away this time.

Swinging open the door, my face fell.

Riven was not the one who stood before me, but some uppity woman.

"Yes?" My tone was icier than intended, but it had no effect on her.

Underneath an extravagant black hat, sun-kissed brown locks spilled from a twisted bun. The atrocity on her head was decorated with dark feathers, flowers, and black pearls. She wore a plum gown, with dark lace and a matching corset that complemented her bark-colored eyes.

She appraised me, pursing her lips.

"You certainly cannot wear that ever again."

I gaped.

She pushed right past me, headed straight for the armoire. Beside the silver piece of furniture was a large mirror, its black edges curving around it like vines. I grimaced, unable to bear my reflection, and instead glared at the woman as she flung open the wardrobe.

"Who are you to be speaking to me like this?"

If she was older than me, it could not have been by much, and she certainly was not above me in *this* house.

She sorted through the dresses, hastily gathering options.

"The only person your brother trusts to teach you proper etiquette. My name is Lady Jocelynn Wrenavia, but more importantly," she said, dropping four wildly extravagant, bright-colored gowns across the unmade bed, "you will need the tailor master later. One of these should work for today. I am told it is a private meeting you are to attend."

I slithered my gaze from the gowns on the bed to Lady Jocelynn.

"Get the fuck out of my room."

She snorted, seating herself on a black armchair by the window. "Once you are not an embarrassment to your name or this kingdom, I will gladly return to my own activities."

Lady Jocelynn crossed a leg over her knee, face painted with persistence. She expected me to bite.

"Were you warned that I am some beast in need of taming?"

I didn't step any closer to the gowns, as I would not be putting one on. For starters, they were hideous. I would love nothing more than to dress in finery like a proper princess, but the first expensive thing I wore would not be someone else's peacockish apparel.

Secondly, I had no idea *how* to get the pile of atrocities onto my body.

Third, I had been dressing myself since I could walk and didn't plan on breaking that streak anytime soon.

She did not shy away from eye contact. "I was warned you would not like me."

"I don't," I confirmed.

I stormed out of the room, slamming the door behind me. She could put the dresses on herself, or burn them for all I cared.

The hallway was just as dark as the room, yet cool and comforting. Gentle light trickled in through slender panes, and the stone architecture twisted like the forest along the walls.

If they wanted me to act like a princess so badly, then so be it.

"Take me to my brother," I barked at the first Blademan in sight.

Lady Jocelynn followed, her shoes aggressively clicking on the floor behind me. The guard glanced her way, then shook his head before walking in the opposite direction.

He'd blatantly ignored my order.

Turning on my heels, I faced Lady Jocelynn.

"I am not—"

Shadows filled my mouth, squeezing my throat tight and cutting off my words. Rage filled me as I struggled for air. She was Dark Natured. A Nightcastor, like Beck.

"Is it not exhausting?" she asked. "Carrying on like a juvenile? War is brewing and there are men with a great deal of money and resources who are going to make decisions soon. You have the chance to be a part of those decisions. If you are to represent our kind and this kingdom, you must present yourself respectably. Everything you say, do, and wear should exhibit who you are and what you stand for. You are dirty, reek of mildew, and look horrendous. Are you going to keep acting like an adolescent, or are you going to bathe and get dressed like a lady?"

Her hand relaxed and the shadows loosened, but still remained near my throat. I considered using my own Nature on her, curious how she would like it.

As my anger died down, shame replaced it. She was right. I'd known since I met Clarke that this would be coming. I could not keep spiraling, or my new life would be no better than my previous one.

Women could be so vicious. The idea of being vulnerable with anyone, especially someone who'd stuffed shadows down my throat, seemed ludicrous. Yet I found myself relaxing. She was just another woman. Dark Natured and trying her best to manage it, like me.

"I don't know how to put one of those contraptions on, and I prefer to wear clothing that is my own. And when I *do* purchase a dress, I'd like it to be a darker color. They look better on me." My gift to her was honesty.

Lady Jocelynn adjusted her hat, shadows falling away.

"I can help you get one of the dresses on, or I can find a simpler one from my closet while you bathe. It will take the tailor master time to design something more suited to your tastes, but I'm sure he will create something to your liking."

Our energy shifted.

"I'll borrow something for today."

"I shall return to your room shortly, Lady Elorengail."

She started to walk away, but I was not done. "Lady Jocelynn."

She stopped in her tracks. "Yes?"

"I go by Elora. You should also know, if you ever put a hand or *shadow* on me again, I will drown you in a tub of my Nature. Are we clear?"

"As long as you never storm the halls dressed like a soggy rag again, sure."

She clicked her heels down the hall, and while she attempted to hide her shit-eating grin, I caught it anyway.

Who had bet against her, for her to be so delighted at my compliance?

———

A few short hours later, Riven returned as promised. Silence lingered between us as he ushered me out of the manor. Other than my room, the stone hall, and the stairs leading right down to the entrance, I hadn't managed to see much.

We rode on horseback to the House of Sterling. Riven led us inside and up a wide, stone staircase. At the end of the hall was the council room, recognizable from my dreams. The sizable rock of a round table sat in the center of muted stone floors. A stunning view of the ocean and the city of Eiden was visible from every angle of the room.

We were the first to arrive. A cool sea breeze brushed the loose silver fabric of my gown across my thighs as I stood unsure of where to sit. I knew Xavian sat at the far side, facing the entrance, and Draven and Avan always sat to either side of him.

The top half of my hair was braided into a bun, courtesy of Lady Jocelynn. Two silver pins in the shape of wings were placed into the bun to represent the Castivian crest.

Lady Jocelynn kept everything else plain. No makeup. No jewelry beyond the necklace from Sitara. The simple gown had soft, sheer sleeves that ran down my arm, and a dainty zipper in the back.

Representing the Dark Natured or not, I was proud like never before.

I felt *pretty*.

Not in the way men back in the Waywards stared on summer nights if I had a bit of cleavage showing, but pretty in the way that I could bear to look at myself in the mirror.

I shouldn't need a dress to feel beautiful, but was it so bad if it made me feel that way?

Riven pulled out two chairs, both on the left side of the table. "The chairs don't bite." He gestured for me to sit next to him.

Cute of him to think I'd be sitting next to him after leaving me with Lady Jocelynn. Instead, I sat on the opposite side, making my disdain clear. He poorly attempted to match it, leaning back in his chair and lifting his brow. Taunting me.

Our silent war was interrupted by Xavian and the rest of his council pouring in, only pausing their conversation to acknowledge my presence with subtle nods before taking their seats. Arthur Pos, the oldest of them, sat next to Riven. Though we had never met, I knew enough from my dreams to not like him.

The redhead, Avan, took the seat between me and Xavian.

Across from Avan, Draven wore an airy, maroon tunic, with his long hair falling to the sides of his shoulders.

Draven was the first to speak, his voice rich and smoky. "It's a pleasure, Lady Elorengail."

"Princess Elora," Xavian corrected him. My twin sat at the end of the table, the view of the stormy grey ocean behind his head of thick, inky curls.

"You're not king yet," Draven argued coolly.

My brother must have had some semblance of respect for Draven, as no daggers were drawn at the dispute. "I'll be enacting the deed by nightfall."

"The plan was to meet with the rest of the lords before claiming your title," Arthur Pos reminded.

Riven had told me the meeting wasn't until next week. Why wait?

Avan glanced between Xavian and Draven while spinning a silver coin on his thumb. Riven focused on me, but I tried my best to not pay him any mind.

"That was before my brother died," Xavian tossed a scroll on the table. "And before the cunt queen sent this."

The rest of the table jumped up, scrambling to grab it first. Riven was the champion, and quietly read it before tossing it to Avan, whose words fumbled out of his mouth the second he touched the parchment.

> Xavian Steele,
>
> Per Queen Delaina Lyonaire, heiress to Jade-hill, Ruler of Drakington and the Castivian Terri-tory, it is hereby declared that all creatures born with Dark Natured blood be sent by ship to Drakington, where they will be a pivotal part of the war efforts.
>
> The Queen expects a swift response and dili-gence in clearing the lands of such kinds. If you prove yourself to be inadequate, a new Keeper of Castivian will be assigned.
>
> Drakington also requests this quarter's tax payments as early as possible, as war does not pay for itself, and the Sapphires are a constant threat at our borders.

My stomach curled. Clarke wasn't even cold in the ground, yet she'd wasted no time. I should have found her while I was within the walls of Lyonsreach and slit her throat myself.

Avan read on about further expectations and threats before finishing, setting the missive down and staring back at the rest of the council.

Arthur Pos adjusted his spectacles. "I agree with you, *Your Grace.* The sooner you declare these lands independent, the better."

"I'm pleased you've found sense during your swim."

Arthur's nose crinkled as he snatched the scroll from Avan and cleared his throat. "I can have the legalities and crowning ceremony prepared for this afternoon. We can all see the King's Mark, should anyone question the legitimacy of the deed. But there is another pressing matter to discuss that cannot wait..."

I tried to pay close attention, but Avan kept spinning that stupid, distracting coin. Just as Payn had.

Xavian waved his hand. "Go on, Pos."

I shot a glare at Avan, whose coin was spinning even faster.

"You both need spouses and heirs. Immediately."

The coin stopped.

"Who?" I blurted.

Riven's eyes sharpened, and Xavian rubbed his forehead.

"Me?" I asked.

Draven gave me a knowing glance.

"Yes, you and your brother. You didn't expect to have no further bloodline, did you?"

Arthur's reality check stung like a burnbee.

Riven promptly pulled out a smoke and lit it right there at the table. Xavian held out his hand expectantly, lighting one as well.

"Ale, please!" Avan yelled. Staff flowed through the doors a moment later with goblets, glasses, and refreshments.

I downed my first before they finished circling the table and signaled for another.

"Goddamn, Princess. We're not running out anytime soon," Avan whispered.

"Give me a few hours and we'll see about that."

Xavian was silent until he finished his smoke, flicking the ash right onto the table. When it was finally burnt to the blunt end, he dropped the bud into an empty glass and steepled his hands.

"I will not force the princess to marry."

The council stiffened.

"I will, however, do my duty and marry. I'd like to start communication with any Lestivian noble families who are not entirely entwined with Saffron." Xavian's voice was that of a leader who had trained for this his entire life.

"And Lestivian's have sexy, thick accents, and thicker asses," Avan added.

Draven let out a heavy sigh, tracing his finger along the rim of a glass of red wine.

The entire premise of the conversation was overwhelming, but of course Xavian was going to do the noble thing. That was what royals did.

As much as I hated to admit it, Arthur was right. Our bloodline ended with us. If we started a war to keep this land and defend the Dark Natured, it would be crucial to have heirs.

There was no guarantee we'd survive, but we could create something that outlives us.

Death no longer scared me.

This meant so much more.

"Your Grace, Whimcastor Hold has already offered their eldest son and heir as a match for the princess," Draven pointed out. "They are arguably our most populated hold in Castivian and our highest taxpayers. They would be valuable assets. If we turn down their offer, they may turn us away when we need men."

Arthur Pos nodded in agreement.

Xavian's voice silenced the room. "Whimcastor Hold will bow to their king, betrothal or not, or it will cease to exist. My sister is not a chess piece, nor livestock to be sold."

My face paled. Never in my life had someone stood up for me in such a manner.

Arthur Pos shook his head. "We would be fools to turn away—"

"I'll do it," I interrupted.

Everyone turned to me, but the only eyes I could meet were Riven's. He exhaled slowly, smoke brushing my face.

My desire to help did not change the desire I held for him, or whatever had sparked between us.

He burned his piece out on the table, leaning forward. "Has the wine affected your senses, Princess?"

I gathered myself, as Lady Jocelynn had advised, before saying something that would not represent myself well.

There were too many people suffering and dying for me to be picky about how I contributed, whether it pissed Riven off or not. Maybe I was being impulsive, possibly desperate, to make something of myself in comparison to my brothers. Or perhaps it was Lady Jocelynn's speech that brought me clarity. One thing I *was* positive about was how sick I was of being the victim. Standing out of the way while people like Xavian made ties with Lestivia, Amzee and Zephy protected ships of the Dark Natured, and even Arthur Pos spent his time tending to our kingdom.

"If I wed the heir to Whimcastor Hold, will it help with the war?"

Avan coughed. "Uh, yeah. They forge our fucking weapons."

Xavian kicked the top corner of Avan's chair, sending him falling back.

"It could be beneficial, but nothing is guaranteed." Xavian eyed every man sitting at the table one by one, daring them to speak again before I gave my answer.

Sitara and her village did not die for nothing. Beck did not lose Arielle for nothing. I did not leave the Waywards and cross the Sea of Blades for *nothing*. War required weapons and men, and if Whimcastor Hold had such resources, I would not be the one standing in the way.

"I'll do it."

CHAPTER 32

A REQUEST

"Castivian history is as unruly as the land itself. The records are chaotic; the literature often poor."

— *DREARY NIGHTSONG, THE ONYX SCHOLAR*

MY FIRST CONSCIOUS NIGHT AT XAVIAN'S HOME— *our family* home, he'd given me a tour of the stone scaled manor, and had seen that Riven and I were paid well for delivering the deed, and that as a council member, I would receive regular compensation.

None of it felt real, but I was proud to pay for my new wardrobe. I had also visited a glamour shop and purchased a basket full of cosmetics and a few pieces of silver jewelry.

The day was young, and I sat for tea in a black gown with a silver-threaded corset, similar to the look the woodland tailor had created. The tailor master in Eiden had been incredibly understanding of my wanting to continue the style. The skirt was not as voluminous as Lady Jocelynn's, but it was long, loose, and comfortable.

Lady Jocelynn refused to pay me any compliments, but she did not try to convince me to change it, unlike most other things about myself.

Three days prior, when she had first invited me to take tea with her overlooking the training grounds, I was hesitant. Not because of her abhorrent demeanor, as that was to be expected, but because of the experience I endured the last time that I drank Castivian tea.

She assured me there would be no hallucinogens, since we had much to accomplish and little time for poppy brain.

Three days had passed since the private ceremony was held to name Xavian king, and since then, Lady Jocelynn had been tasked with teaching me what to expect each day and how to not stick out like a sore thumb among nobles. We had less than a week until the meeting with the lords, my betrothed being one of them.

Having a betrothed to begin with was nauseating, but I had made my bed and I was fully prepared to lay, wallow, and fuck in it.

"Why were you late today?" Lady Jocelynn asked, focused on a crow that sat on the arm of her chair. Another was on the circular iron table between us, anxiously waiting to be fed a piece of powdered cake or lemon tarte. Lady Jocelynn was so fond of her crows, we hardly ever spent time inside.

"My nightclothes needed a wash."

The afternoon wind brushed my hair against my back and tickled my nose with the smell of steeped lavender and sea salt.

It would have been preferable if the breeze picked me up and carried me with it. Instead, I was forced to watch Riven absolutely wreck every man who dared to spar with him, while also enduring Lady Jocelynn's endless lectures about Castivian policies and procedures.

"It is a waste of time to wash your own clothes."

"And yet I will do it, regardless." I had learned that Lady Jocelynn chose her battles.

"Then do it earlier," she ordered. Shadows swirled around her like smoke. She never bothered concealing her Nature. How appealing would it be if I did the same, with poison dripping from me as I walked?

"I would be glad to, and you will be glad to join me."

She finally met my gaze. "I will do no such thing."

"You think you're too good to wash your clothes alongside the Princess of Castivian?" I fired back.

I was *not* too proud to use the title to win an argument. If Fate wanted to throw royal heritage into my lap, I would make proficient use of it.

In the middle of the training grounds, Riven watched over a spar between two tragically under-trained recruits. The brotherhood seemed to be growing every day. His eyes shifted up, shamelessly locking on mine.

One second.

Two seconds.

Three seconds.

A trainee called for him. He broke his focus and turned away.

In my lap, I picked at the skin on my fingers.

"Were the Waywards that terrible?" Lady Jocelynn pestered as she gave a crumb of tarte to the crow.

"In what way?"

"The men."

"The men?"

She pursed her plum-colored lips. "They must have been dreadful if Sir Riven has caught your eye when your options as princess are limitless."

"Are you blind," I began, lifting my tea to my lips, "or do you prefer ugly men?"

"Sir Riven is a pleasant enough sight, but he's such a dog."

"Don't say that," I snapped, clinking my cup down.

She stared at Riven curiously, as if he were low-hanging fruit. She was already married, I had learned, to Lord Draven.

"Is it that you wish to be loved? Or do you simply need to know you *can* be loved?" she finally asked.

"Stop."

Her face was shaded partially by her feathered hat, her painted lips frowning. "Do you wish me to be authentic with you, or say what you want to hear?" Another crow landed on her finger.

"I want you to quit being rude."

"It's not my job to be pleasant." She shrugged. "My question was sincere, though, about the Waywards. I'm intrigued by them."

I laughed. She hated everything about the way I was, and yet she wanted to know about the worst three years of my life.

"Why?"

"You are the first person I have met who has lived in the

infamous Waywards. I host a show once a month where I discuss worldly matters. Your insight would be a nice touch."

Riven began sparring against Lord Avan. They wore no helmets, and Lord Avan's red curls glistened compared to Riven's chestnut, windswept strands.

"A show for talking?" I asked to appease her, my eyes still locked on the training grounds.

Unnatural shadows clouded my vision with darkness, blocking my view. I snapped my head to her.

"Pay attention," she said.

"I asked about your show, did I not?"

"I would like for you to come. It's this weekend at the theater. You will need to be dressed appropriately, especially in the public eye."

Thanks to her pestering, I had missed whatever happened between Riven and Lord Avan, as Riven was now sheathing his sword and walking away.

"I've had enough tea." I said, shooting to my feet and scanning for ways he could have gone.

"You know, if you chase something, it will only continue to run."

I would rather run than watch everything I want pass me by.

"I'll come to your show. Now please leave me be."

She shook her head and shrugged, and that was enough for me. I hurried across the terrace and into the fortress hallways before practically flying down the stairs. It was cool inside, the stone floors solid under my quick steps.

Out of breath, I rounded a dark corner and slammed into Riven's chest.

He cursed, gripping me by the elbows.

"Watch where you're walking," I admonished, yanking my arms free.

"I could hear you making a ruckus all the way from upstairs. Yet I should watch where *I'm* walking?"

My face heated. "If my shoes are so loud, then you should have *moved* out of the way."

The corner of his lip rose ever so slightly. "Really?"

"What is this?" I asked, throwing my arms up. "What are we doing?"

"Our duties."

"Was finger banging me in the tavern part of your duty?"

He lowered his chin and stepped closer. "Do you want me to apologize, Princess?"

No. Of course not.

I crossed my arms. "Yes. Apologize."

Riven's eyes darkened as he brought his mouth dangerously close to mine. "I'm sorry, Princess Elora, for pleasuring you with my hand until you sang for me."

Attempting to hold back a smile, I cleared my throat. "I suppose I can forgive you, if you do something for me."

He straightened his posture and surveyed our surroundings. "What's that?"

"I want another chance at being trained."

I would not watch day by day, eating tarts and sipping tea as training went on for a war that I'd helped start. Death had come close to stealing me away too many times to trust that I was safe. Never again did I want to feel as pathetic as I had in the Waywards, sitting in my own vomit, my best friend fleeing while a Sapphire was ready to make his kill.

He took in my dress before running his eyes over my neatly brushed hair. "You don't have to wield a sword to be useful, Elora."

"Is that a no, *Sir* Riven?"

Shaking his head, he conceded. "Fine."

He set off in the direction of the training grounds, flicking a blade in his hand. "Let's go."

Oh.

He thought I'd meant immediately.

CHAPTER 33

I'LL TELL YOU EVERYTHING

"The Crow's Whisper is the most elite of shows in Eiden. Tell us, dear reader, are you fortunate enough to attend?"

— *EXCERPT FROM THE CASTIVIAN CHRONICLE*

XAVIAN AND LADY JOCELYNN SAT ACROSS FROM EACH other on the terrace, equally disturbed. They both sipped ale in horror as I tried for the twenty-second time to raise a sword and perform a singular slice through the air.

It was too damn heavy.

"Try the wooden pell instead, *please.*"

Riven had been begging for me to give up on the actual sword since attempt number four.

"No," I hissed. The children were training with wooden pells. That would be more embarrassing than failing a hundred times.

Xavian had yet to say a word, but I could sense his disappointment. His skills were marveled at across the kingdoms, while I was only suitable for being struck by arrows.

Riven just wanted to help me. He would lift the sword for me if I would let him.

But that would defeat the purpose.

"It's because of this vexing dress," I insisted, gripping the hilt of the sword once more, the pointy end dragging against the grass. "And I refuse to ruin it."

"I see."

He didn't see *shit*. I would like to see him do anything worthwhile in a gown.

I tried once more to lift the sword, but again, the weight of the bladed monstrosity dragged my arms down.

A chair screeched, and Xavian's voice barked across the training grounds. "Lift the goddamn sword!"

He had roared the command so intimidatingly that my pathetic arms found it in themselves to rise.

I cried out as I leaned into my swing. My muscles whined, but I held that sword up all the same, arms shaking.

I smiled. "I'm doing it."

A small boy with a wooden pell ran up, laughing as he hit my sword with his, knocking it to the ground.

Mother of fucking Moons.

The brunette child giggled as he ran off with the other little gremlins. I faced the terrace, fists clenched. Xavian's face was blazing red. He rubbed his hand over his beard and turned to Lady Jocelynn.

"I don't like this," I mumbled.

"You don't have to do it," Riven said, just loud enough for my ears.

"Then what am I supposed to do?" My response was the opposite. Brash and loud enough that it would be difficult for neighboring trainees *not* to overhear us.

I was tired of being useless. I hated trying to use a sword. *Really* hated it. I also hated watching others practice, unless it was Riven.

Even so, my helplessness was mortifying when everyone else adapted quickly, especially the children. If there was going to be a war, then there would be swords. If I didn't know how to use a sword, then there would be no use for me beyond marriage, but... was that all I would do? Was it terrible to be disappointed with that?

I wanted marriage and children, yes. But living in the shadow of my brother's accomplishments felt so... sad.

Riven picked my blade up from the ground and tossed it into a black barrel. My face fell.

"Sorry I wasted your time," I said.

Perhaps I was better off in the Waywards, sewing and slinging ale and waiting to freeze to death, if I didn't starve first.

His eyes softened, voice still quiet. "You saved yourself more than once. You saved *us*. You have survived every bad day you've ever had, and in just the short three years I've known you, there have been many, but you have *never* failed to make it to the next. You are not useless, Elora. You are invaluable, especially to me."

My eyes darted away.

What was I supposed to say to that?

"I'm going to find a Blackheart to train you," he decided.

It hit me then who was on the training grounds. There were plenty of other Natured and Natureless.

But no Blackhearts.

Questions flooded my mind like a river, fast-moving and overwhelming.

"Why aren't there any here now?"

Come to think of it, I hadn't noticed very many Blackhearts at all since arriving in Castivian.

"Because they don't want to be, I suppose. Not a single one has signed up for service. Rumor has it, they've been moving up north."

Why in the hell would they be cold by choice?

Riven rubbed his hand along the back of his neck, trying to mask his frustration with silence. He wanted to help me, but had no idea how.

Lady Jocelynn had claimed to have a show. If people in Castivian enjoyed it, maybe she had influence over them. There had to be Blackhearts in the capital. If she could convince them to join the guard, we could figure out how to train ourselves properly.

"Are you two unwell?" Lady Jocelynn interrupted, her plum gown flowing elegantly as she approached.

"I'll tell you about the Waywards for your show," I blurted.

"Oh?" Her lips tipped.

"If it'll convince more people to join the Brotherhood, then yes. If they know what will happen to them if we lose, maybe they'll fight for it. Especially the Blackhearts."

She hesitated.

Riven let out a rare chuckle. "Lady Jocelynn's show is about petty gossip. She doesn't touch on the subjects that actually matter."

Her eyes darted up at him, shadows swirling around her ears and wrists. "That's not true."

A knot formed in my stomach at the thought of her using my experience in the Waywards as mere gossip. When living there, I never would have imagined that across the Sea of Blades, people would talk about my miserable situation for entertainment.

"Come on, Jocelynn. You and I both know what your shows truly are. Don't play the princess for a fool."

Her shadows shot up to her neck, rolling off her collarbones like steam. "Riven, you know nothing about my show, especially now. You have not been here for three years. Things have changed. Princess Elora, if you tell me what message you want the capital to hear, I will prove to you the difference I can make."

Was she trying to convince me or herself? Either way, I would not turn away an audience. The people of Castivian needed to know the truth about what transpired within the Waywards, and what freedoms had been taken from the Dark Natured.

"I'll tell you everything I know over... afternoon tea?" I offered. We had already sat for morning tea, but it was clear Lady Jocelynn could lounge on the terrace at any hour. Thankfully, the weather was lovely, with scattered clouds drifting across a pale cerulean sky.

"Perfect."

"I'll have to see this show for myself." Riven gave her no mercy, aiming skeptical eyes at her.

Lady Jocelynn's shadows swirled out farther, threatening Riven, but he didn't flinch. "Princess Elora needs an escort anyhow, as she has already promised to come. Don't forget to dress appropriately for the theater, Captain."

I shifted my heated face away. Had she just set me up on a date? Surely there were other Blademen that could escort me.

"Of course, Lady Jocelynn." Riven's disdain for Jocelynn's show, or maybe just the woman in general, was as clear as a Stonesender's tears.

Their issues were not my problem. If this idea worked, we could find ways to host her show up north, too, and to the east and west. If we rallied enough of the Castivian people, Delaina wouldn't be able to take this freedom away, nor would Saffron likely have the men to stand against us.

For those odds, I'd do whatever needed to be done, whether it be lifting a sword a thousand times, or forcing a smile for the theater.

CHAPTER 34

BLACK ROSES

"Only a bastard would not want any for himself."

— *LORD DRAVEN WRENAVIA, AS HEARD IN
THE HOUSE OF STERLING*

MY HEAD POUNDED BY THE TIME AFTERNOON TEA WAS
over. Recalling the past three years, pushing myself to open up
—it was more difficult than I'd expected.

Lady Jocelynn wanted every unpleasant detail she could
squeeze out of me. The more disturbing, the more interested
she was. She promised it was important for the people to know.

When our tea session finished, Lady Jocelynn dismissed her
crows and excused herself. She had much to do before the show.

With a weight on my mind heavier than any sword, I left the
terrace and made my way back. I could have requested an escort,
but in truth, I wanted nothing more than to be alone.

From the high perch of the Silver Circle, the city below

bustled with life. There were still hours before sunset, but music played, orbs of light bounced around in the streets, and people crowded through lantern-lit walkways. Smoke escaped chimneys as family dinners were being prepared.

My shoulders sagged. I wanted to scream. *"Enjoy it, it might not last forever!"*

I scaled the charcoal steps to Xavian's—our home. The word *home* was not yet a comfortable one. It never had been. How could home be so many places and yet none at all?

The foyer was empty. Streaks of light peeked through the dark curtains and onto the hardwood floors. Thick blankets were strewn about the long, grey couch, evidence that Xavian had been there at some point today. He often lounged with paperwork while snacking on platters of meat and cheese.

He was not here now, though, unless he had retired to his bedroom early. He may still have been at the House of Sterling, or had plans down in the capital.

Exhausted and hollow, up the steps I went, down the hall and into my bedroom. I undressed and threw on a loose, white nightgown, and for the first time in a very long time, I took a nap before nightfall.

———

I dreamt of bladebreathers. A real dream, with my own voice. Singer in my hand, Amzee and I soared over the coast of Lyonscliff, fit to wage war on Queen Delaina.

"Ready to win this thing?" Amzee called from Zephy's back.

Win.

We could win.

My eyes flew open. It was so obvious what could aid us in the battles to come.

Bladebreathers.

Amzee had said it herself. Why wasn't the council more worried about recruiting riders instead of endless days of practicing swordcraft?

I slid to the edge of the bed, rubbing my eyes and glancing out of the large arched window. Light twinkled throughout the capital and into Bastard's Bay. The moon sat high above, peeking through long, wispy clouds.

I must have slept for a while. It was late enough that Xavian would surely be home. Without the pressure of the rest of the council, maybe we could figure out a plan to recruit more riders.

I threw on a pair of soft black pants and a violet sweater, and hurried down the stairs.

A candle burned on the dining room table, flickering shadows and warm glows against the charcoal walls. Two dirty dinner plates were abandoned in the kitchen sink.

He had eaten and was not alone. The fireplace in the living room still burned, and several whiskey glasses were left on the coffee table, ice nearly melted.

Muffled voices echoed off the walls, but it was difficult to identify where they were coming from. I followed the sounds all the way to an open window behind the couch.

Just above the living room, Xavian was in a heated debate with a woman. They must have been on his bedroom balcony.

"You cannot do this!" The woman angrily sobbed.

Xavian sighed. "Fiera, I have told you before. This is my

duty. It's a sacrifice I am making for you and everyone else in Castivian."

"I do not care about duty or sacrifice! I'd sooner pray for Delaina's good health before I would want you to marry some Lestivian whore on the grounds of politics. After three winters, I should be the one you're marrying. Not her!"

Oh.

It was about the marriage thing.

I had been avoiding thinking about my own arranged marriage. I certainly hadn't considered Xavian's.

"It's not about what you want," Xavian interrupted another sob. "I love my people, and I will not let my own desires keep me from winning this war."

"Then what about me?" she screeched. The pain in her voice was the kind only love could cause.

"What do you mean?"

I wanted to smack my brother in the back of the head for asking such a stupid question in response to a simple one.

"What happens to me? What happens to *us* after they ship your bride here? You say you love your people, but what about me?"

I held my breath as a heated silence filled the air.

"You will be my past, Fiera. I will be a married man and a busy king with a war to win."

I pressed my palm over my mouth and took a step back from the window. I could not bear listening any longer. Instead, I went to the kitchen and cleaned their dinner plates, then the whiskey glasses. And when that was done, I scrubbed the counters—anything to distract myself.

Anything to drown out the unbearable cries of heartbreak.

Xavian was sacrificing his relationship with Lady Fiera for his arranged marriage, while I paid mine no regard, wanting Riven.

Saying it, even to myself, felt dirty. The man who had been intimate with my best friend, the knight loyal to my brother, a knight under my employ that would soon have to serve my own husband. I felt sick.

A knock at the door rang out against the wreckage in my mind. I set down the cleaning rag and hurried to answer it.

"Riven?"

He stood with black roses in hand.

"I know you had a hard time today, and you'll probably think I've gone mad, but I thought you might like these. You cannot kill them with your Nature. They're special, like y-"

"You have to leave."

I never thought I'd be interrupting him saying exactly what I wanted to hear. Just an hour earlier, I would have been blushing and sneaking him upstairs.

"What?" Riven's gaze softened before becoming cold, like a protective shield.

The guilt ate at me from the inside out.

War is no place for pretty things, Prince Payn had said all that time ago.

The bouquet of roses was the most beautiful I had ever seen, and the only flowers that had ever been given to me.

But I couldn't take them.

I forced my face into a cold, bored frown.

"You're... dismissed." The words, the *order*, felt wrong coming out my mouth.

Riven shook his head. "I don't understand. What's wrong now? You don't like flowers?"

My chest tightened. I wanted to run away and never show my face again, but there was no running from this. "I don't want your flowers. I'm betrothed. I said you're dismissed."

He took a step back as if I'd hit him. "Tell me what I did."

He was hurt, and it was my fault. "*You* are wrong for me."

He had protected me, fought for my life on multiple occasions, tied my hair up when I was hurt, warmed me back to health, and so much more. It was like stabbing myself in the chest.

"Whatever it is I did, I'm sorry. I wanted to be good enough."

With that, he dropped the flowers and turned away, trailing out of the Silver Circle. I closed my eyes and exhaled slowly to keep from crying.

I needed a drink.

Dragging myself back inside, I frowned at the distant arguing of Xavian and Fiera raging on. Everything was a mess.

I laid my elbows on the kitchen counter, rubbing my temples. At least the view of the city was pretty.

Twinkling lights, a peaceful harbor, and... a bladebreather.

Red mist trailed behind Zephy and Amzee as they soared over the capital. They dropped low, landing on a tall building.

CHAPTER 35

THE DARKEST ALLEY IN ALL OF EIDEN

"Bladebreathers have not been employed for war in centuries. They are creatures of poor temper and rarer trust, far more dangerous and costly to sustain than their worth allows."

— *URGENT CORRESPONDENCE TO KING XAVIAN STEELE*

NO ONE QUESTIONED ME AS I STORMED OUT OF THE Silver Circle with no escort.

I yearned for girl time outside of these heavily political morning teas. I had never been one to seek comfort, but Amzee felt safe. Though maybe I was trying to fill the void Luna had left. I wasn't sure anymore. But I also did not care enough to sit down and sort through those feelings. Not today.

Using only orb light and my limited knowledge of Eiden's layout, I proudly turned down Violet Way. It was a notoriously lively part of town, popular for its nightlife. It was not yet late enough to be dangerous, but I wasn't afraid of the dark or the scum that lingered in it, anyway.

They should fear me.

Darkness lurked under my skin. My mind was the true cage, cruel and relentless.

Down the lantern-lit street were breweries, taverns, brothels, nightclubs, and smoking lounges. Light Natured, Dark Natured, and Natureless all poured in and out of establishments, hopping from one place to the next.

A group of fashionable Stonesenders stood outside of a brick building. It might have been the one Amzee had landed on, but doubt fluttered in my chest. Zephy was nowhere in sight, and it could have been any of the ten other buildings that looked similar.

The Stonesenders stood in a circle as they smoked, passing the piece around while idly chatting. Red and violet lights flashed from inside the building as a couple staggered out of the door, hand in hand, shadows covering the man's crotch. I tried not to stare, but what a weird way to hide a boner.

"Aye, lovebirds. Might as well shadow yer whole bodies, not just his prick, ya know?" one of the Stonesenders called out jokingly, his tone laced with familiarity.

The girl drunkenly giggled, stumbling down the street while gripping her stout partner's hand. He turned back with a wide smile, lifting his middle finger to the sky.

"If you wanna see mah dick so bad, come watch from the corner, Rockney, ya cucky blub!"

The Stonesenders all laughed, especially Rockney, shaking his head and coughing out puffs of smoke as the Nightcastor couple disappeared into the streets.

"Love that guy," Rockney said, passing the smoke to a short girl with a mossy dress.

If I kept watching from a distance for any longer, they would be calling me the cucky blub next.

Amzee was either inside the building or not. Best case, these people would know and I wouldn't have to go searching for myself. They seemed popular enough to recognize a woman who rides a winged creature. Worst case, they ignore me, I fail to find Amzee, then go home and bang my head against the wall to the beat of Lady Fiera's sobs.

I mustered up precious energy from my limited social reserve and approached the tipsy group of socializers the same as I would any other group of Stonesenders back in the Waywards.

Their voices quieted as I approached. The skin on my chest flared hot as each of their grey eyes shifted to me.

"Sorry to interrupt, I was just wondering if any of you have seen a particular Flamecastor tonight. Blonde, tall, chipper beyond reason. She rides a bladebreather."

The tallest of them twisted his lips and rolled his eyes.

The girl with short brown hair, pebble-lined spectacles, and the mossy gown crossed her arms. "Rude to begin with her Nature. Maybe give us a name?"

I blinked as my face shifted with confusion. Rude? Was this considered rude?

Rockney looked down at me with glossy, drunken eyes and a silly grin.

"Fascinating accent... but were yer not taught manners? Not polite to describe someone by their Nature first. Kinda seems like ya think yer Flamecastor friend's an object," he said. The moon reflected off the shiny rocks beaded into his hair.

I swallowed, admittedly embarrassed and a little shocked. It had not dawned on me how unadapted I was to Castivian culture before this moment. I had even forgotten how rough my speech was in comparison to the lilted speech of most in the city.

Rockney's accent was stronger than anyone I'd interacted with in the Silver Circle, but it was still Castivi, no doubt. From what I could remember of the map Lady Jocelynn insisted I study, he was probably from up north in Iron Forge. She'd mentioned how it was heavily populated by Stonesenders, and maybe that was far enough to create an accent shift.

My accent wasn't the reason why they were peeved at me though, my words were.

I discreetly picked at the skin on my finger as I cleared my throat, praying my words would match my sincerity before I made the conversation worse.

"I'm Drakish, and where I come from, *it does* matter what your Nature is. I'm sorry for being offensive," I said, heart thumping. "My friend's name is Amzee. If you haven't seen her, then I'll be on my way."

Back in Drakington, an apology coming from a Blackheart wouldn't have gotten me anywhere, but this was Castivian. If I didn't give myself a chance to change and grow, I would forever be stuck in the same caged mindset I had run from.

The girl with short hair tilted her chin up approvingly. "Ya, Amzee's inside."

I sighed in relief. That was all I needed to know.

After a quick thank you, I left them to their festivities and pulled open the heavy door.

The bar bustled with heavy drinking, heated card games, and drunken laughter. The air smelled of sweat and liquor. My eyes struggled to adjust to the dimly lit room, the glow of red and purple making it difficult to spot Amzee. I weaved through the cluster, dodging sloshing drinks.

Amzee sat in a dark corner, deck in her hand and coins laid out on the table for betting.

She was playing against *Beck*.

A slick smile spread across his face as I approached the circular high-top table. "Well, if it isn't my old friend from the wicked 'Wards," he drunkenly chuckled. He must have been working out and eating more since arriving in Castivian. He looked healthy and *strong*.

Amzee's eyes lit up. "Oh, you know Elora, too?" She tapped the chair next to her for me to sit, so I did.

"Of course. She was on the ship with us. I was stuck with her in the ol' obsidian prison before that. Almost died together once, actually, now that I recall... small world." Beck laughed. He carried it all so well, the pain and baggage.

I was envious.

"We did *not* die," I agreed, not quite as optimistically as him.

The guilt of rejecting Riven forced itself to the forefront of my mind, stinging worse than a Drakenhornet. My mind fed on that pain, longing for more.

The last time I'd been in a tavern with Beck, Luna had been there.

"Are you okay?" I heard Amzee's voice, but I sat staring at the table.

No, I was not okay. But saying it felt risky, like they would think I was just craving attention. That was the last thing I wanted. What I desired was a future that wasn't hollow. To sleep without dreading morning. I wanted to care about myself, but I had no idea how.

"I don't know," I mumbled.

Without a second thought, Beck slid his glass to me. "For you, immediately."

"How can we help?" Amzee set down her cards.

If they thought I was worthy of such kindness, I must have been fooling them, because there was a cruel darkness inside of me. The real me could never deserve sympathy or affection. Sooner or later, they would see the truth of who I was deep down, and leave, just like everyone else.

Sweat pearled on my palms. I couldn't keep up with the racing thoughts or the overstimulating sounds. I should have stayed home and gone to sleep.

"You don't have to talk about it if you don't want to," Amzee said gently. "Do you know any card games?"

I grabbed the glass in front of me and shot the liquid back, embracing its burn. "I'd love to play if you don't mind teaching me."

Amzee got right to the instructions while Beck ordered more drinks.

As we played, Beck delighted in telling us about his future plans. Maybe it was to distract me, or maybe it was to distract himself.

He'd been taking full advantage of his Nature, lurking

around enough to hear there might be a ship going back across the Sea of Blades soon. A discreet trip to bring back refugees. There were already people getting out of the Northern and Western Waywards in small groups, thanks to the Rogue Drakers. Beck explained that ever since he'd found out about the ship, he'd been trying to figure out how to sign up. If Rogue Drakers could get people out, so could he.

"There are two different Waywards?" Amzee asked, sorting through her deck.

"Three," I answered. "North, south, and west. I've heard south is alright, west is supposedly the worst." Thinking about the people still stuck in the Waywards made the alcohol sour in my stomach.

"How do you know that?"

With the back-to-back questions Amzee had, I considered inviting her to Lady Jocelynn's show.

Beck took over. "Because, love, we'd hear rumors from the Drakers, and we kept getting more work. Supposedly, the reason we got loads added on was because the people in the west 'Wards had been dying out." He slapped a card down onto the wobbly table.

Amzee cracked her neck. "Well, I'd love to come help again. Zephy, too, if they'll allow him."

I wanted to help as well, even if it meant crossing those sickly seas again. The possibility was unlikely, though, since I'd probably be in a wedding dress when the ship left the harbor.

"I'm sure they'll take you, Amzee," Beck said. "I don't know about your bladebreather, though. You know how hesitant everyone is about them."

Amzee's lips straightened.

"He's very loyal. Maybe if they started allowing blade-breathers to be used regularly in the upcoming war efforts, we'd have a chance at winning." It was uncharacteristically snippy, but graceful nonetheless.

"I was unaware they were frowned upon," I admitted.

"It's... difficult to bond with one. A few too many mishaps have people—including King Xavian Steele, weary of bothering with them. That's why they're left alone in Moonhill."

Moons of Glory, I wanted so badly to visit Moonhill.

"Alright, enough war talk. More drinking. And Elora, it's your turn." Beck waved his hands at the cards.

"But I want to learn more about the bladebreathers."

Amzee grinned. "I'll show them to you. We can go up there soon."

A few rounds of drinks later, I got the hang of the game. Every time I thought about Riven, I drank more.

So much so, I thought I was hallucinating when he and a few other members of the Brotherhood walked through the door. It was a sobering sight as they sauntered right up to the bar. He hadn't noticed me in the corner, watching—wishing we were splitting a bottle of wine in a snowed-in tavern and laughing about terrible bard music.

Beck glanced at me skeptically before subtly turning around. "Ah," he said as he looked back at his cards.

Amzee scanned the room. "What?"

"Elora is in the dumps about that man at the bar. The tall one."

"Beck!" I gasped.

He placed a card on the table and shrugged. "Am I wrong?"

"All of this brooding over a *man*?" Amzee's eyebrows nearly touched her hairline as she dramatically gagged and clutched her chest.

It was horribly embarrassing. I was prepared to defend myself when my head began to spin, my mind taking me elsewhere.

Training grounds. Moonlight and torches guided my motions. I was in another body—-Xavian's, sword in hand. I felt so angry. I wanted to break something, just to burn away some of the hurt that tore at my soul.

Just as fast as it took me, I came back—eyes flinging open in the tavern.

"What the hell was that?" Beck gawked.

I shook my head, uncomfortable in my own skin. "This weird bond thing I have with my twin, I think." Did they even know Xavian was my brother?

"What?" they asked in unison.

I don't know why I tried to explain it. They would not understand. *I* didn't even understand.

It was as if Xavian's emotions were merging with mine. As if everything was heightened. I wasn't upset—I was devastated. I wasn't missing Riven, I was *longing* for him. I'd never felt like this before.

"Wait, isn't that your guy?" Amzee blurted, nodding at a group of women by the bar crowding around Riven. Their voices were inaudible, but he stood shaking his head as one of them stroked his arm.

I couldn't stop staring. I couldn't control my rising rage as another woman smiled and laughed with her mouth wide open, nose scrunching towards Riven.

My palms darkened, veins beginning to bulge.

I had controlled myself in the Waywards, and I could control myself here.

I compelled myself to stay put and watch everything I wanted in a person be found by another.

The brunette fawned over him, her friends giggling and blushing too. Riven shook his head again, shooting back a full glass of dark liquor.

Riven did not drink, yet there he was.

"Life is too short to sit in a dark corner," Beck said, voice low and eyes stern.

He knew what it was like to lose someone.

"I'm not here to judge," Amzee assured, raising her hands in defense.

I had survived so much, but I wasn't sure I could survive another moment of that woman's hand on Riven's arm.

"I'm not ditching you guys to go bother with him."

Amzee shuffled the cards. "We'll be fine."

Beck began stacking empty glasses.

"Do I need to drag you up there myself?" she pressed. I shook my head and swallowed my pride.

The ground felt a little wobbly as I stood. The girl's hand traced down Riven's bicep. He ordered another drink.

I pushed past smelly, drunk patrons and marched up to the bar. I reached right between the girl and Riven, yanking him towards me.

"I told you I'm not interes—" Riven began as he turned around, stopping the moment his eyes melted on me.

There were so many things I wanted to say, but not in the tavern. Not in front of all these people.

My hands were shaking. "Can we talk outside?"

Riven nodded and stepped away from the bar, abandoning his drink.

"Wait your turn," the woman snapped at me.

Lethally slow, I turned to her. As we made eye contact, we both registered the same thing. I glanced down at her arm to confirm. The reminder of my name on her skin looked irritated, like she had tried scratching it off.

"You... Drakish Blackheart bitch. How dare you show your crooked face!"

Riven stepped forward, towering next to me. "If you say another word, you will find your tongue on the floor."

The darkness in his threat intimidated even me.

"What's so special about her?" she asked, assessing me with pure disgust.

"You'd be wise to never again ask such an offensive question about the Princess of Castivian. Next time, you'll be facing the king."

Her wretched face went pale as she backed away. She mumbled apologies and explanations, but I didn't care.

I gave a reassuring nod to Amzee and Beck, and left with Riven.

The streets were quiet, the brisk breeze brushing the backs of my arms. It was comfortably cool, unlike the stuffiness of the warm tavern.

He broke the silence first. "Her arm? Did you do that?"

Of course he had noticed.

I wasn't ashamed, nor did I regret it. I had been treated like something to discard or be afraid of my entire life. The act of marking my name into her skin only touched the surface of the anger I'd wanted to unleash in retribution. Not just from her, but everyone like her.

"She deserved it."

He had nothing to say to that, and didn't hint at whether or not he agreed.

Through cobblestone streets, winding flowered pathways, and down alleys, we walked. We were both a little unsteady, but nothing terrible. I had walked home in far worse conditions in the Waywards. The silence between us wasn't awkward, but comforting. Occasionally we bumped into each other, granting a subtle smile or side eye, but an hour or so went by before either of us actually spoke.

"Enough," Riven said abruptly. We stopped in what had to be the plainest, ugliest alleyway in all of Eiden.

I turned to face him. The alley gave us little space between each other. It was difficult to see, save for some moonlight and distant lanterns. The silence was unnerving, and it smelled earthy from the growth of weeds along the walls. "You decide to confront me *here*?"

"You decide to turn me away the day I bring you flowers?" he shot back. "After you chased me down earlier, then sought me out again the same night?"

I'd never heard him sound so...hurt.

I didn't want to push him away. Surely he knew that.

I braced my hands behind me, in physical pain as I forced my mental wall down.

"I'm scared to have things...or people that I want," I whispered.

Riven tilted his head. "Why is that?"

The answer was simple. "Because they are unbearable to lose."

And I had lost so much.

Riven grabbed my hand. "You won't lose me." His face was sharp in the shadows. "I keep my oaths."

Stepping closer, I led with my heart, black as it may be. Worrying about the betrothal could wait. Fear could wait. The world could wait.

I lifted up on my toes just as Riven leaned down, delicately grasping my jaw with both hands as he kissed me. His hands were so warm against my cool skin, his mouth even warmer as it trailed down my neck. Heat fired through my core.

He pulled away, only to slowly back me against the wall.

Gazing into his eyes felt more intimate than any touch I had ever felt from a man. I wrapped my arms around his neck as he reached down, picked me up and brought his mouth back to mine. The cool stone against my back was a relief against the fire burning inside of me. He kissed me fiercely and methodically, sliding his tongue against mine and tugging at my bottom lip.

Each kiss made me crave more.

I ran my fingers through his hair as he snuck a hand up my loose shirt. His mouth moved back to my neck, then behind my ear. He gripped my hips, pushing me further into the wall.

"We have to stop," he breathed.

What the fuck?

"Why?" I snapped.

He let out a breathy laugh, brushing his lips along my jawline.

"The first time I fuck you will not be in an alley," he murmured.

"You're too prim for an alley, Sir Riven?"

"You are a princess, Elora."

Not giving me a chance to retaliate, he slid his hands into the sides of my pants, pulling them down. A shiver rushed through me.

In a swift motion, he lifted me onto his shoulders and pressed my back into the wall.

His mouth found its place between my legs. I sighed, gripping his hair. He licked and kissed me with perfect pressure, sliding his tongue with such devotion that my legs shook against my will. I smacked a hand over my mouth to hold in my cries.

Riven held my legs in place, squeezing them as he worked. Pleasure didn't begin to describe the feeling. He held me up as if he were starved, feasting until my body went limp.

Afterwards, time did not feel real. Euphoric and exhausted, we walked side by side back to the Silver Circle. He made sure I got home safely and gave me a respectable nod goodnight as I sleepily ascended the steps, bashfully hiding my smile. I picked the flowers up off the ground, locked the door behind me, and grabbed a glass vase from the kitchen. I set the arrangement on my nightstand upstairs, pleased with almost everything.

I put my orb beside the vase, tapping it until it glowed a faint blue. With the black roses illuminated and the moon smiling from the window, I fell asleep grinning back at it. The night itself had been better than any dream.

CHAPTER 36

MOONHILL

"The late King's own brother has forsaken him in death! A heretic! A usurper! He dares to claim Castivian for himself! Shame upon his name!"

— *Kolson Strange, Minister of Spirit*

I awoke in the late morning. The sun sparkled radiantly over Bastard's Bay, reflecting off the ocean in gold smears like Lyonheart magic.

Reeking like a brothel, I stumbled sleepily out of the heavenly comfort of bed, making the dreadful mistake of glancing in the mirror. My knotted hair could rival a ratty tavern mop.

A thorough bath was necessary before anything else.

I took intentional time to wash my hair and moisturize my skin with a vanilla scented oil. Picking my outfit for the day was easy. I'd been dying to wear a black and violet gown that the tailor master delivered to the house just a day prior. I adjusted the thin straps of my dress and smoothed the flowing lace layers of the skirt down before applying cosmetics.

I was still experimenting, but I liked darker shades on my eyelids, and colors that matched my dress on my lips. I deserved femininity. Cleanliness. Maybe even beauty.

I placed a black chain around my waist, attaching Singer and the orb at each side. While they may have thrown off the elegance of my outfit, I preferred them with me.

Taming my hair took an excessive amount of time, but after I finished combing through it, I decided on my usual style.

By the time I was ready, it was midday.

I had wanted to discuss the bladebreathers and Moonhill with Xavian, but he was surely long gone by now. As king, his agenda was consistently full.

That was okay, though. I could go to him. He'd likely be at the House of Sterling.

I held the skirt of my dress up as I descended the steps and stopped by the kitchen for a light breakfast. Perhaps a muffin. I had been enjoying those. Especially plumberry.

"Late night?" Lady Jocelynn chimed from the living area.

I jumped back a step. "For Fate's sake, I nearly pissed myself!"

She was perched elegantly on the couch, elbow resting on an overstuffed grey pillow, with her hair swept back into a low bun and an exotic hat atop her head.

"No need for such dramatics, or soiling a perfectly fine gown. That one suits you, by the way."

"Thank you."

She studied me for a moment, looking me over. "Anyhow, I

was concerned when you missed tea. Your brother mentioned you were out until dawn."

I did not care for Xavian sharing my business. Especially with the most judgmental person available.

"It was...a long night indeed. We'll have to reschedule tea for tomorrow."

Her face went sour. "My show is tomorrow. Or have you already forgotten?"

"I presumed it was in the evening."

"It is, but for an event like this, I will be preparing and rehearsing all day. My cosmetics, naturally, will be flawless. For the guests, it begins in the evening, yes. Sir Riven should know that." She sighed dramatically, crossed her legs, and folded her hands in her lap.

"No need to pout. We'll be there. I'm sorry you went out of your way to check on me." I grabbed a muffin from a black wicker basket on the counter and took a hearty bite, crumbs scattering.

"And what are you dressed up for, if not our daily tea?"

I swallowed, setting the muffin down on a loose napkin. "I plan on discussing Moonhill and the bladebreathers with my brother today. I'd like to visit as well. I understand it's only a few hours' ride north. The more riders we gain, the better chance we'll have against the Drakers and Witchlords."

"The king is unavailable today."

I snapped my eyes up. "Maybe to you."

Her king. *My brother.*

She sat poised for an argument. "Unavailable' means unavailable. You will have to wait for your little Moonhill trip." Crows flew back and forth outside the tall windows.

Xavian had not told me anything about being busy today. He told me hardly anything at all.

"What's he so busy doing?" I pressed. Of course he had things to do, I just wanted to be included. He was the one who dragged me here in the first place. Over our few shared meals together, he had promised to discuss controlling the dreams and going over our inheritance. Neither of which had happened yet.

She considered her words carefully. "He's spending the day tending to... personal affairs. Loose ends, I suppose, before the meeting in a few days."

Personal affairs. I rolled my eyes and took another bite of muffin. So he was either caught up with Lady Fiera and her tears, or tangled in other matters I probably didn't want to know about. Still, I was every bit as grown as he was, right down to the hour—and had more resources at my disposal than I could ever have imagined. I could just go to Moonhill on my own.

Amzee had offered to take me, but it could be weeks before I ran into her again, and I had no way of contacting her. I could ask Riven, but he would be busy training new recruits.

There was so much to be done. Everyone was busy, except for me. They had purpose. I did not. I would find mine if it was the last thing I ever did.

"Sounds like I'll be going alone." I patted the crumbs away and poured a glass of water from a silver pitcher on the counter.

Lady Jocelynn scowled. "You cannot go to Moonhill alone."

"Why not?"

Shadows danced around the flowers and feathers adorning her hat, cascading off her dress and pooling on the floor.

"Because you are the Princess of Castivian, engaged to the heir of Whimcastor Hold. Are you really that dense?"

"Exactly. I'm the Princess of Castivian, and you believe you have the authority to tell me what I can and cannot do. Are *you* dense?"

The shadows wrapped tighter around her like a protective blanket.

"Hm. Good luck, then. Would hate to hold the blade-breather chaser back."

Now she was going to treat me like I was doing the work of a commoner? No, I would not stand for it. I would never again let anyone believe that my actions were beneath them.

"You're coming with me."

She laughed. "I am *not* going to Moonhill."

"Yes, the fuck you are."

She glared, and for the first time, I think she truly despised me.

———

Three hours later, I rode horseback on Kostini, with Lady Jocelynn beside me on a black mare. We hadn't spoken much, except for her making her displeasure known after I hadn't been sure about which direction to go.

"That is why you should be studying your maps," she'd lectured before taking the lead.

The trees around us swayed, as if waving hello and goodbye. Signs were nailed to posts every so often, pointing in the directions of various villages and small towns. The sky was a beautiful shade of blue, clear of clouds, and perfect for riding a bladebreather. I shuddered with excitement.

The final hour of our journey offered little to admire. Fewer villages and hardly any directionals until finally, there was a solitary plank nailed to a dying tree.

Moonhill.

I urged Kostini forward, catching sight of the clearing through the trees ahead. He seemed to sense my eagerness, and I leaned into his stride as he galloped. Lady Jocelynn did not share my enthusiasm and stayed trailing far behind.

Coming out of the woodline, there were open grass fields for miles. No houses or establishments.

Only bladebreathers, laying out in the sun and circling the skies in quick jaunts.

Black, red, blue, green, orange—every color of scales and fur.

My hands trembled. It was the very essence of my dreams—a landscape that could promise a better future. With the bladebreathers at our side, we could rescue the prisoners still trapped in the Waywards and forge vibrant new communities here. They were our chance to start anew.

"Elora!" a spunky voice called out.

Amzee walked alongside Zephy, waving from across the clearing.

Lady Jocelynn caught up, her chest blotching red.

"There are so many," she said, holding tightly to her reins while I dismounted.

My orb glowed faintly, as if it wanted to see the bladebreather's just as desperately as I did.

Amzee made her way to us. "I wasn't expecting you to come this soon. I'm impressed." She grinned. "Who's this?"

If Lady Jocelynn didn't care for me, she was certainly going to detest Amzee, but she would have to get over it. "Amzee, this is my brother's friend, Lady Jocelynn."

Lady Jocelynn frowned. "That is what you see me as?"

I wasn't sure what else she expected. It would have been worse to introduce her as Lord Draven's wife.

"It's so nice to meet you. The red cutie over there is Zephy." She pointed to her bladebreather, who had run off to fly with a smaller, young one in the sky.

Lady Jocelynn grimaced at the beasts.

"We could try to find your match. Both of you, if you want. So few people are willing to try anymore. I assume that's why you've come all this way," Amzee added.

My heart skipped a beat.

"I needed to see Moonhill and the bladebreathers firsthand. Now that Lady Jocelynn and I have witnessed their magnificence with our own eyes, I'm hoping my brother, King Xavian, will have an incentive to advocate for more riders."

Amzee didn't react to my brother's identity, as if she already knew.

Lady Jocelynn and her steed backed away. "I will be going nowhere near them. I have children and a husband waiting at home." She stuck her chin up at even the idea of trying to match with a bladebreather.

Amzee smiled at me. "Well, we can certainly try with you, Elora. Lady Jocelynn, you're welcome to watch from the woodline if you'd feel more comfortable."

"I don't need comfort. I need both of you to hurry up and

either live or die so I can make it back for evening tea, if your brother does not kill me first."

"No need for dramatics," I said. I'd had enough of Lady Jocelynn for the day. "Amzee, what do I need to do?"

Actually approaching a bladebreather was slightly terrifying. I wasn't exactly sure of their temperament, or what to say or do.

"Well, it's probably best if we approach the youths. One near Zephy's age would be ideal."

Pointing down the valley, Amzee noted two little bladebreathers, one black and one green. "Zephy plays with them a lot. We could walk down there first and see how it goes."

"How long do they take to mature? I don't want to take a baby into war."

She laughed. "I wouldn't call them babies. They're very young adults. They'll fully mature in the next year or two."

"I'll follow you then."

Lady Jocelynn rubbed her temples disapprovingly, but didn't try to stop me.

"Moons, this is thrilling!" Amzee exclaimed, linking her arm with mine as she led me through the field. I shared her excitement, but nerves churned in my stomach.

If Amzee could do it, then I could too.

We were about halfway across the field when a shadow loomed over our heads. Amzee tensed, letting go of my arm as a massive beast landed in front of us. The ground shook. It bared its sharp teeth and released a thunderous growl.

I froze.

"Don't move another step," the bladebreather warned, her wicked voice dripping with violence. Her silver scales gleamed like armor in the sunlight. She towered over us, at least five times the size of Zephy.

Amzee and I both took a step back, her face pale.

Zephy soared down like a hawk, scooping her up with his claws and fleeing. She hollered for him to put her back, but he whimpered and whined, carrying her off to safety.

Lightheaded, I held my shaking hands up.

"Who are you?" the beast boomed.

I swallowed down the lump in my throat. "Elora. My name is Elora. Who are you?"

She stepped towards me. I fell back onto the ground at the sight of her claws.

Behind me, Lady Jocelynn had not yet run for the woods. She sat on her mare, the color draining from her face. She looked at me as if I were already dead.

I shuffled back to my feet. If I was going to die, it would not be cowering.

Not after everything I'd been through to get here.

The bladebreather stood to her full height, peering down at me like I was prey.

"I am Valeska, and these are my kin. You do not hail from these lands, yet you tread upon my grass, seeking to claim one of my own. My children. For what purpose? Greed? Violence? A thrill?" Her dark eyes, edged in the same silver as her scaled body, locked onto mine. A silent threat lingered in the air: a promise of death for the wrong answer.

My voice was shakier than I would have preferred. "I have people that I care for, too. I come from a land where they would do terrible things to creatures like you. I want to be a rider, to aid in the war against them. We could bring riders for all of you. Together we could keep your home, and mine, safe."

It was the first attempt in my life at being diplomatic, and while I wasn't sure I said the right things, it was the truth.

Ashy, metal-tinged smoke blew from her nostrils.

"I have no interest in aiding a man's war. Do you see aid for us here? Do you see sheep or cattle? No. And if we explore other areas for food, we are hunted. You land-walkers are no friends of ours. I only allow the few bonded riders because they have been valuable to us. Keeping us fed, getting to know us. But *you*... You just want to take. Today will be your last day *taking*."

She reared back, metal rippling at the back of her throat.

I turned on my heels, running as fast as I could towards the woodline. Lady Jocelynn was gone, of course. The first three blades plummeted into the ground behind me, too close for comfort. My muscles burned, grass kicking up under my feet.

My wedding was supposed to be next week. The one contribution I could make wasn't even going to happen before I was impaled.

My eyes burned, tears welling as my dream of becoming a rider died.

Valeska bellowed. I looked back as a fresh batch of blades came spearing from her mouth. Dodging them, I fell, narrowly avoiding decapitation.

"Shit," I cursed, dark tears singeing the dirt. I got back up. The ground quaked with each menacing roar. I wobbled, trying not to fall again, but the woods were still too far. I wasn't going to make it.

The clink of metal rose in the back of her throat again, and I knew this was it. In history books, would they include the bastard sister of King Clarke and King Xavian, or would they leave me out altogether?

The blades released from Valeska's throat, a whistle of metal coming at me. Death reaching for the back of my neck.

But death wasn't fast enough.

A mysterious force, either mist or shadow, gripped me with immense strength, yanking me upward onto an invisible steed.

We dashed across the field. Valeska cried out in outrage as I melted into the air itself. I glanced down at my hands, but they weren't visible either. Was I dead?

Racing into the woodline, the illusion faded in waves. I wasn't dead at all. I was on the back of Lady Jocelynn's horse. She sat behind me, panting.

She'd never left me.

I couldn't believe she had held her Nature for so long, *and* extended it to the mare and me.

Sweat dripped from her face and down her nape.

"Oh my God!" I wheezed.

"I'm fine," she breathed, clutching her chest.

"You're strong. I thought that was a goddamn man pulling me up."

She scowled and pushed me off her steed. I shrieked as I rolled onto the ground, a grin spreading across my face.

"Get on your own horse," she rasped.

Kostini stood waiting for me, letting out a huff. I lay on the ground for a moment, catching my breath. "Thank you," I whispered.

I certainly wouldn't be missing her show, not after that.

CHAPTER 37

THE CARRIAGE

"Light or dark, Nature's wasted on violence alone."

— *KING XAVIAN STEELE*

WHILE SHE MAY HAVE SAVED ME FROM THE bladebreather, Lady Jocelynn had no such mercy with my brother. She immediately informed him of what had happened at Moonhill, with special emphasis on how she would never, *ever* return, no matter the circumstances.

Xavian wanted to march up to Moonhill himself and wipe out the bladebreathers, as if that would be an easy feat.

After a long and exhausting argument, it finally ended with a firm "no" to using them in the coming war. To say the whole affair was disappointing was an understatement. Our kingdom's own crest, the beast we proudly displayed on our flags—treated as a blight.

I had attempted to convince myself that the trip to Moonhill was a nightmare, and that the queen of the bladebreathers never tried to end my life on that field, but that was not the case. It *had* happened, and the chances of me ever being a rider like Amzee or even seeing more people become riders was unlikely.

But nothing was impossible. Maybe Valeska would die before I was too old to climb onto a bladebreather's back.

Riven would arrive soon, and surprisingly, I was looking forward to an evening out. I'd spent hours perfecting my cosmetics, being intentional with every color, brushstroke, and angle.

A light violet shimmer swept over my eyelids, and a touch of clear sparkles dusted my cheeks and nose. My lips were glossy, and my hair was tied into a voluminous bun with delicate, loose strands framing my face and spilling down my back.

I marveled at the woman in the reflection. It wasn't long ago that I couldn't stand to look at myself in a mirror. The Castivian black gown hugged my frame down to my navel, and from there, the skirt fell to the floor in heavy layers.

A firm knock pounded on my bedroom door.

I took one last look at my face before opening it.

Xavian stood in the hallway, balancing a black tiara on the end of his pointer finger. It had crystals embedded all along the front, like stars on a clear summer night.

"You have to wear this."

I shifted awkwardly. "You don't wear a crown. Why do I have to?"

He unceremoniously plopped it on my head with no regard for whether it was straight or messed up my hair. I took hold of it, walking back to the mirror to adjust it properly.

"Because I haven't attended a public event as a *prestigious* guest since becoming king. Lady Jocelynn has spread the word far and wide that the Princess of Castivian is attending. So, *Princess*, wear your tiara, and don't let anyone rip it off your head. It's expensive and new."

I would be the first in history to wear it. The first Princess of Castivian.

It was surreal... and maybe not undeserved.

The bastard daughter.

People would say it, if they were not already. The world had said it about Xavian, but he was used to it. His whole life he'd grown up in Clarke's shadow. At least he was respected as a warrior and leader. I was nothing more than Clarke's bastard sister. If I didn't have the King's Mark, no one would even believe that much.

I tensed my hands on the vanity, staring back at someone I hardly recognized.

The tiara was beautiful. If someone else were wearing it, I would surely know they were regal. I supposed that was the point.

In the reflection, I made eye contact with my brother, who still stood in the doorway. "Lady Jocelynn did say appearances for such matters are important."

"Jocelynn is usually right about these things," he mumbled, as if she had given him the same speech.

She had emphasized multiple times in the past day how wealthy some of the attendees would be, and how the men and materials they could provide would be invaluable. If all I had to do was dress up, it was the least I could do. Or so I kept telling myself.

My smile fell flat. "Xavian?"

"What?" he snipped, as if he had somewhere better to be. He was grouchy today, even for... well, him.

Maybe he wasn't the best person for moral support, but he was the only one who might understand the immense pressure closing in on me.

"I know you're still upset about the bladebreather incident, but..." I stopped myself, shaking my head. Why were vulnerable moments such torment? Why could I not just get my words out?

"What is it?" he pressed.

It was like a wall was blocking my speech.

"Tell me."

I swallowed. "I'm worried I'm not doing enough. I keep trying to find a purpose, like yesterday in Moonhill, but every single time, I fail. I'm afraid I'm going to fail again tonight." I stared back at myself as I spoke, searching through seas of black oblivion in my own eyes, hoping to find a spark of light.

"That's ridiculous." He plopped onto my bed, dark curls falling around his face.

"Thanks for the advice, Your Highness," I said, narrowing my eyes.

He scoffed dramatically. "You crossed the Sea of Blades to deliver the deed, nearly died every damn day, and you are doing your duty by accepting a betrothal. By this time next year, Castivian may have another heir, and you'll have contributed more than anyone else could for this kingdom. Get a grip on your pride. Act like you represent lands worth fighting for. We are the last of the Lyons blood."

"But what about my actual *purpose*? Just being an heir can't be my entire life?"

Yes, I was getting married. I'd already resolved not to bother the man beyond fulfilling our marital duties. Like most men, he surely had plenty of mistresses and other affairs to keep him occupied. I only hoped he would leave me alone, apart from producing an heir.

One child. For now.

Xavian sighed and rubbed his head. "Some people get so caught up trying to find their purpose, they forget to actually live. Don't let that happen to you, Elora."

He didn't understand what I was saying at all.

Thankfully, a knock thudded downstairs. I glanced at Singer and the Orb on the nightstand, then back in the mirror. They would clash entirely with the elegant outfit.

I left them safe where they belonged and followed Xavian down the stairs, holding my dress and trying to keep the tiara from slipping right off.

Xavian answered the door with a sharp eye, cracking it wide.

My breath hitched.

Riven stood tall in a black, lavish jacket and pants that hugged his muscular build. Heat flashed through my core. His hair was slicked back, offering a full view of his tan, freckled skin and soft eyes.

"Don't make me fucking kill you later," Xavian mumbled.

"You should come with," Riven taunted, noticing Xavian's loose white shirt and baggy pants.

"Ha. I have correspondences to tend to, and a brothel

calling my name—but thank you for the invitation." Xavian flopped down on the couch, kicking his feet up on a pillow.

I clasped my hands together and smiled at Riven. "Well, there's nowhere to hide in Hell. Let's leave the king be."

Xavian winced at the formality, but did not argue. Referring to him as my brother, or even by his first name aloud, was still foreign. He'd once been merely a noble to me, so far out of reach from my circle. Now the famed figure was my own twin. It was an adjustment, to say the least.

More importantly than formalities and titles, Xavian was exhausted. He had been working day and night on plans and preparations for the meeting. The last thing he would want to do is come to the theater to listen to Lady Jocelynn talk. He was exposed to enough of that already.

The carriage waiting outside was stunning.

Shiny and black, with large wheels and a sizable cab. Swirls had been carved along the side, just below iron-twisted designs of bladebreather wings. There were no horses or reins. Only two men in fine clothing sitting on the front bench.

Riven smirked. "Have you never seen Lady Jocelynn's carriages? Your brother has one similar."

I shook my head. "How does it move? Where are the horses?"

"Don't need them."

Riven opened the door for me, his pupils dilating as he glanced down at my dress.

I gathered the skirt once more, climbing inside, where the bench seats were cushioned with dark emerald velvet pillows, and heavy black curtains framed the windows. Riven slid in across from me, trying to hold back a smile.

"What?"

He shrugged. "Just you."

"What about me?"

"How absurdly beautiful you are."

I tilted my head down, hiding the heat rising to my face. "Oh. Thank you."

The carriage took off. I scooted closer to the window, pulling back the curtain.

"Are we being pushed?"

Riven laughed. "No. It's the Stonesenders, Jon and Morgan, at the front. They're taking turns wielding their Nature. The wind they create propels us forward, and they've got a lever in between them to take turns steering. Swapping back and forth keeps them from burning out."

"Your brother invented it, actually," he continued. "He first learned how to infuse armor and weapons with different Natures, then he moved on to other inventions. He's gotten quite experimental over the years."

I'd known Xavian spent a lot of time training, planning, and throwing daggers at people. I knew nothing of his inventions, nor experimenting. I didn't even realize he had weapons *infused* with Nature. "I would never have thought of such a clever way to use a Stonesender's Nature," I said.

That's why it was so easy for Xavian to brush me off about finding my purpose. He was good at everything.

I let go of the curtain and situated myself in my seat. Riven's legs were comfortably sprawled in front of him, and he had an elbow propped on the window. I wanted to crawl onto his lap and make an heir right then and there. As a bastard myself, I was perfectly fine keeping the tradition going.

"Have you ever been to one of Lady Jocelynn's shows?" I asked, containing myself.

"I have not."

"Then why were you so adamant on judging it?"

"Because she's boasted about it enough times at the dinner table for me to know she doesn't discuss politics or injustices on a regular schedule."

Dinner table.

The years before the existence of the Waywards, when Riven lived in Castivian, they'd all had normal lives. Eating dinner together and attending council meetings that had nothing to do with war.

I tried imagining it. Xavian, Riven, Lady Jocelynn, and the rest of the council. At *dinner parties,* simply enjoying life away from the mother kingdom. They were all willing to give up that peace for the greater good.

The carriage ride was smooth. The outside world got louder the further into the capital we went. Beyond the taverns, port, and brothels, we rode down streets with two-story townhouses and manors with so much property space, there were front yards. There were restaurants with people eating on the roof under the starlit sky, shops that had closed for the evening, and jovial music coming from the window of a lounge.

Riven leaned forward. "That's where your dresses come from," he said, his face close to my shoulder as he pointed to a boutique showcasing various extravagant gowns.

I should visit it myself sometime. The tailor and his husband were always kind when they came to the house, as I'd needed to be measured twice now. I'd never considered asking where they operated.

The walkways were clean, and the shrubbery was maintained. There were no drunks stumbling about the streets, and the people walking on the sidewalks wore fine clothing. Something told me *this* side of town didn't have to worry about the nighttime riff raff.

"That's Lady Jocelynn's home." Riven nodded towards a black manor, with a wide yard and iron fencing. It was elegant, simple, and so... her. With skinny arched windows, a grand double door, and crows sitting on the roof.

"Do she and Lord Draven not live in the Silver Circle?"

"*His* home is in the Silver Circle," Riven said. "Lady Jocelynn insisted on having her own residence near the theater. She bounces between both."

That was certainly peculiar but also exciting to hear, given I had my own marriage to endure soon. Which house did her children live in? Or was it both as well?

When he said she lived close to the theater, he meant it, as a moment later the carriage slowed.

The massive building was white and silver, a stark contrast to the carriage. Grand pearlescent stairs led to the door where crowds poured in. I swallowed, my stomach knotting.

"What's wrong?" Riven asked quietly, placing a hand on my knee. A chill ran down my spine.

The people going into the theater wore regal gowns, expensive jewelry, and tailored suits.

"They all have expectations I don't know how to meet."

I was in no shape for fancy conversations with the wealthy, even after tea with Lady Jocelynn every day. The last thing I wanted was for my stupid mouth to ruin the favor of the rich.

Riven leaned closer and brushed his thumb along my cheek. "You are perfect. They're lucky to lay their eyes on you."

I smiled sheepishly, shaking my head. "I'm not worried about my appearance. I've disguised the street rat in me. I'm concerned about conversations, and what they'll think of me."

He laughed and sat up, cracking open the door. "Blade-breathers do not seek validation from mice."

With a smoke already out of his pocket, he held out his hand. I caught a glimpse of the knife tucked away inside his jacket. "Ready?" he asked.

I took his hand and held my tiara in place as I ducked out of the carriage. I'd crossed the Sea of Blades, killed a warlock, escaped the Sapphires, and survived a bladebreather attack. I would not cower to a theater.

CHAPTER 38

THE CROW'S WHISPER

"Following the tragic fire that claimed both her kin and her betrothed, Lady Jocelynn Valeria—the last of the Crows, is soon to travel to Eiden to wed Lord Draven Wrenavia, whose formidable reputation precedes him."

Archived segment from The Castivian Chronicle

WITH RIVEN'S HAND AT THE SMALL OF MY BACK, WE ascended the stairs. At least fifty sets of eyes watched my every move. Clutching my gown with both hands, I kept my chin up to ensure the tiara stayed on my head. I avoided direct eye contact with any of the onlookers at all costs. At least Riven's protective presence ensured no one came too close.

At the top of the stairs, he held the door for me and— *damn.*

A crystal chandelier hung like the moon above the gilded lobby, where guests chatted among themselves and sipped from sparkling flutes of fizzing champagne. Servers in beige trousers and dress shirts actively buzzed around with loaded trays while handing out theater pamphlets.

Riven guided me forward. "We have balcony seats."

With a subtle nod, I followed him through the growing crowd.

The whispers prickled down my neck.

"Twins, yes."

"Another bastard."

"Tragically sharp features. Xavian's sister for sure."

"A Blackheart, clearly. Look at her hands. You can always tell by the veins."

"I'd heard she was Dark Natured, but a Blackheart... are you sure?"

Riven cleared his throat.

I tried to keep a straight face, but picked at the skin on my thumb. I thought I'd be used to people talking about me after years in the Waywards, but this was different. Before I was hated simply for being a Blackheart, but so were others.

Here I was the sole person being criticized and speculated over like a three-headed pigeon with a piglet hanging out its ass.

"Breathe," Riven murmured, squeezing my shoulder.

In the private booth, there were two chairs, with a note in each seat.

The stage was magnificent from above, though it was almost humorously large, especially imagining Lady Jocelynn talking endlessly while standing on the long platform.

I picked up the note and took my seat, Riven doing the same beside me. It read:

Welcome to The Crow's Whisper.

Beverages encouraged. Willingness to listen required.

Enjoy,
Lady Jocelynn Wrenavia

I grinned slyly and closed the note. "Well, you heard her. I'm going to need a drink."

"Of course," Riven said, back on his feet.

I stayed put while he fetched refreshments, as I had no desire to mingle.

I scanned the area below. White cushioned seats with silver armrests lined the theater. Many were occupied, and more guests trickled in every moment, laughing richly and adjusting their lavish jackets. High above was a bundle of soft white orbs illuminating the room.

There was enough space for a thousand people, maybe more. How long would it take to get to the exit if something catastrophic were to happen? During the Sapphire attack in the Waywards, it had taken me so long to get to Luna and... Riven. Together.

I was going to be sick. I closed my eyes and shook my head, a failed attempt to erase the memory.

The orb lights flickered twice, signaling for everyone to find their seats. From the far side of the stage, a harp played a pure solo before rumbling drums and a group of melancholic strings joined in. The song filled the theater, pulsing through the air.

Golden light danced around the stage, revealing glimpses of musicians in the shadows, dressed in black and vigorously working their arms. The drums intensified, the lights growing brighter and the music stronger until complete darkness blanketed the theater in one beat, bringing with it a jarring silence.

One second of silence, two, three—

Bum, dum, dum, bum, bum, bum!

Blue, violet, and white lights flooded the center of the stage. "*The oneeeee and onlyyyyy... Lady Jocelynn Valeria Wrenavia!*"

Jocelynn exuded extravagance. Her hat made the other ones she'd worn look mundane. Colorful feathers, glittering jewels, and beaded pearls were attached to the side of the headpiece. Her plum and black gown hugged her arms and concealed her chest, while the train was almost the length of a wedding aisle.

Lady Jocelynn held her arms out and flashed a smile to the crowd. "Welcome to The Crow's Whisper! A show unlike any other in Castivian!"

Riven returned, quietly handing me a clear, sparkling cocktail before sitting back in his seat.

"Sorry for the wait," he whispered.

I thanked him, but was captivated by the stage. I didn't want to miss a thing, even for Riven.

The music softened into a haunting melody. The lights dimmed to a low, violet glow, shining only on Lady Jocelynn.

She looked over the crowd with daunting eyes. Then, she sang.

> *Crows alike, crows I like,*
> *Secrets they come and they tell me,*
> *What they know, it's what I hear,*
> *You'd never know what they tell me,*
>
> *Smiles they fade, debts unpaid,*

Secrets that grow and destroy thee.
What I know, you will know,
Open your eyes and you'll see me.

Open your mind to the crows I like,
Truths that are found beyond a page.
Listen close, you never know
What you'll hear from the crows on stage.

What you will scream, when you feel my rage.
What you might know, when the stage lights
  fade.
Caring for secrets, like they care for me.
Whispering Crows are the air I breathe.

Open your heart, sit in your seats.
The crows have something that belong to thee.
Whispers are gifts, unworthy treats.
The crows know exactly where to be

Secrets they linger—wait to be told.
I love to watch it all unfold.
Secrets they give, and then they take
Listen tonight or you've made a mistake

Her song mesmerized everyone in the room, myself included. As it came to a delicate end, a black chair appeared behind her, as if she'd been shadowing it the entire time.

As the stage lights once again grew bright enough to light the entire stage, Lady Jocelynn took a seat.

First, she discussed gossip from prestigious parties around Eiden and a new facial enhancement spa opening down the street. Even though the topics did not interest me, it was hard not to be drawn in. It wasn't *what* she talked about that kept the crowd entranced, so much as the way she presented it all. She was animated, never leaving out a single juicy detail.

She brought a guest onto the stage, a housemaid from a lord's home that had been allegedly robbed. The maid was young, barely twenty, if that.

"Alaya, thank you so much for coming all this way. We are so glad to have you," Lady Jocelynn purred, gesturing towards another chair that had just been carried onto the stage.

Alaya smiled politely, but went a little pale at the sight of the audience. She wore a dark blue gown, simple with long sleeves. Her rusty burgundy hair was tied into a low bun, face clean of any cosmetics—presentably lowborn.

The crowd murmured, but Lady Jocelynn swiftly demanded their attention with sharp eyes.

"To my understanding, you work in Lord Greer Bravestone's home? Employed to complete housework?" Lady Jocelynn leaned in her chair, an elbow propped on the arm.

Alaya sat with her hands in her lap, slouching a little and fidgeting with her dress.

"Uh... yes. I did, but I don't think I'll be going back."

"Oh? And how long did you work for the Bravestone family?"

Lady Jocelynn was direct with her line of questioning, yet

inviting. I could feel even from the balcony the attention she was giving to Alaya. The girl was likely not used to that.

I sipped on my refreshment, noting it was nearly empty.

Riven's tattooed hand was on the arm of my chair, daring anyone to come near me. My core simmered, heat pooling between my legs as his eyes trailed from my face down to my neck and chest, before he slyly returned his attention to the stage.

"They hired me when I was seventeen," Alaya said.

"And you are now?"

"Twenty summers."

"So you were employed to clean the Bravestone manor for the past three years?"

Alaya nodded, her shoulders curling uncomfortably and eye contact faltering. "Yes."

Lady Jocelynn slid a cup of tea to her, smiling. Alaya smiled awkwardly back, accepting the offering.

"Three years is enough time to know the people you're living with, I would think. To our guests in the audience, do you agree?"

Many nods and yeses erupted from the crowd.

"I thought so. Now, Alaya, a week ago, there was a robbery in Lord Bravestone's home, yes?"

Many of the nobles appeared troubled at the news.

"No," Alaya denied. "There was no robbery."

The crowd gasped.

Jocelynn's lips curled up just a smidge. "It was reported that several jewels went missing. Expensive ones. Charged with the crime was Nora Flennett. She tended to the grounds of the property, yes?"

Alaya's face went red, and she shook her head adamantly.

"No—well, yes, Nora was a groundskeeper. No, she did not steal the jewels. No one stole any jewels."

There were more murmurs amongst the crowd. I leaned forward curiously while Riven narrowed his eyes, as if he wasn't sure what might be exposed next.

Lady Jocelynn adjusted her posture. "Then what really happened?"

Alaya no longer appeared nervous. She took a deep breath and clenched her fists, knuckles blanching. "Lord Greer *claimed* jewels were taken seven nights ago. He blamed it on Nora Flennett, but I know that cannot be true."

"And how would you know that?"

"Because Nora was with me that night."

My eyes widened. How scandalous, the housemaid and the groundskeeper. Classic.

"In your chambers?"

Alaya laughed. "No. We were in Lord Hadyn's chambers."

The crowd got eerily quiet, and the smug look on Lady Jocelynn's face suggested we were on the edge of this teacup.

"Lord Hadyn's chambers, as in, Lord Greer's eldest son's chambers?"

"Yes."

"The *three* of you?"

I was beginning to question what the fuck was in the tea she gave Alaya because the young woman confidently nodded.

The crowd boomed with chatter, but after another sharp look from Lady Jocelynn and a finger to her mouth, they quieted.

"Why would Lord Greer blame Nora Flynnet for stealing

jewels from him that night if she was having a threesome with his son and the housemaid at the time of the robbery?"

Alaya contemplated the question, seemingly put off by the phrasing, but determined to say her truth.

"Because Lord Greer caught the three of us in bed the next morning, and Nora's a Stonesender!" she cried out, the words tumbling out of her mouth like rice spilling from a sack. "And, and, and... Lord Greer swore to Fate he'd have her sitting in a cell for the rest of her life for tainting his son with her Dark Nature!"

The room stilled. Shock spread across the many faces seated in the theater.

"Hm," Lady Jocelynn began. "You are distraught over this."

A tear rolled down Alaya's face. "Of course I am! I love Nora. All three of us love each other deeply. Now Nora is in a cell because she's Dark Natured and dared to love someone different than her."

My jaw was tense. Nora's story hit harder than I'd expected it to. It was despicable to think about someone Dark Natured being imprisoned in Castivian.

Things were supposed to be different here. Better than Drakington.

Jocelynn frowned. "That's terrible. I presume Lord Greer didn't fire you?"

Alaya shook her head. "I'm a Lyonheart. He has no issues with Light Nature, not that it matters. I'm not going back. I'd rather work in the brothels or beg on the streets before I work for him ever again. I will seek Hadyn elsewhere."

It was a respectable decision. Surely we could hire her,

although Xavian did not particularly love unnecessary people in his house.

"Thank you, Alaya, for coming all this way to share your story. I'll be speaking with King Xavian Steele about releasing Nora. Both of you can find work at my residence. You may go."

Tears streamed down Alaya's face as she smiled, quickly thanking Lady Jocelynn before scurrying off the stage.

I hadn't expected Lady Jocelynn to offer her a job, and I'm sure Alaya hadn't expected it either.

Lady Jocelynn stood back up, lights concentrating on her.

"We will have a brief intermission before the final talk of the evening. Prepare yourselves, as tonight we will discuss the recent widow Queen Delaina of Drakington already finding intimacy with a new boy toy, as well as a first-hand account of the infamous Waywards recorded from our very own Princess Elorengail Steele of Castivian."

The crowd oohed and aahed.

Lady Jocelynn disappeared, and the lights in the theater brightened. Everyone began getting up to refill refreshments, chat, stretch their legs, and relieve themselves.

"Do you want another drink?" Riven offered.

"If you don't mind."

"I'll be right back."

He took the empty glass and left me free to people watch in solitude. I scanned the room, grinning at different interactions below. I twisted to the side to crack my back, enjoying the relief for only a moment before I caught a glimpse of white hair.

Across the room and a level higher was Prince Payn in a balcony seat.

I was going insane. It had to be just another gentleman with similar neatly groomed hair, enjoying a drink.

Then he turned, our eyes meeting from across the theater.

My heart might as well have dropped through my ass.

Prince Payn was in the capital of Castivian.

His drink was no champagne. Blood trickled from the corner of his mouth, a single drop falling to the floor. He didn't break eye contact with me as he wiped the trail away.

Then, he vanished.

CHAPTER 39

ABSOLUTELY FERAL

"Saffron keeps his secrets well. What we do know is this: his prized warrior, his most loyal weapon, is the one who calls him father."

— MARKER DANE, LORD OF LAWSHIP

PAYN MAY HAVE CURSED BLOOD MAGIC, BUT EVEN that has its limits. He was *here*.

I practically flew up the wide, white staircase before crossing the theater. I ran to exactly where his balcony seats were, searching the booth and area around it. Hissing and cursing.

There was no trace of him anywhere.

I wasn't in his camp anymore. We were in *my* territory, and he was not going to walk around freely as a danger to this city. Much less mock me by showing his arrogant face after what he'd done to the woodland village.

The Sapphires had taken enough.

Clenching my fists, I hurried back down the stairs, checking for hair white as the full moon and an audacity as prevalent as muckbumps in brothels.

The main level was crowded with people parading around in their fineries, gathering drinks and mingling with other socialites. I pushed through, dragging my dress along and securing my tiara.

I spotted him sliding out the front door, unnoticed by anyone else. I didn't want to start a panic or stampede, so I kept my mouth shut as the stage lights flickered, signaling everyone back to their seats.

I couldn't let Saffron's son roam free in the capital. Lady Jocelynn would have to forgive me for missing the end of the show. I knew the contents anyway, except for the bit about Queen Delaina's bed already being filled. She probably didn't even wait for my brother to be cold in the ground before taking another lover.

Keeping my head low among the intoxicated guests, I exited the theater and began searching the streets.

Just a block ahead, Payn strolled away with his hands casually in his pockets. As if his family hadn't invaded and taken over Lestivia. As if they hadn't been killing innocent people in Drakington or targeting defenseless victims in the Waywards as a power source. *As if* he hadn't tied me up in a tree to piss in a corner for days and killed my friends.

I picked up the pace, my blood heating. This piece of shit had killed an entire village of women. Now he just waltzed about the streets of my brother's kingdom with no fear.

As I closed the distance between us, I reached for Singer.

He stopped, turning to face me.

Singer was *not* at my hip.

I'd left the stone club on my nightstand, along with the orb. All because I hadn't wanted them to clash with my outfit.

Plan B.

I reared my fist back and sent it soaring towards his face. He caught it, grasping my wrist and staring me down with dark red eyes.

"You didn't ask permission to touch me, Blackheart."

I bared my teeth and yanked out of his hold. "You didn't ask permission to walk on Castivian land." I grabbed a small rock from the ground and threw it, striking him in the chest.

He didn't react at all.

He stepped closer as I stepped back, searching for another rock. "I don't waste my consideration on what lands Xavian Steele thinks he's entitled to. Hit me again, or even attempt to, and there will be consequences."

The only one who would be facing consequences was him, and one day, his father too.

My palms darkened, poison surging through my veins. He'd killed Sitara. He'd killed them all.

I held my hands out, shrieking as venom exploded from my pores. I'd never allowed such a release before. It sprayed all over his chest, eating away at his black suit.

Payn shook his head, snowy hair glowing under the moonlight.

I was panting, but nowhere near done with him.

"I already told you, you can't hurt me. I spent a lot of time building up a tolerance, just for you. I did a lot for you, but that matters little now, doesn't it?"

"Damn you!" I yelled, bringing both fists to his chest,

beating the poison against him. It melted his shirt off thread by thread, revealing his sculpted chest. Had he cheated to get his build too? Was anything about him real, or was it all blood magic?

He grabbed me by the shoulders as I bashed my venom-covered hands against him like a rabid dog.

"Stop it," he growled.

I screamed, pushing his hands away.

"Stop—"

I clocked him in the jaw, silencing him with my knuckles. My hand erupted with pain.

He rubbed his face, noting the blood dripping from his lip.

I reared back once more, but I wasn't fast enough. He swiped his leg against the back of mine, tripping me backwards. My tiara flew off my head, clanking against the cobblestone.

I winced as I hit the ground, my ears ringing.

Flaring my nostrils, I forced myself up, pointing a finger at him as if it were a deadly weapon.

"*You* are an ugly, sniveling little bitch stuck under your father's heel!" I shouted, enraged that my Nature, for once, was harmless.

His skin remained pristine, not a single burn or any sign of trauma. He should've been dead after the amount of poison I had unleashed.

"What did you just say to me?" he hissed.

I smiled. "I said, *you're an ugly, sniveling little—*"

Prince Payn grabbed my chin, forcing me to face him. His lips skimmed my nose. "Stop."

"No," I spat. "You're a murderer, and I hate you."

"You killed Vyra, and I don't care if you hate me. You fail to appreciate that I was the only one protecting your identity. If anyone in that village would've exposed you, you'd be dead right now, or at least, I'd have killed a lot more people on your behalf."

Letting go of my face, he stepped back and pulled away the lingering pieces of fabric attached to his torso and arms.

I picked up another rock, this one smaller than the last, but I didn't care. I aimed at his head. Unfortunately, he caught it. Rearing his arm back and turning around, he sent it soaring so far it might've landed in the ocean.

When he turned back to me, he was practically steaming.

"You *act* like a lowborn brat, and you're gullible. I hope you realize that."

He walked towards a street of houses. Once again, the *audacity* was appalling. I'd spent years locked away because of people's fear of me, just to have him mock me to my face as if I were harmless.

"What do you mean?"

He ripped a shirt off a clothesline, then continued down the street.

"I meant what I said."

"I'm not gullible."

He scoffed and grinned. "Yeah, that's why you're not in your little seat at the theater next to the Oathkeeper. Instead, you're chasing me down the street."

Payn was the one confused. I was out here to kill him, not chase him. "I'm not letting you go."

He stopped, giving me an incredulous glare. "I think it's clear my proposal is no longer on the table."

"I'm not letting you *live*, dumbass."

He crossed his arms, amused. "And how exactly, are you going to kill me?"

However I needed to.

I mimicked the motions people had used during the midwinter games, bringing my hands together to form a black and violet ball of my own Nature. It was working, although my hold on the floating sphere of venom was somewhat unsteady, and was more egg-shaped.

"Elora... that's enough."

My arms were shaking just controlling the weight of the ball, but dammit, I was going to figure out how to throw it. I tried raising my arms above my head to fling it, but they gave out, splashing the poison all over the ground, barely missing my own head. I cursed and started again.

I rapidly formed another misshapen orb, sweat beading down my forehead.

He pulled a small glass vial out of his pocket and took a sip of blood.

Maybe he was intimidated and needed to fuel up for a fight. Perhaps he wasn't so invincible after all.

The orb wobbled dangerously. I had a clear shot at his head.

Payn vanished for all of a second before he was breathing down the back of my neck. "I said, that's enough."

I screamed, twisting and splashing the venom straight into his face. Black ink stained his pristine hair, dripping from his forehead and chin.

His nostrils flared, red eyes glowing with a promise of violence. I brought my hands together again, ready to form another ball, when he wrapped both of his arms around me, holding me up to face him. His breath was nearly as unsteady as mine as a streak of black ran down his cheek.

"I didn't come here to fight you."

"Then why did you come?"

As I tried to thrash out of his hold, he held on tighter, commanding me to meet his eyes.

"I've been fighting wars for the past ten summers. My youth was sacrificed to conquer Lestivia and other western isles. We both only have so many of our good years left. If you and your brother surrender Castivian now, my father and I can handle Delaina and the Drakers. War can be avoided. We don't need to waste years and bloodshed."

I cackled. Bloodshed? As if he didn't have *vials* of blood in his pockets. He was delusional if he thought Xavian, or anyone in their right mind, would hand over a kingdom to Saffron the Blood Bather.

"The people of Castivian prefer their blood in their own bodies. Are you truly heartless? You've already ruined thousands of lives in Lestivia. You need to do it in all three kingdoms on this side of the world?"

His eyes narrowed. "You don't know me."

"And I don't plan to," I hissed, bringing my teeth to his neck, biting down hard.

He pushed me off, wincing and holding his neck. "No wonder they caged you," he gritted out. "You act like an animal."

With his blood on my tongue, my lips smelled of his skin— a mixture of roses, rain, and regret. The taste was addicting, like the first time hearing a new favorite song. I frowned, ashamed. It must've been an effect of the blood magic.

He had to be dealt with before he disappeared again and hurt other people. Frantically, I started throwing every bit of poison within my bloodstream. One hand at a time, I formed palm-sized orbs, barreling them at his head.

He dodged them, stepping aside and ducking. "You're going to hurt yourself," he warned.

He didn't care if I hurt myself, nor did I care what he had to say. Every drop of venom that had built up inside me over the years erupted like a volcano, from my hands, nose, eyes, and mouth. It was all I could do to aim as much of it at him as possible.

My head spun, my limbs trembling. Soon, my Nature wasn't the only thing coming out of my mouth. Copious amounts of dark emesis pooled onto the ground as I lost control.

I couldn't give up. I couldn't be useless again.

Payn stepped towards me, shaking his head. "Please stop."

"Oh, since you asked politely." I grabbed a handful of the vomit puddle, and threw it at him. He turned, but not fast enough. It hit him in the chest with a wet smack, dripping down his front.

"You're absolutely feral."

My vision blurred, and my hands lost feeling altogether.

"You would be too," I mumbled as the world became shadows and stars.

He clicked his tongue. "Now I'm going to have to find something to do with you, Brat."

I wanted to scream. To tell him not to touch me.

But I couldn't. He picked me up off the ground, pressing my face against his soaked chest. My own poison was scented so deceivingly clean, like freshly watered roses. Did it smell that way to other people, too?

Everything was wet. Had it started raining? I lost sense of what was real, and what wasn't. The only thing I was sure of was darkness, and him. Whether he planned to kill or kidnap me, all I could do was embrace oblivion.

———

Dishes clanked in the distance. My eyes fluttered open, daylight pouring in.

In my room.

I sat up, snatching Singer off the nightstand and surveyed my surroundings. It appeared untouched. I was still in my gown.

If it weren't for the black and violet stains covering the dress, I'd think my interaction with Payn was a nightmare. My blood went cold.

If I was here, then Payn could be in the house. He could've killed Xavian in his sleep. He could—

I ran down the stairs with Singer, tripping over my disgusting dress. My heart thundered as I rushed into the kitchen, only to find the cook prepping breakfast and Xavian sitting on the couch, papers in hand.

It was still early. The food wasn't ready yet.

I sighed with relief. Riven must have found me with Payn and fixed everything.

A wave of chills ran down my spine. Was Riven hurt? Had he been able to kill Payn?

"What in Fate's name is all over you?" Xavian asked, rubbing his eyes and sitting up.

"Vomit."

He squinted at my dress. "Why?"

"Because I threw up. Where's Riven?"

"Waiting for you outside."

"Why?"

Xavian shrugged. "He didn't care for the fact that you came home without telling him or Jocelynn goodbye."

My throat dried. "No..." I whispered, mostly to myself.

"Are you okay, Princess?" the cook asked, her dark eyes swelling with concern.

"No... yes. I just don't understand."

I ran to the front door and threw it open.

Riven was pacing outside.

He stopped, taking in my ragged hair and destroyed dress.

"Why did you leave me last night?" he asked. "Why would you walk home instead of telling me you were ready to go?"

My shoulders sagged. There was no hiding this. No way to sugarcoat it.

"I—I need you to come inside."

Within ten minutes of me telling my brother and Riven the events that had unfolded, all hell broke loose. Members of the brotherhood were posted all along the outside of the Silver Circle, while hundreds were directed to search the capital for Sapphires.

I'd been ordered to sit down and stay put in my ragged dress, makeup halfway down my face. My tiara was gone, but Payn had left me with everything else. How he'd gotten me into my room without being noticed, no one knew. Blood magic was the only logical answer.

Xavian was furious. He and Riven had checked for any sign of Payn, storming through and tearing the house apart, finding nothing but a pure white hair on my nightstand.

"I want every single person knowledgeable on creating wards and barriers to report here by sundown," Xavian ordered Avan. "We will begin immediately. I don't want blood magic able to be used on any of the council's homes, at minimum."

Most of the council was already here. We only awaited Lord Draven.

"The barrier stuff is pretty new," Lord Avan replied. "There's not much known about their creation. Draven's been looking into it. Only small rooms have been warded in places like the castle, to our knowledge."

Xavian ignored him, moving on to the next order. "The guard rotations need to be more effective, *Captain.*"

Riven nodded, still silently boiling with rage. He couldn't believe Payn had gotten to me again on his watch. He refused to meet my gaze, either from his own shame or anger at me for having left him.

Lady Jocelynn burst through the front door, shadows swirling up to her hips and hat clipped onto the side of her head. While her appearance said elegant, her demeanor said otherwise. She pointed a finger at me. "You!"

I winced, but did my best to maintain eye contact. "I didn't plan to leave ear—"

"I don't care about you leaving early! I care about your piss-poor decision-making abilities! You are the princess of a fragile, newborn kingdom. We need you, and you are *determined* to find an early grave! Who needs an enemy when you are actively destroying yourself and seeking danger? Open a book! Learn something! Just because you grew up in squalor doesn't mean you need to act like a petulant, lowbrow, backward delinquent!"

The room fell quiet.

She didn't understand. I was trying to help. To be something more than how I grew up. I wasn't like Xavian, raised in a castle and schooled in decision-making.

"I'm trying my best..."

"Then stop trying! This isn't the Waywards! If you want to act like an animal, then go back to your cage!"

"Jocelynn," Riven warned.

"Don't interrupt me," she snapped.

"Enough," Xavian cut in.

Jocelynn pressed her lips into a hard line. "If no one else will give her a reality check, then I will! Elora, look at yourself, covered in your own vomit. And we all know this isn't the first time. Escorted home in the arms of the enemy? You're lucky it was Payn and not his father. You are betrothed to the wealthiest heir in Castivian! Money that can change our fate in the battles to come! Why do you not realize that you are in a position that thousands of girls would kill to be in?"

I was unsure of what to say. Too many thoughts came to mind, racing through me like a tornado.

"I do realize the stakes," I said, "and I care very much about winning this war. I actually know people in the Waywards. My friends were killed by Sapphires."

"Then act like it," she demanded, pointing her finger one

last time. Then she straightened her posture and patted her dress down with gloved hands.

My face heated with overwhelming embarrassment. I wanted so badly to be someone that other people would be proud of, but the more I chased that feeling, the further it was from my reach.

Everyone but Jocelynn awkwardly looked away as I stood and dismissed myself to take a bath. There was nothing left to say.

Xavian, Riven, and the rest of the council proceeded with planning, while Lady Jocelynn left. I watched from my bathroom window as she got into her carriage. It almost looked like she wiped away a tear, but I knew better.

While she may not have cried, I did. By the time I was ready to get out of the tub, the water was stained pitch black.

I ran a second bath and washed up with fresh water. I cleaned my face, braided my hair, and tossed on a white night-dress with thin straps. I spent the rest of the day taking Lady Jocelynn's suggestion: reading. Tomorrow was the long-awaited meeting, and I'd educate myself as much as possible on Castivian before then.

What was my betrothed like? Was he wondering about me, too? I fell asleep in the late afternoon, dreaming of thick clouds and dreadful storms whisking me away to an imaginary land where I didn't make so many mistakes and didn't feel so much pain.

CHAPTER 40

THE PELL

"Rumor has it that several of society's elite will be arriving in Eiden within the coming days. Merchants and hosts are advised to prepare their establishments accordingly."

— *THE CASTIVIAN CHRONICLE, MOST RECENT ISSUE*

I DIDN'T BOTHER PICKING OUT A DRESS IN THE morning, though I was sad to pass up several of my new ones. Instead, I dressed practically, in a long-sleeved black shirt with matching pants and boots, and tied my hair back in a lousy bun. Singer and the orb were clipped at each hip. Leaving them behind wasn't a mistake I would make again.

Slipping out of the house at dawn, cool morning air and salt from the sea filled my nose. The longer I lived in Castivian, the more it smelled like home. I held onto that feeling, letting it fester into hope. I never wanted to breathe in the death and decay of the Waywards again, and if we won the war to come, I'd never have to.

Nodding to the Blademan posted outside the house, I took off down the street in a quiet jog. I despised running, but I would give everything to never see the disappointment in the eyes of Xavian, Riven, or Lady Jocelynn ever again.

In the evening, all the lords in Castivian would arrive in the capital to attend Xavian's meeting. My betrothed included. I was equally as nervous as I was intrigued to be introduced to him. Navigating my relationship with Riven would be the most challenging part; surely my betrothed had his own baggage to be attended to as well. Political marriages were common. There was nothing to get worked up about.

While I had no actual destination, I kept jogging, letting my mind wander free. I ran when I could and walked when I couldn't. My chest burned, but I knew once I'd gone far enough, I would have no choice but to run the whole way back. Determination, anger, and resentment towards myself was the only fuel I needed.

When I finally made it back home, breakfast was being prepared by Juni, one of the cooks. She smiled at me, far more energetic than I was.

"Oh good, at least one of you will be eating. Your brother already went to the training grounds. Must have a lot of energy to get out before the big meeting!" she beamed, brushing dough with butter.

I needed to get to the training grounds too, but didn't want to disappoint Juni by rushing off. She'd been working so hard on this meal.

"Thank you for preparing food this early. Can I help with anything?"

She laughed herself damn near to tears and adamantly refused. Everyone seemed to be keeping me away from the kitchen ever since I'd made a foul-smelling, overcooked soup a few days ago.

As she finished preparing breakfast, I sat at the dining room table, mindlessly studying a map of Castivian. Hopefully, the pieces would click into place.

Once the food was ready, I invited Juni to join me at the table, but she, of course, declined. Picking up my plate, I excused myself to the ocean-facing terrace, barely making it to the table before scarfing down a flaky croissant.

Sitting outside was bittersweet. Lady Jocelynn hadn't invited me to tea overlooking the training grounds like she usually would. She'd probably be uninterested in my company for several days, if not longer. Whether or not she was involved in the meeting later, I wasn't sure.

All I knew was it would begin an hour before sundown at the House of Sterling, in the same meeting hall where members of the brotherhood were initiated.

Lady Jocelynn had told me plenty about it. It was the oldest room in the kingdom, built by the first bastard to ever rule. The rest of the House of Sterling had been constructed around it.

After breakfast, I went straight to the training grounds, ignoring blank stares as I crossed the yard wearing pants instead of my usual dresses.

Riven had a new group of initiates, so I did my best not to draw his attention. I passed quietly by, then past another practicing group, not bothering to join them. Instead, I went to the far back corner where the children fought ferociously one another with wooden pells.

As I approached the small group, they turned their attention to me, scrunching their noses up in the sunlight.

"Are we in trouble?" one asked, his pell dropping to the ground.

I shook my head, pushed my pride aside and grabbed a small pell of my own out of the barrel.

"I'm quite bad at using these," I admitted, waving the training stick around. "I was hoping you all could teach me what you know."

The four children were tickled pink, and took the task at hand with the utmost seriousness and diligence.

A boy named Ryder, the eldest of them, instructed me to hold the pell above my head while running a lap around the training grounds. I was hesitant until Kyla, the youngest, insisted she would go with me.

"There is no shame in runnin' like a war-ri-or," she said proudly.

Warrior.

I winced at the word. Sitara had wished every day for a warrior. The woodland village had claimed me to be one.

"You're right," I said. "Let's go run our lap."

Kyla couldn't have been older than six, but she did exactly as we were instructed. With little black bangs and pigtails frolicking around her face, she ran next to me with her pell held high above her head.

When she started to tire, I slowed with her, but that was no good to Kyla.

"No," she demanded. "We speed up, not slow down. Just like the boys do."

I ran at her pace, which was surprisingly fast. With shaking arms and red faces, we made it back to our corner of the training grounds, ready for another task.

There was a twinkle in Kyla's eyes as she set down her pell and stretched her arms out. A literal twinkle, like a star chasing the moon.

She was a Nightcastor.

Not all of them had it, but it was a telling sign they used their Nature often.

She would certainly be impressive one day, assuming she kept up her training and continued working on skills *outside* of her Nature. Combining the two would make her a force to be reckoned with.

I wished I wasn't starting so late, but thankfully, I had help, even if it came from adolescents.

As the rest of the children finished their laps, Ryder began instructing us on wielding a sword—well, pell. We all stood there, me with twice the height of little Kyla, holding our practice swords as the oldest child went over the rules.

"So, uh, what my father says is that you have to hold tight to your weapon, so it doesn't go fallin' on the damn floor," Ryder recalled.

I held back a smile. The other children admired Ryder like a victorious leader, though he couldn't have been older than twelve. Even so, he had our small group pair up and begin practicing against each other. I partnered with Kyla.

She boldly smiled. "The biggest versus the smallest. *That* is cool," she declared, holding her pell firmly.

"Begin!" Ryder called.

Kyla was fast and fiery with her attacks, forcing me to work up a sweat just to keep up with her. Despite her being a child, the spar was challenging, but not hopelessly impossible. It was a starting point that I'd desperately needed.

"I have something I know," Kyla chirped.

I parried. "What do you mean?"

"You asked us to teach you what we know, and I know something."

I suppose I had said that.

"Well, go on then," I said, out of breath. She was tiring too, her chest rising and falling heavily and face blazing red.

Kyla hit my pell, blocking me efficiently. "Sometimes, biting works."

"Biting?"

"Mhm. In fights with boys, sometimes I've won by biting them."

I winced at the memory of tasting Payn's flesh. "Oh, okay. Thank you."

The other children sporadically gave me tips as we switched partners. From 'in a tussle, turn your head in the direction you want to go,' to 'if you spit, they get distracted for a second.'

I caught Riven watching me with the children a few times, but he never walked over to judge or question it. He minded his own training groups, leaving me be.

Several hours went by before Xavian graced me with his brotherly presence.

"Elora," he called out, walking over. His black suit was polished beyond his usual attire. The top was decorated with a silver ruler's pin on the left side of his chest, with matching buttons going down the middle. His curly dark hair was groomed neatly behind his ears, and he'd even trimmed his beard.

"What do you need?" I wasn't done training yet, if that was what he was going to ask.

"We have a meeting in a few hours."

The cloud-scattered skies overhead weren't becoming dark yet, just a bit overcast as the afternoon settled in. I still had time.

"I remember the meeting," I assured him.

"Then remember how to get ready for it."

"Excuse me?"

"We're busy!" Kyla yelled.

I whipped around.

Was she not aware Xavian was the king? Back in Draking-ton, we couldn't speak to the Draker's like that, much less a king. I would have to explain to Xavian that she was young and didn't understand. I could teach Kyla the proper—

"Your mother is going to want you home soon as well, Kylarove. We have company this evening," Xavian said, giving her a stern look.

I took a meaningful glance at Kyla, honing in on her brown eyes and the little shadows around her ankles.

She was a spawn of Lady Jocelynn. She'd probably known Xavian her whole life, like an uncle.

"Nooooo," she whined.

"Yesssss," Xavian mimicked.

Kyla glared defiantly. "No."

With that, she disappeared, shadows coiling where she had been. I held in a laugh as the grass softened where her steps trailed straight out of the training grounds. She had more control over her Nature than most of the adult Nightcastors back in the Waywards.

Xavian shook his head. "Are you going to run off with your new friend, or go home and get dressed?"

I shrugged, as my training partner was long gone. "I still have a few hours."

"So use them to get ready. Mentally. Physically. We need to be every bit of what this kingdom represents when the lords step into the House of Sterling."

"What do we represent?"

I squinted as the sun peeked out from behind a cloud, nearly blinding me. Xavian was so kind as to step in the path of light, casting a shadow over me.

"Strength. Tonight we show that our bloodline is an unyielding force, and will continue to be for ages to come. There will be no option but to follow us through the storm against the blood bathers and the Nature blamers."

CHAPTER 41

THE MEETING

"Strange, isn't it, that Blackhearts can weep? Even their tears run dark, as if their sorrow remembers what they are."

— *JON HARVINGTON, GOLDEN SCHOLAR OF LYONSCLIFF*

THE DRESS THAT HAD BEEN SENT TO THE HOUSE WAS nothing less than a work of art.

"You've come quite far."

I startled at the sound of Jocelynn's voice.

She stood in the doorway behind me, assessing. Her lips pressed together and her hands folded in front of her.

"Thank you," I said, turning back to the mirror. Now wasn't the time for excuses or apologies. Now was the time to pull myself together. To be a princess, whether I knew how or not.

While the skirt was a sleek, night-sky black, the dark corset was made to appear as if slender blades held it together instead of lace. The neckline was high and modest, though sleeveless. I wore black gloves and had styled my own hair, per usual.

My cosmetics were the best I'd done yet. A sharp but short winged eyeliner paired with a shimmery silver eyeshadow. I'd used a neutral-colored gloss on my lips, and a light blush.

"Your brother has a new tiara for you, since you misplaced the last one."

Guilt trembled through me.

"I didn't misplace shit, they stole it."

"Because you left the theater alone," she fired back.

"Because I witnessed someone fleeing who had murdered people I care about, and I'm not over it. Sorry that for the past three years, I've not had the freedom to run where I wish or hold men accountable, but now I can at least try. Even if it makes me look crazy or immature to you."

Her face tightened. "You're not in the Waywards anymore," she said gently, before leaving. A tattooed hand caught the door.

The air seemed to escape the room as we stood across from each other, his eyes admiring me from head to toe.

His shoulders lowered—his gaze soft. I closed the distance between us, reaching my arms out before being swept up in his embrace. I shouldn't have left the theater, but that didn't matter now.

Riven held me tightly, his heart beating wildly in his chest as if he was afraid to lose me.

Meeting my betrothed was inevitable. It was not only a duty, but an honor. We both knew it was the right thing to do, and while I *would* go through with it, I didn't want to let Riven go.

He rubbed his thumb along my back. "I'm not sure I can stomach this," he admitted quietly.

"At least I'm not the one with stomach issues this time," I joked.

"The princess is irresistibly beautiful *and* funny." He laughed, flopping both of us onto the bed.

I shrieked playfully as we landed. Our eyes were level as we lay on the mattress.

He swallowed, scanned my face solemnly, and ran his thumb down the center of my lip.

Our smiles met as he kissed me, unafraid and unruly. He wasn't worried about my Nature, my mistakes, or my moods. To feel wanted was intoxicating and addictive. I wasn't sure I'd ever be able to let this moment go, much less him. I didn't want to get out of bed. I didn't want him to stop kissing me.

But we had to.

I could hear Xavian shouting orders in the hall. He'd be at my door soon.

Riven pressed his lips to mine once more before reluctantly pulling away.

We left the room unnoticed, just in time to load into the carriage outside. I held Singer with me like a baton. People could question it if they wanted, but I wouldn't be caught picking fashion over safety again. My orb was chained to the bottom of my corset, dangling along for the ride.

———

The grand stone building awaited us. Full companies of

armored men lined the gates, displaying the emblems of their respective houses across their chests and banners.

Once the carriage came to a stop, Riven opened the door and gave me one last longing glance.

Chest tight, I pulled him back in by the collar and closed the door.

"What's wrong?" he asked.

Everything wrong did not matter at that moment, only him.

Still gripping his shirt, I dragged him forward and kissed him fiercely. He met me with the same desire, gripping my waist and bringing my weight onto him. A moan escaped me as he held me tighter, his needy tongue swiping against mine.

We took advantage of every second, knowing that once I met my betrothed, we might never touch again. With his hand at my back, he buried me in his embrace, letting my neck fall back as his mouth trailed behind my ear.

A knock sounded on the outside of the carriage, startling us both upright.

"Are you ready?" he asked.

I nodded, holding back any sign of sorrow. I straightened my tiara, pulled my dress up, and stepped out of the carriage with my head high and face composed into calm indifference.

We followed Xavian into the House of Sterling, down several hallways, and finally through the circular stone door of the Initiation Hall. I'd never had a reason to see this area of the fortress before; most of my time having been spent on the terrace with Lady Jocelynn.

The foyer was a long and narrow room of stone columns. Compared to the rest of the House of Sterling, it was cool and dim, with light only glimmering in from the glass-dome ceiling. The sun was setting, pouring an orange glow delicately against the columns. Voices chattered nearby, just through a daunting set of obsidian double doors.

Blademen stood on both sides of the entrance, ready to open the doors, but Xavian ordered them to wait. He waved for me to stand at his side and organized the rest of his council, Riven and Lady Jocelynn included, behind us in a proper formation.

Xavian studied us once more, then nodded. He'd never looked more tense, yet he'd also never looked more powerful. He stood tall with a silver crown atop his tied-back curls, the picture-perfect image of a king. Maybe it was wrong to think, but Clarke wouldn't have compared. Xavian was fearless and strong. He hadn't sent the Dark Natured to be imprisoned. No, he was determined to free them.

This was the first step.

The Blademen opened the doors to the packed hall. Inside was the longest, oval-shaped table I'd ever seen, with almost every seat filled.

I couldn't meet the eyes that stared as we walked in, as many of the guests had stood in respect for Xavian's arrival. Instead, I held Singer at my side, focusing on breathing and walking normally as we made our way to the farthest section of the table.

Once we'd crossed the silent room, Xavian sat at the end with Lord Draven next to him, as usual.

The rest of the council filed in. I took my place with Lady Jocelynn on my left and Riven on my right. With Singer situated in my lap, I nervously patted my skirt down.

There was no point in worrying. All I needed to do was be here. I didn't have to say anything except greet my betrothed, though that wasn't necessary either.

I hadn't yet glanced around—to wonder which one he might be.

Xavian stood as the rest of the room took their respective seats.

Lady Jocelynn sipped from her glass. I immediately drank from my own, relieving my suddenly dry throat.

"I appreciate you all being here," Xavian began. "I know some of your travels were long and difficult this time of year."

As I sipped the water, I slowly searched the table of men, regretting not having paid enough attention to Lady Jocelynn's lectures on Castivian. She'd tried teaching me about all of these people, but I had no idea who was who or which emblem represented what.

Some of the men were broad and burly, while others were slender and tall. I could tolerate the idea of marrying a few, but most seemed decidedly unappealing to share a bed with. I continued scanning around the table as Xavian gave his introductory speech.

Too old.

Looks drunk already.

There's no way in hell I'm sleeping with him.

I silently searched, one man at a time, until striking blue eyes brought me to a sharp halt. I spit my water back into my cup, my hand shaking as I tried not to interrupt Xavian's moment. A mocking dark brow lifted directly across from me.

"What is the matter with you?" Lady Jocelynn gritted out quietly.

I whispered back. "There's a Witchlord in here."

Lord Ansel sat with his eyes locked on mine. I couldn't wrap my head around why or how. My heart beat rapidly, fear colliding with confusion.

Lady Jocelynn shook her head and shushed me.

This was bad. So bad. How did Riven not *see* him right there? Surely he remembered the Witchlord.

"My sister and I are proud to say we will join our great house with Whimcastor Hold. With this union," Xavian announced. "Castivian will build its newfound independence on a formidable foundation."

I could feel the color draining from my face. There probably wouldn't be a wedding at all, because the Witchlords had infiltrated.

Next to Ansel sat a middle-aged man dressed in a light grey and blue tunic. He nodded with pride.

"My son, Lord Ansel Whimcastor, is honored to be taking Princess Elorengail's hand in marriage. We hope to solidify the union while we're here, as much work will need to be done back in Whimcastor Hold. That is, if you desire troops in a timely manner, Your Grace."

I was going to faint, or just fall over and die altogether.

Riven placed a firm hand on my thigh as he leaned over, voice low. "Breathe. Everything is okay."

Everything is *okay*? Did he know Lord Ansel would be here? Had he known something pivotal and not told me *again*?

Furthermore, how could Lord Ansel be the heir to Whimcastor Hold? The last time I saw him, he was in proper Witchlord's attire. He *was* a Witchlord. He was supposed to be across the Sea of Blades and in the Waywards.

Instead, he sat across from me, no longer making eye contact but paying attention to Xavian. The same could not be said for me. I could not listen to a single thing with Lord Ansel sitting there, clean-shaven with dark hair combed like a proper noble.

Lady Jocelynn leaned over me, smacking Riven's hand under the table. "Pay attention," she hissed.

My palms were going dark, a feeling all too familiar when I was afraid. I focused keenly on Lord Ansel as Xavian continued to speak. If he were to try to hurt my brother, I'd be ready. Payn may have been immune to my Nature, but Lord Ansel surely was not.

"I see all are here but Bravestone. Any word from Lord Greer?" Xavian asked, now sitting. He balanced the pommel of a dagger with his palm, the tip pressing into the table.

"They've pledged to Delaina," a large man with frizzy, auburn hair and an untamed beard said. He wore dark green, as did the two men on either side of him.

"Thank you, Lord Regby. Is there anyone in this room who feels the same? Or have you all come to wisely pledge your loyalty to me?" Xavian's voice carried boldly through the hall.

My stomach would never recover from the knotting. Aside from the presence of the Witchlord, our lives and so many others depended on this kingdom uniting as one. Not dividing.

One by one, the lords of each house stood, declaring their loyalty to 'King Xavian Steele.' Arthur Pos, Lord Draven, and Avan all observed sharply, prepared for if someone did not.

When it was his turn, Lord Regby pledged proudly to Xavian. As he sat, the next lord rose from his seat, an average-sized man with balding, sandy hair. He wore a gold tunic and a lilac jacket, accompanied by three men in matching attire.

"The Court of Flora will not stand for this treachery! Xavian Steele," he spat. "Is a bastard born, usurping—" A whistle soared across the table, before a dagger sank in between the man's eyes. He fell forward, blood splattering on the stone table.

The three accompanying men froze, gaping in horror.

"Who are each of you to him?" Xavian asked, holding another dagger.

"Cousin," one choked out.

"And your stance?"

"I'm—I'm loyal to Castivian. And you, Your Grace, I swear," the lankiest of them said.

The other two scowled, disgust riddling their gazes.

"Hm, and you two? Who are you to the dead man?" Xavian asked, lazily pointing to each with the dagger.

"Sons! And we don't bow to Dark Natured loving bas—" Xavian's dagger plunged into the man's heart before he could finish.

His body fell to the floor as Xavian unsheathed his third dagger.

The last son held his hands up innocently. "I do not wish to die, nor do I care for Queen Delaina. You, you—you have my loyalty, Your Grace," he stammered.

Lord Regby snorted, pouring his glass of water over the blood on the table, rinsing it away from him. "What a puss," he chuckled.

Xavian sized up the two remaining men, and he waved

them off. "You're stripped of your titles. Get out, and drag your kin with you."

The Flora Court men departed without another word, a crimson trail of misplaced loyalty following behind them.

With their chairs freed up, Lord Regby used one to prop his feet on for the rest of the meeting.

The remaining houses all pledged their loyalty, with Lord Ansel's father being among them.

I kept my eyes on the Witchlord while Xavian discussed plans for reassigning the two fallen holds, and what resources each of the houses present could provide to the Crown. He stressed that we needed every man possible for the war to come. Natured or not.

After hours of discussion, drinks, and formalities, the meeting came to an end. As Xavian dismissed the lords, Ansel spoke into his father's ear. The Lord of Whimcastor Hold stood, his company all following behind, except for Lord Ansel.

My jaw tightened. The only people left were our council, Lord Ansel, and Lord Regby, who had moved in closer, plopping down in the seat next to the Witchlord.

I swallowed. "Xavian, I have something to say."

I'd held my tongue for hours. I didn't know why Lord Ansel was here or what he was planning, but I wouldn't let him get away with it while I sat silent.

"Go on."

With the small group of us left, Xavian's 'around company' face faded, and the exhaustion showed in his true expression.

I pointed Singer across the table. "This man is not the heir to Whimcastor Hold; he is a Witchlord from the Northern Waywards," I said, deathly serious.

Lord Regby burst into laughter, while Avan looked ready to crawl under the table.

"Father, I beg of you," Avan said. The similar red hair was telling enough that they were related, with the same strong nose, too.

Lord Ansel rubbed his hand over his mouth, avoiding eye contact with me.

"He's not a Witchlord, Elora," Xavian said.

My fists curled. "Yes, he is. He was in the Waywards with me, and he gave me this orb!" I snapped, unclipping it from my waist and holding it up as proof.

I was sick of being a diluted version of myself in the hopes of gaining an ounce of respect. I was tired of being disregarded. I *knew* Lord Ansel. A thousand years could go by and I'd still recognize him.

"I was supposed to be retrieving you," Lord Ansel cut in.

"Which you did not," Xavian pointed out.

"What do you mean 'retrieve me'?" I demanded.

"I saw you a year ago, when Xavian requested some counseling on his horrid Waywards dreams. Once I laid eyes on you, I sought to retrieve you." Ansel shrugged, taking a healthy sip from his glass. "There was no need for you to be there. We've known this war would come, just like many of you were catching on in the Waywards. I willed you to look in the mirror, thanks to your bizarre dream bond, and I was able to find you after. It's all simple, really."

"Sounds confusing, actually," Avan mumbled.

Arthur Pos clicked his tongue. "While I don't know why the twin heirs have sporadic intertwined memories, we know the Dreamsouls are able to see those memories if they go into your dreams. So if I were you, Princess, I'd stop bickering and questioning unimportant matters, and start learning how to shield my mind for Fate's sake."

"Who the fuck was talking to you?" I yelled.

Lord Regby let out a deep chuckle.

For once, Lady Jocelynn did not intervene. She sat with her arms crossed, as if she'd already warned someone this was a terrible idea. I was their punishment, and she had no intention of stopping me.

Riven's shoulders were stiff, and his eyes dark. "You sent me to watch her for three years, with orders to bring her if Clarke were to fall, or if told otherwise. It made no sense to send Lord Ansel. His show of being a Witchlord was unnecessary and now confusing for the princess."

Ansel chuckled darkly. "Oh, you did more than watch her, Oathkeeper."

My face flared with heat.

"He escorted me across the Sea of Blades!" I shouted. "Don't insult him."

His light blue eyes twinkled. "If I'd have known that escorting you included orgasms, maybe I would've followed through with bringing you myself."

"Your claims are outrageous!" I exclaimed, embarrassed and enraged. How would he know about us? Surely Riven hadn't told anyone.

Ansel held his hand up. My orb snapped out of my grip, flying through the air and into his palm. "I didn't take you for a shameful liar, Blackheart. I made this orb. I can see through it, anywhere, at any time."

"Enough," Xavian warned, dagger in hand.

Lady Jocelynn scoffed. "Oh please, Ansel. We all know what you've been doing lately. Don't act so sentimental about your betrothal now."

Avan grinned. "Yeahhhh, sleeping with the queen is brutal work, man."

"You've been fucking Delaina?" I hissed.

The man I was intended to marry had his dick tainted by the wretched queen?

"For Fate's sake," Riven said under his breath.

Arthur Pos was equally revolted as he was alarmed.

Xavian, at his wits' end, lit a smoke.

"It was an inside job," Ansel said, leaning back in his chair.

"Well, rumor has it, you went thoroughly inside." Avan nodded in cheers.

Ansel waved away a pipe Avan offered. "I needed to know her plans. I attempted unraveling Princess Clayvarie's dream as well during my time in Lyonsreach, but she's deeply entwined in the Blackheart nightmare. We'll have to retrieve her at some point to continue my work here. Just don't send *that one* to do it," Ansel said, gesturing to Riven snidely.

Riven was lethally quiet.

"What are the queen's plans, then?" Lord Draven asked, adjusting the cuff on his velvet button up.

Everyone quieted. Whatever her plans were, they surely included the worst possible outcome for Blackhearts. There would be no mercy for even the innocent if they shared the same Nature as the man who had poisoned Princess Clayvarie.

Ansel pulled out a scroll and unrolled it onto the table. It was a map of Drakington.

"Cutting off Castivian taxes from her vaults has left her in need of money. She made a fool's deal with Saffron. At the end of spring, she's set to sell the Dark Natured of the Southern Waywards to the Sapphires. They're preparing 'camps' in Lestivia as we speak."

Delaina was a sick bitch. I had known whatever she was planning would be horrible, but selling innocent people, including children, to bloodthirsty thieves was disgraceful.

"And she thinks Saffron will leave her be after this?" Xavian asked, shaking his head.

"She's convinced they can be business partners," Ansel replied.

Poison dripped from my gloved palm onto the table. Those were people, not livestock.

"Saffron will not stop," I said, balling my fists in my lap to try to contain the poison. "His son said so himself. He will not be satisfied until he's king of the three kingdoms, or dead."

Xavian twirled his dagger on the table as Ansel pushed the map to him.

"Your Grace, if we can redirect the vessel leaving this week to an area close enough to the Southern Waywards, myself and a few others can infiltrate before the Sapphires arrive. Send enough ships to hold the Dark Natured ten days behind us; that's all we'll need. On the tenth day, we'll ensure that the people have a way to escape onto those ships."

While I was from the Northern Waywards, not Southern, they were surely set up similarly. It would take a massive fleet, and would also require overtaking the Drakers and seven Witchlords. The task he was suggesting required inside knowledge.

"Uh, where are we getting these ships?" Avan asked, peering at the map.

Arthur Pos groaned, adjusting his spectacles. "I will supply twenty ships."

Xavian glowered skeptically. "In exchange for?"

"*You* find my daughter a respectable match. And no more *relations* with her."

Xavian considered this, shrugging. "Deal. Lord Avan, you're engaged."

Avan choked on his ale, grasping at the stem of the goblet.

"I'll supply forty ships, and the men to man them," Lord Regby interjected. He gave Lord Pos a gnarly side glance. "In exchange for my son to be freed of his engagement to the barren one."

"Deal. Pos, your ships are unneeded. We'll negotiate a new match at a later date. Next," Xavian said, taking a drag of his smoke.

Riven followed suit, lighting his own.

"I'll be going," I declared.

Horrified looks struck everyone in the room except for Ansel, who tilted his chin with intrigue.

I would've never volunteered to go back to the Waywards before, but this was different. I knew what was at stake. I refused to sit on my ass while Ansel became the hero.

"*You* are making heirs," Lord Draven said coolly. "Your brother's betrothal won't arrive from Lestivia for months, maybe years at this rate. We need a bloodline established."

I leaned forward. "I wasn't asking for permission. I have two distinguished individuals who will want to go as well. Oh, and my *personal guard*, Sir Riven. He has excellent Draker knowledge that will be useful for our venture."

I rubbed Riven's shoulder with a smile. Ansel shook his head, biting back an amused grin.

"I'm most certainly not going," Lady Jocelynn interrupted.

I rolled my eyes. "I'm fully aware."

She'd never voluntarily leave her home, and that was perfectly fine. She had children and a life to maintain here.

I did not.

"Elora, you have a duty to marry," Xavian reminded.

He was right, and I would, while making sure I got my bargain's worth.

"I will keep my promise, but I will also go on this trip. Also, while we're discussing important matters, I want livestock sent to Moonhill regularly."

I wasn't sure why, but I *needed* to be more confident in front of Ansel.

Arthur Pos shook his head. "We should not be feeding the bladebreathers. They're the rats of the sky."

My eyes narrowed. "Says a man who would cower in the face of one. They're hungry. If you all want me to feed Castivian with heirs until Xavian's wife steps in, then feed the bladebreathers."

"It will be done," Xavian decided, raising his hands in finality.

A grin tugged at the corner of my lips. At least I'd done one thing right.

"My father will want us wed before we depart for Drakington," Ansel said bluntly, rolling up his map.

I'd expected as much.

"It will be arranged in the next few days," Xavian said, finishing his smoke. "Focus on gathering your crew in the meantime. While you all are absent, myself and the rest of the council will deal with the traitorous holds. They'll need new leadership, and... remodeling."

"Alright, enough wedding planning. I've got ships to prepare," Lord Regby announced.

I didn't give a shit about the wedding. I needed to ready myself for the trip back to Drakington. I also had to inform Amzee and Beck that they'd been selected for a mission that could save thousands.

CHAPTER 42

THE WILTING SILENCE

"Usurper Xavian Steele and his inkweed sister are murderers! It is said that he unleashed his vile Blackhearted twin upon the Flora Court nobility! She has spilled blood upon the sacred stone of the House of Sterling. She is darkness itself, wicked and without remorse!"

— *KOLSON STRANGE, MINISTER OF SPIRIT*

KNOCK, KNOCK, KNOCK.

Groggy and mentally exhausted, my eyes fluttered open. It was dark, the sky just barely purpling before dawn. Rubbing my face, I forced myself to sit up in bed.

Knock, knock, knock.

"Yes?" I called out, tense.

"Princess Elorengail, you have a guest. He's taking coffee in the parlor now," Maya, one of the housekeepers, said through the door.

I relaxed back onto my pillow. It was likely Riven, as he'd promised after the meeting that he would find and deliver my message to Beck and Amzee. The rest of the council didn't want to chance another *Prince Payn* situation with me venturing out into the city.

The decision had been fine with me. The time it would have taken to find them could be used to catch up on reading, since Lady Jocelynn agreed to resume our tea lessons until my departure in a week.

It was impressive, but not surprising, how fast Riven must've found Beck and Amzee. I appreciated his efforts, but would've appreciated it more if he'd waited until a reasonable hour to tell me.

In my lilac nightgown, I practically dragged myself through the dim hallway and down the stairs.

Sat in a dark armchair across the room was Lord Ansel. He placed his cup down and locked his angular eyes on me.

"Oh, absolutely not," I said, taking a step back. Having coffee with Lord Ansel at this hour, or in general, was comical.

"We need to talk."

I scoffed. "No, we don't. You had plenty of time to talk to me in the Waywards. You could've told me who you were. *Or you could've told me who I am*, but instead, you played pretend. You forced me to compete for my life at Orb Hazy, then made me feel grateful for your little gifts. I will do my duty and marry you, but I have no interest in speaking with you, especially before sunrise."

Lord Ansel let the wilting silence linger between us for only a moment.

"I didn't realize you sleep in now, Blackheart."

I stilled.

The terrible wintry nights of the Waywards and my dark lonely mornings flooded back to me. I never slept later than dawn while within the obsidian walls.

He didn't attempt to stop me when I turned away and returned upstairs. I grabbed Singer off of the nightstand, laced on a pair of boots, and stormed back out, still wearing my nightgown. It was strange to not have the orb clipped at my waist, but worse to know he'd been using it to spy on me all along.

The heavy front door to the house slammed shut behind me. I wanted Ansel to *know* I was leaving.

Slivers of burnt orange peeked over the horizon. A Blademan stood in front of a grey and silver horse-drawn carriage at the end of the yard, lantern in hand.

"Princess?" he called out.

I politely grinned, gesturing to the carriage with Singer. "Lord Ansel requested I take his carriage to the House of Sterling, as he'll be inside taking coffee with the king for some time."

"Lord Ansel is leaving himself without transport?"

"Yes. Is that not something you'd do for your betrothed?"

He shifted awkwardly, but opened the door for me. "I suppose."

The ride to the House of Sterling was swift, and I relished the whole way that Ansel would have to walk.

Once at the stone fortress, I didn't bother going to the terrace. Lady Jocelynn wouldn't be there for hours. Instead, I threaded through the halls and out the side door, sneaking off to the barracks down the street.

Several Blademen were already up for the day, walking

around outside their quarters, carrying weapons and lugging out trash. I approached a larger blond man with bags under his eyes.

"Where's Sir Riven?"

He eyed me cautiously, then nodded his head back. "Over by the stables."

Riven stood next to Kostini in the stall, brushing his coat. His eyes softened at the sight of me, concern peeking through.

"You're up early."

I crossed my arms. "Lord Ansel was in my living room."

"Ah."

I approached Kostini, petting his mane. "Can we go somewhere? Just for a few hours? I don't want to worry about war and expectations, just for a little while."

"If that's what you want," Riven said softly.

"I need to be back by lunch," I added, handing off Singer briefly as I mounted. Missing midday tea with Lady Jocelynn might warrant a grudge she'd never let go of.

Riven held back a smile before hopping up behind me. His tan hands reached for the reins in my lap, his mouth brushing my ear. "Hold on."

Kostini bolted.

Through the capital's streets, the brotherhood's presence was much more noticeable than before Prince Payn's infiltration. I kept my head low, not wanting to catch any attention, especially not that of someone who might report back to Lord Ansel's father. Whether I liked Lord Ansel or not, the betrothal was important.

After expressing my concerns to Riven, he cut right, ensuring we'd take a more discreet route. I didn't care where we were going. Anywhere I wouldn't be reminded of my responsibilities to wed and breed would be fine by me.

Riding along the outskirts of the waking city, we veered down a rocky path, where thick, grassy patches led to the sea. We were so far from the port, I had to squint to make out the ships in Bastard's Bay. The coast was just ahead. Blue, green, and grey, simmering waves rolled onto the sandy shore in a song of endless repetition.

I squinted. Further down the beach, a boulder rested in the sand, carving its way out into the sea. It blocked the view of the shores beyond, as if protecting the land itself.

Kostini came to a stop where the grass turned into shell-scattered sand. Riven had chosen a perfect location, secluded and serene. The sun had just barely entered the sky, reflecting shades of pink and yellow on the water.

There was nothing even close to this beautiful in the Waywards.

A bitter ache dwelled in my chest thinking of the years wasted while beauty like this waited on the outside. There were still people stuck inside those walls.

It wouldn't be that way forever. I was certain of it. We'd start with the Southern Waywards, and eventually, we'd get everyone out. I had to believe in us, because the moment I started doubting, destiny might follow suit.

Riven planted his feet on the ground first, then offered me a hand. I gladly took it, letting him guide me down. I unlaced my boots, leaving them on the wispy grass before embracing the cool sand between my toes. It was freeing—standing on the beach in a flowing nightgown.

Riven did not appear free at all. He'd dressed himself for a full day of training.

"Oh, don't tell me you're keeping your boots on," I complained.

He sighed. "Fuck it."

He removed them along with his black uniform and dropped his weapons to the ground.

I turned away in an attempt to be polite, hiding my flushed cheeks.

His muscular build was on full display, save for his grey shorts. I wanted *so badly* to know what the tattoo said on the bottom of his abdomen, but couldn't bring myself to look long enough to find out.

Instead, I walked towards the water, Riven following. The thin material of my dress blew against my legs in the wind, but I didn't care.

I watched curiously as cold water ran over my feet for all but a moment before the wave returned to the ocean.

Riven approached, and we stood quietly while another calm wave crashed and simmered out, water running past our ankles.

His hand brushed against mine. An accident, but powerful enough to ignite a flame from the ashes inside of me. I didn't pull away, and despite his brief hesitation, he laced our fingers together.

"There's a cove in there," he said, pointing to the boulder in the distance.

Truthfully, I would go anywhere with him. If he wanted to show me the inside of a huge rock, I'd do it.

I nodded, and he guided us down the beach, walking hand in hand.

As we approached the boulder, Riven assessed it silently, as if he might change his mind.

I frowned. "What's wrong?"

He scanned our surroundings, considering his options. "It requires a short swim to get inside the cove. I don't want you having to get your dress wet."

"It will dry. I'll be fine."

Releasing his hand, I walked straight into the ocean. He didn't argue, but hurried ahead protectively, guiding us around the rock. Following its edge, the water came up to my chest. The ocean was cold, but not unbearable. I'd had plenty of baths that were worse. It wasn't until we were on the far side where the boulder's cave opened up that I needed to truly swim.

Following Riven's lead, we entered, passing around a corner, where it became an enclosed cove. Light poured in from above, illuminating the space. Stone platforms surrounded the edges of the water, flat rocks wide enough to walk on.

Riven climbed out first, then helped me.

My nightgown clung to me, but it was worth it. It felt as if I'd entered a secret room, where mermaids would gossip and brush each other's hair. The water was clearer—more blue, and without waves, completely calm.

"Look," Riven said, pointing up.

Along the round opening in the ceiling, thousands of violet and blue crystals were embedded in the stone. I sighed in awe.

"How did you find this place?"

Riven sat with his back against the rock wall, while I kept on the edge, my feet dangling in the water.

He shuffled uncomfortably. "My mother showed it to me when I was a child. It was my reward for learning to swim."

He'd never talked about his family before. I'd figured he had one somewhere, just never thought to ask about them. "Your mom sounds nice."

His head hung low. "She was."

My lips pressed together.

"What happened to her?"

"Um," he said, voice wavering, "I don't want you to think of me differently."

"I won't."

Our eyes met. He wanted to confide in me, but something was stopping him. I'd never given up on him before, and I wouldn't now.

"I promise, Riven."

He was silent for a while, rubbing a hand over his mouth, before he exhaled in surrender.

"She got sick, but not a plague or cold. It was her mind," he said, tapping the side of his head. "She started saying the most unusual things, sometimes screaming for no apparent reason. She needed to be watched, because she couldn't be trusted by herself anymore. My father, he—"

His jaw flexed, eyes darkening.

I sat patiently. There was no need to push him. I was there to listen, nothing more.

He rolled his shoulders back and cleared his throat. "My father waited until I was out processing goat meat, because he knew I'd be busy for hours. My mother loved goat stew, and I wanted to do what I could for her. When I came home, she... she wasn't there. I found my father burying her out back."

My face fell. "Did she hurt herself?"

Riven's knuckles went white, the words erupting from him.

"No. My father slit her throat. Said he couldn't handle being married to a mad woman."

What a disgusting piece of shit. I'd heard similar stories in the Waywards, of families turning on each other. If one got the winter sickness, they'd go ahead and kill them, hoping to contain it and not waste food on someone bound to die. Riven though, he grew up *here*. It just went to show there were terrible people all over the world.

"I hope you never spoke to him again."

Riven frowned. "I killed him, Elora."

My blood turned cold, not because I judged Riven, but because of the weight his decision clearly had on him.

"One might say that would have been the noble thing to do, for your mother."

He looked so defeated and ashamed—his dimple entirely absent and brows knitting together. "There was nothing noble about it. I murdered him with my bare hands, like an animal."

While unfortunate, it was nothing I hadn't already been hardened to. Far worse happened in the Waywards all the time. Hell, I'd killed a man with my crotch, and would do it again in a heartbeat.

Pulling myself up, I scooted closer to him, snuggling my head onto his shoulder and wrapping my arms around his bicep.

"He deserved it," I said, smiling. I was proud of Riven for sending him to an early grave.

Riven tilted my chin up with a finger. When he met my eyes, all I felt was warmth and security.

"I stand by you, no matter what," I assured him.

He brought his lips to mine. Chills erupted the moment we

made contact, and he held the back of my neck, kissing me deeper.

I pulled him closer, throwing our weight off balance. He pushed against me, lowering my back to the ground. His mouth trailed to my neck as he hovered above me, in between my legs —his hand traveled up my thigh. With my head against the flat stone, I gazed upward.

There was only him, the crystal cove, and soft light.

"I can take you back," he murmured in my ear.

"Not yet," I said quietly.

A warm kiss met my collarbone as his hand braced on my rib cage. "Tell me what you want."

Wasn't it obvious?

"Everything."

I'd be a married woman soon enough, but at this moment, I was just a girl falling for Riven without a way to stop it. I'd tried to stop it. For Luna's sake, I'd avoided looking his way for years, even when tempted. Even lately, I'd tried convincing myself I was better off sticking to duty and nothing more.

But it was impossible to push him away. There was *nothing* I could tell myself to stop the torrent of feelings.

My body begged for him somehow even louder than my heart did, my pulse racing as his hand navigated through the flowing slits of my dress, finding my center.

"Is this okay?" he asked, his voice unsteady.

As soon as I nodded, he slipped a finger inside me.

"I want to hear you," he growled. A soft moan escaped my lips, and he grinned.

As he teased me, I tugged at his shorts, making my wants, my needs, known. *More.*

He'd wanted to be honorable, but we were far past that.

As he slowly removed his shorts, I finally had a full view of not only the thick muscles trailing down his abdomen, but also his tattoo. There, displayed above his pelvis, read:

Show Time.

He leaned down, kissing me softly before entering me.

I'd had sex before, plenty of times, but I'd never felt my entire body ignite the way it did when Riven moved inside of me, maintaining eye contact, lips parted and pupils dilating.

Marriage be damned, there would be no separating Riven from me.

I'd fight for it, hide it, protect it in any way I could. The gossips could judge it. Ansel could hate it. I didn't care.

From the moment Riven's body connected with mine, I was done for, and he was my unraveling.

Chapter 43

Puddles

"The heir to Whimcastor Hold is soon to wed the Princess of Castivian. A daunting match they will be."

— *The Castivian Chronicle*

As promised, the wedding had been arranged swiftly.

Three days had gone by in a blur before I was standing emotionless in a plain, long-sleeved white gown. A silver veil had been placed on my head at some point, as well as silver flats on my feet. I hadn't said a word since sunrise, not that most people bothered saying much to me outside of instruction.

Aside from Avan. He had already so graciously informed me that Riven had been in his cups since sunrise.

I wished I was vowing myself to him today instead, but we'd both known that was not in the cards. But Riven had no need to fear losing me. I wouldn't let that happen.

Ansel's intentions were apparent. He was going to fuck who he wanted to fuck, as he'd already stooped so low as to bed Delaina. I would take no questions or judgment from him.

Ansel and I stood between two pillars on the stone floor of the House of Sterling. An evening breeze blew in through the open windows, a welcome moment of air between us.

His wedding suit was his family's notorious light blue and grey. His father was present alongside other prominent members of Whimcastor Hold, while Xavian and our council stood behind me.

While most royals usually wed in temples, Xavian had made an example out of my ceremony. There would be no more worshiping the Fates by force. He'd declared the people of Castivian free to follow their own religions and practices, and could gather in their temples and churches. As long as they paid their taxes, he couldn't care less.

Xavian would no longer involve the Crown in religion. It was a message to Drakington.

"I refuse to worship any God who stands idle as atrocities are committed against children and the innocent," he'd declared. I wasn't sure if he was talking about Clayvarie or myself as a child, or both. Either way, he made a compelling argument.

Arthur Pos had put up a fuss, per usual.

"The people will call you heretics!"

"Let them," I'd replied, defending my brother. It made no difference to my sex life, sleeping arrangements, or dinner plans if the Crown were attached to the Gods. Plenty of people prayed in the Waywards, yet they were still caged. I stood by Xavian's decision.

Time crawled as Lord Draven recited our titles and read off our traditional vows, officiating the match. Ansel avoided meeting my gaze, his attention drifting to the darkening sky outside the open window. His father, on the other hand, smiled proudly at his son. Satisfied with their family's role in shaping this fledgling kingdom.

For a moment, I felt sympathetic for Ansel. This wasn't something he'd wanted either. Luckily for him, I would require very little, if anything, from our marriage.

"Do you, Lord Ansel Whimcastor of Dreamsoul, vow to bind yourself to Princess Elorengail Steele of Blackheart?"

They'd left my mother and father's last names out, only claiming my Castivian bastard title. Ansel's shoulders tensed, but that was the only sign of his hesitation.

"I do," he said, quiet and sharp.

A sire approached with a silver tasselled pillow, holding on it two rings.

Lord Draven eyed me. "Do you, Princess Elorengail Steele of Blackheart, accept this ring, binding yourself to Lord Ansel Whimcastor?"

The ring was a thin silver band with an embedded light blue stone. It glinted in the soft torchlight.

"I do," I said faintly.

Lord Draven exhaled, as if a weight had lifted off his shoulders.

With his jaw tight, Ansel picked up the dainty ring. His hand was twice the size of mine. He held me gently, similarly to the way he had all those months ago in the Waywards, when he'd checked my palms for a leak.

I swallowed nervously as he slid the ring onto my finger, tension running through me like lightning.

I did the same for him, quickly placing the silver band on his finger.

Lord Draven cleared his throat. "By the privilege vested in me by King Xavian Steele, I pronounce you Prince Ansel and Princess Elorengail Whimcastor, husband and wife. You may seal your bond with a kiss."

With my hands clasped together at my navel, I barely lifted my gaze to meet Ansel's. His sharp eyes were resolved to see the task through.

He glanced away briefly before sliding his hand around my waist, tipping me back and pulling me into a kiss. He smelled like the air just before a storm.

He pulled away, and I looked down at my feet as the entire hall cheered for our matrimony.

An extravagant dinner commenced at Lady Jocelynn and Lord Draven's home, just for our council and the Whimcastor family. Ansel and I sat next to each other in silence at the head of the long, black table while a quartet played in the corner of the ballroom-sized dining room.

Lady Jocelynn gossiped with Ansel's mother, a tiny, dark-haired woman named Kyomi, about the happenings of Whimcastor Hold, while Xavian and Avan played a relentless drinking game.

Arthur Pos was pleasant for once, happy I'd gone through with the wedding. He and Lord Draven sat a few seats down, going over supply plans for my trip to Drakington. While they both thought it was a terrible idea, they at least hoped I'd become with child during the time spent with my new husband.

I highly doubted I'd be taking part in any marital activities in the Waywards, unless it was with Riven.

Ansel's father, Lord Eiren, walked by as others enjoyed their wine and roasted chicken, and placed his hand on Ansel's shoulder.

"Don't forget the consummation ceremony after dinner. Eat light."

Xavian interrupted from his seat. "I don't think an audience is necessary."

I blinked. If I tried to escape the ceremony, my future children's paternity could be questioned. My entire marriage's legitimacy could be thrown out, or worse, the Whimcastor's could pull out of their end of the deal. It would be too easy for them to claim our marriage was never legitimate.

"Let them watch," I said with a sparkling smile. I mustered up every bit of charisma I could as I grabbed my glass and took a healthy sip of wine. "My... handmaidens, and Lady Jocelynn of course, have prepared me for the ceremony," I lied.

Jocelynn rolled her eyes as Lord Eiren smiled in approval of the "virgin" princess his son had wed. Ansel shook his head, grabbing his fork and taking a bite of roast. Xavian was plainly disgusted, waving us off and returning to his game.

Once Lord Eiren returned to his seat at the other end of the table, and as the festivities continued on, I turned to Ansel.

"I have very low expectations for tonight. All you need to do is—"

"I'm a grown man," Ansel said harshly. "I know what to do."

I held my hands up in defense.

He laughed to himself.

"What?" I asked.

"You do know an orgasm is caused by electricity sent to your brain, right?"

Barely able to keep my jaw off the floor, my face went hot. "Interesting."

I wished he hadn't told me that. In fact, I hated my rising curiosity.

I spent the rest of the evening in silence, not daring to taunt Ansel again. Xavian seemed to be genuinely enjoying himself, celebrating and drinking with his friends, while Lady Jocelynn was completely in her element, effortlessly hosting the event. The shadows of banter, raised glasses, and boisterous laughter danced along the gothic wallpaper in the chandelier-lit space. Was this how things were before the kingdoms had begun to fall apart?

Since the Wrenavia's were hosting the Whimcastor's in their small castle, the consummation was expected to happen upstairs, in the room made for Ansel.

I had no plans of sleeping in the manor. After the deed was done, I'd go find Riven, hopefully not drunkenly passed out.

As dinner came to an end, Lady Jocelynn took me in her arm, guiding me through her home.

"My consummation was also witnessed," she said. "I understand you may feel modest or—"

I shook my head. "I'm fine."

I'd been forced to be naked in front of several Drakers during my check-in process for the Waywards. I'd stood nude in front of an entire village with poison running down my legs.

Countless men had seen me bare in my life. I didn't give a shit about councilmen watching me. In fact, I wanted them to see, to *know* I endured a loveless fuck for the sake of Castivian. No one would ever be able to question me, my loyalty, nor my future children.

Prepping me in the large bedroom first, Lady Jocelynn gave me a soft white nightgown with a thin purple bow on the front. It was meant to keep my modesty for the viewing.

I laughed. All of this was so ridiculous. Maybe it was my way of coping, but I couldn't be nervous. It was Ansel for Fate's sake. *He* should be nervous. I couldn't wait to lay there, expressionless, while he tried to prove his manhood by claiming a wife.

I periodically giggled while Lady Jocelynn gave me concerned glances. Seated on the bed, I leaned against large pillows with dark grey cases. The entire room had a similar color scheme, dull and dark. The windows were ceiling high, the open curtains revealing the moon clouded over the ocean in the distance. There was no point in closing them. I'd have an audience either way, and I doubted the sea cared much for intimacy.

There was a knock at the door.

"You don't have to do this," Lady Jocelynn whispered, keeping the door locked. "We can say the alcohol has made you sick. You can consummate another night, in private."

She, a noblewoman who had endured this same scenario, was concerned about me. I was bred into this world tough as any shield, and raised tougher.

"This is my duty," I declared adamantly, any trace of amusement gone. "And I am perfectly capable of enduring it."

Lady Jocelynn straightened her posture, composing herself. "Good. We'll talk tomorrow."

With that, she unlocked the door.

Within a moment, ten men stood at the far side of the room as Ansel approached the bed, unamused. Arthur Pos, Lord Eiren, and his men all waited attentively, while Avan was the only one who'd brought a drink. He sipped at it through a child-sized straw.

"The consummation may begin," Lord Draven announced.

I'd sat on top of the blanket, but now I wished I'd gone beneath it. As I assessed the situation, my legs rapidly slid out from under me, the back of my head dragging down along the mattress.

My eyes widened. Ansel wasn't getting in the bed; he was pulling me to the edge.

"Is the center not suitable for you?" I ground out quietly.

He tilted his head to the side as he unbuttoned his pants. "I'd hate for the sheets to need changing this late in the evening."

The familiar warmth of a new cloud blanket surrounded me, radiating into my neck and shoulders—rolling in a massaging motion.

My hands couldn't move. The blanket held them down. Ansel placed his own hands on my knees, spreading them apart.

His eyes flared with surprise. I hadn't bothered wearing anything under the nightgown. Fully on display, my pulse quickened as he brought his thumb directly to my clit. With his opposite hand, he held himself, the tip of him just barely brushing my entrance.

"What are you—"

The cloud blanket sent a quick electric shock of cold air over my skin. He pressed his thumb down, lightning striking through my body the precise moment he thrust inside.

I cursed as an ocean erupted from me, splashing Ansel's white shirt with a loud smack.

The audience gasped. Avan fucking *clapped*.

Evidence of my orgasm puddled around us, dripping onto the floor.

With unsteady breaths, I tried to speak, but lightning rippled through me again, in sync with him, jolting every part of me with fiery euphoria. I couldn't think straight—couldn't move my arms. There was nothing except for intense release, over and over and over again. Thrust, by thrust, by thrust.

By the time Ansel finished, rumbling a low moan, the mattress beneath me was drenched, and the floor was likely the same. As Ansel caught his breath, the cloud blanket evaporated. He firmly tugged my dress back over my wobbly legs.

Zipping his pants back up, he glanced at his shirt and then at me, before slowly shaking his head. "I need to change."

The wide-eyed audience said nothing as Ansel stormed out of the room, leaving the door wide open.

I glared at the councilmen, nostrils flaring.

Avan winced. "Okay, okay, the ceremony is over. Shoo now," he said, waving people out with his drink still in hand.

Once everyone else had exited, he approached where I still lay on the edge of the bed and peered at the floor.

"Well," he began, examining the puddle. "Let's not tell Sir Riven about this."

My face burned, and I nodded, too exasperated for words.

Avan left, but Jocelynn walked in.

"Are you alright?" she asked, hurrying to my side.

"Yep."

She let out a startled breath, taking a step back and lifting the skirt of her dress protectively. "Oh my word, let me send someone in with a mop."

I covered my face with my hands, shaking my head.

———

Jocelynn allowed me to exit the premises discreetly from the kitchen, sparing me a word or even eye contact after the puddle incident. I stepped outside into a light rain, thunderous vibrations still reeling through my body. Crossing my arms, I jogged back home.

There were no lights in the windows, but there was an overly conscientious Blademan posted by the entrance.

Riven stood there in the rain, bags under his eyes and hair sopping wet, waiting for me.

I'd never seen him look so broken.

While I had no words of comfort to offer, I did have my presence. I approached him, tilting my head up.

"Escort me to my room, Sir Riven."

He nodded somberly, but led me up the stairs all the same. We both tossed our wet clothes to the floor, and shamelessly entangled ourselves in bed, skin to skin. Nose to nose.

I fell asleep, but found no peace.

Instead, Xavian delighted in sending me a fond memory. Examples of him moving out of the way when an arrow was nearing him, over and over again.

I woke up frustrated and exhausted, even after my night full of training. I should've sent him a memory back, perhaps the one where I'd saved Beck's life in the midwinter games. I'd been the one to stop a hurling object from killing him. But no, I had no control over what Xavian could see. Only *he* had the privilege of learning how to control it.

As my brother, I hoped for both of our sakes he hadn't been subject to watching anything too disturbing. Shaking my head, I gave my best effort to erase that horrifying thought.

Light shone through the windows in my quiet room. Riven was gone for the day. He'd probably left to train the new recruits hours ago.

I was sore in a way I had never been before, and tired in a way I was all too used to.

I dressed for training, needing it now more than ever if I was going back to Drakington.

The entire house was empty. I treated myself to a piece of buttered toast and a solitary cup of spiced tea before heading out. The herbs soothed the aching silence in my head. It was as if my own brain had shut me out. I couldn't bring myself to care about most things, but I did care about proving myself to be just as noble and worthy as my brother by the time I returned from Drakington.

There was a shred of doubt, and even a little fear, that I wouldn't make it back at all. I slammed that thought away and tossed my plate in the sink. After I'd washed and put it away, I opened the front door.

My husband was standing there with his hands in his pockets.

"No," I snapped, walking right past him.

"No?"

"No, I don't want to talk to you," I clarified, reaching the stone pavement.

"Why?"

"Because I have nothing to say to you." He was no more than a stranger to me, and no less than a liar.

Surely he'd mock me about my body's response, or force me to stay put with his stupid clouds. He caught up, stopping in front of me.

"We have to trust each other. You can have your freedom and your preferred company. I don't care to control you, Blackheart."

I wasn't sure *what* he cared about.

"I will never trust you, *Witchlord.*"

He rolled his eyes back in annoyance. "Would you have preferred I pretend to be a Draker? Like your lover?"

I stepped back. "No. I would've preferred something else."

"What do you mean?

"I meant what I just said."

He rolled his eyes again, even more dramatically. "Yeah, I get that, but could you please expound?"

I leaned forward. "Expound? Is that even a fucking word?"

He shrugged. "Expand upon what you meant by 'something else'."

I threw my arms up in the air. "I don't know, but having my first impression of my betrothed as a Witchlord was an insane decision."

He scoffed. "Bold of you to think I wasn't scoping out my options. You're lucky the queen is mad, or I might've taken her up on her proposal. Destiny, of course, gives me the choice between a Blackheart with no sense of self-preservation and affections for a Blademan, or an ill-minded widow who plans mass murders for self-care. Oh, and of course, the *slightly* less insane of the two of you doesn't even appreciate my choice."

"You are rude."

"Rich, coming from you."

"What is your problem with me?" I hadn't done anything to him. I'd simply minded my own and refused his presence unless otherwise necessary.

He formed a new blue orb between his hands, his Nature rolling and illuminating. He held it up, keeping his eyes on me. "I want to be on the same page, but you make it irritatingly difficult."

I was tired of men telling me what page to be on. I had no intention of letting him boss me around. His only saving grace was that we were soon be stuck on a ship together. It would be easier to just go ahead and get both of our expectations out of the way.

"Go on with what you want to say."

He stepped closer, his dark hair towering over me. My body responded to the familiarity, reminiscing of the night before. I tried to find something ugly about him, a distraction, but it was more challenging than expected.

"I meant what I said before. I want us to trust each other, or at least try. I promise to protect you when I can, but you cannot go running off in the night without telling me. It's not safe. I don't care if you keep your habits and... company. After this war is over, we can have separate residences, if that's what you wish."

It sounded too simple.

"What about when we have children? Where will they live?"

He sighed. "Let's focus on surviving first."

"Fine. This is a truce then?"

He held out his hand in answer. I let out a huff that could rival Kostini's as I grasped his hand, firmly shaking it. He grinned, sending a trickle of lightning all the way to my tailbone.

"Deal."

———

After only two short days spent training with the children, tangled in the sheets with Riven, and attending lunch meetings, I was aboard a ship, taking in the capital of Eiden as we sailed away.

Beck, Amzee, and Riven were beside me. Ansel was somewhere on the ship, but hadn't felt sentimental about watching Castivian fade away in the distance. I watched Xavian standing at the port, until his body became a blur.

"I'm going to miss Zephy," Amzee sighed, elbow on the edge of the ship.

With our mission being as discreet as possible, we couldn't risk bringing a bladebreather. I'd thought maybe she'd decide against going, but she'd been eager for the opportunity. Zephy would be fine, especially with the food Xavian promised to keep sending to Moonhill.

Lady Jocelynn hadn't opted to watch us depart, but she had woken up at dawn to have tea with me. My parting gift to her was a friend suggestion. I'd described Trista and where I'd last seen her. With a little cleaning up, Trista would be the perfect person to accompany Lady Jocelynn. I'd half-expected her to shoot down the idea, but instead, she wrote the information down and wished me a safe trip.

With me, I had friends and a lover beyond anything I'd ever expected, but I still found my eyes stinging as my brother disappeared from view.

I should have spent more time with him. I wanted to know him better, and give us the chance to be siblings beyond just survival. If I returned home in one piece, I'd make more time for him. I'd loosen the grudge that was not his burden to bear.

I smiled, just barely, as the capital shrank into the distance.

"What are you smiling at?" Beck sassed, knocking me with his elbow.

I grinned a little more, eyes still burning with tears I desperately tried to hold back. "I just feel so lucky that I have a family to come back home to."

Amzee leaned against my side, locking her arm with mine. "The future is ours to claim, and our home is ours to protect."

Our home. For the first time, I had something to miss. More so, I had something to live for.

"We *are* coming home after this," Beck said confidently.

I nodded with certainty. Yes, we would.

PART 4

CHAPTER 44

NOSTALGIC, YET HORRIFYING

"No man, nor giant, could hope to climb the obsidian walls."

— *A MODERN HISTORY OF THE REALM, BY*
JON HARVINGTON

THE PASSAGE ACROSS THE SEA OF BLADES WENT BY faster and smoother this time around. I wasn't as sick, and the weather was far more pleasant.

I spent my nights reading Castivian histories in my room or playing drinking games with Beck, Amzee, and occasionally, Riven.

Ansel never indulged in such activities, at least not with us. He did, however, require my presence during the day.

Amzee, Beck, and I stood at the rear of the ship while Ansel carried on with instruction. Every morning for weeks, our small group trained. We never bothered with blades, only honing our Natures. Ansel insisted if I were to be getting off this ship with them, I should at least be able to wield my Nature within reason without becoming sick.

We each practiced forming orbs between our hands, strengthening them until they reached the size of a dinner plate, then shooting them out to sea.

As we faced the ocean, Ansel stood behind us, reminding me to lift my elbows or complaining about Amzee's improper form, as her orbs often took on the shape of a heart. Ansel insisted that forming them into anything but a sphere was a waste of time and energy on the battlefield, and she needed to break the habit. Once she'd started aiming for circles, they became tube-shaped.

When I pointed out the drooping length of her orb, she was taken aback.

"Well, Elora, yours are too small. Try making them this large and see if they don't misshape. The weight is heinous, truly."

She was right. Mine were the smallest out of the three. Any larger than my thumb and they became ovalish.

Amzee threw another red flaming droop out into the ocean as I tossed my petite oval of poison. Meanwhile, Beck hurled a sphere of smoke.

"Oh, that splash was fantastic!" Amzee mused.

"I thought so myself," Beck bragged.

My orbs needed work, but my stamina was increasing. It took far longer for the sickness to hit, and even longer for me to actually vomit. Ansel tested the limits often, which, as unpleasant as it was, was helpful.

I'd asked to use Singer for the exercises, but Ansel refused. "What if you misplace it?" he'd lectured. "Or if it's taken? Don't cheat yourself."

I had no choice but to accept he was right.

While the training wasn't enjoyable beyond a few small victories, it became easier with each passing day. It was invigorating to know I had some means of protection. I never wanted to find myself at a Sapphire's feet again, vomiting and helpless.

Outside of training, the most challenging feat was attempting to distance myself from Riven. There were too many lingering eyes on the ship to risk rumors that my marriage was illegitimate. Aside from the occasional glance, it was best I avoided him unless in a group setting. He was busy with planning anyway. For what? I didn't know.

Even knowing it was best to stay away, I often found myself sneaking into his room when all but the night shift sailors were asleep. Every time, without fail, Riven would be out of bed in an instant, locking the door behind me.

One night, he pressed me against the door as he kissed me, before carrying me to the bed. On another occasion, the waves were so rowdy that he just tossed me onto the mattress before lifting the back of my shirt and biting his way down from my neck.

Every time he fell asleep holding me, as if I were his to keep.

He always woke first, dressing and disappearing for the day without a sound. We had very few actual conversations, which was probably best for both of us.

Amzee cleared her throat. Everyone was staring at the blob between my hands, waiting for me to toss it.

"This is a bad one," I admitted, frowning at the wobbly, violet orb. I threw it and it sizzled into the water.

Ansel had his hands in his dark cloak pockets, glancing around.

"We will make landfall early tomorrow. Meet me in the planning room after dinner. Make sure your things are gathered."

Amzee lit up at the news, while Beck gave a respective nod. I followed suit, trying to remain confident as the reality hit.

We'd be back on Drakington soil in less than a day. A kingdom where I did not have any rights. More so, I was going back into the cage. Voluntarily.

I swallowed. There was a very real possibility of not making it back out.

A gentle zap hit my shoulder, bringing me back to the moment. I snapped my head to Ansel, who had already dismissed the others.

He came closer. Thin, loose strands of his hair billowed in the wind.

"Worst case, we fail," he said sternly. "Best case, we bring the entire Southern Waywards population back to Castivian."

I rested my forearms on the edge, admiring the horizon. "Much worse could happen."

His elbows next to mine, he leaned his tall frame down until our faces were level. "You will make it back home."

Fear knotted in my stomach. "How could you know that?" I asked quietly.

He stared for a moment, his eyes somehow becoming icier. "If you weren't to make it back, I would have to be dead. And I have no plans of dying in the Waywards."

He gave me one last piercing glance before walking off without another word.

Chills ran through me as I once again thought of the worst.

No one ever planned to die in the Waywards, yet they did.

———

My appetite was entirely shot. I sat at a long table with Amzee and Beck, who were in the middle of a drinking game. They both scarfed down rolls and ale, formulating the most diabolical belches I'd ever encountered. Amzee had the giggles so bad at one point, I thought she might've had a hard time breathing.

They were truly celebrating our impending arrival, while anxiety had completely ruined me.

I'd asked to be here. I wanted to bring the Witchlords and Drakers crumbling down, and to bring the people of the Southern Waywards back to Castivian. Why was I overcome with this terrifying feeling?

I sat in silence with my arms crossed and feet propped up on a dining chair while Amzee and Beck continued their festivities. Riven showed up after a few minutes, and then finally, Ansel.

The lantern-lit room was just barely big enough for the table, with only a few decorations, including a map on the wall.

Riven sat next to the chair I'd propped my feet on. Ansel directly across from me. Riven kept his eyes on Ansel, as if to deter him from glancing my way.

"The marked map," Ansel requested, holding a hand out.

Riven silently passed it over.

Ansel unrolled it, placing Amzee's glass on one corner and a few coins on the other.

He leaned over the table to point to the Southern Waywards. "We need to get here, then, we will port..." He slid his finger across—"here."

"Hm. Not too far, huh?" Beck said, nodding in approval.

Ansel shrugged. "Only a day's distance, maybe less. The

ships traveling behind us will be porting right outside of the Southern Waywards. If we fail, not only will the people of the Southern Waywards suffer, but the fleet will be at risk."

Lord Avan's father's fleet. We needed those ships for the coming war, not just this.

I turned to Ansel. "Then what's the plan?"

"Once we make land, Sir Riven will meet with his contacts and enter the Southern Waywards posing as a Draker. He should go unnoticed while wearing his mask."

Beck nodded as he listened. Amzee scanned the map while Riven flipped an unlit smoke between his fingers, surely awaiting the moment we could leave the tight, windowless room.

Ansel continued, "I will be in Witchlord attire, as I still have my pin. We will arrive at the gates of the Southern Waywards with the three of you bound as any Dark Natured captives would be. I will claim to be a Witchlord from the Northern Waywards, meant to be on leave for the spring traveling down south, when I found the three of you criminals. Of course, I'll need to include that my travel plans have been ruined, and I'm not expected back at the Northern Waywards until Summer. Thus, I'll be seeking residence for two weeks before returning north."

I lifted my brows, impressed.

"Wow, you know how to come up with a lie," Amzee beamed.

That he did.

"It's only a good lie if they buy it," Beck pointed out.

"Then I suggest you three prepare to be believable prisoners."

He wrapped up the meeting, instructing us to be ready before sunrise and to pack light. We wouldn't be able to bring anything into the Waywards.

I chose not to spend the final night on the ship with Riven. He needed rest. Instead, I tossed and turned in my own bed. It was as if the closer we came to returning to those obsidian walls, the more my mind and body rejected it.

Just as Ansel promised, we made landfall before sunrise. All day we travelled through the spring woods. Every so often, Amzee would ask Beck and I about what it was like in the Waywards. She could probably tell it didn't help either of us to talk about it, so eventually, we all got used to walking without conversation.

Riven had set off on his own path hours prior. We could only hope to find him within the Waywards.

The closer we got, the worse my anxiety became. At nightfall, we stopped only for a few hours to sleep in the woods. We had nothing to use for comfort, and didn't bother risking a fire. I attempted to sleep with my head pillowed on my arm, but failed miserably and volunteered to keep watch instead.

After the brief rest, we continued on until the ever dreadful walls peeked through the woodline.

"Ah, Amzee, love. Remember when you asked how tall the walls are?" Beck asked.

"Yep."

"That tall," he said, pointing ahead.

For the first time, Amzee looked nervous, her face losing its usual glow. I tried giving her a reassuring glance, but we both knew there were good reasons to be afraid.

Ansel however, spared no time for fear. Instead, he pulled rope out of his satchel and winked at me. "Ready, prisoners?"

He was shockingly good at tying knots, having the three of us bound within minutes. The sky darkened, and the last opportunity to return to the ship had passed. We were nearing the gate, and had surely already been noticed by Drakers.

I kept my head low as we arrived, my palms shaking.

A Draker stood guard, face hidden by his mask and hood.

"You're early, Lord Zaren. We weren't expecting you for a few more weeks," he said, sounding too jolly for the Waywards. "You've brought prisoners with you as well?"

I swallowed. We hadn't planned for Ansel to impersonate another Witchlord.

Ansel, legitimately annoyed and exhausted, rolled his eyes. "I've had a long day. Get these animals processed and get me the keys to my house."

The enthusiastically foolish Draker moved promptly to open the gate. "Of course, of course, Lord Zaren. Welcome home."

I held back a smile as the gates dragged open. Ansel was unsurprisingly good at improvising.

He walked freely through, while Amzee, Beck, and I were herded to a crumbling grey building off to the side.

Processing had been degrading the first time I'd done it, and the second time was no different. They stripped us bare, checking for weapons and contraband on or inside of us. I kept my head forward, face resting naturally in a glare.

The Drakers examined Amzee and me beyond necessity.

As one of their gloved hands grabbed the curve of my hip, my nostrils flared.

"Angry one, isn't she?"

Another laughed, turning his attention to Amzee. "Hey, Flamecastor. You're a big one. Soft belly, lumpy hips. You'd make a decent wage at the brothel down the street. I'll make sure I come visit you."

Amzee didn't cower, nor did her face flush. She smiled, eyeing his crotch and biting her lip. "I wonder if it would... melt off in the heat of the moment."

He drew back a step, disgusted. "Send them out. Enjoy the shithole, *inkweeds*."

They kicked our piles of clothes out the door, not even allowing us to dress in privacy. Amzee cackled as we grabbed them and ran behind the building to get dressed. Beck immediately shadowed us, allowing us some modesty.

"What a bunch of masked freaks," Amzee said.

I nodded in agreement.

Once we were dressed, Beck took the lead on finding Keeper's Street.

It was nostalgic, yet horrifying to walk through the Waywards.

Bars, shops, brothels—all marking which Natures were allowed. Children, frail with dark circles under their eyes, scanning the meandering pavements for things to collect or sell. Dark, gloomy, deteriorating buildings stacked on top of one another lining the overcrowded streets.

An hour went by before we found Keeper's Street. It was like a cheap version of the Silver Circle. The loop of houses with bulbous black and gold roofs was freshly maintained for the Witchlords, and Ansel was inside one of them.

"The one all the way to the right," a familiar voice said. I turned around, grinning at the Draker. It had been some time since Riven had worn the uniform, but I'd recognize his voice anywhere.

I nodded to Beck, and he quickly shadowed all of us, including Riven, as we hurried to Ansel's assigned residence.

The door was unlocked. As we entered, Ansel was sitting in a brown leather chair, smirking. We each picked a spot in the spacious living room, Amzee and I falling onto either side of the couch.

We'd made it. Part one of the plan was complete.

"I do love a full circle moment," Beck mused, propping his feet on the oak coffee table.

"The full circle," Ansel said, "will be when we return home."

Chapter 45

Blood

"The Princess is said to be spending her honeymoon within Whimcastor Hold. The Chronicle extends its congratulations to the newlyweds."

— *The Castivian Chronicle*

Amzee and I each claimed a bedroom upstairs, while the men fell asleep wherever they saw fit. Each space in the house had been claimed for some purpose; even the dining room had transitioned to the planning room.

I melted into my pillow. Of all places, the Waywards was where I finally hit my point of exhaustion.

We all woke early to have our first meeting inside the 'Wards. Once we were sitting around the table, I felt the true weight of this mission, and just how much was on our shoulders. Thousands of lives were at stake, including our own.

As the meeting commenced, it was made clear by Ansel that

we each had a job to do. Riven would be meeting with other Rogue Drakers throughout the day, organizing operations for when the ships arrived. We would also inform any Drakers joining our side that they would receive safe passage and pardons once they reached Castivian. Riven was silent as usual, nodding and dismissing himself from the meeting first, disappearing into the Waywards.

We knew from Riven's contacts that there was a group of Dark Natured already planning an uprising. Amzee's job was to find them and be our contact. She was excited for the task, exuding confidence that she'd be able to do her job and recruit more rebels as well.

"I'm a people person," she bragged.

"That you are," Beck agreed.

He had a task as well, aside from shadowing us in and out of Keeper's Street.

With Beck's natural gift of observation, Ansel trusted him to search for any weak points in the walls or otherwise. He would also report to Amzee any information on meeting spots and other rebels if he were to come across them.

Informed of their tasks, Amzee and Beck left together, shadowing in silence out the front door and into the rowdy streets, leaving me as the sole person sitting across from Ansel in a now too-quiet room.

His dark hair curtained the sides of his face as he surveyed the parchments in front of him.

I crossed my arms. "What am I to do?"

He gathered the documents into an orderly stack and placed them neatly in the center of the table. He went over to the door frame and leaned on it, eyes locked on me.

"This house is vulnerable. It has our plans, and that information is too valuable and dangerous for anyone else to see. Beyond that, I'll be gathering weapons to store here, enough to arm the rebels. We can't risk losing the stash. You'll be staying here. "

"I didn't realize I'd come all this way to sit in a house for two weeks."

He slid his hands in his cloak pockets. "Someone needs to be here."

The glorious story I hoped to have seemed unlikely, and while I wanted to push for a more important task, I'd rather sit in the house than be the whining burden of the trip. What good was it to have a different job only because I'd begged for it?

"Fine."

"Thank you."

My knee jittered up and down, moving silently to the beat of my increasing heart rate.

"What do I do if someone comes here?" I asked quietly. The question came not from fear, but genuine curiosity.

From his pocket, he pulled the small blue orb with my chain still attached, rolling it on the table towards me.

"You handle them, and notify me immediately."

It was the same one Ansel had watched me through the entirety of my travels. It was shocking he felt confident in my abilities to handle an intruder, but even more shocking that he expected me to take his orb back.

"I don't need you spying on me," I said sourly.

He gritted his teeth. "I don't *care* what you do. What I need is for you to use the orb to summon me if someone infiltrates this house."

I took a deep breath, tapping my arm as I considered.

"Elora, you're my wife. If someone tries to harm you, I need to know. How else do you expect to get in contact with me?"

My leg stopped bouncing, fingers stopped tapping. I grabbed the orb awkwardly and clipped it at my waist. "Okay. Can we be done with this conversation?"

He shook his head. "I'll see you this evening, Blackheart."

I rolled my eyes, propping my feet on the table as the front door closed behind him.

The silence marked the beginning of what would surely be the most boring two weeks of my life, while the others organized the destruction of the Southern Waywards from the inside out.

I spent most of the afternoon studying Castivian history, while occasionally scanning the maps of Drakington that Ansel had left on the table.

As the afternoon carried on, I found myself upstairs laying in bed, propped up on my elbows and staring out of a crack in the dark curtains. Behind Keeper's Street was a small training yard. Witchlords and Drakers filled it, all working on different weaponry.

Ansel was with another Witchlord, but neither were using their Light Nature. They wielded swords, wearing only tunics instead of the usual heavy cloaks.

Ansel fought just as I'd expected of someone with the privilege of being trained his entire life. Quick, balanced, intentional—

I winced as he sliced the other Witchlord's forearm, an accident surely. They paused their training, and while I couldn't tell what they were saying, it all seemed friendly. While the other

Witchlord set his sword down, walking away to heal his arm, Ansel carried his own in another direction.

I could barely see what he was doing, but he appeared to be... cleaning his sword?

Squinting was no use. I sighed, closing the curtains and tucking myself under the heavy black covers. The bedroom was not homey like back in Castivian. It felt dim and lonely.

I *was* lonely. I closed my eyes, forcing myself to sleep, even if it were just to pass the time.

"Wake up," a low voice said, gently moving my shoulder.

I snapped upright and out of the bed, fist held back and ready to swing. With my brain still half-asleep, I nearly lost balance in the dark.

"It's just me. Sit down, Blackheart," Ansel said, grabbing me by the waist before I fell.

I smacked his hand away and sat back in bed, pulling the blanket over my lap.

"What time is it?" I yawned.

"Midnight."

I frowned.

Ansel sat on the end of the bed, still wearing his black pants and tunic. His hair was tied back in a neat bun. It had grown much since we met.

He made himself comfortable, paying no mind to my disapproval. He laid six vials of blood out on the bed.

Breath hitching, I leaned forward. "Why do you have these?" That was Sapphire behavior. Singer was within reach, just on the nightstand.

"I need them to dream."

Did I know so little of Dreamsouls and how they use their

Nature? He unscrewed the first one, swirling the small amount of blood within.

"Please tell me you are not about to drink that."

"It's not so bad."

I grimaced. "That's what Sapphires do."

Ansel rolled his eyes. "Yeah, well, they got the idea from us and turned it into something despicable. I can only enter someone else's dreams if I have their blood. I spent all day getting a sample from each of the other Witchlords. I'm going to find out if any of them could be swayed to our side."

I lay back on the pillow. He hadn't been cleaning his sword earlier to be prim. He'd been collecting blood.

"You're telling me you drank Charles the Imp's blood?"

He gave me a vile glare, shaking his head as if I'd reminded him of a foul memory. "To find out if he was lying about you."

"Where's everyone else?"

Ansel downed the first vial, making an unpleasant face. "You can't hear Amzee snoring down the hall? She went to bed a few hours ago. Beck and Riven are still out."

I yawned, adjusting myself on the pillow. "Why are you here telling me all this?"

He'd gathered up the remaining vials, laying them out neatly on the dresser.

"I don't trust anyone else on this side of the sea. It's been a long day. I will need you to wake me if the dreams become too intense, which they shouldn't."

There were moments I didn't even trust myself, yet here he was, trusting me. I felt a pinch of guilt, thinking about the effort it took for him to get all of this blood, and how he was so far from his family and friends.

"Okay."

He finished laying his things on the dresser before pulling his tunic off, thick muscles rippling across his pale skin. I turned away, hiding my face as he got into bed.

I considered asking him to sleep on the floor, but that would be ridiculous. He'd already been inside of me, and furthermore, he was trying to dream for a reason. I didn't want to make it more difficult.

As far as the option of me going to the floor, that was absolutely not happening. I'd spent enough nights without a bed that I knew to always be thankful for one.

A cloud wrapped around me, a cool breeze smoothing down my hair.

"Goodnight, Elora."

"Sweet dreams," I replied, eyes wide open.

I held the blanket to my chest like a lifeline, staring at the wall until Ansel's breathing became heavy. When I was sure he was sleeping, I quietly turned over, watching him.

His angular, almond-shaped eyes were closed so gently—his skin smooth and relaxed like silk as he slept. His thick eyebrows even managed to appear softer as he softly snored.

The muscles of his broad shoulders protruded in his sleep. I took it all in—the powerful man before me appearing so vulnerable.

I tossed onto my back, eyes settling on the blur of the dark ceiling. It wasn't long before Ansel swiftly woke up, shaking his head.

"The first will not be swayed," he said, before downing the second crimson vial.

Sitting up, I braced my hands on the mattress. "Are you going into each of their dreams all in one night?"

"That's the plan," he confirmed, laying his head back down.

"We can't afford for you to burn out," I whispered.

A grin spread across his face, as if he were holding back a laugh.

"What's funny?" I snapped.

He shook his head, eyes peeking open. "It's humorous that you think six dreams would drain me."

I turned away, hiding my blush.

Ansel did exactly what he said he would. He dreamt with all six of the other Witchlords' blood, and felt confident only two could be swayed.

He updated our group in the morning as we dined in the planning room. Amzee and I had made a breakfast of eggs, toast, and jam.

We were in the kitchen when Riven had finally arrived back, bags under his eyes. Amzee had sent him to her room to sleep, and he'd only offered a nod before retiring.

Beck sauntered back into the room after pouring hot water for his tea. "Hmm... So when the time comes, it will be three against four Witchlords?"

"That's if Ansel is able to convince the two to join us," I reminded him.

Amzee popped a piece of bread into her mouth. "I can be very convincing," she offered between bites, thick blonde hair spilling out of a bun on top of her head.

Ansel was entertained, but not bought in. "I will handle the

Witchlords. Each of you have your own tasks. The ships arrive in one week. Every minute counts."

Everyone except for *me* had a real job. I couldn't tell if I was truly watching the house, or if it was watching me. I wouldn't put it past Ansel to claim it's a real job just to ensure my womb stays safe.

I spent the morning cleaning up, thinking about my Castivian history books, identifying the gaps in my head where I needed to reread in the evening.

Around noon, Riven woke, and while I wanted to request he lay me out on the planning table and tend to my princessly needs, I lingered in the bathroom until he was gone. I couldn't be a distraction. Lives depended on us.

The sun set by the time Ansel and Beck returned, shadowing through the front door with sacks of weapons in tow: swords, daggers, and even mallets. My eyes widened as the heavy weight of them hit the floor in front of the fireplace.

Beck was winded, while Ansel flashed a devious smile. "Well, Blackheart, now you'll be guarding the house *and* the weapons."

I met his stare with a smile of my own. The plan was working.

Beck sank into the velvet couch, cracking his neck. "Amzee and I found groups that we'll be able to distribute to the day before the ships arrive."

Everything was coming together. There were people willing to fight within the Waywards, and we could put blades in their hands. I thought back to my days in the tailor house, where two Drakers would guard while *dozens* of us worked.

Two Drakers could not have contained dozens of us.

It was all an illusion, one I had every intention of seeing fade when those gates opened.

To my surprise, Ansel privately pulled me aside. He sat with me for over an hour, going over his entire day and every interaction he'd had with the other Witchlords. One of them was secured, while the other needed more convincing.

I was quiet most of the conversation, taking it all in. He did not treat me like I was less than him, but as his partner. It was such a simple, but serious concept. I wasn't quite able to grasp it.

Five days went by, each smoother than the next.

Amzee grew the rebellion numbers every day.

Beck had created a map, marking points with low security and weak spots in the walls.

Riven conspired among the Rogue Drakers, and while he did not talk much about it, he spent some of the longest hours out in the Waywards.

Ansel secured both of the Witchlords, promising high-paying positions in Whimcastor Hold upon our safe arrival to Castivian.

All while they worked tirelessly, I stayed inside. I studied and copied the map Beck had made. I cleaned, rested, meditated —well, I tried to, at least. Most of the time I lay in bed in silence until I eventually fell asleep.

I also practiced with my Nature, with and without Singer. I only managed as much as I could before burning a hole in the floor, but at least it was something. Staying busy was the only thing that made the time go by.

Then one day, as I was studying with the fireplace lit and stew on the stove, the blue light of Ansel's orb went dark.

I grabbed it, tapping it in a frenzy.

Nothing. Lifeless.

I tapped it again—spoke to it even. "Ansel?"

Nothing.

No one was home yet, and it was well past dark. My heart thundered in my chest. The ships would arrive in less than two days. We had to be ready for them.

A terrible, deep instinct weighed me down as I stared at the dark orb.

Bolting out of the comfort of my chair, I made for the heavy sacks of weapons in the living room. They were my responsibility.

I ran to the kitchen, finding a simple hammer under the sink. I yanked the rug away from the floor in front of the fire, before kneeling down and placing the back of the hammer in between planks of hardwood. It took some grit, but I pulled six planks up.

I would never be able to carry the entire sacks. Instead, one by one, I moved the weapons into the floor. Some were heavier than others, and all I could do was drag them. When I'd unloaded all five sacks, I put the floor back and replaced the rug.

My anxiety picked up, unfathomable scenarios becoming real in my head. I put my boots on, sliding Singer into one. The lifeless orb wouldn't blend in inside the Waywards, so I hid it within the depths of my armoire.

In all black, I exited out the first-story window, becoming one with the night. The last time I'd used a window as a door had been with Riven. My stomach churned like spoiled milk thinking about the possibilities of where he was now.

I made it safely into the winding streets. It was dark, moon-light and the occasional lantern being the only light. Rowdy taverns held the night owls, while many paths remained mostly empty. I peered inside each establishment, searching for my friends or my husband... or Riven.

I had no success.

As the night went on, less and less of the stacked buildings remained lit.

The hair on my neck stood as I resorted to searching down an even darker alleyway. My eyes had adjusted, but it wasn't enough. I crept forward, listening closely for any sign of my group.

Singer hummed in my boot—a warning.

I pulled her out, gripping her with both hands as I swung around. The stone club lit up as my Nature coursed through it, illuminating a crimson spray as Singer smacked into her target.

My attacker's body dropped dead.

He was not the only one behind me. A group of unmasked Drakers stood there, weapons ready.

"You're good at hiding, Princess," one rumbled like thunder.

Panic engulfed me. They knew I was here, and they knew who I was, but there would be no running. I could fight or die.

I chose to fight.

Screeching as my Nature ran through me and into Singer, I wacked a second Draker in the face, death swallowing him before he could move.

I tightened my trembling hands around my club.

"It's clear why you pack of swine hide behind the mask," I taunted.

There were seven Drakers. My Nature was wanting after the first kill. It was ravenous. I took a step towards them, marking my intentions like a bloodstain on a fresh sheet of snow.

"Now, which one of you fucking idiots wants to die next?"

I caught a glint of fear in *their* eyes. At that, my Nature hummed in pleasure.

They *should* be scared.

That small moment of hesitation was enough. Shadows danced along the alley walls as I sprayed down the first three bastards with forceful black mist, poison violently suffocating their screams.

I cackled as I stepped over their limp bodies, approaching the remaining four who still held their swords high, but were slowly retreating.

"You are just as dark and evil as they say your kind to be," a bald one with small, circular eyes sputtered, sweat beading off his forehead.

I stepped through a shallow puddle.

"Oh yeah? What makes you say that?"

He wielded his sword as if it were a shield. "You killed four men and you laugh!" the Draker spat.

"Because I like when men die after they try to kill me. I think it's funny." I smiled. "Don't worry, I'll laugh for you too."

With that, I sprinted. The maskless Draker squealed like a hog and dropped his sword. That was fine. He had no need for it once I cracked Singer against his skull.

His body smacked onto the ground.

The remaining three bolted out of the alley in a full retreat.

Smirking as their bulky footsteps faded into the distance, I stuffed Singer into my boot and tied my hair back, hoping to better blend in.

I turned around, nearly running right into a tall and cloaked figure. I gasped and took a step back.

Wild, brassy hair was tied up on the man's head, and his dark brown brows pulled together at the sight of me.

I should've ran with the Drakers.

"Your ol' Whimcastor isn't the only Dreamsoul in the realm," the Witchlord said, his yellow teeth peeking out.

I formed a misshapen ball of mist that could rival Amzee's droops and threw it towards his chest.

He grunted, raising a fist and summoning a dark cloud of grey. It swept my poison away before it could hit him.

"It's late, Elorengail. Time for bed." His dick hardened through his pants as he said my name.

An overwhelming sense of fatigue drowned me. I fought against it mentally, but physically my body was out of my control. My knees sank like anchors, shoulders following quickly behind.

I ground my teeth together, pleading for my limbs to work. The Witchlord snorted, nudging my chin up with his wet boot. I willed desperately to keep my heavy eyelids open, vision blurring.

"They call you the dark heir, you know."

"Who?" I breathed.

"The people, and one day, the histories."

He pulled his foot away, letting my face fall to the cold ground. Reality and darkness collided. I could not fight any longer.

CHAPTER 46

NO MERCY

"There are whispers, too many to count, of Elorengail Steele. She is no princess, but a dark heir. They say she brands her name upon the skin of her victims, tempts men toward rivers steeped in poison, and carried off a babe as its mother fell to her doom."

— *THE LYONSCLIFF PRESS, URGENT EDITION*

IN THE VOID, THERE WERE NO DREAMS OF CASTLES OR training.

There was only darkness. Was I dead? Was this my eternity? I couldn't move or speak. Only think and wait.

After what might've been an hour or a year, the faintest swirl of silver and black glimmered in the distance. It moved like a wraith, spindling and sliding through the void.

I wanted to call out to it, but I did not exist beyond my mind.

My soul pulled towards it. I needed it like it was a missing part of myself.

The silver swirl got closer and closer, until a sound echoed from it.

Xavian's voice.

"Elora..." he called quietly. He was so far, but the swirl was right there.

Closer, my soul pleaded.

As if it understood, the swirl molded into me, revealing that I was nothing but a wisp of violet.

When the silver began to blend with me, reality and darkness blurred together. I could hear, and my vision slowly returned.

"Holy tits, I think it's working," Avan exclaimed, his red hair unruly. He appeared utterly exhausted.

We were at Lady Jocelynn's house, sitting in the parlor. There was a black coffee table, with parchment and an ink pen on it.

"Princess Elorengail, are you in there?" Lord Draven asked calmly. He sat in a black armchair across from me.

I wanted to speak, but I couldn't. I stretched my fingers—Xavian's fingers. It was difficult, and being in his body felt like holding a heavy weight. I couldn't do this forever.

I grabbed the pen.

The weighted words came out sloppy as I scratched them across the page.

'We tried.'

My consciousness was forced back, the whisper of my

brother's spirit rushing past me as we crossed soul paths, never meeting.

I sucked in air as my eyes flung open. I yanked my arms—wrists bound.

Cursing, I frantically pulled against the black cuffs holding me to a table. My legs cuffed apart.

There were no windows in the cool and dingy room, and only a single torch cast shadows across the cinder walls. As I caught sight of the two men across the room, my breath halted.

Ansel and Riven were against the wall, both bound by the same cuffs.

"Easy," Ansel warned quietly.

"Don't tell her what to do," Riven bit out.

By the looks of the both of them, bruises and cuts along their arms and faces, it hadn't been easy getting them here.

"Where are we?"

Riven's eyes were dark, torchlight barely glowing within them. "Under the Southern Waywards."

I frowned, glancing at the low, dark ceiling. There was one rounded door, likely locked. Aside from the table, the room was empty. The stench of bodily fluids was horrid. What horrors had the walls within this room seen?

"What day is it?" I rasped. "Where are Amzee and Beck?"

"The ships arrive tomorrow," Ansel said, face full of quiet fury.

Days.

It had been two *days*.

"Where are Beck and Amzee?" I asked again.

Ansel's head hung low, dark hair falling over his face. "I don't know."

"Likely dead," Riven said curtly.

My lips fell into a flat line. "No, they're not."

Neither Ansel nor Riven mustered up the energy to argue with me.

"You have lightning. Break the cuffs," I urged. Had he forgotten his Nature?

Ansel shook his head. "They're obsidian, coated with something I presume. I can't use my Nature. Neither can you."

A hollow feeling echoed through me. My Nature, the one I'd cursed myself for having for years, wasn't there when I tried pulling it to the surface. It felt like the very lungs I needed to breathe had been ripped from me.

Pulling harder against the cuffs, I winced at the burn of my skin tearing.

"There's no use," Ansel mumbled.

I swallowed, trying to think.

The heavy door opened. A healer with a grey jacket and white gloves walked in. Behind him was a woman in a gold gown and a satin lined, bronze cloak.

Brown skin, caramel hair, and hawk-like eyes stood before me.

Queen Delaina herself.

I watched her from the table, eyes tracing her every move.

"I would've thought they'd clean you up a bit in Castivian," she droned.

My face twisted. "Why do you care what I look like?"

She clasped her hands together and gave a half smile. "It's just pathetic to see that Lord Ansel is with the filthy likes of you after making love to me. But... I suppose he is just a man, after all."

Turning, she scowled at Ansel. "You left my chambers in the middle of the night like a common whore. Did you think I wasn't aware of your wedding? And you actually thought it wise to bring your new bride back here?" She snorted. "Well, at least you're pretty, Ansy."

He refused to look at her, much less speak. I was speechless myself. I had no part in Ansel and Queen Delaina's history. She'd just been married to my brother, for Fate's sake.

She snapped her head back to me. "This isn't about me and Ansel," she said coldly. "It's about you and your bastard brother."

"Are you so offended by us," I began, "that you would go against your late husband's wishes?"

She scoffed. "Clarke didn't even know you. But I knew him," she said, dragging her finger along the table. "I knew Clarke better than anyone, and let me assure you, I am not an idiot like him. You should've never been allowed to live to begin with. All of you Blackhearts. You're vermin!"

The more Delaina talked, the angrier she became.

"You are the vermin," I snarled. "Selling and murdering the Dark Natured like cattle."

She slammed her hand on the table, barely missing my face. "Your kind hurts little girls! All of you Dark Natured blights are a plague that cause nothing but grief!" she yelled, voice cracking. There was a pain there, so deep that no light would ever find it.

I was quiet long enough to let the room go still.

"There are little girls in the Waywards, too."

She smacked me across the face, scowling at the hurt it

caused her own hand. I was too angry to feel pain—too stunned to care about anything other than escaping.

"If you kill us, Xavian is going to hunt you down and string you up like forest game," I warned.

She rubbed her palms together. "I owe Xavian Steele and our friend Ansel a present. Killing you would be too easy."

Riven's eyes darkened as he struggled against the cuffs.

"Xavian's not much of a gift person."

She was not amused by my response. Instead, she locked me in her sights.

"Your brother will watch me win. An heir for an heir, Blackheart."

My brows knitted together in confusion. We had no heirs to give, nor had we taken hers. What had happened to Princess Clayvarie was terrible, but a crime I did not commit.

"I don't have any heirs."

She slid her hand along the table once more before turning to the door, giving the anti-healer a nod. "And you never will."

Ansel's head shot up. "Touch her, and you're dead," he warned.

The false healer paid him no attention as he began setting tools out along the table. A guard held the door open for Delaina as Riven yanked wildly against his cuffs.

"I'm returning north, but I highly anticipate hearing all about Xavian's tantrum when you return to him spayed, just before I take my lands back," Delaina called as she headed out.

"You worthless, spiteful bitch!" I screeched, voice cracking. "You cannot cage people and be anything but evil. You are irredeemable! You are a murderer!" The door had already closed, but I prayed my voice followed. "You are the one with a warped mind! You are the one with a *black heart!*"

My chest rose and fell rapidly. Riven and I locked eyes, his anger rivaling my growing fear.

This was my legacy. There was so much I couldn't do, but growing our bloodline was supposed to be my opportunity.

My arms trembled as the man pulled out a knife, similar to those used to prepare fish.

I frantically thrashed away from the blade, but there was nowhere to go.

Riven jerked against his restraints like a wild animal, cursing the man and his honor. Every threat in the book was thrown out, but the false healer did not waver.

I'd been scared before, but now I was petrified.

Ansel scanned the room, cursing himself as he tried to think.

"I'm so sorry, Elora," he croaked as the blade entered me.

Burning met tearing agony as he began the procedure. There was nothing I could do to stop it.

I tried to cry out, but it was not my voice that screeched from within my soul.

It was my bloodline.

Every woman who had come before me—the royals on my father's side that had endured birthing heirs, and the Black-hearts on my mother's side who'd done the same. My ancestors cried out with me, their wrath unrelenting.

"The river of our blood does not end here!"

My legs shook uncontrollably, teeth jamming together.

The screams became louder.

"The river of our bloodline does not end here!"

The false doctor jerked his knife upward.

"Do not let our bloodline end here!"

Their spirits fueling me, I sat up fast, my teeth reaching the false healer's neck before he had the chance to move. Following the advice I'd received from a child, I bit down as hard as I could, ripping the artery from his neck. His knife fell to the table, just in front of my boot as he grabbed at his neck.

It was mere seconds before he was cyanotic, blood pouring out of him. He tried to make it to the door, but failed, his pale body falling to the floor.

"Riven," I whimpered. I kicked the knife towards him, the pain of the first cut settling in. It was the worst thing I'd ever felt, sending contractions through my abdomen and lightning pain in my back.

He caught the knife between his knees and raised it to his mouth.

Ansel stretched his long legs toward the false healer's boots.

I panted, my head spinning.

Ansel used nothing but his legs to drag the lifeless man's body closer. When his jacket pocket was within reach, Riven leaned forward, using the knife clenched between his teeth to knock the set of keys free.

Ansel groaned as he twisted his body just enough to grab them with his restrained hand. Fingertips grasping the keys, he slid them along the side of his cuff. The restraints released.

I'd never seen a key like it, nor did I care to question it. Ansel jumped up, crossing the length of the room in two strides and sliding the key along each of my restraints.

He looked me over, both of us aware of the pooling blood.

"She needs a healer," Riven snarled. "Not a Dreamsoul."

I'd never witnessed such anger from Riven, violence radiating through his eyes.

"Get his restraints off," I said.

Ansel seemed ready to leave Riven to his fate, but with a reluctant sigh, he stepped over and released him.

Riven stood and brushed his hands off, all before drawing his fist back and punching Ansel in the jaw.

"Riven!" I yelled.

Ansel smiled as he kicked Riven in the chest, knocking him to the floor.

Riven grabbed the knife that had been used to cut my insides, and hopped to his feet.

"Enough!" I snapped.

Riven glanced at me, then at the blood dripping from the table. He threw the knife to the corner of the room, then pulled his black shirt over his head and brought it to me.

"This might help with the bleeding," he said.

I sighed, shoving the shirt between my legs.

"But I'm still not done with you," Riven snarled as he snatched the knife back off the ground and pointed it at Ansel.

"Oh, for fuck's sake," I cursed.

Ansel stepped forward. "Try it, *runt*."

"What did you just call me?"

Ansel swirled a small bolt of lightning on his finger. "Are you as deaf as you are dull?" he taunted.

Amzee came bursting through the door, with Beck shadowing in behind her.

They both stopped and stared at the cloth stuffed between my legs, Riven with his shirt off and knife clenched in hand, Ansel holding lightning in his grasp, and finally, the dead body.

Amzee shifted her weight. "Did we just walk in on some weird sex thing?"

Riven grimaced.

"No," I answered firmly.

"The Princess needs a healer," Riven grumbled, walking over to the table. He gave Ansel a menacing glare before cradling me in his arms.

"I can walk," I said.

"But you won't."

Riven carried me out of the room, with Beck leading the way. I had plenty of questions, but exhaustion outweighed my curiosity.

I focused on Riven instead, our faces close enough that I could nearly taste the honey in his eyes.

"You look so angry," I whispered.

His dimple peeked out as his lips remained in a flat line.

"I should kill him for dragging you into this mess—for bedding the queen, then taking you as a bride. He should have his balls nailed to his dome for what's happened to you."

I finally knew why Riven chose to be quiet most of the time. The space inside his mind was often so dark, he chose to not subject anyone else to it.

We understood each other in that way.

"I need Ansel for heirs," I mumbled, eyes fluttering. Tears crept into the corners of my eyes. It was as if my body knew the damage had already been done.

Riven's face tensed, and he leaned his cheek onto my forehead. "You are enough, with or without being able to create something more," he said softly.

I wiped a tear away with my sleeve before it could get the

chance to scald Riven's bare chest. As he carried me through weathered hallways, Amzee held a flaming orb in her hand behind us, illuminating the area.

Drakers' bodies were scattered along the floor. Amzee and Beck must have torn through the Waywards to find us. She would have to tell me the story another day.

This was the one time I was thankful my blood wasn't venomous. While it would've been convenient if the Sapphires ever tried to drink it, it was a small mercy that I wasn't hurting Riven as the shirt between my legs began to drip.

"How much further?" Ansel called to Beck.

"Almost out."

"I'll have to take her to Jaime," Ansel planned aloud.

Jaime was one of the two Witchlords on our side. He was a Lyonheart, just as Clarke had been. He might be able to fix me.

I shuddered. There would be no mercy for Queen Delaina.

She would die for this. If I couldn't create life, then she didn't get to live hers. No amount of troops, ships, or Witchlords could save her from me.

Up stone steps we went, exiting through a door that led to an alleyway not far from where I'd been captured. The underground cellars were practically hidden in plain sight. Did the Northern Waywards have these as well?

Amzee dimmed her light, casting subtle, golden shadows on our faces.

Beck analyzed our group, particularly me. Riven still held strong with me in his arms, blood completely soaking the shirt between my legs.

He reached out to me. "I can't shadow us all there at once. We only have hours before dawn and the ships will be visible. I haven't been in a piss-soaked cell for days. I can take her to the Lyonheart."

Beck may have been more slender than Riven, but I'd bet he was just as strong.

"I'll meet you there, make sure there's no trouble with Jaime at the very least," Ansel said quietly. "I don't need to be shadowed."

Riven held me closer. "I will not leave her again."

Beck nodded, glancing at Amzee for a brief moment and back to me in Riven's arms. "Then I'll need you to run, Sir."

Riven readjusted me. "I've been waiting to use my legs all day. Let's go."

———

Just as Ansel had promised, Jaime welcomed us into his home and worked quickly while Riven watched for threats.

The healing felt strange, the magic swirling around my abdomen and legs like warm liquid being poured over me.

Lord Jaime's blond hair was combed back, curling just slightly behind his ears. He was already dressed in his Witchlord's cloak and armor, ready for battle. As quiet as he might've been, he was polite and concise when he needed to speak.

I didn't mind the silence as I lay on the hardwood floor, a couch pillow resting under my head as I stared at the high ceiling.

I'd told Beck about where I'd stashed the weapons, and requested he return my orb. He promised to distribute everything swiftly, and he must have, by the rate at which he returned to Keeper's Street, orb in hand.

With Riven by my side and the orb healthily glowing, I sighed in relief.

"I've done what I can," Jaime said, offering me a hand.

My long, ragged shirt braced against my knees as he pulled me to my feet. There was no blood trailing down my legs, and no soreness in my abdomen or back.

"Will I be able to have children?" I asked frankly. I didn't need my feelings spared. I needed the truth.

He picked the pillow up from the floor, tossing it over to the couch. "I don't know, but if you do, consider Jaime for a name," he joked, refusing to meet my eye. Swallowing my tears, fire crept up my chest. There was no time for weeping, only requital.

"The sun will rise within the hour. We'll need to take you to a ship first," Riven said delicately.

I shook my head. "No. I will go last, or not at all."

His hard eyes softened, but he nodded at the order and handed me a fresh set of clothes.

Amzee and Beck shadowed back in through the door, Amzee's hair now braided back with a red ribbon running through it.

She brushed herself off, eyes bright at the sight of me standing.

"I found a purple ribbon for your braid!" she chimed, holding it up and shaking it around like a worm, holding out her own braid with the opposite hand as an example.

I crossed the room to hug her.

"I'm so glad you're okay," I said. "Though, I never doubted you."

She squeezed me tight. "I'm glad *you're* okay. Now, please hurry and wash up before I have no time to braid your hair. I had to arm wrestle three men to win this ribbon!" she exclaimed, wiggling it around again. Even the darkness of the Waywards couldn't dim Amzee's fire.

Mine had only just ignited.

The queen would be wise to remember that even the smallest fires burn like hell.

CHAPTER 47

TERRIFYING, BEAUTIFUL, DANGEROUS

"Pray for your queen. She weeps for her late husband, while his kin turn their grief to sin."

— *KOLSON STRANGE, MINISTER OF SPIRIT*

DOOR TO DOOR AND WINDOW TO WINDOW, AMZEE'S rebels snuck along the alleyways, clinging to the shadows, slipping notes into homes. They'd spent all week prepping the messages, waiting until the very last moment to distribute them to ensure a traitor wouldn't ruin it all.

When dawn crept into the sky, every single family in the Waywards had been informed of what was to come.

There are ships set for Castivian waiting in the bay. Make it to them. Stay only if you wish to be fed to Sapphires. Fight if you wish to be free. When lightning strikes, it's time to leave.

The people had a choice, and I prayed they would make the right one.

Orange and pink light peeked over the horizon as I sat crouched on top of the highest building. Beck and Amzee did the same at my side, each of us waiting for the light to hit the sea. If the ships hadn't arrived as planned, this would all have been for nothing.

Singer was clasped in my hands, and I was thankful the Drakers hadn't bothered removing my boots to find the stone club.

Hope soared in my chest as the sun illuminated our saving grace. As Lord Regby had promised, there was a daunting fleet of ships just beyond the obsidian walls, waiting in the bay.

With the touch of withering shingles under my palm, I held steady as Amzee lifted her hand to give the signal. Fire flickered from her palm.

We watched with bated breath as Riven led his Rogue Drakers to the gate. They swallowed up the command—snapping necks, slicing throats, and dragging the bodies of the gate-watch away.

"Brilliantly done," Beck said, voice hushed.

I grinned as Riven and a few other unmasked rogues pushed the gates wide open.

Amzee held her hand high once more, this time towards Keeper's Street. She opened and closed her palm, flashing fire three times. We waited. One second. Two. Three.

Lightning illuminated the skies before striking the wall. Blue and white glowed within it, followed by blaring thunder. The wall held, but the signal was loud and clear.

Rushing from homes and rumbling the ground below,

came hundreds of Dark Natured, running for the gate. My pulse skipped a beat as the hysteria began.

Families carried everything they could. Small children were dragged along by their wrists, desperate souls racing for their lives through the streets. Bumping into and bickering amongst each other. It was madness.

"I'll be back," Beck announced, shadowing away.

Beck, Riven, and the Rogues shouted over the crowds, a late attempt to form lines and stop the pushing, but it was no use. The Dark Natured squeezed out of the Waywards, the gate not wide enough to be practical. It would take far too long to get everyone through.

A horn sounded, echoing through the 'Wards.

The Witchlords were coming.

Amzee and I lay flat on the roof, consumed by panic at the sight of mothers pushing through crowds with crying babies in their arms, and the elderly dragging behind, their families begging them to move faster.

"The wall needs to come down," I muttered. She silently nodded, but we both knew there was no way to do it; otherwise, it would've been done already.

Crowds came from the far end of the Waywards, while true Drakers rushed from their barracks in the east and west.

"Send the signal," I ordered. This was the last thing we had planned.

Everything after was up to Fate, the Mother, our Nature, and blades.

Standing now, Amzee did not flicker a flame signal. She instead held a small, black bow with an arrow drawn back, the tip infused with her Nature. She narrowed her eyes, target in sight.

Amzee released. The flame-tipped arrow left a smoke trail as it soared over buildings and crowds. It flew straight through a third-level window of the barracks, meeting its mark.

I held my breath.

One second. Two. Three.

Explosive flames erupted from the windows. Half-dressed Drakers leapt from high stories in an attempt to escape death by fire.

As bodies splattered against the ground, rebels armed with the weapons we'd supplied raced to the posts and remaining barracks, prepared to protect those who could not protect themselves.

Civilians screamed as the living Drakers charged with swords held high, rebels meeting them with roaring cries of vengeance as they fought for their freedom.

Blood painted the Waywards.

I rotated slowly, taking in the carnage and chaos.

The Dark Natured were not prepared to wield swords, and it was horrifically telling.

At the gate, Riven was forced to abandon his post to help with defence and pushed his way through the crowd.

Just a few streets over, Drakers sliced through the Dark Natured like feeble mice. The people crammed around the exit, trampling each other as they realized the fate coming for them. Riven yelled over their cries, warning them to stay calm, but his words were washed away by the frenzy.

Ansel, Jaime, and Lord Syler would have to be our saving grace. They were the only Witchlords on our side, but that didn't count for nothing. They were waiting for the other Witchlords to exit their homes.

Thunder shook me off balance, forcing me to crouch as a dark shade of blue illuminated the sky. Lightning webbed the sky, before striking near Keeper's Street. The battle of the Witchlords had begun.

Ansel wasn't the only Dreamsoul here. I'd known that and cursed myself for forgetting.

I scanned the Waywards, wincing at the losses. "It's time to move."

Amzee nodded. "Thank goodness."

We were supposed to wait until Beck and Riven returned, but how could we sit and watch? King's Mark and Lyons blood or not, Xavian could make his own heir. How could I ever consider creating more lives if I didn't try to save these?

Scaling down the building, we dropped the last few feet into the madness.

"Please, Fate, help us!"

"Just know I love you."

"I'm scared."

I gripped Singer, lip curling at the fear around me.

They didn't deserve this.

All of this death at the hand of Queen Delaina and the Sapphires. Disgust and rage flowed through me like the blood in my veins.

"Follow us!" I shouted, lifting Singer and cutting through the crowd. Amzee raised her hand, fire leading the way. Side by side, we strode through the streets, not allowing anyone to rush through. Amzee knew the people. They trusted her, and thus they trusted me.

The first group of Drakers charged us, masks on and swords drawn.

Pointing Singer, I released my Nature through the stone club, my poison eating up the distance.

Amzee followed suit, holding her palms forward and shooting flames. The Drakers screamed as they succumbed to fire and darkness. Some rolled around on the ground as they burned, while others slit their own throats.

I turned back. "Take their weapons! We must protect each other!"

"You heard your Princess!" Amzee shouted.

Inspired tears filled eyes across the crowd as lightning collided against its own in the sky, booming thunder.

With this group close enough to the gate, we were needed elsewhere. Hopefully, they would wield the weapons well.

"Let's return to a higher vantage point," Amzee called to me over the mayhem.

I followed her to a nearby building, scaling the side quickly. As we made it to the top, my heart which had been so full of hope, shattered.

Drakers from outside of the Waywards were on horseback, riding for the port. They were going to kill all of the escapees before they even made it to the ships. My orb flashed at my hip, lightning cracking in the sky. I looked down at it, and there Ansel was, his face in the orb itself.

"Ansel?"

"We lost Lord Syler. We were able to wound one of their Lyonhearts, and they retreated to heal him. We have to spread out. Lord Jaime is already nearing burnout."

Amzee's face fell. "So he's the last Witchlord we have? Against four others?"

I sucked in an anxious breath. Only maybe five percent of the Waywards had made it out of the gate so far, and Drakers were still chasing them down. More bodies lie dead in the streets than were outside the walls. One of our Witchlords was gone, the other nearly useless after spending all night healing me.

Ansel couldn't fight forever.

I attached the orb at my waist and rolled my shoulders back. "Then we spread out."

Amzee did not appear pleased. "I'll go east. You go west?"

I nodded, my stomach already twisting. Every corpse on the ground was a tally in my mind for the cuts I would give Queen Delaina. That anger fuelled me as I climbed down, building inside of me and radiating through Singer.

All battle strategies fled my mind as I rampaged through the uneven streets, casting my Nature at every Draker in my path. I had no thoughts of nausea—no consideration for fatigue. They were mostly in groups of two or three, all too happy to have an excuse to kill the Dark Natured.

I was pleased to return the favor.

Screams echoed in my head, so much so that I started confusing real ones with imaginary.

I didn't know these Waywards well, and although I'd studied the map, it was different now. I'd killed almost twenty Drakers, but I was having a hard time finding them. I needed a higher viewpoint.

Climbing the side of the first building, I scanned below

until I found Amzee near the center of the 'Wards, surrounded by rebels. They protected her as she vomited.

Beck shadowed in next to her, emesis running out of the corner of his mouth. My breathing was unsteady, the adrenaline waning and nausea rising.

I tapped the orb frantically, receiving only a flicker in response. Light-blue lightning struck a building near Keeper's Street.

I had no idea where Riven was, but I knew we were crumbling.

There still had to be ninety percent of the population inside.

My eyes stung as I spotted two women around my age, both sliced through the chest. Deceased next to one another while still holding hands. They didn't deserve this. They were supposed to make it to Castivian.

"You're harder to find than I thought," a familiar voice sounded behind me.

I swiveled, eyes narrowing on the enemy Dreamsoul.

"I'm getting bored of men chasing after me," I snarled, wielding Singer. God, I was tired.

The Witchlord held his hands up. "Let's make this easy and painless. You get down with me, we put you in a nice little room until the Sapphires arrive to retrieve you, and then maybe we can even have a drink."

I charged towards him.

"Fine. The hard and painful way," he grumbled.

"Just the way I like it," I taunted, swinging the club.

He dodged the blow, and I fell against the roof. I winced,

forcing myself to tuck the pain away until later. I jumped back to my feet, smoke billowing into the sky as nearby buildings caught fire.

The Witchlord had to be weak as well, or he would've already forced me to sleep. Lightning sparked between his fingers, threatening me.

I charged him, because fuck wasting time to spar. If I was going to die, so was he, right now.

His face twisted as we collided, both of us grunting from the impact. He fell on his back at the edge of the roof, and I landed on top of him.

"Just where I like my whores," he snarled. The glint in his eyes was the same one all mindless men had when they wanted what was between my legs.

"Really?" I teased.

He hardened under me at my response.

His face reddened, lust clouding his good sense. Leave it to a man to face death with desire. Though who was I to pass up such an opportunity? Would the historians write about this moment? The Witchlord and I on the roof?

I reached for his pants, gripping his waistband. "I mean, if we're going to die anyway."

His eyes roamed from his sword, to my hands, and finally— my body. "You *are* a little whore."

I lowered my gaze shyly, focusing between his legs. I tugged the zipper down, revealing the subpar, veiny creature within. Not appealing in the slightest. My eyes stayed locked on his face as I lowered my mouth, tongue reaching out. His eyes rolled back as I sucked down.

What a fucking dumbass.

Years worth of withheld poison erupted from my mouth. I reached for Singer, bashing the stone club onto his hand that held the sword. He screamed as I bit down on his pathetic excuse for a dick.

My poison flooded into the bite wound. He tried to yank my braid with his only usable hand.

I laughed, spitting a piece of penis onto his face.

"As if I've never had my hair pulled."

Blood and poison dripping from my mouth, I pressed Singer into his shoulder, forcing him to release my braid. As the poison burned through his body, he shouted slurs and curses, the last bit of damage he thought he could do.

It was useless. Heirs did not concern themselves with the opinions of dickless men.

As he guppied on his last breath, I stood, using my arm to wipe the poison from my mouth.

I took in the disarray across the city. The gates were too crowded. There were too many Drakers. I had no idea where any of my friends were anymore. The people within the Waywards had given up hope. Some retreated back to their homes, while others held their hands above their heads in surrender, begging for mercy.

Even worse, four archers were perched across different buildings, all with their elbows cranked back, aims pointed at me.

My eyes stung, a hot tear rolling down my face. Years worth of anger clawed its way up my chest.

Amzee and Beck were burned out. Riven was nowhere to

be seen. We were overrun by Drakers. The gate was too small. Four arrows would go through my skull if I didn't surrender. Worst of all, I was going to die with subpar penis breath.

The archers whistled a warning. *Surrender or die.*

I would rather die.

A roar erupted through the sky like nothing I'd ever heard, rattling my brain. I snapped my head to the sound, shoulders dropping.

Flying at a high speed with their wings drawn back were two bladebreathers—Valeska and Zephy.

My knees buckled.

Valeska screeched, her sights on me. *"There you are,"* she called through my mind.

On her back was Lady Jocelynn.

I couldn't believe it. The woman who didn't even want to ride to Moonhill—who had no interest in leaving Castivian. The woman who had children at home and a life to live for.

She had crossed the Sea of Blades for this. And she wasn't the only one.

Xavian was behind her, while *Trista* rode on the back of Zephy.

My brother and friends were here. Lady Jocelynn was *my* friend, not just Xavian's.

Zephy barked a blade out with precise aim, sending an archer to the ground before diving into the streets. Trista held on for dear life, red hair blazing behind her.

Amzee ran to him, spirits high. There was *hope*, and that was stronger than any burnout.

Valeska came to a halt in front of my building, flapping her wings and blowing smoke into my face. I stood frozen in awe.

She was everything I'd imagined a bladebreather to be.

Terrifying, beautiful, dangerous.

Xavian spared no time for niceties and conversations, leaping from her back to a nearby rooftop, blades in hand.

Valeska's shimmering eyes bore into my soul as the world tore itself apart around us.

"You sent food to Moonhill?" she demanded to know.

"Yes."

"Why?"

Shrugging, I maintained my firm footing and gave her an honest answer. "I've been starving before."

She lowered her wing, allowing Jocelynn to slide down.

"I stink like dirt and sweat, my Gods!" she scowled, shadows wisping around her as she made her way to the roof.

Steam puffed from Valeska's nostrils and she pulled her wing back once more. "Your friend was very worried for you. She rode to Moonhill alone, confronting me with not a weapon in sight but her whip of a tongue."

Jocelynn brushed herself off, refusing to look at the scene around us, complaining to herself. My heart swelled in admiration of her actions. Of Valeska's, too.

"And you came," I said to Valeska.

"I have come to claim you as my rider, if you will choose me, Princess Elorengail," she said, silver scales reflecting the lightning above.

She would claim me, all because I had done something as simple as send food?

There was not a single doubt in my mind. "Then I choose you."

Her large eyes marveled, head tilting curiously. "There are

younger bladebreathers back in Moonhill, if that is what you'd prefer."

I stepped forward, fearlessly placing my hand at the bridge between her eyes. "I choose *you*."

Black, silver, and violet mist fluttered as Valeska and I became a united force, our instincts clicking together like puzzle pieces. It was so seamless, so natural. How had we not been that way my entire life?

"The wall needs to come down," she acknowledged, our motives colliding. It was unlike anything I'd ever experienced.

Lady Jocelynn scoffed. "I'd say so. We'll be fighting for weeks with that measly exit," she interjected, pointing to the crowded gate.

"Get on," she ordered, her wing lying down like a bridge. "I can't fly long without a rider."

I faced Jocelynn. "Are you coming with me?"

She confidently shook her head. "I do not possess the desire to ever have my feet off the ground again, thank you. I will make my way to the ship just fine."

"It's dangerous down there," I warned.

She rolled her eyes. "I'm a Nightcastor."

Fair enough.

The moment I'd been waiting my entire life for was right in front of me. Valeska craned her wing, awaiting me.

From the moment I touched her, my Nature bonded with her—fueling her. It was like a magnet. The pull was so strong that if I were to fall off, it would have had to have been on *purpose*.

Once seated behind her neck, I felt energized, not afraid,

looking at the scene below. We were getting the rest of the Dark Natured to Castivian, no matter what.

A similar energy rolled off of Valeska—the anger she felt on my behalf.

She let out a roar that could rival the Gods, then soared full speed at the wall.

CHAPTER 48

A VERITABLE NIGHTMARE

"The walls are indestructible. They must be, to keep such creatures inside."

— MARKER DAIN, LORD OF LAWSHIP

"BRACE!" VALESKA ORDERED.

Wind ripped past. The world became a storm of obsidian and screams. I should have been afraid, but how could I be? We moved faster than my own legs could ever take me. The ground was far below, where no one could reach me.

My Nature charged through my veins, surging as we plummeted towards the obsidian barrier.

One of us was going to come down. Me, or this fucking wall.

"Don't doubt us," Valeska echoed as she pulled my Nature through her, splashing it from her wings as we smashed into the wall with bone-rattling vibration. I closed my eyes, and my legs held tight, though my Nature would surely keep me in place.

Valeska flapped her wings, flying upwards.

"Are you alright?" I asked, hiding my face in her neck, afraid to look for myself.

"I may not be a fresh hatchling anymore, but I'm not that fragile. We're turning around. The west end needs an exit too."

Too.

I glanced below. She had plunged through the wall like an anchor. Glee spread through me as we flew back for a second round.

Civilians cheered, running through their new exit and charging for the ships.

We crashed through the wall once more, and this time I forced my eyes to stay open, watching the wall crumble.

Valeska held strong, once again ascending after the hit.

"The Drakers! Outside of the Waywards! They're targeting those who have escaped!" I pointed below. Rebels fought the troops of Drakers nearing the beach. Valeska growled, nosediving.

I buried my head against her as the speeding winds pulled at my skin. With no warning, Valeska spun, spiraling towards them, forcing my head upright as she erupted countless blades at the masked men.

Valeska's satisfaction trickled into my mood as she landed on the beach, shaking the ground.

When she roared, the Drakers' knees wobbled, some of them dropping their measly swords.

They wielded weapons. We *were* weapons.

"Retreat!" one of them yelled, yanking back on the reins of his horse.

I lowered my chin, glaring. Forfeit was not good enough for me.

Join me, or join those who've crossed me.

Every moment they spent fleeing, they solidified their choice. My lips curled back, rough Drakish accent loud enough for the cowards to hear. They had caged and betrayed their *own* people.

"End them."

Blades rippled from Valeska, shooting like darts. As the Drakers tried to flee, Valeska released blade after blade, until they were nothing but a pile of memories who had made the wrong choice.

With the path to the ships clear, more and more Drakers retreated, even those within the walls. They were losing hope.

"Take me to the center."

Valeska followed my command, landing in the middle of the Waywards.

My brother was fighting in glowing black armor. Riven fought nearby, and Amzee soared overhead, sinking blades into archers. Most of the Drakers were concentrated in the center of the 'Wards, all second-guessing their decisions as Valeska screeched.

I dismounted, sliding awkwardly down her wing. "Clear the path behind us. I'll help my brother."

Valeska huffed steam in response, plundering into the streets and sending men screaming for their lives. I pulled out Singer, whacking the first Draker to come at me.

Across the street, Riven locked eyes on me in awe. I smiled, my feelings for him surfacing—

Time slowed as two archers in blue cloaks grinned from atop the building. They both cocked their arms back and released.

One arrow soared towards Riven. One for Xavian.

I'd stopped a flying object before, in the midwinter games. I'd saved Beck. I could stop an arrow—

I screamed, dropping Singer and holding both of my palms up. My Nature erupted, forming a misted orb. I needed two at the same time. I needed more, but my body denied me, forcing me to make a choice. My brother or Riven.

I threw it with all my might. My poison soared through the air, swallowing up an arrow and melting it into the ground.

The other went through Riven's chest.

His knees hit the ground, hand grabbing at his heart.

"Riven!" I cried. I ran to his side, trying to hold him up by the shoulders. Xavian was somewhere behind me, calling for Riven to hold on.

Prince Payn appeared above us, looking down on me, unbearably calm.

My eyes hardened as Xavian reached for a bow off the ground.

"Your debt is paid," Payn called out, downing a vial of blood and vanishing from atop the building.

His words echoed through my mind. *You will learn what it means to be an heir.*

"No," I breathed. We had bladebreathers. We had Xavian. It was time to win, not *die*.

Blood trickled out of Riven's mouth. His face was horrifically pale, sweat dampening his cheeks, lips turning blue.

Xavian cursed, helping me lay him down.

Amzee ran over, as did Zephy and Valeska, circling us. Daring any Drakers to come near.

Red coated my hands as I frantically tried to stop the bleeding.

"I'm sorry," he mumbled.

I didn't want apologies. I wanted him. I wanted *us.*

"No," I snarled. "You promised I wouldn't lose you. You... you're the Oathkeeper!"

Blood flooded from Riven's mouth, choking him. His eyes flared with fear, refusing to meet mine. He grabbed at his chest, every inhale a stridorous nightmare.

I screamed for Xavian to help me, and he was already sitting Riven back up.

"I–" Riven coughed, gripping my hand.

"You what?" I breathed.

His eyes closed, weight dragging against me. His hand went limp, warmth fleeing his skin.

Xavian brought his fingers to Riven's neck. My jaw trembled.

Riven's next breath never came.

"You promised me." My throat was dry, arms shaking.

"We need to keep moving," Xavian said gently.

I eyed Riven's sword on the ground a few yards away.

"He needs his sword."

"Elora, he—"

"He needs his fucking sword!" I cried.

With heavy steps, I went to it—a grand and heavy sword

that he'd surely spent many years with. Tears rolling down my face, I grabbed the hilt and lifted, screeching as I forced my body to endure.

I didn't let it waver as I carried it over and laid it next to his body.

I knelt down once more and rested my head on his chest, my eyes closed.

Amzee hugged my back. Then Xavian joined, and then Beck. Until we all held on for one final moment.

I refused to look at Riven's body any longer. I stood, hands shaking, facing the Drakers who were still bold enough to challenge us.

Picking up Singer, I approached them.

"When you meet the Gods, tell them to stay the fuck out of my way," I growled before pointing Singer, misting twenty of them. I didn't give a damn about the inevitable burnout.

Revenge consumed me.

Back to back with my brother, he with a sword and I with Singer, we remained at the center of the Waywards with Valeska, striking down any Draker that dared try to pass through. Xavian was here, a *king*, doing what my father and Clarke never would have.

We were an unstoppable force, and as the weight of the battle shifted in our favor, more and more of the Dark Natured safely boarded the ships.

———

By nightfall, I was staring at the stars, lying on Valeska's back as we flew over the Sea of Blades.

Grief numbed me from the feelings of victory.

The freedom of being able to go home had a price. So many had paid for it. Riven had paid for it. Valeska roared in tribute for him, releasing a dozen blades into the sea in his honor.

With the burning Waywards long behind us, I clenched my eyes shut, wanting to disappear.

The orb flickered.

I held it up, tapping it.

"Care to join us?" Ansel requested. "Just for a moment."

I swallowed, clipping it back to my waist. I was not the only one who had lost someone. I needed to be there for my people.

Valeska dropped us to the forefront of our fleet, perching lightly on the end of the ship.

Celebrations were happening on the deck. Liquor and food had been served. People were singing, kissing, holding each other. The world around me was a blur compared to my grief. I tried to at least focus on conversations where Xavian and I were being thanked for our leadership, with promises from the Dark Natured that they would join the brotherhood upon arrival to Castivian.

Late into the evening, Ansel proposed a toast.

I stood with a strong pour in hand, staring out into the sea.

"To the famed bastard twins of Castivian, King Xavian Steele and Princess Elorengail *Whimcastor*, for their triumphant victory at the Southern Waywards!" Ansel cheered.

He'd already changed and cleaned up, his piercing blue eyes cutting through the crowd.

"And cheers to my wife, for a successful bonding to a blade-breather!" he added.

Beck stared, arms crossed from across the deck. I drank deeply. Ansel offered to grab me another.

As everyone else celebrated, I planned my revenge.

Delaina thought me to be a monster? I'd become something far more frightening—a veritable nightmare.

My revenge is inescapable.

EPILOGUE

"She is no princess, but a blight, hellbent on poisoning the Crown. She is darker than Saffron, crueler than the bastard who defied me. Let her name be known only for its evil. Elorengail Steele—the Dark Heir."

— *QUEEN DELAINA LYONAIRE, DECREE BEFORE THE CHURCH OF FATE*

LUNA SAT TREMBLING, ROPED AND BOUND TO A CHAIR in the middle of the woods, surrounded by dark blue tents.

Prince Payn sat on a chair in front of her with a tiara in his hand. The campfire cast a warm, shadowy glow on his angular face, his eyes red in stark contrast to his snow-like hair.

"You've saved yourself a lot of trouble answering my questions so far," Prince Payn murmured, leaning forward in his seat. His finger traced along the tiara.

Luna kept silent.

"So let me get this straight. You managed to escape the Northern Waywards. Before that, you lived with a girl named *Elora*," he paused, as if saying her name sliced open a bitter wound. "After your escape, you what? Whored around taverns thinking you wouldn't be captured?"

Luna closed her eyes, lip quivering as she nodded. "Please don't kill me," she begged.

Payn rolled his eyes and stood. "You Blackhearts are so dramatic. I'm not going to kill you. I have a job for you."

Luna perked up. "What's the job? I'm experienced in many things," she promised suggestively.

Payn grimaced. "Nothing like that. You'll learn more later. For now, I have one more question. After you answer, I'll let you change into clothes that aren't soaked in piss. Fair?"

She nodded graciously. "Whatever you want."

Payn cut the restraints off in a clean slice. "Come with me."

Luna did as told and followed the blood prince through the heavily guarded camp. When he stopped, he drew back the opening of a tent.

"Tell me everything you know about my idiot brother."

Luna gaped at the limp body lying on a table, bandages wrapping his chest. If it weren't for his shallow breathing, she would've thought he was dead.

TO BE CONTINUED

Acknowledgments

Thank you to everyone who knew wholeheartedly that I would write this acknowledgment letter one day—even when I didn't believe it was possible. There were nights soaked in tears when I was certain I'd never finish a book, never be good enough, never see the end of the story. But you believed for me. And without you, this would not exist.

To everyone who has supported my wild little corner of the internet. My found family, thank you. When I first started sharing stories, never knowing whose feed they might drift across, I could have never imagined I'd find a community so kind, so supportive, and so delightfully bonkers. You are my favorite kind of chaos, and I love you all dearly.

To my friends, you know who you are. I would unravel without you.

To Sydney, Reed, and my father: we made it out of the bad years.

To my Nanny, I wish you were here.

And finally, to all the creative little beans out there: write your story. You have no idea who might need it.

Love,
Pixie

About the Author

Pixie is a writer from South Carolina. She enjoys a stormy night on the coast, video games, bubble baths, unusual dolls, an iced matcha, and all things whimsy.

instagram.com/pixer.ella